Shameless

SHAMELESS

OFF-LIMITS LOVERS
Book Two

LORE TOWNSEND

Shameless
Paperback Edition

Love N. Books Press
An Imprint of Wolfpack Publishing
1707 E. Diana Street
Tampa, FL 33610

www.lovenbookspress.com

Edited by My Brother's Editor

Shameless was originally published as Shameless Lover in 2024 by Lore Townsend

Paperback ISBN 979-8-89567-633-2
Ebook ISBN 979-8-89567-632-5

For the hopeless romantics…

Before we begin...

This love story leans a bit to the kinky side, especially when it comes to the bedroom scenes. I mean, that's why you're here, right? All the wild and crazy spice that some of us can only dream about.

Just wanted to note that, while I've done my best to include safety and consent wherever necessary, this is a work of fiction and should not be taken as a guide or manual for the BDSM lifestyle. The characters in this story get up to hijinks that may not be safe or recommended to try between your own sheets without preparation and conversations about safety.

That being said…if you have fun on this wild ride and want to join the rest of us who enjoy similar fantasies, you can find us in Lore Townsend's Romance Club on Facebook.

Love you!

Welcome to Faraday Island

If this is your first time checking into The White Sands Resort, you're in for a treat. Avery and Franzeska's love story is a fan favorite, and one near and dear to my heart.

Here's a series cheat sheet, just for fun.

The owners of The White Sands Resort:

- **Dominic:** The chef
- **Sam:** The general manager
- **Ben:** The lawyer
- **Avery:** The wild card
- **Reina:** Dominic's fiancée. You can read their love story in *Off the Menu*.

Places you'll go:

- **Faraday Island:** a fictional tropical island with the climate and geographic features of a small island off the coast of Belize (where I was when I started writing this series)
- **Saubry Village:** The town on Faraday island.

- **Merit Island:** The small island next to Faraday where the guys own a house.
- **The White Sands Resort:** the four guys purchased the abandoned resort over a decade ago and reopened it as a high-end beach destination.
- **Raft:** The high-end restaurant located inside the lobby of The White Sands Resort.
- **Reef:** The casual fare restaurant located poolside on the lower level of the resort.

Shameless

Rule #1

MAKE GATSBY PROUD

FRAN

"Better get that mask on, girlie, or they ain't letting you off this elevator."

The words are spoken to me by a round, middle-aged woman in an enormous orange-feather bird mask who I'm fairly certain is drunk.

We're packed in the elevator with at least ten other masked people, some of whom have gone the full costume route. I'm pressed right up against a Where's Waldo. There's a sexy Santa in the far corner.

I turn my own mask over and over in my hands. It's a small black and white bird mask, soft plastic glued with what I'm hoping are fake feathers. It's my first and only purchase so far on my new island home, snagged from a vendor's booth in town after being told that this annual rooftop Halloween party is not to be missed.

Halloween in a black bikini, white mini dress, and a few plastic feathers. Definitely not in Kansas anymore.

"Let me help you." The same orange bird masked woman

from earlier has abandoned her creepy as hell black ski-masked partner and shoved her way through the tightly packed elevator toward me. I hand her the small mask, and she ties the black ribbons behind my head.

"Thank you."

"Remember, don't ever take it off. That's the rule."

"Rule?" I was told to get the mask, I didn't actually realize it was a requirement.

"The *only* rule," the woman gushes excitedly in my ear. "Have fun."

When the elevator dings at the top floor, I'm left behind by the rush of excited guests hurrying out onto the rooftop patio. I take my time following, glancing around at the wild, Mardi Gras-inspired decor.

Oh, and the enormous, clear-bottomed rooftop pool.

It's already half filled with bikini-clad ladies and floaties of various shapes and sizes. I smile at a giant popsicle and a pink flamingo. I spotted this pool from the ground floor walkway—it's hard to miss—but I figured it was part of a private suite or something.

Now that I'm up here, it seems to be two private suites. I'm on the south building of the resort, with the elevator and large sliding glass doors leading to an interior space with food and a full bar. I can see across to the north building, where music is pumping and there's a dance floor set up. The pool bridges the gap, hovering impressively in the open air.

I do have my bathing suit on under my dress, and I'm tempted to hop right into the cool, clear water, but there's something else calling my name.

Food.

I've only had a few snacks I snagged from the little bodega in town, and I'm starving.

The orange bird mask woman promised there would be buffets, and here they are, laid out like a cornucopia of riches throughout the giant main room of the rooftop suite. It's like someone was planning a wedding for a million people with an unlimited budget. Seems overboard, but I'm not exactly complaining. I eagerly load up a small plate with shellfish, decoratively sliced veggies, and fruit.

Snagging a glass of sparkling wine from a passing waiter's tray, I make my way over to the walkway surrounding the pool, heading toward the music and the party that's already well underway.

Damn, real crystal glasses? Who's throwing this party? Gatsby?

I spend a few minutes enjoying my fancy little meal and people watching before abandoning my empty plate and turning my attention to the dance floor.

The place is pumpin'.

There's a live DJ spinning reggae hip-hop mixes and at least a hundred people, all in masks and not much else, getting down on the dance floor.

I'm mesmerized watching them when I feel someone come up behind me.

"Enjoying the party?" a male voice asks over my shoulder.

I turn to find a man in a red and black tiger mask and a black linen suit. His mask, like mine, covers three-quarters of his face, leaving just his mouth visible.

It's impossible to see his features, but the way he looks, filling out his expensive-looking yet casual suit, hip cocked to one side with his hands tucked in his pockets, tells me a bit about him.

Youngish. Older than me, but not old like my parents.

Fit.

Rich.

And that voice. Smooth like velvet.

"I am, yes. Is it your party?"

"Mine?" he asks with a surprised laugh. "Not exactly."

I glance around wondering if I'm ever going to get to meet the host. The man responds to my distraction by stepping back into my line of sight.

"Care to dance?"

"Oh, I was probably just going to watch."

"What's the fun in that?"

I glance back toward the mass of gyrating people and decide that I could dance for a few songs. I mean, there's a man who's probably handsome inviting me out on the floor after all.

"Okay."

I let him lead me by the hand to the center of the fray.

I'm not generally the kind who jumps out on the dance floor, especially at such a rambunctious party, but it feels different here. Maybe it's because we're all wearing masks, but it doesn't feel like everyone is watching me. My self-conscious tendencies are able to take the night off.

Maybe that's the point.

No, that's definitely the point.

"Are you going to tell me your name?" I'm not sure why I ask. It's not like I care all that much. This is a dance floor-only kind of relationship, and I'll forget all about him tomorrow when my new job starts.

"No," he answers simply.

I laugh in surprise. "What do you mean no?" I never expected him to actually not tell me.

"No means no. Didn't they teach you that back in the States?" His tone is sly and flirty, and he leans in as he says the words, grazing each one down my neck.

I shiver. "Yeah, I guess I've heard that before." I manage, my voice as weak as my knees.

"You can make up a name to tell me, but don't you dare tell me your real one."

I pull back and look him in the masked face. "Why not?"

"Because this isn't that kind of party, love."

Something settles over me then, a feeling I can't quite place, but it zings excitedly in my chest. "What kind of party is it?" I ask.

The man leans in close once more and whispers in my ear.

"The kind where you can do anything you want and not have to worry about the consequences."

There's something both eerie and electrifying about his words. What he's suggesting is just the kind of freedom I've been dying for after years of living in cramped quarters with a family who has something to say about everything I do.

I'm not exactly the kind girl who does wild things, but somehow, his words release something wild in me.

When the song ends, I gesture with my head toward the bar set up at the far end of the dance floor. "I'm going to grab a drink." I toss the words out as though I couldn't care less if he comes with me. My heart leaps into my throat when I feel him take my hand and guide me through the crowd.

He orders us shots without asking, and I take mine without complaint.

Ordinarily, I would insist on ordering for myself, or at the very least knowing the contents of my glass, but this night is anything but ordinary.

Cheers.

We take one more shot, then head back out to dance, the distance between us all but erased by the alcohol.

When he pulls me close for the next song, he pulls me really close.

Instead of needing my space, all I need right now is this man's hands on my body. I place them there as we sway to the Caribbean beat. The noisy crowd around us fades away as a bubble of magic rises up from the floor to encapsulate us.

Two people. One moment.

I catch myself gazing into his eyes and quickly look away.

"Want to take a swim?"

I glance over at the pool, lit up from the inside with blue LED lights. It's teeming with mostly naked people. "Eh, it's a little crowded."

What catches my eye is the rooftop suite, looking almost like a mini mansion perched up on the roof of the resort. The masked man must follow my gaze.

"Care for a tour?"

I narrow my eyes at him behind my mask. "I thought it wasn't exactly your party."

"Doesn't mean I don't know my way around."

"Yeah, okay."

He starts to pull me off the dance floor, but I hold back.

"Just a tour, though." I'm not fooling anyone, not even myself.

Rule #2

STICK TO THE PLAN

FRAN

We stop at the bar for a glass of sparkling wine before heading across the patio toward the half-open set of sliding glass doors leading into the first level of the suite. Men and women alike clap the man on the back or shoulder, calling out drunken greetings as he pulls me through the giant living room and toward a set of stairs. I try to catch his name in the shouts, but these people are apparently well-versed in the rules.

Up we go into the darkness of the second floor. When we reach the landing, we're in a hallway lined with closed doors.

"How many rooms would you like to see?" he asks, his tone signaling that he knows exactly why we're up here.

I know as well. "Just one will be fine."

As soon as the door closes behind us, he presses me against it, and our lips finally meet.

To call the feeling electric seems like a sorely lacking cliché. The kiss is more like molten lava.

I'm already hot from dancing, and now I'm on fire.

And a teeny bit drunk.

This dress will not come off fast enough.

The masked man drops to his knees before me and takes the hem of my dress in his teeth. He pulls it up to expose a few more inches of thigh and looks up at me.

I nod.

He raises up enough on his knees to be able to pull the dress over my hips. My black bikini bottoms feel skimpier than ever, now that they're the only thing standing between me and being exposed in front of this complete stranger.

"Take them off," I command in a voice I don't recognize.

The words earn me a smile, however, and the power of it all shoots straight to my brain.

He pulls them down roughly, just enough to take in the sight of me. His lips graze lightly over the lips I shaved this morning —just in case—so softly that my whole body screams for more. When I buck my hips toward his face, he pulls away and stands.

Before I know what's happening, he's got both of my hands in his and is pinning them overhead against the door.

"What do you want from me?" he asks.

The question is unexpected, and I feel a sudden burst of nerves at the idea that I will have to tell him what to do. I thought he was just going to, you know, do things.

I suppose I could just tell him to do that.

"I want to lose myself in this." It's something I heard in a movie once.

I can't see enough of his face to get a satisfactory idea of the reaction my words have on him, but I imagine his eyebrows going up in surprise.

Hell, he wouldn't be the only one surprised by my brazenness.

All I can see are his darkening eyes, and his lower lip clenched between his perfectly straight teeth.

His hands tighten on mine, and he presses his body close. "I'm going to take that as a request for me to be in charge?"

I nod. He can't see my face with his pressed into the crook of my neck, but I know he can feel it.

As he brings his face back to center to look me dead on, he licks along my ear and collarbone, leaving a trail of wetness and goose bumps behind.

"I'm happy to be in charge, love. But I need you to acknowledge that you understand you're still in control."

I nod.

"Say it."

"I'm in control."

"And if you want me to stop?"

"I'll tell you to stop."

He nods and considers me for a long moment, the tiny bit of face I can see not giving away his full expression.

Then he pulls me by the hands and shoves me roughly on the bed, letting go of me as I fall backward.

Let the games begin, I guess.

He walks forward until he's standing between my knees where my legs dangle off the edge. He pulls up roughly on the bottom hem of my dress, and my hands fly up to save my mask from being pulled off with my garment.

"Sorry, love. That was a close one." He tosses my dress aside without a glance toward where it lands. "I forgot to tell you the only rule I have. If you take that mask off, it's over."

"What if you take it off of me?"

"I won't do that."

"Okay."

"What about you?"

"Me?"

"Any rules?"

"Oh." Jeez, do I have any rules? After just telling the strange man in a mask that I want to lose myself in him it feels silly to all of a sudden start listing off rules, but I do want to be able to offer something. He did, after all.

I take a deep breath. I generally save my one condition for

later on in the evening, when the condom-covered cock is a bit closer to its target. But what the hell. May as well lay it out now.

"I…I want you back here." I roll onto my knees with my ass facing him and slide my hand down one of my cheeks.

His response is immediate, grabbing me by both hip bones and pulling my ass right up against the erection in his pants. He holds me there and thrusts a few times. My body explodes with the anticipation the movement creates.

"You like it back here, love?"

"Yeah."

"Well, we're here to get you what you like."

I relax when I realize he's not going to argue. It's not like I spent my college years whoring my asshole out, but of the handful of guys I managed to get this far with, most of them had to be talked into it.

Not this guy.

Still holding my hip with one hand, he pulls my black bottoms down around my knees and spreads my cheeks, brushing his thumb over my tight hole. "I think you and I are going to get along just fine."

I can barely breathe now that his hands are beneath my bathing suit bottoms, sliding over my bare, screaming flesh. His fingers make their way forward, one of them finding my clit. "Can I touch you here?"

"Yes." *God, yes, please.*

He slides his fingers back to my pussy entrance, hovering softly over what I know damn well is a very wet hole. "Can I put my fingers here?"

"Yes."

In they go, the wetness I was anticipating allowing his fingers to slide right in. I can't imagine it's more than two, but they go deep fast.

"Fucking glorious."

I squeeze my eyes closed and hold my breath.

Only to have the air knocked out of me as I'm pulled to my feet. The man holds my back close to his chest and reaches around to free my breasts. When the bikini top is discarded, he takes one in each hand. I'm pinned here by his tight grasp, his fingers working my taut nipples, his still clothed erection working my backside.

Torturous suspense, but the very best kind.

Then I'm being walked to the end of the bed where the man presses my hips up against the plush, padded footboard. Coincidentally—or perhaps not—it's the perfect height to bend me over at the waist, and he does just that.

"Stay there for a second, I'm going to go look for some—"

"Oh," I say, remembering too late that I forgot to tell him. "I have some lube. It's in the little pocket of my dress."

In the tiny hidden pockets where most women carry condoms, I carry single-use packets of silicone lube. To each their own.

I can say with one hundred percent certainty that this man is prepared in the condom department.

I can just see out of the corner of my eye from where I wait, bent over the bed, the man rustling up my dress and locating the packets. I ambitiously packed three for this party. He brings them all, tossing them on the floor next to my left foot.

"You are not how I expected my evening to go, you know?"

"I could say the same thing about you." I want to sound cool, but it's hard to talk with my ribcage bent over the footboard.

"Says the girl with three packs of lube hidden in her dress." I can hear the smile in his voice.

He's got me there.

"Wishful thinking," I say, trying to recover a bit of my dignity. Or, as much dignity as I can manage bent over spread eagle with my asshole about to get primed.

"Wishful thinking indeed."

I feel his hands slide down the backs of my thighs as he

kneels. The man wastes no time in sucking my clit straight into his mouth, and I scream in surprise and pleasure.

"I wish I knew what you were thinking right now." His words are a brief pause in his contact with my pussy. He dives back in without waiting for an answer.

The fingers that were inside my pussy before slip right back in and curl into my body. Between them and the way he's sucking at my clit, mixed with the anticipation, I'm going to be coming in seconds. I breathe deeply to try to slow it down.

The man seems to realize this and slows himself. His sucking turns to licking, up and around my electrified nerves. His fingers slow as well, gripping harder inside me, but sliding only an inch or two in and out. It's really all he needs. Somehow, the cunnilingus magician already found the only spot inside me he needs to touch.

The slow pace is only ramping me up more quickly, as his movements get more and more specific—and more and more ideally placed.

"I'm going to come."

"That's what you think, love."

What? That sounds like a challenge, one I am happy to rise to. I suck in a breath and hold it tightly as his tongue gives me just enough…

But it's not enough.

He's one step ahead of me, lightening the flick of his tongue on my clit just as he starts fucking me hard with his fingers. And it's so good, so fucking good. My poor pussy doesn't get enough attention, only what I can offer her myself. It's not exactly normal behavior for a man to fall to his knees and give like this. And this guy is giving it all he's got.

It's not enough to bring me that last bit, but I can't find even a shred of care anymore. He could just do this forever, orgasms be damned.

My body doesn't get the memo, however, and I can feel my hips pressing back, chasing more clit stimulation from his tongue. As I move closer to his face, he pulls back just a bit, keeping me at the distance he wants me. I only have a few inches of play before I can't move toward him any more without surrendering my position over the footboard.

I cry out in frustration and pleasure and excitement. The sound is primal, animalistic, and nothing I've ever heard come from my own mouth before.

I hear him return the growl between my legs.

"You're lucky I want to fuck you so bad, love. I could keep this going all night."

I say nothing, honestly content with any direction this whole thing takes, and suck in a deep breath, preparing myself for the big O I feel coming.

But nothing could prepare me for this one. Fractured bits of sound escape my lips as I plunge off the cliff of pleasure and into fully uncharted territories. The man between my legs feels the second I tip into it, and he changes his tactics to one of prolonging, rather than instigating.

And prolong it he does. His fingers just in the right spot, his tongue now soft on my clit, the pulses of pleasure go on and on, lasting so long that I laugh a bit, clenching my eyes closed and allowing him to take me farther and farther.

When I finally emerge on the other side, sensitive and breathless, I'm astounded.

"Okay, okay." I laugh, and he stops.

What the fuck just happened?

It seems I've been failing miserably at my vibrator game. I had no idea an orgasm could last that long. Maybe I've just been getting myself there too quickly. Something about the tease and denial made my body break in a whole new way.

It's probably better that I don't have a chance to catch my breath before the cold lube hits my backside. It almost feels like this is an extension of the activity, rather than a completely new one. He orgasmed my body open and now he is going to fill it.

And all I have to do is dangle here.

Princess fucking life.

I hear his clothes hit the floor and remember with surprise that he's been fully clothed this whole time. I try to get a glimpse of his naked body behind me, but he's just out of sight. All I see is a flash of golden hair-dusted calf, a few tentacles reaching toward his foot from a tattoo I can't see fully from this angle. Something about the black ink sparks my mind, though, and I struggle even harder to turn and see the full thing. It's futile. Oh well, I'll see him when we're done.

Fingers enter my body first, bringing my mind back to the task at hand. The first one is cold, but it slides well in the ultra-high-end lube.

"Tight little hole, love."

It's extra tight because I'm making it so, giving his finger a little squeeze. I'll do the same thing to his cock soon enough.

I get two fingers next, as he works more lube into my body. He's prepping me like a perfect gentleman, and my heart melts at the gentle touch he offers. I relax my muscles and open up for him as he strokes my insides.

"There she is," he freaking coos as his fingers fuck my tight hole a bit more easily.

The tear of a condom wrapper makes my breath catch once more.

This is really happening. I'm getting fucked by a complete stranger at a party on a tiny island that I moved to only yesterday.

Plot twist.

When his tip swirls at my hole, my clit comes back to life. My whole body comes alive, as if it was waiting in the wings this whole time and now wants a piece of the action.

He presses in, and I let him, staying as relaxed as I can to encourage him to bury himself in me. It's a long, slow, delicious slide, and he makes it in on his first try.

"Fucking hell, love."

I agree, sir.

He pulls out and thrusts back in quickly and then seems to catch himself, offering a few slow pumps to get me used to it.

"I'm ready," I say. I can't wait another second.

"She's ready..." he murmurs behind me, continuing his long, slow thrusts.

I can tell he's trying to keep himself from coming right off, and it's certainly appreciated. Most guys come in seconds the first time they make it into my tight hole, apologizing profusely for the lack of proper fucking. They just can't help themselves, once inside, they fuck like crazy for a few, and that's that.

Not this guy. He's tempering himself to the feeling. I can hear his long, slow breathing timed perfectly with his sliding in and out of me.

Franzeska, you may be in for it this time.

God, I'm so ready.

The man brings his hand down between my legs and presses his fingers back inside my pussy. It's even wetter now after my orgasm, and they slip right in. His thumb presses down on my clit, the nerves there very sensitive still, but somehow ready for his touch.

With the other hand, he takes hold of my hip bone, his fingers gripping tightly in a move that could almost be called painful—if my body had any sensory receptors to spare. Right now, it's all focused on the three most important things happening.

I never got to see his cock, but I can tell it's a big one. The first slam of him to the end rattles my bones. I get another one before I've recovered from the first. They're coming more quickly now as he finds his rhythm.

The fullness is so extreme, borderline too much, with his massive cock pounding into me, his fingers fucking my dripping pussy. I'm suspended in a place between orgasm and screaming where there is no breath, no rational thought, no time or space.

There's only him and me.

With my eyes closed and breath held, I take all he's got. I can't tell how many fingers have slipped inside me, it could be his whole damn fist for all I know. Suddenly he's curling his fingers the other direction, toward where his cock is buried in my ass. I can feel him feeling the slide of his tip through the thin wall that separates the two entrances to my body.

For a second, the sensation of him touching himself through my flesh is the only thing I can focus on, breath still ragged, eyes still closed. Then suddenly, his thumb hits my clit, pressing down hard until he hits the bone and holding my bundle of nerves there as he thrusts his cock deep inside me over and over.

I'm coming again suspended in time. I can't move a single part of me, face still covered by my mask and shoved into the bed, the plastic sliding painfully to one side, feathers threatening to poke my eyes out if I dared open them. My hands grip the blankets below me for leverage as my lower body is immobilized by the spearing it's taking from the man's cock.

All I can do is hold my breath and ride it out.

As I do, my body clenches down hard on all the muscles down there, and I hear him react to my now much tighter hole. I clench back there even harder in response.

Feeling him come apart during my orgasm is a delightful treat I never even knew I was missing out on in life. I'm breaking open as the waves of pleasure tear me apart, and he's filling me with his cries, his cock, his seed.

I'm never going to recover from this.

Our bodies finally still, and we hover, locked in that moment for so long, I lose track of time. When he finally slides out of me, his cock retreating at the same time he pulls his fingers free, I am left feeling wide open and cold.

I can't move to comfort myself, and the sudden need to curl to the side overtakes me with what I know sounds like a sob but is actually just how my breath sounds when I let it out for the first time in what feels like forever.

The man's arms pull me up immediately. He lifts my limp body from the footboard and walks me around to the bed where he lays me down.

"Will you fix my mask?" I haven't regained all the blood in my arms yet, and they're too tingly to manage the task.

He stands for far too long of a pause, looking down at me, before leaning down and righting my little bird mask.

"I don't want to break the rules." Who knows why I say it. Rules are the last thing on my mind right now.

The man walks into the en suite and comes back with a warm, wet towel that he uses to clean me while I lay on the bed, watching him.

His red mask covers enough of his face that I wouldn't have known what he just went through with me if I hadn't been there to witness it.

He's still naked so I get to glimpse the body I was craving a look at back before he ripped my whole world in two.

He's sculpted and bronze like a man who lives in the sun. The sheen of sweat on his skin only works to highlight the chiseled lines of him, the patches of golden hair, and the black ink scattered over his skin.

I can see the full sea creature now, the one who owns the tentacles I glimpsed before. The ink is oddly familiar. I feel a flash of déjà vu, as if I had seen the thing before in a dream. I smile at the thought of having a premonition of this particular night, how very fitting that would be for my state of mind lately.

I've been single, alone, and focused on myself for so long I can hardly even remember the last time someone's hands were on my body.

Fat chance of that ever happening again. I could go fifty years before my next fuck and not forget his hands. I let the memory bathe me in dopamine once more, any concern I had over the strangely familiar tattoo fading as I continue to take in the perfect specimen below the mask.

He sees my smile and returns it with one of his own.

I wish I could take that smile and tuck it into the secret zipper pocket of my dress.

Because I know I'll never see it again.

I watch as he crawls up onto the bed next to me, placing his back against the headboard with his knees bent.

Someone else's headboard.

Someone else's bed.

Someone else's suite.

The realization hits me like a punch to the gut.

There will be no tender moment of curling up and falling asleep together after this. We are just two strangers who fucked in an empty hotel room at a party.

The owner of this room is not going to appreciate finding us here when they stumble up to bed.

Against the screaming protests of my body, I pull myself upright. I'm a bit woozy for a moment, but I breathe through it. The man lunges forward, intent on catching me if he needs to, but I steady myself.

Getting to my feet is another story.

I'm hyper aware of the man watching me as I collect my tiny scraps of clothing and quickly get myself dressed. I don't know what to say, so I say nothing.

After I pull my dress over my head, careful not to dislodge my mask, I look up to find him standing. He's not close enough to touch me, but the slightly forward position of his arms tells me that he would like to be.

I hesitate, considering walking into those arms, but catch myself just in time. The yearning feeling in my chest is enough of a red flag to keep me from indulging it. The last thing I need is to let myself think for a moment that this is something it's not.

"That was fun." It's a stupid thing to say, but I don't know what else to do. The man hasn't said a word, and with his mask still in place, I can't read his expression. For all I know, he's impatiently waiting for me to leave.

"No," is his surprising answer.

I swallow hard. "No, it wasn't fun?"

"No, don't leave like this."

I laugh softly in relief. "Well, I can't tell you my name or take my mask off, according to the rules, so I think I better just go."

"We'll change the rules."

My jaw clenches with indecision. Just a second ago, all I wanted was for this man to snuggle up with me and sleep the night. Shouldn't I be happy that he now wants a proper introduction?

I am happy. I'm just…

I take a deep breath and let it out slowly.

He seems to take my hesitance as an invitation to move forward with the introduction. Hell, maybe it is.

"I'm A—"

"No." I hold up my hand and stop him. "No," I say again, this time with more confidence. "This party has one rule. We aren't breaking it."

"I made that stupid r—"

I hold up my hand to stop him once more. I don't know why I can't just relax into whatever this is, allow this handsome and obviously interested man to unmask me and take me into his arms.

Maybe that's it right there. I can't be taken into anyone's arms right now. I came to this island for a reason. I'm here to take the first step toward the rest of my life. I have a concrete goal. I've been given the opportunity of a lifetime to achieve it.

I will not be derailed by a man.

Albeit a handsome, perfect in nearly every way man.

But I can't actually know that. Sure, the guy is an excellent fuck, but what if he turns out to be controlling or douchy, or… my eyes flick back to his calf tattoo and then jet away once more as if burned by an ember.

No.

Better to walk away now, as hard as it is. I'm going to have to be able to make hard choices in order to make it on my own. To run my own company. This is just the first one.

I start to walk toward the door in lieu of answering, not

trusting anything that might come out of my mouth. He catches my hand for a split second, not holding on to me, but making enough contact to make me pause.

"Give me a chance," he says.

And, by god, I almost do.

Instead, I run.

Rule #3

CHIN UP, WALLS HIGHER

AVERY

"Father, Padre, Père, Vater. To what do I owe this honor?" I sing out as I answer the phone, ducking into a small alcove so I can hear over the wind rushing off the ocean.

"Oh, grow up, Avery. You're nearly a forty-year-old man. When are you going to stop answering your phone like a goddamn teenager?"

I grind my teeth. Why did I answer at all? "Big words from a man who wasn't around enough when I was a teenager to know what I sounded like."

Why did I have to say that? Why did I let him know he got to me?

I should hang up now. Cut my losses.

"For the love of God, Avery. When are you going to get over all that? It's ancient history."

"Yes, of course. Anyway, what can I do for you?" Better to just agree and get this over with. "I assume you weren't calling to check on the status of my manly phone answering skills."

Frederick heaves a sigh so heavy I can hear it over the breeze. "I got married."

"Oh. Congratulations?"

Another sigh. "You know, the least you could do is be happy for me."

Oh, no. I could do a hell of a lot less than that.

"I'm happy for you, pops. What's the blushing bride's name?"

"Her name is Mimi."

"Well, give Mimi my best."

"That's not why I'm calling."

I roll my eyes up to the sky and wait. Whatever this is, it better be good. I can see the party on the beach starting without me, tanned bodies stripping off cover-ups to reveal skimpy bikinis as they run toward the ocean.

"Mimi has kids. Her oldest one, her son, is getting married."

"Goodness. Double congratulations are in order."

"Cut the shit, Avery."

I don't bother to respond.

"Mimi was thinking that The White Sands would be the perfect location for the wedding."

I pull the phone away from my face so he can't hear my surprised laugh. "Oh, is that what Mimi was thinking? And what does the happy couple think?"

"Mimi's son is very…obedient."

Unlike his. He doesn't need to say the words aloud. They hang in the air between us.

"Okay, well…"

The guys and I have talked a lot about hosting weddings at the resort in our quarterly meetings. The property is perfect for it, with its enormous center courtyard that leads straight onto the beach, two full restaurants, and enough rooms for all of the bride and groom's dearest family and friends.

If I remember correctly, the last conversation we had about it hinged on the idea of needing to find someone to run the program—book the vendors, coordinate, that sort of thing.

Dom flat out refuses, and Sam is far too busy to take it on. I suppose one wedding would be possible, assuming we could find a wedding planner to run the show. "I'll just need to check in with Sam."

"I already did."

Of course he called Sam first. Why would I expect anything else?

"Oh, perfect. So, you're just calling me to…"

"Can't I call and have a talk with my son?"

You can, certainly. You could have been doing this my whole life, but you haven't.

I say nothing. After the silence stretches on for a few moments, I hear another sigh.

"There's something else."

"Oh, goody. What other bombs does my dear old dad have to drop on me? Any new children you forgot to tell me about?"

"You know what? Forget it. Sam can tell you."

And he hangs up.

All in all, a pretty good chat with the man. Certainly the longest we've had in years.

As I tuck my phone back in my pocket and head back out to the beach, I make a mental note to call my mom soon. Last time I talked to her, she was still living in Paris with Rene or Jacque or whatever young French boyfriend she had at the moment.

She rarely marries any of them. She has sense. I never understood Frederick's need to always *marry* them. I mean, hasn't he learned his lesson yet?

Hell, maybe the man just really likes divorce court. There must be something about battling your former loved one in court to make sure they leave your home destitute that really appeals to the bastard.

Luckily for me, I learned those lessons through him. It took exactly zero marriages of my own for me to learn that I'm just not the marrying type. Sure, I enjoy the occasional girlfriend, even keeping some of them around for a while—as long as we can stand each other. But that's where I draw the line.

Love, lust, copulation—life's great pleasures. What's the use in signing legal documents over them?

I wade into the ocean after my friends and dunk my head in the warm salt water, washing away the conversation. There will be a wedding, which means a visit from Dad and his new bride, but that's all in the future. Nothing I can do about it now.

Best to focus on the present. The ocean, the sand, my upcoming dinner reservation.

And the girl from last night.

I've been trying in vain to put that whole situation out of my head all day. I just can't let it go. She was everything I'd ever dreamed of, dropped from the sky and into my lap.

I went to the party without a date hoping something crazy might happen, but I never could have imagined the night going like that. I'm usually the one calling the shots and blowing women's minds with my adventurous bedroom prowess. Last night, however? I got fully schooled.

I broke my own rules at the end. I just needed to know who she was so I could find her again. But she bailed, like she had every right to. I suppose it would have been just a matter of time before she got tired of me anyway, even if she had agreed to take off the mask and stay the night.

Maybe I'm better off not knowing.

Those kinds of thoughts used to be much better at consoling me. Something happened last night that shook me in a way I'm not used to.

And not even the ocean can wash it away.

Rule #4

ROCK BOTTOM HAS A BASEMENT

AVERY

After a riotous swim with the group of friends who flew in for the party and would be flying out later this afternoon, I head back to the resort to shower and change. It sounds like I need to get Sam alone for a minute to hear whatever else Frederick was too chickenshit to say to me directly.

My room at The White Sands is on the second to top floor, the corner unit facing east. I could have pulled rank and snagged myself a top-floor suite, or even a west facing sunset room, but even I know better than that. Those rooms bring in enough on their own to keep the lights on around here, and I have a very vested interest in those lights.

When we signed the papers to purchase the run-down resort eight years ago, I definitely got talked into it.

Not that I was upset about it, but owning a resort on a tropical island was hardly my dream.

It was, however, an opportunity for me. An opportunity to change.

I may have spent the last decade and a half as a free-wheeling adventurer, living out of a suitcase, hopping from one blonde beach babe's bed to the next, but The White Sands looked like it could be the beginning of a new era for me.

I certainly couldn't have asked for a better group of guys to go into business with. These three are my lifelong rocks, the people who were there for me when everyone else bailed. The ones who would answer the phone when I called.

Not that I do all that much calling.

It's funny, the longer you spend on your own, the less you seem to need people around.

Something about this felt different, though. I found myself dreaming about the resort—the projects I'd help tackle, the locals we'd hire, the community we'd build. Committing to something like this was a first for me, but hell, my life is one long string of firsts.

This was just my newest adventure.

I signed those papers knowing that freedom was just a plane ride away if things didn't turn out all sunshine and roses.

And, much to the dismay of the other three guys, that plane arrived the first year we were open. It's not that I don't love The Sands. It's not like I don't visit as often as I can.

It's just that the one thing I've learned to be true in life is you're better off leaving before you get left.

After a quick shower, I'm jogging down the steps to Sam's office. When I blow through the door, it's not Sam I find. It's a strange woman.

Strange as in, has yet to make my acquaintance. Not strange in any other way. As a matter of fact, the woman is pure perfection. Young as sin—the best kind—tall, muscular, with long dark hair falling over her shoulders in beachy waves.

"Good afternoon," I start as the woman looks up. "I was just looking for Sam."

She smiles at me, and it's glorious. Lips so luscious, I want to lick them like ice cream.

"He ran down to the front desk," she says.

I flop into one of the comfy chairs against the far wall and cross one foot over the other knee. Casual cool guy stance. "Well, it's a pleasure to make your acquaintance…"

"Oh," she says, blushing just a bit. "I'm the new wedding coordinator. Or I hope I am. I mean, I am." She smooths down her skirt with both hands and stands a bit straighter. I struggle to keep my eyes on her face. "I am coordinating the wedding."

Oh, wow. This whole thing is further along than I imagined. I guess things move quickly when you work all day, instead of sleeping till noon and then swimming in the ocean. Dear old dad really chose the right man for the job.

I'm back on my feet and approaching her before I can tell myself to stop.

Taking one of her hands in mine, I bring it idiotically to my lips. She tries to pull away for a moment, looking hesitant, but relaxes into my grasp after I shoot her my most charming smile. I graze my lips across her knuckles and resist the urge to bite down.

I am about to learn the name of this little siren when good ol' speak of the devil Sam comes through the door.

"Nine should be fine for that—" He stops short when he sees us standing there together.

The woman pulls her hand sharply down and out of my grip and offers Sam a smile and nod before turning on her heel to make a quick exit. As she does, her loose brown hair makes contact with my face, and I inhale.

Plumeria and sunshine.

I'm transported straight back to the night before, with those smooth thighs spread before me over the bedrail, the black and white bird mask covering eyes that must have been squeezed tight in pleasure as I fucked her tight little hole into orgasm after orgasm.

I open my eyes just in time to take in the long hair, pale purple nails, smooth pale legs with freckles. All checks.

By Jove, I think I found her.

She is a brand-new resort employee, but what the hell. Destiny is destiny.

She's gone before I can get another word out, but I'm not concerned. I have the full lead on her, and it sounds like she's more or less a permanent fixture here on Faraday. At least until after the wedding.

My biggest fear was the new love of my life being a day-tripper who had already hopped on a jet somewhere never to be seen again. This is the best news I've gotten…well, in a long time.

When I turn to Sam, I'm elated. He must read it on my face because he lets out a laugh and sighs. "Sit," he says.

I find my chair again.

"I talked to your dad."

"Yeah, he told me. I tried to congratulate him on his third… no, fourth…marriage, but he hung up on me."

Sam shakes his head. "You know, Ave, the man's not going to be around forever. Maybe it's time to set aside some of these old wounds."

Leave it to the guy with no father to not understand how important it is for me to stay mad at my father forever for everything he's ever done.

Oops, better not say that one aloud, Avery, you fucking asshole.

"Sounds like The White Sands is hosting its first wedding. We've been talking about it since day one." I try to bring the convo back to business, but I'm having trouble reading the look Sam is giving me. "It's a good thing, right? I mean, sure, it's family, but he'll still pay out the ass for this party. And we can use the pics for promo. I mean, this could be the start of something big."

"Yeah, it's going to be great. It's just…"

It's then I remember that there was one last big reveal Frederick left up to Sam. "Lay it on me, Sam. I can take it."

"Mimi has three kids, her son who's getting married here, an older daughter who is married and has kids, and a younger daughter who graduated from college a year ago. She's an aspiring wedding planner."

Damn. I can see just where this is going. "No way, man. That wedding planner you already hired is smoking hot. I won't stand by and let you fire her to bring on some nepotistic kid."

Sam is quiet long enough that my mind starts following the trail of breadcrumbs. It takes me a second, but he lets me get there.

That woman.

The daughter.

The wedding planner…

Oh.

Well, shit.

I sit back in the chair and bite my lip. I need to say something quick to pass off my shock as something else, but I can't find a single word in this entire brain of mine except…

Fuck.

Avery, you jackass. You just fucked your new stepsister.

Better not say that.

"Great," I manage. "Well, she seems…competent." I stand, Sam still giving me the 'what the hell's wrong with you' eyes. "I'm just going to go…for a second to…you know."

I make my escape on the wings of that brilliant statement.

Once in the hall, I let my head drop back and close my eyes, taking my first full breath since my brain clicked into gear and solved that little mystery. Mimi's fucking daughter?

Jesus.

This might be an actual problem. It's not often that I encounter one of those, or at least one that I can't throw money at.

I'm not sure there's a sum that will make this one go away.

That's Mimi's daughter. She's going to run the wedding for her brother here at the resort. Frederick will be here. I will be here.

I get a bit lightheaded and gasp in another breath, wondering briefly how long it's been since I took one.

Good ol' body, ready to throw in the towel.

It's not that bad.

I mean, it's hella bad.

Like, really bad.

Not the worst thing I've ever done by any measure, but the worst thing that I am one hundred percent guaranteed to be caught having done in front of all my friends and family.

Well, hold on now. Is that really how it has to go down?

I mean, it didn't seem like she recognized me, right? And the night before, she ran out of there when I tried to get her name, so it's not like she wanted to meet up for a date or whatever. She wanted to keep herself anonymous. And she didn't know that it was me in there.

In everywhere…

So we'll just leave it at that.

I can keep her secret. Our secret. I can keep it together. Do this stupid wedding and then get on with my life. I never have to see any of these people again after the wedding, if the last thirty-nine years of my life have been any indication.

Okay. I steel my resolve and straighten up. I run my hands through my hair a bit and rub my cheeks. This is going to be fine. I can do this.

Rule #5

KEEP THE MASK IN PLACE

FRAN

I got ass fucked by my new stepbrother.

Perfect.

So fucking perfect, Franzeska.

Of course I did. I mean, what else would I have done on the eve of starting this new job, which my mother and her rich husband pulled strings so I could get? Go to bed early and get a good night's sleep? Wake up at dawn to go for a run? No, no, no. Not Franzeska. I was doing shots and getting fucked by one of the resort's owners—my new boss—who also happens to be my mother's husband's son.

Leave it to me to screw this up royally. I mean, was there even another option? It's been weeks since I gave the family some reason to gossip about me at Sunday dinner. Perfect Leon and his perfect fucking fiancée. Perfect Anna and her…well, her kids are actually pretty perfect, but that's beside the point.

I thought I was taking a step in the right direction. I know everyone gave each other the classic "what's Franzeska up to now" look when I announced that I was using my business and design degree to start my own wedding planning company. They couldn't understand how it was any different than the catering job I had been doing through college. They actually expected me to take an internship at one of the business firms and design business card logos for the rest of my life.

As if they'd never met me.

Well, they've never really met the real me, I guess.

The one I keep hidden behind my perfect daughter mask.

No wonder I sank into my role of masked stranger so easily at the party the night before. I feel like I've been playing that part my whole life.

I reach my room and collapse inside against the closed door, finally letting my emotions out. I want to scream, but I can't do that with the shared walls surrounding me, so I settle for crying.

When there's nothing left but dry sobs, I haul myself off the floor and into the shower. As the water hits my face, washing away my tears, I start to feel better.

I did something stupid, but it's going to be okay. I mean, he clearly didn't recognize me.

He would have said something, right?

The guy isn't exactly mister subtle, at least not from what I learned in my internet stalking.

His Instagram is a slideshow of his fantasy life—beaches, helicopters, parties, far-flung destinations. He's the ultimate trust-fund playboy. Last night was probably just a blip on his radar. I'm sure he does stuff like that all the time. It was his freaking party.

I mean, the four of them own this place together, so I guess technically he wasn't lying when he said it wasn't exactly his, but untechnically—he was absolutely lying.

He was just saying whatever he needed to say to get what he wanted. That's what men do.

Well, two can play that game.

As I dry off and pull on soft shorts and a bikini top, preparing to lay out on my deck, I solidify my plan.

I'm just going to say nothing.

I'm going to go down there and do an epically badass job on stupid Leon's stupid wedding, and it's going to launch my company. Hell, I'm going to do such a good job that couples will be lining up outside my door to hire me.

Maybe I'll even have a door of my own for them to line up outside of by then, instead of this hotel room door.

Perfect plan.

I can do this. He's just a freaking guy. A one-night stand. It's not like it's my first. I'm going to pretend the whole thing never happened and go on with my life.

I'm still repeating those words like a mantra when I collapse on my sofa with a tiny travel-sized vibrator in hand. It's not a big deal if I go one more round with this baby and the memories of the night before, right? It's just in my head.

Sure, it was the hottest night of my entire life, and I will probably be masturbating to it until I'm dead, but I can let it go. I can be grateful that it happened, so I have something to fantasize about.

That's pretty pathetic, Franzeska.

It's not pathetic. It's fine.

I'm fine. This is all going to be fine.

Rule #6

YOU HAD ONE JOB

AVERY

By some stroke of luck—good or bad, I can't tell yet—she's down at the Reef Café when I swing in to grab dinner.

"Hey," I greet her, standing over her chaise lounge, turkey sandwich on a plate in my hands.

She tips her enormous floppy hat so that she can peer up at me. At first, it's possible she thinks I'm a waiter, but she gets there. "Oh, hey."

And then drops the hat back into place.

I set my plate down on the table next to her chair and drag another lounge chair over. It's horrendously loud as the metal legs scrap against the cement pool decking, drawing attention from all over. I ignore the stares and flop down. If I'm going to make this "friendly stepbrother" act work, I need to be proactive about it. Hiding in my room or avoiding her will only make me look guilty.

"We never got properly introduced earlier. I'm Avery."

She is silent and still for a long moment—too long—before pulling her hat off and rolling her face to the side to face me.

"Franzeska."

I open my mouth and close it again stupidly, trying to process that name. "Fran...*zeska?*" I give the zeska a little extra emphasis and a smile.

She turns her head back to the center. "That's right. My mom is a crazy bitch."

I laugh in surprise. "Whoa, whoa, whoa. I don't know if I like you talking shit about my new stepmom."

That earns me a smile. A tiny one, but I'll take it.

"So, Franny—"

"Don't call me Franny," she snaps, still not looking in my direction.

Now there's some of the fire I remember from the night before. I immediately start planning for ways to get more of it—when I catch myself. I'm supposed to be nice here, not trying to get her riled up for my own devious sexual purposes.

But hell, you can't teach an old dog new tricks.

"Fran? Franz? What do people call you? You can't tell me that everyone calls you Franzeska."

"My friends call me Zesk."

I nearly choke on the breath I'm taking as I try not to laugh. I fail miserably. "*Zesk*?"

"That's right."

"Well, your friends sound very cool and hip," I say, cringing as I age myself, "but I think I'll go with Fran."

She sits up and turns to me in one slow, fluid motion like a cat. "You will not call me Fran."

"Well, I'm certainly not calling you Zesk."

"You can call me Franzeska then."

"But why would I do that? It's so long and nicknameable. What about Ska? Anz? Nze?"

She lays back down and pulls the hat over her eyes. "If you call me any of those names, I'm going to hate you."

With a smile, I stand, pulling the hat off her head and tossing it on her lap. "If you make me call you Zesk, I guarantee you will start to hate that, too."

I grab my sandwich and exit the pool area through the door to the café where I emerged from.

Ha! Take that. I got the last word. Sure told her.

Oh, wait. That wasn't really the point of that little meeting, was it, Ave?

I was supposed to introduce myself to the daughter of my father's new wife. Not start World War III over a stupid nickname. What the hell is wrong with me?

I stop halfway through the café and turn on my heel, preparing to march back out there and apologize. Start over.

But when I get to the door, I'm frozen in place.

Franzeska must have slipped into the pool the second I left her because she's now pulling herself athletically up the side, climbing out of the clear blue water. It drips down her absolutely perfect, curvy body and pools around her purple toenails. I almost lose consciousness for a moment when my mind flashes back to the night before, and how I slid those legs to the side to gain better access to the treasure between her thighs.

Fuck! Shit!

Stop!

But it's too late.

My ship has sailed.

I can only hope that everyone will be kind to me when I'm carted off to the mental institution when the strain from trying to keep my cock out of my stepsister finally pushes me over the edge.

I need to leave the island.

Just get on a boat or a plane and go far, far away from here.

But even as I think it, I know it's not going to happen. I have been the one championing the wedding program since the beginning. It's the perfect project for me at the resort—sporadic bursts of work instead of the daily grind, schmoozing people, and problem solving.

All of my greatest strengths.

If I bail on this wedding, the guys are never going to trust me to take one on in the future. They're going to be a little surprised by my level of involvement, especially considering the fact my father is the one signing off on expenses, but who am I if not a man full of surprises?

As much as I like running, I don't think that's an option this time. Instead of avoiding Franny, like every instinct in my rational brain is telling me to do, I'm going to have to lean in. Be around her every day. Be so helpful that she will never for a second suspect me of being a dirty stepsister fucker.

I can't find a middle ground—this is an all-or-nothing kind of situation. Since I can't run and hide, I'll have to sink my claws in.

And my teeth.

Now that sounds great.

Alarm bells go off between my ears, but I hit the button to silence them. This is a perfect plan.

Rule #7

CHANNEL YOUR INNER ADULT

AVERY

Sam looks up in surprise when I walk into the meeting room. "Hey Ave, what's up?"

I try to hide my annoyance at his question. "There's a meeting. I'm here for the meeting."

"It's nine a.m."

I glanced around at the empty room and then back at Sam. "Isn't the meeting at nine? The woman at the front desk told me you had a wedding planning meeting at nine."

"I mean, yes, there is a wedding planning meeting, I just wasn't expecting to see you here. Or up, for that matter. I think the last time I saw you at nine a.m., you were still up from the night before."

He's not wrong there. But things are different now. "I'm going to help."

"You're going to…help."

"Yeah, Sam. I kinda own this place. Isn't it time I had a job here?"

"*You* want a job?" His emphasis on the word "you" makes me scowl. "You've never had a job in your life."

"Well, there's no time like the present."

Sam sits back in his chair and considers me. "And what kind of job did you have in mind?"

"Wedding program director."

Sam nearly spits out the sip of coffee he just took. "Wedding program director."

"That's right."

"Do you have any idea what a job like that entails?"

"Directing wedding stuff."

"Wedding stuff."

"Sam, I'm a learn as I go kinda guy. I just know that since this wedding is being put on by my father, and it's celebrating the love and commitment of my new brother, I should be involved."

"As the wedding program director."

"Exactly."

"Okay."

The way he collapses so suddenly gives me pause, but not enough pause to come to any real conclusions about what it might mean. "Great. I'll start now. At this meeting."

I sit in a chair and look around. "Is anyone else coming?"

Sam considers me carefully, and I raise my eyebrows back at him.

"What?" I ask.

"This just seems suspicious."

"Can't a guy want to help out at his estranged father's new wife's son's wedding?"

"I will find out what's going on here."

The hell you will.

This guy may have been one of my best friends since I was learning to tie my shoelaces, but I know how to keep a secret.

While he and the other three guys were learning to run businesses and communicate professionally, I was learning how to smuggle dehydrated reptiles through customs and convince pirates not to murder me.

I've got this one in the bag.

She breezes in then, bringing the scent of plumeria and sunshine with her.

I'm instantly transported back to when I had my hands on her, and I try to shake it off.

I fail and shift a bit so my now bulging crotch is hidden better under the table.

"Morning, Franny."

Her head whips in my direction. "I told you not to call me that."

"I know, I know, I just can't get used to *Zesk*. It just won't roll off the tongue, you know? Zesk, Zesk, Zesk. The more times in a row I say it, the worse it gets. Like I'm trying to rid my mouth of something—"

"Thank you, Avery." Sam shuts me up with a stern glance. It's probably for the best. "And good morning, Franzeska. Thanks for meeting with me…us…to go over the preliminary plans."

Fran is smiling exclusively at Sam now, as if he's the only person in the room. "Thanks, Sam. I'm excited to get started."

When she speaks those words to Sam, I can see the genuine happiness in her face. This wedding stuff really excites her. She's happy to be here. For the first time, I consider what an incredible opportunity this is for a young wedding planner.

The White Sands is one of the premier Caribbean destinations. Our restaurant, Raft, won the Pendleton award last season, the highest honor a restaurant can receive. We've been almost completely booked out since. For this young woman to be planning a wedding here, well, it's a career-making opportunity.

One I'm making fun of left and right.

So, I make a new promise to myself. Even though I think marriage is an abomination, and this wedding is probably a sham, I am going to take this seriously.

So fucking seriously.

More serious than I have ever taken anything in my life. I will throw myself at the mercy of the wedding gods and bleed whatever it takes to make this wedding the smashing success it needs to be to make Franzeska happy.

Money. It's usually money I need to bleed.

Which is handy, considering that's pretty much all I have to offer.

I glance over and see Franny getting out her smart leather portfolio and setting her pen and pencil on the side in precise, straight lines. Sam has already arranged his yellow legal folder in front of him with two pens. They both came prepared with folders and extra fucking pens.

I glance at the empty table in front of me. Shit.

"Oops." I jump up, drawing all the attention in the room to myself. "I forgot my papers and stuff. Give me just a sec." I dash out the door and down the hall to HR.

"Carol, hey, good morning, you're looking lovely today."

"What can I do for you, Avery?" This woman has my number. She has been on staff since day one and has witnessed many of my island escapades—and the paperwork necessary when one of those escapades involves a resort employee.

"I need a fancy folder and paper and pens. A few pens."

She gives me a long look, and I gesture that I'm in a hurry. Finally, she rolls her eyes and lets out a sigh, reaching below her desk and pulling out a purple portfolio with a gold dolphin embossed on the cover. She slips a yellow legal pad inside and holds it out to me.

I hesitate. "Is that the only one you have?"

"I have work to do, Avery." Again, that tone from someone, insinuating that I have never worked a day in my life.

Well, I haven't, not exactly, but I do work at things.

I work out, for instance.

I work to learn how to say basic phrases in the language of

every country I land in on Duolingo. That's a hell of a lot of work.

I grab the folder and pluck three pens out of the cup on her desk. "You're the best, Carol."

I duck out of her office before she can reply.

Once in the hall, I pull the legal pad out of the portfolio and place it on top, covering the shiny gold dolphin. There. Very professional.

When I get back to the meeting room, Sam and Fran are talking. I sit back down in my chair, arranging my folder and *three* pens—take that, fools who only thought to bring two—on the table in front of me. "What did I miss?"

They both stare.

I swallow and glance down at my new set up and then back at them. "What?"

Sam recovers first. "We were just chatting about Franzeska's time on the island so far. She got into town earlier this week and is staying at the resort."

Sleeping in the same goddamn building as me. Perfect.

"Oh, lovely. I hope your room is to your liking?" I want to sound like a gracious resort owner, but I know I don't. "What did you get up to last night?"

Why the fuck I ask that is beyond me, but it's too late to take it back.

The poor woman blushes, obviously, and glances down at her portfolio. I follow her eyes and let myself really take it in for the first time.

The folder looks worn, used—well loved. The soft leather of the binding is creased from being opened and closed so many times. Two loose leather straps that must hold the thing closed drape to the side.

I imagine her long, slender fingers wrapping the straps around the folder to keep it closed after spending an afternoon filling the pages inside with ideas and inspiration.

As her fingers graze over the flat cover, I can make out a

small brand in the very center—a single word. Her fingernail catches in each of the letters as she drags it across the surface. I can't tell what it says, but there's no hiding what the folder represents. This is everything to her.

That simple leather portfolio contains all her hopes and dreams. All the pressure and wishes she's placed on her future. It must look so bright from where she's standing, with not enough years under her belt to know the truth about life. About the world.

Suddenly, the only thing I want is to protect this woman from ever having to find out. It's ridiculous, but I can't help it. My primal instincts, the ones I thought were only good for fucking, scream at me to protect.

"I went to town and did some shopping. Then I relaxed in my room."

I glance up from the place where her fingers are still touching her portfolio and meet her eye. I have no intention of calling out her lie, but I notice how easily it rolls off of her tongue.

God, Avery, don't think about that tongue right now.

"Well, let me know if you ever want to...if you need anything, I mean, I know this island like the back of my hand."

The hand that was smacking her ass while she screamed last night.

The silence lingers until Sam clears his throat. We both look over at him.

"As you know, Franzeska," Sam starts. The way her full name rolls so easily off his tongue makes me envious. Will I ever be able to call her that and not have it sound like a taunt? Not likely after the scene I made down by the pool. Why am I like this? "This is the first official wedding we will be hosting at The White Sands. There have been other, smaller affairs, elopements, that sort of thing, but this is the first big one. It's something we have planned on adding since day one, but we just haven't had the time to properly implement it. This opportunity is sudden, but it's a good one for us. It gives us a chance to get the first one out of the way and see how things go. I know this is a big opportunity for you, as well. This is your first?"

I turn back to Fran and watch her transform from bratty little sis into a calm, polished, professional. It's fucking spectacular.

"This is the first solo wedding I have put on, yes, although I have worked many. I was the assistant planner for McCree Events in Hartford for the last three years, and I graduated with a degree in business and design. This wedding will be the launch of my new company, Franzeska Events."

And it will be the world's greatest success. I'll make damn sure of that.

"That's great," Sam says, and I nod stupidly, as if anyone cares what I think. Besides, it's not like this is a job interview. This girl knew she had the job before we did. "Have you had a chance to look around the property and get some ideas about the set up and flow?"

"I did a bit of looking around yesterday and this morning, but I will still need to do a thorough walkthrough and take measurements—"

"I can help with that," I interrupt. Franny barely glances my way before going on.

"...and I do have some ideas that I want to incorporate." She opens her portfolio, and I can see that the thing is filled to bursting with loose, unlined paper, covered with notes and sketches. She pulls out a few, passing them toward the center of the table. I make a grab, but Sam's hand is there first. I slide my chair closer to his so I can see.

"The first sketch is how I see the altar coming together. I think that it will fit perfectly on the path that leads from the pool to the beach, but I'll have to measure to be sure."

The drawing she's referring to is a masterful pencil sketch of an elaborate arch of flowers with the ocean in the background.

"This is great," I say.

She doesn't acknowledge me.

"The next one is what I envision for a welcome area. We

aren't anticipating a huge number of physical gifts, most of them will have been ordered and shipped directly to their home, but I do want an area where people can leave cards or whatever they brought, and I can put the guestbook there as well. I haven't decided whether we will have disposable cameras or Polaroids, but that's where they will live."

I look up from the incredibly detailed drawing of a table decorated with flowers, driftwood, and candles prepared to question whether she really thinks disposable cameras or Polaroids are really appropriate—I mean, this isn't a high school graduation party—but the earnestness in her eyes shuts me up before I even begin.

There will be enough cameras and Polaroids for every guest to have their own. It will be the best documented party in history if I have to fly to the mainland and procure the damn cameras myself.

"The couple didn't choose specific colors. Honestly, they didn't pick much of anything. The groom, Leon, doesn't have much of an opinion about the wedding, and his bride, Cynthia, hasn't ever traveled out of the country. She got a bit overwhelmed just looking at pictures of the resort. After I told her my ideas, she said that she trusts me and wants the wedding to be mostly a surprise."

"That's a bit unusual, isn't it? For a bride-to-be so hands-off?" Sam asks.

Fran gives a solemn nod. "It sure is. I think the situation might be different if we were planning this at a church or hotel in the States, but as it stands, she's happy to show up and enjoy the beautiful wedding, without being overly concerned about the details."

"How does a woman who's never traveled and who imagined getting married in a church in the States get roped into a tropical destination wedding?" I ask, genuinely curious.

I can tell Franny doesn't want to answer me, but even she can understand that it's a valid question. "This whole thing was mostly my mother's idea. Then Frederick got involved, and the rest of the family started talking about how impressive it would be, and before long, she agreed. It's possible she's just in it for the pictures. I mean, she's going to be able to make a lot of Hartford socialites jealous with her posh Caribbean wedding."

"That's fair. Okay, so we don't need to be double-checking all of our plans with the couple as we move forward?" Sam asks.

"Nope. I plan to send her photos as we go along to keep her involved, but I want to honor her desire to have the finished product be a big reveal when she arrives. I do know that they both want the wedding to be beach formal and incorporate the natural beauty of the island. That will be whatever local flowers we can get at the time of the wedding, and the colors of the beach and ocean. I know The White Sands has gone with whitewash and green as its color palette, with some Caribbean blue thrown in here and there, so we'll try to match the wedding decor with the resort as much as possible."

"You want the wedding to look like the resort?" I ask, glancing up from the sketch.

"We want it to *match* the resort," she says smartly, her eyes resting on me for the briefest moment.

"Why would you want it to match the resort? It seems like you would want it to stand out. If the colors of the wedding are the same as the colors of our planters and umbrellas, it will just look like a regular old day around here."

Franny is glaring at me with barely concealed contempt. "I think it will be beautiful."

"Well, we can pencil your idea in for now, but we'll keep this line of dialogue open."

"We?" she practically hisses at me.

"Yes, we. I'm the wedding program director. Didn't Sam tell you? So, we'll be going over the plans together. I'm happy to hear all of your ideas, which look great so far, but the final decisions will be made as a team."

She does a fantastic job of keeping her cool, I have to give her credit for that. I guess while I was spending my formative years getting my way in every conceivable situation, she must have been dealing with unqualified asshole men swooping in to steal her thunder. I don't envy her that.

She can go ahead and hate me for now. When she sees what an excellent job I can do with problem solving and getting people to do what I want, she's going to be happy I forced her to be on my team.

"Perfect," she manages to get out through clenched teeth. "As I was saying, I will need to find out what flowers will be blooming in late February so I can plan—"

"We'll head into Saubry and talk to Marta, the flower farmer, but I'm fairly certain it'll be bougainvillea and orchids. Both come in a variety of colors, so you'll have a selection. We'll have a selection," I add with a smile.

The looks I'm getting let me know that they are both surprised I know anything about flowers, but when you're as fond of the ladies as I am, you learn a thing or two about flowers.

"That would be great, thank you," Franny says, expertly offering gratitude for something she didn't need or ask for from the man steamrolling her.

I need to cool it a bit. But do I even know how?

"It sounds like you have a lot of great ideas, and you'll just need a week or so in the resort and on the island to get things settled," Sam smoothly takes control back like the actual professional he is. "Let's meet up again next Tuesday and go over some final plans, then we can start arranging vendors and getting orders placed. We will need to finalize the menu soon after so we can get that catering order into the café."

"Sounds great," Fran says with a smile just for Sam.

He stands and glances nervously at me before collecting his notes and exiting. Franny is also gathering her things, but I haven't left my chair.

"Sorry to spring this whole teamwork thing on you—"

Her head whips to face me. "Are you?"

I open my mouth to reply, but she's already storming toward the door. "Wait, wait, wait. We got off on the wrong foot, sis."

"I'm not your sister," she hisses, hand on the door.

"I mean, not technically—"

"Not in any sense of the word. My mother married your father. That's all. We are not related."

I'm tempted to keep arguing the point, though for the love of God, I can't imagine why, since I can still feel the clench of her tight muscles on my now stirring cock. I decide to let her win this one. "Yeah, I know. I was just giving you a hard time."

"Why?"

She's got me there.

"I'm not sure," I admit, getting to my feet. "Can we start over?"

She doesn't want to let it go, but after a moment she does. What choice does she have? "Fine."

"Hey. I'm Avery. I'm Frederick's son. I own this place. I hear you are going to be launching your new wedding planning company by coordinating your brother's wedding here. I just so happen to be launching my career as a wedding program director for the same wedding. It's my first job…ever…so I was hoping you'd be willing to help me get off on the right foot."

I can see her lose the battle she's been fighting not to smile. One corner of her mouth tics up just enough for me to see that I've found my way in. "What do you say?"

"Avery." The gravity of her tone grabs my full attention. "This is really important to me. I know it might seem like a silly game to someone like you, but for me, this is everything. An opportunity like this could make or break the rest of my life."

My heart goes out to the beautiful woman in front of me. To think that anything that happens in your twenties could make or break your life, well, she's going to find out the hard way that this is only the beginning. I open my mouth to say something nice, but she's not done breaking my heart.

"I'm not like you."

"A forty-year-old man? Don't let it get you down, love."

"You know what I mean. You just rolled in here and decided to make up a job for yourself for God only knows what reason, and you can do that because you own the resort. You're rich and can do anything you want. I don't have that luxury. I need this to go well so I can support myself."

I crinkle my forehead and cock my head. "You do realize that your mother married the man who bankrolls my irresponsible lifestyle, right?"

She rolls her eyes. "It doesn't work like that."

"How does it not work like that? He's rich, they're married. It's pretty simple math."

"Not everyone is interested in being supported by daddy for their entire lives."

I cringe at the blow.

Franny's face takes on a look of pure satisfaction at my reaction. "I am planning to launch my company and create a wedding planning empire. Not sit around all day and spend someone else's money."

The dagger twists, and I struggle to suck in my next inhale. When I exhale, though, I let the pain go. It's nothing I haven't heard before. People think all kinds of things about my life, only some of which are true. I usually don't bother correcting them, but this dig hits a bit too close to home.

"It's more complicated than that." I don't know how much time I'll have with this woman, and for some reason, what she thinks about me feels important. "I do things, just not typical work things. Like, for instance, I own this resort."

She rolls her eyes and shakes her head. "Whatever. I just need this wedding to go well."

"I will do everything in my power to make sure it goes off perfectly. It'll be the wedding of the century, rivaling any horseshit royal wedding."

I earn a small smile for my trouble.

Finally, she nods.

I'm in.

Now, all I have to do is keep my hands to myself, not let her find out it was my cock in her ass at the party, and not fuck up this wedding.

Easy.

Rule #8

YOU HAVE NO ONE TO BLAME BUT YOURSELF

FRAN

Avery talked me into taking a trip to Saubry to look at flowers and "get the lay of the land" as he put it. While I know that I'm much better off being shown around by someone who seems to know everything and everyone on the island, my anxiety levels are high as I drop my water bottle, extra sunscreen, and a handful of local currency into my bag.

This man is just so unpredictable—and now we're working together—so my perfect plan of avoiding him completely has gone out the window.

I need a new plan and fast.

The idea that I could just avoid him and not let him realize it was me at that party was probably too good to ever have been true. Wishful thinking. All I can do now is keep my defenses up and let him know that I'm not someone he can fuck with.

Or fuck.

Again.

Sigh.

I tuck my phone into the pocket of my shorts. It mostly doesn't work here unless I'm on someone's Wi-Fi, but just having it close brings me comfort. Besides, I need to be able to take pictures of anything that strikes as inspiration for the locally inspired wedding palette I'm putting together.

And…after a bit of consideration, that palette might have to waver a bit from my original design. I'm not looking forward to the *I told you so* I'm sure to get from Avery when he realizes he was right.

He's waiting for me in front of the resort, leaning against a very nice looking green and black golf cart chatting with a security guard. When he spots me, he straightens and smiles.

I smile back, of course. Friendly. Friends. Relations of a sort.

I can do this.

Avery mimes opening a car door, and I slip into the passenger seat of the cart. He mimes closing it behind me.

On his way to the driver's side, he stops to say something to the security guard, clasping the man's hand as they clap each other on the back. I watch him closely, his knee-length flower-print Bermuda shorts and cream linen shirt hanging open in the front, exposing glistening golden skin with a dusting of lightly colored hair.

There's a tattoo on his side just visible from the front, and I have to look away to keep from blushing at the memory of the man fully bared before me. There is something so intimate about tattoos, about running your hand over one while someone takes in your naked body and you take in theirs. The image becomes a tattoo on your memory.

Avery climbs in beside me, and I look over with what I hope is a matter of fact smile on my face.

This is my friend, my coworker, my kind of boss, my kind of stepbrother. We are going to town. This is a matter-of-fact situation, and I will act professionally. The floor drops out from under my stomach as his legs swing in and another tattoo enters my field of vision.

The octopus on his calf.

The tattoo I have been looking at in pictures for years. That torso piece is relatively new, but the leg tattoo has been there for a long time. I should have recognized it. I did recognize it. I just wasn't able to place it in time. And even if I was, would I have said something then? Called him out? Told him who I was? Grabbed my clothes and bailed? Doubt it.

Jeez, Franzeska. You would have knowingly fucked Frederick's son.

The biggest problem is that somewhere, deep down, I did know.

Avery never would have known who I was at that party. He told me flat out in the office that he'd only learned about my mom and us kids when he talked to his dad that morning. He made an honest mistake.

I made a different kind of mistake.

Ever since my mom started dating Frederick nine years ago, I've been more or less obsessed with my new stepfather's jet-setting, absentee playboy son. Frederick always had a story about why Avery wouldn't be at holidays, or why we hadn't met him at all yet. It only added to the mystery of the man—and my attraction to him.

My high school years—and some of college, let's be serious—were filled with fantasies of the man showing up at Christmas or to my birthday party. He'd be so enamored with me that we'd end up flirting, getting along so well. And then dirty things would happen. Dirty things always happen in these fantasies.

When Frederick took to one of his tirades and conquered the objections my whole family had about me being ready to take this job planning Leon's wedding—effectively handing me the position—I knew Avery would be here. He owns the damn resort.

Not that I want to admit it, but there's a teeny tiny part of myself that knew exactly who the handsome man putting his hands on me was at the party. It's the exact thing I've dreamed of him doing since I was a teenager.

But that was then, and this is now.

It's one thing to fantasize about an out of reach celebrity in your childhood bedroom. It's quite another to put your entire career—and the opportunity of a lifetime—on the line for a chance at a couple of rolls in the sheets.

Nope. It's not happening.

This guy has promised to use his power and influence to help me pull off an incredible wedding in a place where things are a bit more difficult than the States. I should just be grateful and accept his help. Not that I needed help, really, but I have it, so that's that. I'm one thousand percent sure I could have done this on my own, but I'm not. I'm doing it with Avery's help.

We pull out of the circular drive and onto the bumpy street. It's only a few hundred feet before the road turns into coral dust, so I enjoy the smooth ride while I can.

"I can't wait to show you the island."

I look over at Avery and smile. He's radiating joy and excitement like a child. My first instinct is to thank him, but I don't want to thank him. I didn't ask for this tour or any of his assistance. He just decided he would be on the wedding planning team with me and inserted himself there.

He inserted himself all right…everywhere.

Oh god, don't think about that now. The man is literally two inches from me.

"I'm looking forward to seeing more of it." I say instead, forcing my eyes back onto the road, away from the bare skin of his chest as his unbuttoned shirt blows in the breeze of the golf cart.

Avery plants a strong, tan hand on my thigh where it rests on the seat mere inches from his own. I stare at it, trying to breathe around the sensation of my skin melting under his touch. When I look up, he's looking at me. Something in my expression makes him pull his hand away quickly and place it back on the steering wheel.

An awkward moment hangs in the air.

I want to break it, but luckily, I don't have to.

"So, uh, flowers?"

"Yes," I say, too quickly, grateful for the segue into something less intimate. "Flowers. I can't wait to talk to the flower farmers and find out what will be available and which colors we can work with. I think that just having the party be white with multicolored flowers is going to be so beautiful."

"Not white, green, and teal to match the resort?"

I look over, the detective in my brain searching for any hint of condescension in his tone or expression like I'm accustomed to getting every time I open my mouth around my family, but I come away clean. "The white is going to match the resort. But I am imagining big bouquets of pinks, purples, yellows, oranges, with the greenery, of course. It will be wild and carefree. Like confetti. Like a garden."

"Sounds lovely."

Again, I pull out my tiny magnifying glass, going over his words to make sure he's being genuine. Not making fun of me.

I find nothing.

"Have you given any thought to the menu?" he asks, unaware of my tone sleuthing.

I have, of course, given hours and hours of thought to the menu, but I'm hesitant to share too much. I still have not fully allowed myself to trust this man. I'm still waiting for him to tell me that what I'm planning is stupid and take my wedding away. Hand it over to a proper grown-up to plan.

I take a deep breath and let it out. When I glance over, he's looking at me with that kind, open expression that I've seen so often in photographs. I always imagined how easy it would be to talk to the man with that expression, but faced with him now, all I feel are nerves. I'm starting to sweat.

"I haven't really had a chance to eat at either of the restaurants on property. I want to hold off making any decisions until I get a feel for their style."

"You know, you don't have to go with the restaurants at The White Sands."

I look over at him sharply. "What do you mean? The wedding is at the resort. I just thought that catering was part of the deal."

He shrugs. "There is no deal, really. We've never done this before. It's not like you all signed a bunch of contracts for food and beverage minimums or anything. I mean, I'm sure that kind of stuff will be required for future weddings, but this is our wedding. We don't have to play by the rules."

I consider this in silence for a few moments. I don't hate the idea of bringing in local food for the reception. It's not something I'd thought about before, but now that I'm picturing it, I'm liking the idea more and more.

"Besides," Avery goes on, "the locals here know how to feed a party. Raft isn't going to cater the wedding, and Reef, while they certainly have the capability, hasn't ever done it before. You're going to be looking at the standard shrimp cocktail, Caesar salad, chicken or fish rigamarole." He shrugs again. "I mean, it's up to you, but..."

He really had me up to that last little statement. The part where he all but said that if I choose to get the wedding catered by the resort then I'm throwing a cookie-cutter yuppie party.

"As the owner of the resort, I would think you'd be a bit more complimentary of its menu options." I say primly, annoyed but not wanting to let on. I can't let him see that he got to me.

"Ah, the restaurants are fine. They're grand. They do their job. But we need to do our job, which is to throw the wedding that is going to launch the career of one Franzeska Miller and Franzeska Events. Someday, they'll have an actual wedding program director whose job it will be to sell the happy couple on shrimp cocktail, but that's not today. Today, anything goes. Consider me your free pass."

I look out to my right, where I can see the ocean in the distance. It's the only separation I can manage from the man when we are stuck in this tiny golf cart, speeding down the dirt road. If he happened to stop the cart for even a second, I think I would run.

"We'll have lunch in town at my favorite pit barbecue chicken place. There is also a bakery where the owner makes these caramel cookies—"

"Okay," I say suddenly, needing him to just stop being so wonderful for just one goddamn second. "Okay. That all sounds good. We'll go there."

He's silent for the rest of the trip, but I can feel his eyes on me. I know if I dared to look over, I would catch his gaze, but I don't.

Avery parks in front of a white cinder block building a few blocks into the small, colorful town.

"Is this the jail or something?"

He laughs. "No, this is Mackenzie's place. He does all the importing to the island. We'll be meeting with him for sure, once we figure out what we need to bring over from the mainland."

"Oh." I hadn't really considered how things get to and from a place like this. "So, he, like, has a boat or something? Planes?" I don't remember seeing an airfield, but there must be one.

"Shipping barge. There is a dock at the far end of the island, opposite the resort. The less picturesque side. He runs a route between here and Houston. Anything you can get shipped to Texas, you can get barged to Faraday."

Now that is a useful piece of information.

I relax a bit as Avery pulls down a few of the bricks in the wall I've built around myself.

I even feel him do it, but I don't object.

"What's first?" he asks.

I thought he was going to be in charge of this whole tour, so I'm happy to get to choose. "Let's get a coffee and then look at flowers. It's a bit early for lunch."

"Yes, ma'am. When you say 'a coffee,' I get a picture in my head of an iced Starbucks kind of thing. Is that what we're going for?"

He must be making fun of me, but again, I catch no hint of mocking in his tone. "That is what I was imagining, yes."

"Perfect, I know just the place."

He holds out an arm, gesturing for me to walk down the little brick path toward the street ahead of him. I do, and he follows close behind. As we walk the four blocks or so past little shops and food carts, Avery buttoning his shirt as we go, the owners and patrons all call out greetings to him as he smiles and waves, asking about their children.

He leads me up to a little window in a yellow building with a coffee menu posted on the side. In the end, I order a simple iced coffee with milk. The idea of being handed a blended drink with whipped cream and chocolate sauce like a ditzy teenager is too much.

I make a mental note to come back to this particular window on my own some time and get one of those.

Avery orders nothing, but ends up with some kind of green juice, forced on him by the older woman working the window, who passes it to his waiting hands with a glowing smile. I do not miss the large bill he slips into the tip jar.

The flower shop is next door.

"Marta!" Avery calls as we make our way into the makeshift shop consisting of rows of flower crates in a large, oblong shape. The exquisite scent of flowers is almost overwhelming in the small, sunny room. There are so many colors, so many beautiful, exotic plants to look at. I set down my coffee to take pictures of everything.

"This is Franzeska. She's the person in charge of the very first wedding at the resort. And possibly many more." Avery gives me a wink and one of his gunshot smiles that hits me just where he's aiming.

I die a little, right there on the spot.

Get it together!

"Hello," I say to the woman he's talking to—a short, older local woman with a colorful scarf wrapped around her large twist of braids. "Your place is so beautiful."

The woman finishes what she's doing and gets up from her stool with considerable effort. She walks over to me, still a bit hunched, and takes my hands in hers. "You and I, girl, we're gonna to be friends," she says with a deep accent.

I laugh in surprise but nod eagerly. "I'd like that."

"Nowhere else you get flowers like this. Other people, they have flowers come in on boats. Mexican flowers, same flowers they ship to the States, that's what they have. Not here. These flowers, all from Faraday, some from Merit, some from Jamaica. These orchids are from Belize."

"They're incredible. This is definitely what we want for the wedding. Can you tell me what will be blooming in February?"

"Mostly the same. This, the bougainvillea." The woman reaches out to touch the brilliant fuchsia flowers of a tall vining plant in a pot by the doorway. "This will be in all colors. February is perfect. Much easier for flowers then. Most flowers here are very delicate. The orchids are in the greenhouse on my property and my sister's property on Merit. We grow those for you anytime."

I like the sound of this. "One of the things I'm hoping for is to be able to build a large arch out of flowers for the couple to stand under for the ceremony. Is there a colorful flower that can be cut with stems long enough to build an arch like this?" I pull the drawing out of my portfolio, still juggling my phone, and show her.

The woman's face beams up at me. "Bougainvillea. I will grow that for you. The flowers here, most are not like the States, where there is a long rose or long daisy that you cut, and it lives for a short time. These plants will be alive at your wedding. I will grow the bougainvillea up the arch, and it will be alive."

"So, two pots at the ends of the arch and living flowers

growing up and over the top?" It's not something I had considered before, but I love the idea.

"Yes, yes. You come to the farm tomorrow and choose colors. Then we will build the arch and grow the flowers."

I look up at Avery, excitement swelling in my chest. I want to tell him how perfect it's going to be, how excited I am to go to the farm and choose the colors, but the look on his face stops me short.

He's watching me with what could only be described as adoration. But it couldn't possibly be that, could it? His eyes are soft and filled with joy. The smile on his lips is just barely there, a bit lopsided as he seems lost in whatever thoughts he's having. Whatever it is, I know for a fact it's about me. He watches me with undivided, unabashed attention.

I have to look away, suddenly unable to speak. Luckily, the flower farmer is already moving back to her stool, clapping Avery on the arm as she passes. "This is a good one, good girl. You bring her up to the farm tomorrow in the evening."

"Yes, ma'am," Avery replies, never looking away from me.

I can hardly breathe under his gaze. I snatch up my coffee and make a clumsy exit, thanking the woman over my shoulder as I practically run for the street. When I turn, I find Mr. Suave himself strolling smoothly out of the shop behind me, seemingly without a care in the world.

Out here in the blazing sunshine, I'm breathing better and can think more clearly. Whatever flirting I thought was going on in that shop must have been my imagination. I was having some kind of heat induced flashback brought on by my proximity to him in that small, confined space.

"You okay?" he asks, cool as a damn cucumber.

"Yeah, of course. It was just so beautiful inside there."

He looks at me with those eyes again, the dark ones. The fuck me eyes. "Beautiful doesn't even begin to describe it."

"Avery…" I have no defenses against this man's charms, but

I feel the need to at least feign fighting him off. I want to be able to tell myself later that I tried.

"Ready for lunch?" he asks, as if nothing just passed between us.

No, for fuck's sake. I'm not ready for lunch.

It's eleven in the morning. I'm holding a still full, dripping iced coffee, and my gut is completely full of turmoil and lust and anxiety. I am not ready for fucking lunch!

"Yeah," I say, as coolly as I can manage considering all of the gut baggage. "Lunch sounds great."

"Let's take the long way. You can see one of the best gardens on the island if we walk down the beach."

Oh, how perfectly romantic. Sure, just a nice stroll through a garden where you can take my hand and pull me into your waiting arms. Or the beach, where we might just get wet and have to take our clothes off. I think I would be safer alone with a serial killer.

"You can also finish your coffee," he adds.

"Yeah, yeah. Yeah." It's the only word I know right now, apparently. Avery raises his eyebrows at my sudden fluster, and I struggle to regain control of my brain. "I'd love to dip my toes in the water. I missed my chance to swim in the pool." The rooftop pool on the patio where this man swept me off my feet.

"Oh? Which pool was that?"

There is definitely a tone there now, but I don't have time to play Nancy Drew. I have to think fast. "The one at the…resort."

"Ah, yes," he says smoothly, as if he only just remembered that the resort had a pool. "The elusive resort pool." He holds his hand out as if he expects me to take it.

I'm paralyzed, breath stuck in my chest. What is it going to mean if I take this man's hand right now? It hovers in the air in front of me like a poisonous snake. One I have no choice but to grab onto.

As I do, Avery pulls me into motion on the pale, sandy street and then lets go. I let out my breath in relief and manage to keep walking even though I feel the paralysis his touch causes taking over. One foot in front of the other.

We walk in silence for a few moments.

"Tell me about your mom?" he says finally, breaking through my filthy thoughts with the worst possible question.

I cringe.

He laughs. "That bad, huh?"

"No," I say quickly, shaking my head to release some of the pent-up tension from my face. "She's not that bad. It's just…" I pause, considering how much I really want to tell this guy about myself. I decide on a short and sweet version of the actual truth. Something about his manner, and the fact that we are on an island in the middle of nowhere, so far from everything familiar, inspires that much in me.

"I'm the youngest, so there have already been two perfect examples in our family of how to become an adult. I guess my mom just expected me to be like them. High-powered career or mother and housewife. When I started on my own path, it's like the whole family went into damage control mode, secretly plotting among themselves about how to get me back on the right track." Well, shit. So much for short and sweet. I sigh and shake my head.

"And here I thought you came from a long line of wedding planners. Born and bred."

I laugh gratefully at the way he lightens up the mood. He always knows what to say. "Nope. Black sheep here."

He laughs and pulls me in for a side squeeze. I freeze and hold my breath till it's over.

"What about you?" I have to get the subject of conversation off of me. "I mean, I know your dad pretty well, but he doesn't talk about you much."

I see my words land and catch the tiniest bit of a flinch in his features before his face expands into a smile. I can't see his eyes well enough to know if it reaches them. "You probably know the guy better than I do."

"What happened between the two of you?" I've always wanted to know, but could never ask Frederick, of course. I imagine a big blow up or a tragic falling out.

"Nothing. Nothing at all."

I wait to see if he's going to go on. When he doesn't, I push. I'm not proud of it, but I've waited years for this story. I want a little more than that. "Nothing at all? You guys don't talk, seem to kind of hate each other, and nothing happened to cause it?"

"He just wasn't around. I guess he didn't latch onto being a parent. His work took him away a lot of the time, I'm sure, but even when he was home, he just wasn't interested in being involved. He and my mom were never very good together, and she was usually off on her own travels doing God knows what. The three of us just lived separate lives, pretty much since day one."

"Day one being the day you were born?"

He nods.

I grimace. "That's awful."

"Yeah, well, the story doesn't inspire much sympathy for me, as I'm sure you can imagine, so I don't rag on about it. Just try to tell people about your terrible childhood as a billionaire heir and see how bad they feel for you."

There's no mistaking his tone now. It's lonely. Sad.

I reach out and grab his arm, but he doesn't stop walking. My fingers slide off as he moves away.

"We're almost to the beach, let's keep moving." He speaks the words without turning.

After a deep breath, I hurry to catch up.

I feel bad that I caused this tension, but I'm also rejoicing in it. It has saved me from the other kind of tension I had been feeling since the flower stand. Or maybe since the golf cart ride. No, it was since the day before when I first realized who he was, and he smelled my hair. No, no, it was definitely since the night at the party when he was fucking me. Yup, that's definitely where the tension started. Hard to even see it now over the ancient family drama I just stirred up.

Avery kicks off his flip-flops when we reach the sand and scoops them up. I follow suit. He leads me down the gentle slope to the shoreline. Our silence should be comfortable, as we take in the gorgeous scenery, but I'm racked with nerves. I need to keep talking, if for no reason other than to shut my mind up.

"Your dad has always been really nice to me." It's true, even though I might still have said it if it wasn't. Of all the men my mom dated since my dad died, Frederick is by far the best. When she announced that they were getting married, I was excited.

Avery glances over at me, his expression unreadable. "That's great. I'm glad to hear it." He sounds genuine.

I ramble on. "He used to come to our house in Hartford a lot. He was always there for Christmas. When they got married, they moved to his house in Aspen. They're there most of the time now. I went for Christmas last year."

"Aspen, huh? I've never been."

"That's not the house you grew up in?"

The house in Aspen is a massive estate, definitely large enough to have raised a family in. Frederick told me one time that he had owned it for many years. I guess I was wrong to assume that was where Avery had lived. I laugh at myself in my own mind for all the time I spent searching the house for any remnants of him. Trying to guess which room was his and claiming it for my own when I thought I figured it out.

"Nah. He bought that place right after his first divorce." It doesn't need to be said that the divorce was from his mother. I hold my breath, waiting for him to go on. I feel a bit like a paparazzi with all of my personal questions, but I desperately want to know. "I grew up in New York."

"Oh, at the Paramour estate?"

He looks my way sharply. "You've been there?"

I shake my head quickly. "No, but Frederick mentioned it once."

He nods. "It went to my mom in the divorce."

"Where do you live?" Finally, I've made it to the real question. Sure, I'm deadly curious about his upbringing and familial strain, but what I really want to know is about his life now. I've gleaned all I can from Instagram captions. I want the truth straight from the source.

"Here and there."

My heart sinks as he dodges the question. I take a deep breath and push on. "You don't own a house?"

Now it's Avery's turn to take a deep breath. He doesn't want to talk about this, but, to his credit, he's not going to shut me down. "Well, I own a house on Merit with the guys, but to be honest, that's mostly Ben's house. He was the one behind the project, getting it built and furnished. That was a total mess. It's his money pit." He pauses, not looking at me. "I own one-quarter of the resort, and I have a room there that's all mine. And I travel a lot."

"So, you just, like, Airbnb or something?"

I see him shrug out of the corner of my eye. "Yeah. Something like that."

When I don't respond, he finally elaborates. "I stay with friends a lot, hotels, and yes, Airbnbs. I like being in new places, meeting the hosts and resort staff."

I'm not sure what to say to this, so I remain quiet. In my wildest dreams, I never imagined that he was going to tell me that he doesn't live anywhere. That he travels constantly. Not homeless, exactly, but kind of. Speaking of which… "Where's all of your stuff?"

Avery laughs. "I have some stuff at the New York house. If I called anywhere home, it would be there, although I haven't been back in a few years. The staff keeps the place up." He pauses, glancing over at me. When he catches my eye, I look away quickly. "I'm a good packer, but I also have a bad habit of buying clothes and other stuff when I arrive somewhere and then leaving it behind."

A mental image of him traipsing across the globe, a trail of clothes and toiletries in his wake makes me smile. It's a sad smile though. I can't imagine not having a home to return to.

Like an idiot, I go ahead and say so. "I can't imagine not having a home to return to."

He's quiet for a long moment, as we walk through the sand, the tide lapping gently at our feet. "I spent a lot of years living in a house, waiting for the people I loved to come home. I don't go for that anymore."

It breaks my heart, but I try not to fall over dead in the sand. I hold it together. Reaching out, I take his hand and give it a squeeze before letting go.

"The garden I want to show you is right up here."

As much as I wanted this conversation to start, I am now so very relieved to have it be interrupted. "Great."

Avery leads me up to a fence line that runs along the top of the sandy beach. I see immediately why he wanted to bring me here. The flowers, arches and landscaping are immaculate.

"Wow. This place is so beautiful."

When I look over at Avery, he's looking at me, a look similar to the one he was giving me in the flower shop. The difference is, now, I don't feel claustrophobic or like running. I breathe in the look in his eyes, and my chest expands.

"I'm really glad I met you, Franzeska."

I smile at his words, but the tone of his voice is so sad, my heart breaks even more. I can no longer look at this man and see the carefree, fun-loving traveler who has been smiling at me from the internet for all of these years. I don't know how I ever saw that. This man is so, so much more. "Me too."

I'm paralyzed by the intensity of the energy between us, but Avery's stronger than me. "Come on, let's go get some food. We can come back and meet the people who live here another day. It doesn't look like they're home."

I nod, not trusting a word that could come out of my mouth. They bounce around in my mind like trapped bees.

I don't know what I was imagining when I thought about what a pit barbecue place would look like, but it certainly wasn't this—a shack on the beach with a big hole dug in the sand and a group of young guys standing around it with no shirts on, smoking and drinking sodas, laughing and handing out paper boats filled with meat.

As we walk up to the ruckus, I see a table being cleared for us under the shade of a palmetto tree. A woman waves us over and pulls the chairs out for us to sit down.

"Welcome, Ave. Who's your friend?" A big man who's clearly in charge walks over to our table like he's the king.

Avery stands and offers a much tighter embrace to this giant, sweaty, half-naked man than I would have, no matter how impolite it would be to refuse. Luckily, I'm not offered the same greeting. The man smiles down at me where I perch on a rickety black metal chair and takes me in.

"This is Franzeska," Avery offers an introduction. "She's putting on the very first wedding ever at The White Sands."

The fact that he doesn't introduce me as his stepsister isn't lost on me.

The man is looking at me more curiously now. "Your wedding?"

I smile back up at him. "No, it's my brother's wedding."

The man nods and turns his attention back to Avery. The two men share a couple of very specific and meaningful facial expressions before the man nods and turns back to me. "Very nice to meet you."

Then he walks off toward the grill.

"What was that about?" I ask, my curiosity meter back on high.

Avery shrugs and smiles. "Chef Kuramo and I have been talking about getting something going at the resort for a while. I think he's wondering if this might be his opportunity."

"This is *my* opportunity," I remind him.

Another cocky smile. "Yeah, well, maybe you'll spread the love around."

I like the way he insinuates that this is entirely my decision, even as he brought me right to his friend's restaurant to sample the very food he thinks we should have at the wedding.

I decide to keep an open mind.

Drinks arrive first. Cold Cokes in glass bottles with expertly folded napkins around the necks and blue plastic straws.

Close behind is a chicken feast of epic proportions. I laugh as the men parade over and place dish after dish on the table before us.

There's a whole roasted chicken split into parts, the skin glistening in shades of red, green, and black, signaling that a dry rub went on before it hit the grill.

It smells amazing.

On the side, we have rice, beans, slaw, three kinds of salsa, limes, sliced radish, cilantro, and handmade flour tortillas.

Any thought I might have had earlier about not being hungry disappears.

No one waits next to our table to see if we like the food or need anything else. They drop the feast and retreat back to their grill, watching us out of the corners of their eyes.

"Holy shit." It's all I can think to say.

"Language, Fran."

My mouth drops open in embarrassed surprise, but when I look up, Avery's eyes sparkle with mischief. I shake my head and look back down. There's still the same energy from earlier, but it's transformed now, turned into something familiar. Something dangerous.

I reach for the food to avoid reaching for him.

It's just as incredible as it looks. I eat way more than I ever imagined possible, downing loaded tortilla after tortilla, pausing between bites to breathe and moan in pleasure. Avery eats as much as I do, probably more, with just as much enthusiasm.

When I'm ready to explode, I sit back in my seat and let out a sigh.

"You're never going to get a meal like this at the Reef Café," Avery says.

"That's for sure." I got room service when I first arrived, and while the club sandwich was lovely, it was not this. "They can do this on the beach at The White Sands?" I'm eyeing the hole in the ground filled with coals, with the grill pulled over the top.

"Dom would need to get involved, but yeah. That's the idea."

"They can pull this off for a hundred people?"

"You expecting a hundred people?"

"Invites went out to one-thirty-four. So, yeah. A hundred, give or take."

"I have no doubt. This style of food is designed to feed a crowd. We would order the ingredients in bulk through the resort, and these guys would prepare and cook it right on the beach."

I glance over at the pit again, remembering the incredible presentation of the chicken and all the sides. The photos would be epic.

Anyone can offer a buffet of crudités and guacamole. It would be something special to be able to offer this unique, local experience.

"Let's do it."

"I knew you were going to say that."

"Oh, did you now?"

Avery nods with a smile. "How could you say no?"

"What's Dominic going to think of these guys cooking on his beach?"

Avery looks sharply up and to the left. I wonder briefly if it's the male version of an eye roll. "He's going to be Dominic."

"So, hard sell?"

That killer smile is back. "I didn't say that."

I narrow my eyes at him, but it has no effect. All I get is another smile before he's out of his seat, heading over to the group of guys to exchange more handshakes and back claps. I see a casual exchange of money take place. When he returns to the table, he takes me by the hand and pulls me out of my seat. "Ready to walk back?"

I am worthlessly flustered being this close to him, so I just nod.

"Nice to meet you, Franzeska," the big man calls out to me as we make our way back down the beach. I smile and wave in response.

"I'm taking credit for this idea," I say finally, after walking for a bit in silence.

Avery laughs. "I wouldn't have it any other way."

I glance over to see if he's mocking me, but he seems genuine.

"Thank you."

His immediate release of all credit for the idea to me inspires feelings in me. Fuck, what about this man doesn't inspire feelings in me?

I get a sideways smile in return.

We swing back by the flower shop on the way to the cart, and I grab a few bird of paradise stems for my room. Avery wants to grab some things at the grocery store, so I follow him through the air-conditioned aisles, sneaking a couple of kombuchas and exotic looking snacks into his basket.

When we arrive back at the golf cart, the seat is crazy hot from the afternoon sun, but Avery has a large beach blanket in the back that he lays over the seat so I can sit down. He helps me into the cart, which is unnecessary, but so lovely. I sink back into the seat and close my eyes, allowing myself to pretend that this is my life—that this is my man—for exactly five seconds before I open them and shake it off.

Not my life.

Not my man.

"Where'd you go there?"

Leave it to Mr. Considerate to notice my five-second fantasy. "Oh, just tired."

"Well, let's get you back for a nap."

He pulls us out of town and onto the dirt road back home.

No, back to the resort. Not home.

The wind from our motion feels incredible, and I close my eyes again, letting the breeze wash over me. I feel Avery's hand on my leg again, and I tilt my face up to look at him.

He doesn't pull it away this time.

I relax into the seat, my eyes closed, and let myself sink back into the fantasy.

He keeps his hand on my leg for the whole drive.

Rule #9

GOT SOMETHING TO HIDE? HIDE IT BETTER

AVERY

We swing into her hotel room still laughing from some dumb joke I made in the elevator.

My self-confidence is at an all-time high after spending the entire day in the pleasant company of this beautiful woman. The best part is, since I'm not trying to get her into my bed, I really can just be myself.

A beautiful woman that I'm not trying to sleep with. Now there's a first.

We're in her room for exactly two seconds before I spot the black and white bird mask sitting brazenly on the coffee table.

Fran sees it at the same moment I do and sheds all of her natural grace as she lunges across the room and shoves the thing under the sofa.

Very smooth, love.

When she straightens and turns back to face me, I can see an ocean of warring emotions in her expression. Her blazing eyes dare me to speak, but I can't think of a single thing to say so I just stand there stupidly.

Finally, she breaks the silence. "Did you know?"

I still can't find my voice, so I maintain my silence, drawing a long, slow breath inward.

Fran's defensive expression melts into anger. "You knew this entire time and never said anything? You've just been antagonizing me and inserting yourself into this wedding, and the whole time you knew? Why didn't you say anything?"

My eyes shift downward as I struggle to kick my mind back into gear.

Say something, you jackass!

But I can't. Anything I say right now is going to make it worse.

All I want is the easy, happy feeling of one minute ago. I want it so badly my chest aches.

"How did you know?"

This question leaves her lips on a softer note, one so filled with sadness that I bring my eyes back to hers and finally force a few words out.

"It's a tiny little mask, Fran. It barely covered your eyes. The entire rest of you was showing." I try not to draw my eyes down and then back up her body, but I can't help it. She folds her arms protectively over herself as if she can hide.

"I can't believe you."

"Hold on now, sis. I saw the way you lunged to hide that mask. You can't pretend that you didn't know. You definitely knew."

She juts out her chin in a look so adorably defensive that I almost drop to my knees.

"Don't call me sis," she hisses.

I open my mouth to retort, but then I catch the look in her eyes. I've grown accustomed to seeing those eyes blaze, challenging and feisty, but they're now filled with what I can only call shame. Maybe even fear.

The actual weight of this situation settles down on my shoulders, lowering from the fantasy cloud of "no one's ever going to find out" that I put it on before.

I start to feel like an asshole for…well, for acting like an asshole.

"What are we gonna do now?" I ask. I'm happy to do whatever she thinks is best, but I can't read her mind.

"Do? We are not going to do anything. We've done enough already. Why don't you just go off on one of your trips and forget all of this ever happened. And if you want to come to the wedding, I'm sure you'll be invited."

"Wait, what? I am the director of wedding programs. I'm not going anywhere." So much for doing whatever she wants.

I'll do anything she wants that involves her and me. Together.

But why, Avery? Why don't you just leave?

"Avery, damn it, we both know that's a job you made up in order to…wait, in order to what? You already knew that I was the girl at the party when you made up that job so that you could steamroll my wedding. Why did you do it? I thought you were just trying to be nice and get to know me. But if you already knew, why didn't you want to get as far away from me as possible?"

It's the same question I've been asking myself since the second her plumeria-scented hair hit me in Sam's office, and I realized just what I'd gotten myself into. I haven't come up with a single answer for myself, so I certainly don't have one for her.

I shrug.

Fran's mouth falls open, and she regards me like the absolute atrocity of a human being that I am.

Then, as I have already witnessed several times in our short relationship, she transforms.

With a deep breath, she pulls her mouth closed and lifts her posture. On the exhale, she smooths the emotion from her face and smiles.

Holy fucking shit!

Women are seriously the scariest creatures on the planet. I would know. I've seen a lot of the planet.

"Fine," she says, all traces of the fight gone. She's calm, cool, and collected.

I, however, am still a self-deprecating mess, having been given exactly zero ability to pull myself together and regulate my emotions by my barbarian hunter ancestors.

"Fine what?"

I'm a toddler throwing a tantrum in front of my mother who has seen this kind of behavior before and is completely unmoved.

"Fine, fine. This just is what it is. What happened, happened. You are going to work with me on this wedding whether I like it or not, so I guess I'll just make the best of it."

Straight to the goddamn heart.

I hang my head as the pain from her words hits me.

I'm just a problem she has to deal with.

How did I get here?

She stands statue still as if she can wait forever for me to get it together.

"Can we start over?" I hedge.

"We already started over."

"Again? Can we start over again?"

"And what's going to be different, Avery?"

Okay, I seem to be getting somewhere. I decide to throw myself at her mercy and hope for the best. "Well, the party stuff is all out in the open now, so there's that."

Not a word from Fran, so I push on. "We hooked up at a party, no one knows but us, and we don't have to let it ruin this. I mean, it's not like it was a bad hookup." I look up into her unwavering glare. "You can't tell me that you didn't have fun. I know for a fact you did. Several times."

"I had fun."

"Great, perfect. Me too."

"Your point?"

What the fuck is my point here? I'm flailing. "My point is that we made a fantastic team in that bedroom, and we are going to be an even better team on this wedding."

Her arms cross, and her expression shows no signs of warming at my words. "I don't need you."

"I beg to differ."

Fran balks. "Give me one reason why I would need you for this wedding to be a success."

I thought you'd never ask, my love.

"Everyone on this island knows me and loves me, as you saw in town. I can get anything you want from anyone. I know the island and the resort by heart. I have the key to every door, and I know what's hiding in every closet."

"So does Sam."

I laugh. "Sam? Sam's so busy you'll be lucky to get a meeting once a week with that guy. Me? I'm one hundred percent yours. Twenty-four hours a day. Not a goddamn thing to do in the whole world except help you."

She cocks her head to the side, and I see the steel walls lowering.

"I've spent my life traveling, which is the greatest education in troubleshooting and communication you can ever have. Nothing in life is ever a problem for me. All I see are solutions. Not to mention that I have endless funds available, and I am more than happy to spend them getting you whatever you need, even if it means flying to the mainland to pick things up or building new structures myself. There's nothing out of reach for me."

"Sounds like a pretty nice life."

"Yeah, Fran. It is nice. It's a real fucking nice life. And it could be your life, too."

"What's that supposed to mean?"

"It means I'm not your enemy. I know this"—I gesture between the two of us—"is a…delicate situation, but it doesn't have to be a bad one. I'm not sorry we got together. I think you're incredible. I would do it again right now, even knowing what I know about our parents and their stupid legal agreement."

A scoff from Fran tells me I surprised her with my words.

"It's true. I know bedroom stuff is off the table now, and that's fine. I just want to help. Let me help."

She's quiet for so long that I start to sweat.

"You would do it again, knowing who I am?" she says finally.

I nod. "Like you keep reminding me, love, we're not related. Not in any sense of the word."

She says nothing, sending me back onto uncertain ground. I respond to the threat by saying something stupid, of course. "You wouldn't have?"

"Would I have fucked you knowing you were Frederick's spoiled, playboy son? Of course not. Don't be ridiculous."

Damn, girl shoots to kill.

"All right. Fine. You wouldn't have, but you did. It's in the past. Besides, that spoiled playboy gave you a pretty good time. I didn't hear any complaints."

"I'm sure you never do."

It's meant to be a dig about how many women I've been with, but I take it for the compliment it is. "You'd be correct."

Fran rolls her eyes. "Whatever."

"Whatever…we can put this behind us and work together? Or whatever…you never want to see my dumb ass again?"

She cocks her head, and I see the tiniest hint of a smile.

I'm in.

"You know, the morning after that party, I searched for you. I broke all of the party rules—my own rules—by asking you your name, by trying to get you to stay. And I asked everyone there if they knew who you were. It was like goddamn Cinderella the way you ran out of there and left me wondering. If you'd left behind your undies, I would have gone door to door, asking women to try them on, just to find you."

She's shaking her head, full on amused now, and I'm starting to relax.

"That's ridiculous. You could have any girl in the world."

"Yeah, you're probably pretty close to right about that. But I don't want any girl in the world. I've never had a girl swoop into my night and totally rock my world like you did. I'll never forget that night as long as I live."

She takes a deep breath and a tiny step backward as if I've cornered her.

I quickly retreat. "I know that's not going to be our reality moving forward. I just want to let you know that I can put it behind us if you can."

"Can you, though?" There's something in her voice that I can't quite place, but her tone is so soft that I decide it must be good.

"Can *you*?" I ask, no longer entirely sure that's what she wants.

After a long pause, where we stare straight into each other's eyes, she gives the tiniest, least certain shrug I've ever seen.

Holy shit, Ave, don't screw this up.

"We certainly don't have to put it behind us. You know where I stand on this." If there is the faintest glimmer of hope for a round two, or four, or ten, I'm here for it.

"Avery, that's completely insane." She says the words, but there's no fight in them. I can almost hear the war in her mind.

I decide to stay out of it. I shrug.

She shakes her head, looking down at the floor. "Can you imagine what people would think?"

The clouds part, and the holy rays of light shine down on me.

If what other people think is the only thing standing in our way, I'm home free.

"Doesn't matter what anyone thinks. Especially not here on this island. No one even knows you. No one knows what our parents' relationship is."

"But they're coming to the wedding."

"And we will be on our best, most professional behavior."

She puts her hands on her hips and considers me. "You're serious."

"Quite."

"Why, though? Isn't there a world of less complicated sleeping arrangements out there waiting for you?"

"There's only one arrangement I want."

"The one that if people found out about, they would think we were perverts or at least completely insane."

"Your only arguments so far have been about other people, Fran. What do you want?"

"I want other people to not think I'm insane."

"Really?"

She looks away, a bit flustered. "I mean, yeah. Don't you?"

"Never even crossed my mind."

"Well, that is a nice world you live in, but some of us have to go home for holiday dinners where all of our life choices are put under the microscope. They would have a fucking field day with this one."

"You don't have to go."

She shakes her head. "I do. I want to go. It's just…"

"It's just that when you do, the people there criticize you and make you feel terrible about yourself? Sounds lovely."

"You wouldn't understand."

"Make me understand."

"I…I have to prove myself to them. That's how you get on the other side of the criticism. Once you've proven yourself as responsible and capable of making the right choices, going home for holidays is okay."

"Life goals?"

"Don't be an asshole."

"I'm not the one criticizing your every move, love. I'm the one who just wants you to be yourself."

"As long as that means I am in your bed?"

"No. God no. Whatever you do is perfect. Whatever you decide, I'll support."

That earns me an eye roll and a shake of her head. "It must be nice not to have a family watching your every move, waiting for you to fuck up."

"Was that a '*must be nice not to have a family*?'"

She blushes just a bit. "No, that's not what I meant. I'm sorry. I just mean, it sounds nice to have the kind of freedom you have. No one watching you."

"Oh, love. My whole life is photographed. There are a dozen accounts dedicated to tracking my every move. I may not have parents who care, but I am certainly not immune to people's judgment."

"And it just doesn't bother you?"

"It used to. When I was in my twenties—"

"Oh my god, you are not about to tell me that I'll understand when I'm older."

I was going for something similar to that, but not anymore obviously. "No, no. Of course not. All I'm saying is that we have different seasons in our lives. Our early twenties are a season where people's opinions matter a lot. Late thirties are a season where other stuff matters more."

Her hands drop from her hips and hit her sides. She looks exhausted.

I'm terrified of what she's going to say next so I jump back in. "Don't decide. Not now. Don't even worry about this now. I'm going to head up and grab a nap."

"Wait—you're leaving?"

"Yeah, my deck hammock is calling to me."

I've surprised her by cutting our conversation short, but she definitely looks relieved. I know I made the right choice.

No one is their best being put on the spot like this.

I'll give her some time alone to think about it, and surely, she'll come to the conclusion that a secret affair with her step-brother is the right move.

"I'm going for a swim at about four fifteen down at the beach. It's the perfect temperature and tide combo. If you want to join me."

Stupid to invite her to do something so soon after this conversation. And our trip to town. And our meeting. And the party. Jesus, I hadn't realized until this moment that I have spent almost every waking minute with this woman since I met her.

And all I want is more.

"I'll probably take a nap as well."

I slip my flip-flops back on, hand on the door handle. I glance at her over my shoulder. She's still standing just where I left her, looking slightly shell-shocked. "I think you're incredible. What you're doing with your life is amazing. Your family are fools if they don't see that."

I slip out before she feels like she has to respond. It's not likely that gushing praise from the man trying to get you to sleep with him is going to have a life-changing impact, but I had to say it. It's true.

I think back to myself at twenty-three. Self-destructive, angry, living to spite the man who I felt so wronged by.

Compared to me, Fran could be elected president.

She's so calm and focused on her goals. Hell, she has goals. Not something I had when I was her age.

I pause halfway up the stairs as the thought hits me—do I have goals now? Have I ever had a goal?

I grimace and keep jogging upward.

When the soul-searching thoughts start, I know just what to do.

Throwing open the door to my own room, I kick off my flips and head straight for the patio where my hammock waits. Eyes closed, I let thoughts of Fran overtake my own doom and gloom memories of my aimless younger years. And my aimless last month. Last year.

Hell, my aimless life.

Rule #10

THE ONLY THING TO FEAR IS...LITERALLY EVERYTHING

FRAN

The second Avery closes the door behind him, I collapse onto my sofa.

Fuck.

Fuck!

So much for my stupid steel resolve.

So much for not getting involved with the man and derailing the wedding.

Because even though I know I'm a strong person—a total badass capable of doing anything I set my mind to—there's no way my mind is going to agree to walk away from this.

I can pretend to dither over it for as long as I need to make myself feel better, but in the end, I know what my decision is going to be.

Everyone is going to find out and...

And what, though?

What if Avery is right?

I know this is just my delusion talking, the part of my brain that is dead set on fucking this guy again and again and again, but maybe his words have some merit.

I mean, it's true none of my family are here.

It's true he and I aren't actually related.

It's true we had a fantastic time together.

I grind my teeth and squeeze my eyes closed. So, what's the problem, then?

I catch one of the brightly colored flowers out of the corner of my eye and pluck it from the bunch spilling out of my bag beside me on the sofa. It smells like the tropical paradise I'm in. It's what the air smells like here.

Tears spring to my eyes as I remember sitting on my bed back in Hartford, dreaming of this exact life. Being at The White Sands, planning Leon's wedding, wearing a bikini all day, swimming in the ocean. That girl was so sure of herself. So sure she was going to crush this project and skyrocket herself into the career of her dreams.

Look at me now, wallowing on the sofa because the hottest guy on the planet wants to sleep with me.

I sit upright, tossing the flower aside.

Fuck that.

This is what I have fantasized about for years. The tropical paradise, the wedding planning, and the man.

This exact man.

Sure, it's a little scarier in real life than it was in my mind, but I can handle scary. I will not let a little fear stand in my way.

Besides, it's not like he's proposing marriage here. It's just a little bit of coworkers with benefits. After the wedding, we'll go our separate ways. Maybe then I'll actually be able to find myself a relationship—once I have Avery out of my system. Pining over him has made the last few years tough in that department.

Fine. It's decided then.

Exactly zero parts of me are surprised, but a few are growing more and more impatient. The ache between my legs becomes a throb as I let my mind wander back to the party and transform that night into future nights right here in my hotel room. Or his hotel room. Or on the beach.

With a roll of my eyes, I'm digging in the coffee table drawer for my vibrator.

And there we are in my mind, on the sofa together. I'm wearing nothing, and he's wearing just his shorts. He stands and pulls them off to reveal his already hard cock. It's coming right at me. and I open as he slides it between my lips.

I lick my actual lips and a bit of salt from the sea air greets me as I press the tiny machine into my flesh. The setting is pretty high, but I don't have time to get the app connected to turn it down, so I manage the sensation by touching it lightly to the tip of my clit.

Avery is fisting his cock, pulling it out of my mouth and smiling. In my fantasy, I roll over and the sensation of the vibrator becomes his mouth on my flesh. I press it harder and feel the echo of the buzz in my bones.

Bringing two fingers to my entrance, I imagine it's the tip of his cock, asking permission to dip inside me. I nod, and he slides himself in an inch, right to the spot where my fingers always find during fantasies like this.

I bite my lip as the vibration starts to take me there, my fingers press deep inside me as Avery slides his cock into my pussy.

Inside the place where no man's cock has ever been, except in my fantasies.

My heart beats faster now, and my mind takes me to my hands and knees. Avery's behind me like at the party, but in my pussy this time, pounding into me as he holds tightly to my hip bones.

I come suddenly and so deeply.

I lighten the touch of the vibrator to prolong the spasms of pleasure rocking through me.

Avery doesn't let up, just keeps thrusting as I arch my back and hold my breath, the orgasm stretching on much longer than usual. When it passes, I click the buzzing device off and toss it on the sofa beside me, breathing heavily.

It's not a new fantasy, or even a very wild one, but somehow it took me to a place I've never been before.

I wonder if that's because now I know it's true.

I could jog up one flight of stairs, knock on one door and that fantasy could be happening within minutes. What was once only my bedroom fantasy is now my possible reality.

Not that I am going to let him in my pussy like that, but still. The sucking, the fucking, it could all happen.

It *will* all happen, I decide.

I don't make it to my deck chair for my afternoon nap. It overtakes me right where I sit. It's probably the fragrant bouquet beside me, but I dream of walking through a field of flowers, hand in hand with Avery. I wake an hour later sweating and impatient.

It's time for a swim.

Rule #11

DON'T GET ATTACHED

FRAN

When I make my way down the beach, nonchalantly, playing it cool, at four fifteen on the dot, Avery's already in the water. I stand by his towel and wave.

I planned to make it seem like I just happened to be walking by and saw him there, swimming at the exact place and time he told me he would be, but once I arrive, the whole idea feels ridiculous.

He invited me to swim, and I came.

There's no way around that now.

Laying my towel out next to his, I sit, still wearing my shorts and tee. Avery makes his way out of the water, dripping wet and glistening in the sunlight like a Greek god, blond hair wild with the salt and his uncaring way of brushing it back from his eyes.

This is the most beautiful man who has ever lived, and he wants me. Why, oh, why does he have to be Frederick's son?

"You made it," he says, flopping down on his own towel and facing me, propped up on one elbow. His bicep bulges. My eyes try to stay away, but I can't keep it out of my peripheral vision.

I turn back to the ocean.

"Yeah, I was just on a walk and saw you swimming." I thought I decided to shed the "playing it cool, didn't know you'd be here" act since we both know the truth, but I guess my lips had a different idea.

Out of the corner of my eye, I see Avery raise his eyebrows and smile. "Well, just my luck, then, I guess."

"You said you like to swim at this time? Why is that?" I have to acknowledge our conversation from earlier, so I don't seem like a complete idiot.

"The heat of the day is peaking, and the tide is as well. Brings some colder, deeper water closer to shore. I love getting hot and then diving into the cool ocean. Most times of the day, the water close to shore is near the temperature of the air. Right now, you can feel the difference."

"How hot do you need to be to feel it?" Why, Franzeska? Why do you say these things?

"I don't know, how hot are you right now?" he answers, sounding just as sure of himself as always.

"Pretty hot." I'm lost in this, unable to find my way back to solid, non-sexual ground.

Avery has no interest in even trying. "Well, your first step is going to be ditching those clothes."

I inhale too sharply, and I know he hears me, but bless his heart, he doesn't laugh. Doesn't react at all.

"Then lay out and let the sun soak into your skin until you are so hot, you can't stand it."

I'm already so hot I can't stand it, but most of that feeling is trapped between my legs.

"Okay." I mean, what else is there to say?

I stand and strip off my shorts while Avery watches my every move, not trying to conceal his gaze one bit.

How freeing it must be to do whatever you want all the time and never worry about what people think. To just lay on the beach and openly ogle your stepsister while the whole world watches.

I glance around, but there's no one in sight. Confidence lifting just a bit, I pull off my tee.

I didn't choose my skimpiest bikini—so far that one has been reserved for porch sunbathing only—but they're all fairly skimpy.

This suit is a spray of neon pink, orange, blue, and green tiger stripes on a black background. It's an actual vintage bikini that I found at a secondhand shop in downtown Hartford. A relic from the last time this style was in fashion, I guess.

Avery might have been alive then.

The thought strikes me as comical, and I glance down at him with a smile, getting ready to shoot off a joke about his age, but the look on his face stops me dead.

"What?" I ask, suddenly self-conscious.

"You're the sexiest creature who has ever lived."

"Avery, stop." My words have exactly zero fire.

He holds his hands up in surrender. "Just saying."

I lay down on my towel and stretch out on my back, perfectly aware of what I'm doing now that he commented on my body. I wiggle my hips to create an indent in the sand and stretch my arms overhead.

Avery groans.

I smile.

"You're going to be the death of me."

"Why? I'm just existing."

"Well, you better cut it out."

"Cut out what? Existing?"

"No, love, cut out wiggling those gorgeous hips and arching that back so your tits stand up." As if his words wouldn't have had enough of an effect, Avery draws his finger over the parts he has his eyes on, so softly I can barely feel it. A trail of goose bumps follows his finger across my skin. "If you're not careful,

I'm going to pull those tiny scraps of fabric right off you and then where will you be?"

"Lying naked on the beach with my stepbrother while everyone watches."

Avery laughs and flops onto his back. "I thought we weren't related."

"We're not, but…you know."

"Enlighten me."

"People will still think…I don't know. That it's weird."

"I thought we decided that the only people who know enough to care are a thousand miles away."

He's right, but now that we're out in the open, all of my feelings have shifted a bit. "Your friends all know. And they could've told anyone."

"You can't live inside a bubble, love."

We lay in silence for a while. I can feel him beside me, saying nothing. I'm not brave enough to look over and see if he's watching me, so I just have to wonder.

Finally, I can't take it anymore. "I'm so hot, I can't stand it."

"Me too."

Avery is straddling my hips, pinning me to the beach, before I can even open my eyes and see him coming.

He dips his face down, planting a hand on either side of my shoulders.

For a second, I consider letting him kiss me, right here and now, but the invisible eyes of everyone who could be watching eats at me, and I push him off with a laugh. "Hot enough for a swim, you barbarian."

"Oh, jeez. Why didn't you say so?" He gets to his feet and tries to brush off some of the sand he's covered in, but it sticks to his sweaty skin. He pulls me to my feet and straight into a sweaty, sandy embrace.

I feign disgust and pretend to fight, but there's nowhere on earth I would rather be.

We walk about halfway down to where the waves are hitting the beach hand in hand before I realize what we're doing and quickly drop his hand. If he reacts, I don't look over to see it.

I walk straight into the surf until I'm hip deep and dive.

He wasn't wrong.

The cool blast of the ocean water on my achingly hot, sunbaked skin is the most glorious feeling. When the intensity of the contrast wears off, along with my breath, I surface and spin slowly in place, searching for Avery.

I find him a few feet further in, still standing in thigh deep water, talking to a group of women on the beach.

Tall, thin, fashion model looking women.

"...catching the six-forty boat to the airport," one of the women says.

"Great party!" another chimes in from behind the first. I can hear their accents from where I tread water.

Perfect. Not just models, but actual French models.

"It was so good to see you ladies," Avery responds, not making any move to walk toward them.

I don't know what possesses me, but before I know it, I'm wading out of the deep water and coming up beside him. All eyes move to me.

The feeling of being sized up by six perfect eyes, belonging to three utterly perfect, French Riviera sun-kissed bodies decked out in what is most certainly not secondhand beachwear is pretty surreal. I'm grateful that none of them are close enough to see me tremble just a bit. I hold their gaze.

And incredibly, they just back down. After a few glances each between Avery and I, they wave and walk off without another word.

The conversation was probably over anyway, that's why they left.

Or they were in a hurry to get to their boat.

There's certainly an explanation that's not what it looked like happened, which is that they saw me as competition and scampered off with their tails between their legs.

I watch them walk away and when I look back, I find Avery watching me. He smiles, seemingly unfazed by the exchange of female energy that just took place. I would say that he didn't even notice, but there is something in his gaze that tells me differently. No, he knows exactly what just went down. He watched the whole thing.

Watched me claim him.

I look away.

We swim out to where we can't touch, the ocean washing away some of the nerves I built up during that silent exchange with the alpha females. I should let it go, but I just can't.

"Girlfriends?" I ask.

"Friends."

"You fucked them?" I ask, even though I shouldn't.

Avery cocks his head to the side. "Ahh…"

"Never mind. I don't want to know."

I really don't. It's bad enough that I am behaving like there will be no consequences for my actions. It would be quite another to allow myself to think that this thing between Avery and I, whatever it is, is something that's going to last. That it could grow into something larger than just a realization of my bedroom fantasies.

Not even I am that stupid.

The list of reasons why we could never *actually* be together is so long, I can't even see the end of it.

There's the whole Mom's husband's son thing, which is insurmountable all on its own. And then there's his age—seventeen years my senior. Technically old enough to be my father.

And then there's the man himself. The wild, rootless, playboy who's rumored by the internet to have never been seen with the same woman for longer than three weeks.

Disgusting.

But now that I think about it, also a little sad.

I only have a couple of relationships on my dating résumé, the longest of which was eighteen months. But even in that short time, the guy got to know me. I was able to relax and be myself around someone who knew me.

Has Avery ever experienced that before with a woman?

"I get it." The words leave my mouth before I can stop them.

I'm not entirely sure what I mean by them, and I have zero clue what he interprets them to mean, but before I know it, his hands are on my shoulders, pulling my body to his. Pulling my mouth to his.

It's stupid. Idiotic. Absolutely asinine to be making out in the ocean right in front of the resort, but I could no sooner pull away from him than I could stop the tide. As a matter of fact, right now, with my lips locked on his, his tongue pressed so deep in my mouth that I have to stretch to fit mine in his, I could just stop treading water. Sink right to the bottom of the ocean. Live inside this kiss forever.

I hate myself for being so weak, but it's Avery who finally breaks off. His lips are smiling as he slips under the water, disappearing from sight.

When he comes back up, he's several feet away, closer to the shore. I watch him stop swimming as his feet reach shallow enough water where he can touch. He walks up the beach until he's standing in the gentle break.

He stands with his hands on his hips, watching me. He must see my gaze travel down to his erection in his wet shorts because he looks down as well and shakes his head, smiling. "I'm heading in. It's room 315. If you…if you were curious."

And then he leaves me there, still treading water.

I watch him collect his towel and walk up the beach, rubbing his hair dry before draping the striped terrycloth over his shoulders.

I'm too chicken to speak. Too chicken to move.

I don't trust what I would do if I did.

I stay out past the breakers, treading water until I can't hold myself up any longer. When I finally make it up the beach, I'm sick with indecision.

Obviously, I'm going to go up to his room. I can't even pretend that I'm not. I just can't wrap my head around what all of this means.

Or if it even has to mean anything.

I mean, this is his lifestyle, right? Find a girl he thinks is hot, fuck for a while, and then move on. This time it's me. Why would this time be any different?

And why would I want it to be?

If anything, I should feel safer knowing that there's zero chance I'm going to have to explain this to anyone. It's just fun for now, and then he'll leave.

And that's okay…as long as it's actually okay.

Rules, Franzeska.

Okay, rules. What are they?

One, no getting attached. He's just going to leave.

Two…I can't think of another one.

I guess there's just one rule. Great. That's easy.

I head up to my room on the second floor and throw myself, still in my wet suit, onto the sofa.

What am I doing?

I am here on this island for one reason.

Throw the wedding of the century and launch my company.

This is my one shot at getting it right. My one opportunity to prove to my family, to the world, that I am capable of making good choices for myself. That I am responsible and talented and not some fuck-up teenage girl who needs looking after.

I'm not here to get sucked into a whirlwind romance with the world's biggest red flag.

But it's too late.

I change into a loose white dress and don't bother with a shower or underwear. I'm throwing myself into the lion's den, guaranteed to be eaten alive.

No point in putting too much preparation into my outfit.

I skip the elevator and climb the stairs of shame up to the third floor. I stand staring at the whitewashed wood longer than I would ever admit before my fist finally makes contact.

Here goes nothing.

Rule #12

THERE ARE WORSE WAYS TO DIE

AVERY

I swing the door open, mildly surprised to hear a knock so soon. I remind myself that it could be anyone, but I know it's not.

"That was fast."

I'm a bit nervous and can't stop the words tumbling from my lips. I watch them hit, Fran's mouth dropping open slightly as she intakes a surprised breath.

Then she turns on her heel and takes a step back toward the elevator. I grab her arm and pull her inside, closing the door behind us. "I was joking, love. Terrible joke. I'm sorry."

She's shaking her head but smiling.

That smile nearly brings me to my knees. "I'm glad you came."

"Yeah, I…me too." She's as nervous as I am.

I'm terrified all of a sudden that she's come here to call it off. To tell me this is stupid, and I'm too old, and whatever else.

I prevent it the only way I know how. By pressing my lips to hers.

Fran doesn't pull away, in fact, she leans into the kiss, and I press back until I have her pinned firmly against the closed door. My hands are everywhere all at once, unable to decide where to touch first. I come across her lack of underthings immediately, and this takes precedence.

"Fuck me, Fran. You're naked under there?"

"I told you not to call me Fran," she manages to get out with my tongue tracing her lips.

I slide my mouth down to her collarbone and breathe in her scent. "I'll call you anything you want if you tell me I can slip this dress over your head."

I feel her inhale sharply, deeply, and the wait for her answer is the most delicious suspense.

"Okay."

I strip her of the dress so quickly, she cries out in surprise and laughs.

I drop to my knees before her, lips tracing the bottom of her ribs as my hands slip around behind her to grip her ass. As my tongue finds her navel, she finds her voice.

"Avery," she says softly.

I look up, my mouth still on her belly.

"If you ruin the wedding, I'll kill you."

It's my turn to laugh in surprise. "I wouldn't dream of it, love."

She shakes her head in disbelief at what's about to happen, and I totally understand.

I stand and lift her hand, pulling her off the door and into the room. It's feeling awfully unfair here clothing wise, so I strip off my shirt and toss it in the pile with her dress. "Where to?"

"You decide."

I nod, leading her to the bedroom.

It's decorated in seventies Hawaiian chic, the same furnishings that were in place when we bought the place. All of the other rooms have been updated, but I opted to leave mine as is. I love it.

I sit her down on the faded hibiscus flowers and nestle my

fingers deep in her hair, tilting her head up toward me. "What now?"

"Lick me like you did at the party."

Her words are unexpected and wickedly decisive. I'm more than happy to obey. "Twice in one week, huh? I might have to hit you up for a testimonial later."

The joke sounded better in my head, but as soon as the words leave my lips, I hear the tastelessness of them. "Another terrible joke, I'm sorry. You make me nervous."

Fran coughs out a surprised laugh. "*I* make *you* nervous?"

"Yeah. Are you kidding me? You are literally god's gift to men, sitting here completely naked with your perfectly curved and tanned body, offering me the honor of licking your pussy. Here I am, just some middle-aged beach bum who lives in a hotel room." I drop to my knees and push her legs apart as far as she'll let me. "Guys like me are a dime a dozen. You, however, are a once-in-a-lifetime find. A jewel so rare…" I press her torso gently, and her body obeys by lying back on the bed. Her knees spread all the way now. "…I feel the need to hide you away, so you won't get stolen by pirates."

I finally manage a joke that I don't think is offensive, and I glance up to see if she liked it, but she's giving me a look I can't interpret.

"I could be middle-aged, you know," she says matter of fact.

I open my mouth to respond, but not a single thing comes to mind.

What on earth does she mean by that?

I'm tempted to ask, but she's closing her eyes and settling down, so I guess the moment passed.

I'll just put that one in the ol' vault to talk about later…

I'm sure some future moment will need ruining, and I'll have it in my back pocket.

This moment, however, I'm not taking any chances with.

I drag my fingers gently up her slit, from her adorable rosebud to the tuft of hair on her mound, giving her nerves a little hello. I can hear her breathing change as I graze over the more tender parts, and I wish I could see her face. I'll have to settle for hearing her sing, which I'm hoping will start soon.

Touching my tongue down on the side of her clit and swirling up and around the top, I'm rewarded. She tastes like the ocean and the sweetest fruit, all wrapped up in one squirming, gasping little package. When I finally hear her start to breathe faster and feel her relaxing open for me, I add my fingers to the game, curling up inside her just like I remember from before.

Her tight, wet heat makes me wonder if she got started on her own before coming over, and the thought nearly makes me come in my shorts.

I'm trying to be patient, but the knowledge that on the other side of this orgasm is my cock inside her…well, it doesn't inspire me to take my time.

I work her hard, relentlessly, and she comes apart in my mouth as I lap her up. I don't stop until she's squeezing my head with her knees and laughing.

"Stop, okay, that's enough."

I peek up at her from between her thighs. "You are magnificent."

She shakes her head and lays back, stretching her arms overhead. I stand and unbutton my shorts, sliding them over my massive erection.

All of a sudden, I'm standing over the woman of my dreams, buck naked, with a huge hard-on, staring down at her peaked nipples and wet pussy…and I have no idea what to do.

I mean, I know what to do, of course, but…can I really do it?

"May I fuck you?" I'm not sure I could have come up with a less delicate way of asking that if I had an hour to try, but she nods.

I lean down and slip my fingers back inside her, fucking a bit to get her stirred back up. "You are so fucking wet, love. I can't wait to be inside you."

She flinches just a bit, and I hesitate, waiting for her direction.

"Not there." She reaches down and takes my now drenched fingers out of her cunt and slides them back to her rosebud. "Here."

"Back there, again, huh?"

Fran nods.

I nod.

"Okay, love. We'll do anything you like. We can even try out both if you are up for it," I offer, as if I'm not the one who's going to be falling asleep first. The girl has nearly twenty years on me.

But she shakes her head.

"Just like it back there better?"

A pause, and my interest ratchets up a notch.

"I'm…I really don't want to get pregnant."

"Are you not on birth control?"

"I have an IUD."

"Okay. I have condoms, and between the two, we should be safe."

"Avery, I…"

Her soft words hit me like a bullet to the heart.

Here I am, trying to convince her to do something she just flat-out told me she didn't want to do. I don't deserve her.

"Sorry, I was just trying to understand. It's okay. It's perfect. You're perfect." I pull her body closer to the edge of the bed and flip her onto her stomach. I land a firm smack on one of her perfectly round cheeks. "I can't wait to fuck you."

I have a bottle of lube, but it's in the bathroom. "Get up there on all fours," I tell her and jog into the en suite and start opening drawers like my life depends on it. When the little bottle is in hand, I hurry back.

The sight of her—damp, ocean-kissed hair, bikini tan lines, and pale, round butt, waiting obediently for me on all fours in the center of my bed nearly kills me.

"You are really something."

"You…are…really something too."

I'm surprised by the compliment, but I take it. I also take the opportunity to smack her ass a couple times, and I take the squeals she lets out as I do.

I take it all and file it away in a folder marked Open after Franzeska Leaves Me.

Get it together, man.

The cold lube hits her skin, and I watch goose bumps spread down her legs. I rub up, around, and finally inside, bringing the cool gel in with me. "How's that feel, love?"

"Good."

I've already been balls deep in her ass, so I don't think there's too much need for a warm-up. A girl who has backdoor sex exclusively knows what to ask for if she needs it. I roll a condom down my shaft and get my tip in the game, swirling it up and around her tight hole.

"Jesus fucking Christ, Franzeska." I dip just the tip into her body, the squeeze of her tight muscles making my eyes roll back in my head. "Give me a chance, love. I'm not going to make it long if you don't relax a bit." I feel her let up, and I slide a few more inches in. It's still tight, but not so tight that I have to white knuckle it to keep from coming.

On my next withdrawal, I add a bit more gel and work it in with my cock. "It's feeling pretty wet to me, how's it feeling to you?"

"Feels good. I think you're good."

I trust her. "I'm going to fuck you now."

"So you keep saying."

I laugh and shake my head, the joke taking some of the tension off my hovering orgasm. When I wrap my fingers around her hip bones to get more leverage, they are so slippery from lube that it takes me a moment to find purchase.

Once I do, it's on.

God, the tight slide of her feels magnificent, and she knows just how to move her hips to settle me in deep and keep me sliding just where she likes it.

I want this to last forever—like, literally forever—but I can't slow down the thrusts. I fuck and fuck, and scream her name, all three goddamn syllables of it, until I'm so close to the edge that I pull my cock out sharply and breathe. The sensation mellows out, and I touch back down with my tip.

"You feel so fucking good. I could come just looking at you."

"I don't want you to come just looking at me. I want you to come fucking me so hard I can't breathe."

I lean down and rest my forehead on her back, taking a few calming breaths. "I'm trying, love. I'm trying to hold on, it's just..." I don't need to say it.

She understands.

As if I wasn't already surprised enough, the woman speaks again. "We'll just have to get you through your first one. Then you'll last longer."

Oh, my good Lord in heaven. This dirty talking vixen might actually kill me and my old man heart. Before I can open my mouth and say something idiotic about how I'm going to pass out the second I blow my load, she's settling down on her heels and turning to me.

Her eyes fall to my cock, and she bites her lip. I freeze, unable to do anything but wait to see what happens next.

"Lose the condom."

It's off in a millisecond, discarded to my left without a glance at where it lands.

She scoots back just a bit, still on her knees with her butt on her heels. She pats the bed in front of her, and I climb up, kneeling before her.

"Lube?"

I fumble beside myself on the bed but find the little bottle and hand it over.

She pops the top and squeezes a little river of the silicone gel between her round, luscious tits.

Fucking hell.

I'm fourteen again, watching pornos with my buddies in one of our basements.

I hold my breath, the suspense of the moment a living thing with its hand around my windpipe.

When she reaches for my cock, I let my arms drop to my sides. She takes it in both hands, pulling it toward her chest. I shuffle forward until our bodies press together.

"Okay, this is where you take over." The humor in her voice snaps me back to the present moment. "You got this?"

Oh, I so totally got this. I'll just titty fuck this sexy ass little siren. No fucking problem.

She squeezes her tits together with her arms as I brace one hand on her shoulder and pull her chest closer to me. The lube makes us so slippery, it's not long before my tip pops up between her breasts over and over again.

No problem at all. I can just watch her bite her lip and take my titty fucking like a goddamn champ. No way am I about to blow in her face five seconds into this.

Baseball.

Mom's birthday party.

Spiders crawling on you while you sleep.

It's no use.

"Fuck, Fran, this is so fucking hot." I reach up and fist my hand in her hair tightly, using it as another point of leverage. Any concern I had over being too rough flies right out the window.

"It's going to be even hotter when you come on my face."

"Jesus Christ, you kill me when you say shit like that."

"Do you think you can hit my mouth from there?"

I lay my head back and groan in defeat as I fuck her even harder.

I realize my mistake immediately and look back down, wanting the vision of her peaked nipples squeezing in on my cock burned into my retinas. Reaching my hand down from her shoulder, I take one of those nipples roughly between my fingers.

She cries out, and I pinch her harder, my fist in her hair tightening as I give in to the absolute lost cause.

Even though I had no plan to do so, I find myself tilting her face down toward my tip as I thrust myself over the cliff of my release.

I grunt and thrust and pull too hard on her hair, her neck obediently bending down. Her mouth opens, and I hear myself scream as I come straight into it. Most of the white liquid falls right back out and lands on her tits, but the effort.

The fucking effort.

She opened her goddamn mouth.

My whole body lights up like a live wire as the orgasm passes, the electricity of the moment still pulsing through me as I grow more and more sensitive.

I pull my cock free first, refusing to relinquish the grip in her hair until long after I settle my hips down on my heels. I sit there for a moment, gaping at her, her head still bowed down where I'm holding it.

Then a switch goes off. I release her quickly and take her chin in both hands, tilting her face up to meet mine. Her eyes glow with some kind of witch doctor voodoo lust magic, and my cum is on her cheek, her chin. I glance down and see it falling in drips from her still peaked nipples.

I haven't even had a chance to fully process the scene when she speaks.

"*Now* you can fuck me."

I open my mouth to protest but she's already on her knees before me. I look down and find my cock still rock hard. Praying it's not just the aftershock of whatever the fuck that whole thing was, I raise myself back up to my knees behind her. I snag another condom from beside me on the bed and sheath myself.

My cock miraculously stays hard.

I say a silent prayer to any and all gods that have ever existed.

I pick up the little lube bottle from where it's resting next to my knee. Fran moans as I squirt her with it, reinserting my fingers into her tight hole and adding a couple to her dripping pussy at the same time. I take my fingers out of her ass and slide my tip in their place, leaving my hand in her pussy.

I try out a few slides, my confidence in this erection growing when it doesn't give out on me. Whatever fucking spell she put on me is working because I'm hard as a rock and ready to fucking roll.

I give it to her without any pretense. Having been witness to her wild side twice now, I can say without hesitation that the girl wants to get properly fucked.

The pleasure is a warm glow that starts at my tip and spreads through my entire body, but I am nowhere near teetering on the edge like I was before.

A primer orgasm…

That's all I needed.

Why didn't I think of that?

"Fucking you feels so good, Fran. God, I can't take it, it's so fucking good."

She says something into the bedspread that I can't make out.

"If you need anything, just tell me."

"Harder." I make out from where her head turns to the side.

Jesus, can I fuck any harder?

I abandon her pussy and grab both hips with my hands, giving myself leverage to slam into her.

"Lube," she says, and I slide out, reapplying and sliding back in without missing a beat.

She was right about that. The decadent slickness of her tight channel allows me to feel every ridge against my tip as it makes its way all the way in and then almost all the way out.

"Clit."

I continue to obey Franny's one-word commands like a well-trained dog, releasing one hip to slide my hand down and press a finger on either side of her clit. She screams.

Now there's the sound I want.

Somehow, I fuck even harder, my grip on her hip and her clit the exact leverage I need.

I'm going to come again. It's fucking incredible, but true.

"Lift me up," she says, her upper body rising off the bed as she straightens her arms.

I sink down onto my heels, using one arm around her stomach to bring her onto my lap. As I do, my cock sinks impossibly deeper into her body.

I'm going to die. Right here, right now.

Grand fucking way to go.

"I need you to come for me, love, I can't hold on much longer."

She leans back on my chest, her head lolled over one of my shoulders. Her back arches and her tits taunt me from where they bounce.

Still bearing the streaks of my last orgasm.

One of Franny's hands comes up and clamps down over mine between her legs, guiding my fingers to just the right spot and pressing them much deeper into her flesh than I would have done on my own.

"Fuck me," she says through her clenched teeth.

I'm trying, but I resolve to try harder. I use my arm around her stomach as leverage to help lift her as I thrust my hips up and forward.

I'm going to be too sore to walk tomorrow, but it's all worth it when I hear her breath catch. She holds it for so long I start to worry, but the second I'm about to ask if she's okay, her core contracts, and she tries to buckle forward. I hold her tightly to my chest, continuing my steady pace in and out of her, while also giving her clit some extra attention.

Her cries force their way out through her clenched jaw, her eyes squeeze shut, and her body strangles my cock. Fucking stunning. I would kill to know what's going through that mind of hers as she rides her wave of pleasure to the end.

As soon as she takes a breath, I let go of my resolve and suck in my own. My second orgasm beats down my spine, chasing my first and smashing it into a million little pieces.

My eyes clench so tightly that I lose track of what and where I'm grabbing, simply holding on for dear life as the pleasure seeps through my every cell.

As soon as I regain some semblance of consciousness, I become aware of how tightly I'm holding her and release altogether.

Fran falls from my arms onto the soft bed in front of me. My hands hit my thighs, and I brace myself there, still gasping for breath.

"Damn," she says from under the locks of long dark hair that have fallen over her face.

A short laugh escapes my lips that sounds like someone else. Someone manic. A bit insane. Two seconds ago, I never would have believed that the whole experience could be summed up in one simple word, but she's just done it.

"Damn," I repeat.

"What time do you think it is?"

I struggle to do some simple time math and come up short. "Dinner?"

Fran laughs and rolls onto her back. Her now bared torso is like a magnet, sucking my body down until I'm pressed against her. I have so many needs competing for my attention right now, but they all fall to the wayside as I slide my hand over her stomach and pull her closer to me.

"I've gotta get up," she says, stroking my hair with her hand and making no move to do so.

"Me, too," I reply, my face buried in her ribs, nose grazing the side of her breast. I don't even open my eyes to consider moving.

"I'm going to count to a hundred in my head, and then I'm going to get up."

I pull her more tightly to me. "I'll just yell until they hear us and demand that someone send room service."

"Room service isn't going to help me go to the bathroom." Her voice is light and amused.

"You never know until you ask."

She curls herself tighter against me, pressing her lips to the top of my head. I'm having so many feelings right now, it's hard to sort them into piles I can understand.

I try anyway.

Joy goes here in the pile with amazed and satiated.

Exhausted goes on top of hungry, which I lump in with sore and thirsty.

Contentment goes in the miscellaneous pile with other feelings I'm not used to. I think I see hopeful in there. That one underneath it might be love.

Fran starts to stir, and I hold on more tightly.

She laughs. "I'm going to go to the bathroom, and then I'll come back. You should probably do the same."

I groan, even as the growing condom problem calls to me from between my legs.

In the end, I let her escape.

As soon as the bathroom door closes, I drag myself to my feet, the condom in even worse shape than I imagined. I discard it and use a beach towel from the floor to clean myself and the bed a bit.

I stand in front of the large mirror atop the dresser and consider myself. Pretty okay, all things considered. I feel like a perfect mixture of walking death and sunshine, but I look more or less the same as I always do.

I give myself an all-over shake to get my energy moving again and then pull on some boxers.

Fran comes out of the bathroom still naked, her bronze and white tan lines glowing in the early evening light from the open window. Her hair falls messily over her shoulders, obscuring half of her breasts on each side.

She's a goddess, come to earth to bestow blessings upon me.

Or kill me.

Either way, it's fine.

I walk to her and lift her hair over her shoulders to bare her chest, my hands following the hair down her shoulder blades, down her back, and over the soft mounds of her ass. I pull her to me, eliciting a little laugh. I let it wash over me as her body touches mine once more.

"You're incredible," I say. It's not enough, but I don't know how to say what I'm feeling.

"Stop," she says softly, but I can't tell if she actually wants me to stop. I don't think I could anyway.

"That was the most incredible thing that's ever happened to me." I'm not lying. The list of incredible things in my life is long, but this definitely tops the chart.

She's shaking her head, trying to pull away, but I hold her close. I'm not ready for whatever comes after this. I need to live in this moment a little longer.

"It was just sex," she says softly.

At that, I do release a bit and take a step back so I can see her face. "That was not just sex, love. That was…I don't know that there's a word invented yet for what that was. We'll have to come up with one and send it in."

I've made her blush just a bit, and I lift her chin with my hand so I can get the full effect. Her hazel eyes meet mine, and I see nothing but happiness there.

I wonder what she sees in mine.

After a long moment, she breaks away and walks toward the living room where her clothes are in a heap. I tag along, still on her leash. I need her attention to turn back to me, so I keep speaking. "Where did you learn to do that stuff?"

It's the wrong thing to say, inappropriate, possibly even offensive, and the crinkled forehead look she tosses me lets me know that. It's too late to take it back so I stand in the awkwardness that follows.

"I didn't *learn* to do anything."

I want to badger her to no end, but even I know better. I keep my mouth shut and watch her shake out her dress and pull it on.

Goodbye beautiful breasts.

Goodbye glorious pussy.

Until next time, dear friends.

When she's clothed, she turns back to me. "It's just how it goes in my mind. I made it real life today."

And wouldn't you know, the thought of her alone in her room, pleasuring herself to the fantasy of me coming on her breasts and fucking her up the ass wakes my sleepy cock right up.

She notices the sudden motion in my shorts and laughs. "Really?"

I shake my head, adjusting myself to conceal my erection. "No, definitely not really. There is no way it's serious."

We share a look so intimate, so private, that I almost buckle at the knees. I want to spend the rest of my life in a private moment with this woman. I knew that the moment I laid eyes on her, but now, it's official.

I consider dropping to my knees right now but shake it off.

"We should talk about this." She motions between the two of us, and I snap back to reality. "Whatever this is."

I nod.

"Do you want to talk now…or later?" she asks hesitantly. Something in my demeanor is making her uneasy so I try to pull it together. To calm down. But I can only manage another nod.

I never want to have the talk she has in mind. I want to live forever in this bubble, no talking required. But if I say the word *now* then she'll stay, so I do. "Now's good. Let's talk, and then we can go grab dinner." I try to sound cool and confident, but the look she gives me lets me know I've only partially succeeded.

She flops down on the couch, and I sit next to her. The intimacy of the last hour seems to have waned a bit, so I don't lay directly in her lap, although I want to.

"This for sure crosses a line, and I just want to make sure we're on the same page."

I can almost guarantee that we aren't, but I nod. "Yeah, totally."

She hesitates but goes on. "I think we can do this as long as we can maintain a good working relationship."

I am nodding, the words *we can do this* rattling around in my brain like fireworks.

"For me, that's going to require that you only sleep with me for the duration of…whatever this is."

I open my mouth and then close it. This woman never fails to surprise me. "Yeah, of course. And you? Can I assume you will only be sleeping with me?"

Franny rolls her eyes, and I hold my hands up in surrender. "Just getting clarification on the ground rules here."

"I am not really the one we need to be worried about sleeping around."

I cringe as her arrow hits, but I'm well aware of how I'm portrayed in the media, and that some of it is true. Okay, a lot of it is true. I give her a side-to-side nod that I hope indicates that, while I don't completely agree, I am happy to submit to her rules.

"And we are not going to tell my family."

I nod again, expecting that one. "Other people, though?"

She shrugs. "I'm not planning to make an announcement or anything, but I don't think complete secrecy is necessary or even possible in a place like this. I do need people to take me seriously, though. I need them to have confidence in my ability to do this job. And I am not going to stand for anything that jeopardizes that."

She is full-on boss lady right now, with her stern tone and sharp eyes, and I consider briefly whether I could actually go another round. It's so hot I stutter over my next words. "Of-of course."

She gives me a little side eye, as if considering taking the whole thing back, so I leap into a fully unprepared speech. "It's going to be fine. Great. We're a fantastic team, and most of the people in this place who would care are too busy to take much notice. I'm happy to defer to you on all things wedding. I'm not about to start any squabbles or drama or anything. You and I… it's going to be great. We'll be so professional, they won't even consider that anything else is going on."

I've only partially convinced her, but she's relenting.

Finally, she nods. "Do you have any rules or boundaries or anything?"

Do I?

"Nothing jumps out at me right now, but let's keep this line of communication open at all times, in case anything comes up for either of us. Nothing is off the table. If this is going to work, it's gotta work for both of us." I kneel in my mind as the president hands me a trophy for being the most sensitive guy on the planet.

Fran just nods. "Okay."

And that's that.

I'm in an officially unofficial kind of stepsiblings with benefits relationship with my coworker and the forbidden woman of my dreams. Even I, with hearts dancing across my eyes, am not stupid enough to miss what a terrible, terrible plan this is.

But sometimes in life, the stupidest decisions turn out to be the best ones.

Not true at all, but it sounds good.

No, it sounds totally stupid, but this is what we're doing. Caution to the wind and whatnot.

"How about dinner?"

Fran nods, smiling. And away we go.

Rule #13

IT'S NOT WEIRD (UNLESS YOU MAKE IT WEIRD)

FRAN

After a not-surprisingly wonderful dinner at Raft, I manage to sleep in my own bed, alone, even though it isn't really what either of us want. I just feel like I need a few minutes to think, and I can't think straight when I'm with that man.

And that's a problem.

This whole plan, my whole career, is resting on my ability to think. To pull this off on the level I need in order to launch my business, I need to stay focused.

I thought that giving in to my desperate mind and sleeping with him would get it out of my system, allow me to think more clearly, but I'm not entirely sure that's what happened.

The sex was so good, it became clear right away that we would both want to do it again, and so I launched into a full-on discussion about the rules and boundaries of our new "relationship."

So, now we have a new relationship.

A "girl naively thinking she can be in a sex-only relationship with the hot billionaire she's had a crush on since high school while keeping the whole thing a complete secret from her family because the man happens to be the son of her mother's husband" kind of relationship.

So, you know, no problem.

I've been telling myself it's fine and then rolling my eyes at myself so often I have a headache.

It's fine though. Really. It's going to be fine.

Fine.

I can do this. Modern woman, right? I can have it all.

I don't sleep well, even though I'm exhausted from our bedroom escapades and the bottle of wine we shared at dinner. The roller coaster of my mind runs through the night, never pausing to let me jump off.

I take a cold shower and get dressed. I have a big day ahead of me, taking measurements in the pool patio area and at the beach where the arch is going to go, plus visiting the flower farm later this evening.

I check my phone and find only a few Facebook Messenger notifications from my mom and a few friends back home, not a single text from Avery.

The phone reception here is terrible, though, even if the Wi-Fi is pretty good, so I'm not worried. Not that I'd be worried even if the reception was great. I can go twelve hours without hearing from the guy. Can't I?

I consider running up to his room to see if he's ready.

It dawns on me then that we're going to have to become Facebook friends in order to use Messenger like I do with my other friends and family, and the thought of proposing that…no, just no. I know there's not a chance in hell I'm going to do it. I would rather string tin cans between our hotel room windows.

Actually, that sounds kind of romantic. We could use them to say good night—

Stop. Just stop.

I toss my still-wet hair in a bun and grab my portfolio and bag.

When I swing the door open, Avery is standing there, fist raised as if preparing to knock.

I laugh in surprise and then go a bit gooey in the knees as his face spreads into a smile.

"Hey," he says.

"Hey."

"I couldn't text you, so I ran down to check on your time-frame." He looks me down and then up. "I see you're ready to go."

"Yeah, I don't have reception here."

"Oh, we text through WhatsApp in countries like this. Do you have it on your phone?"

I shake my head.

"We'll get you set up today. It's super easy, and everyone around here uses it. It's just your regular number but it runs through this Wi-Fi app."

Relief at a sunny future with no talk of becoming friends on Facebook glows brightly in front of me. "Perfect."

"Did you eat?" he asks as we make our way to the elevator.

I shake my head. "I was about to head down to Reef to grab something."

"Mind if I join you?"

I shake my head again. It's more than not minding. I want this man attached to my wrist with handcuffs. "We can go over what we need to measure while we eat."

"Very professional."

I am so grateful for his humor, for the way he manages to see through my awkward nervousness and scoop me back into the fold, that I could cry.

I will not actually cry, though. Under no circumstances.

"I'm a little nervous," I admit, even though I'm sure it's completely obvious.

"Me too," he answers, stepping a little closer and bumping my shoulder with his as we walk down the hallway.

Just that one little touch is enough to send sparks of joy and excitement through my whole body.

"We got this, though." He sounds so sure that I believe him.

Reef is much busier than usual, and I stand awkwardly in the doorway, unsure of where to go. Avery comes up behind me and stands too close, looking over my shoulder at the crowd.

"Damn," he says, referring to the mob of vacationers taking up every available seat.

"Yeah, damn," I respond, referring to the way my heart pounds, and I have to force myself to breathe when he's this close to me.

His hand on my arm snaps me back to life. "Why don't you go snag us that bench by the pool, I'll grab coffee and whatever they have sitting around in the back and meet you out there."

"Okay," I breathe, willing to agree to just about anything he says right now.

Avery moves past me and disappears behind the counter, high-fiving the staff and calling out greetings. I can't help but grin at his easy nature with everyone, how they respond to him in kind, graciously offering up whatever they have.

Is that all I've done?

I stifle another eye roll at my ridiculously dramatic thoughts and remind myself of my task. Sneaking past the bathing suit-clad families, I make my way to the only free bench on the whole patio, getting there just in time. The woman I beat out for the seat doesn't look particularly friendly about conceding it to me, but I stand my ground.

Avery appears ten minutes later with two ceramic coffee cups filled to the brim and a brown sack under his arm. I've just finished laying out the list of measurements I need and gaps that still need to be filled in the plan overall. I shift my papers to the side so he can sit down.

"I hope you either like black or with cream and sugar because those are the two I brought."

I smile at his earnest face, looking down at the two cups he holds out. "Which do you prefer?"

He shrugs. "I'm happy with anything. Coffee is coffee."

I take the cream and sugar cup from him and watch as he takes a sip from his black coffee and smile. He isn't just humoring me. I have a feeling he would have been just as satisfied with the sweet, creamy cup I now hold.

I wonder if that sort of thing comes from a lifetime of not having a home with your own coffee maker. You don't have the chance to develop such rigid preferences.

I'm interrupted in my scrutiny of his entire life by the rustle of the brown bag. As he opens the top, the most delicious smell escapes.

"These just came out of the oven," he says, drawing two large muffins from the bag.

My eyes go wide.

"You're not gluten-free or plant-based or anything? I forgot to ask." His hesitation is adorable.

I shake my head and seize one of the steaming muffins.

"I'm not anything," I manage to get out with a huge bite in my mouth.

I glance down at the pile of crumbs forming in my lap, and when I look back up, the man is looking at me with these eyes, like I hung the moon. I have to look away.

But then something dawns on me, and I look back at his beautiful face, glowing in the morning sun. "You know, you look—"

"Don't say it."

He's not upset, but I stop short anyway, feeling scolded. It takes me a breath to recover. "How'd you know what I was going to say?"

Avery gives me a sly smile. "People always get this certain look on their face before they tell me I look like him."

I turn back to my coffee, busying myself with taking a long sip and setting it back down. Until this moment, I'd only really considered the whole stepsiblings thing as a concept. Words that people might object to. I now have an inkling about the deeper implications.

Because, while Avery and his father are distinctly different people, the resemblance is uncanny. It takes a certain light, a certain expression to get the full effect of the similarities, but there is no denying them.

It's a whole new layer to unpack.

Even if I do convince everyone around me that this whole sleeping with Frederick's son thing is a good idea, will I ever fully let go of the fact that the face looking up at me from between my legs is so similar to the pseudo-father figure I've had for the last nine years?

Up until this point, Frederick was the most handsome man I'd ever met. I was so shy when my mom first brought him home because I wasn't used to having men around the house and because he was such a *man*.

When I learned about Avery and started following him on Insta, it was the perfect outlet for my teenage girl crush on my mom's boyfriend. Avery looked like his father but acted like a superhuman. Like every girl's dream, traveling the world, unencumbered by work or kids, or anything really. I lost myself in the fantasy that was Avery. Now that I have him here and am faced with the reality of who this person is, and who he is to me, I'm left to wonder.

What have I gotten myself into?

"Whatever it is, love, you gotta let it go."

I snap back to attention. "What?"

"I can see your mind going a million miles a minute over there. We just acknowledged the fact that I look a lot like my father, your mom's husband, and you disappeared into scared eyes land. Don't go there. It's not a real place. People look like each other. I'm not Frederick. This doesn't need to be weird."

I nod, even though I'm not quite sure I agree. As if my mind wants to make it weird, I open my mouth. "I like your dad a lot.

I mean, not like that, but you know. He was there through some hard years for me, high school drama and graduation. He helped me out."

"I'm glad to hear that."

He does sound glad. I look into his eyes just to make sure. Yup, he's okay. He doesn't hate me for having the relationship with his father that he never did.

Oh my god, this is so weird.

My eyes must go scared again because Avery jumps into his own awkward puddle of words. "Where's your father?"

The air gets sucked right out of me, and I gasp it back in as quietly and ladylike as possible.

There's no way Avery missed that.

"Oh," I start, not looking up from my coffee cup. "He died."

I want to say more, but I can't. It's been years, but somehow, this never gets easier to talk about. One word about my father, and I'm right back on the front steps of our house in Connecticut, nine years old, holding a small jar of bubbles while my mom cries.

"Dang, Fran. I didn't know that." He reaches to pull me closer, but it's impossible with the coffee cups and brown bag spread between us, not to mention my stiff, unyielding body. He lets go and lets the silence stretch.

I take another sip of coffee and regain the ability to breathe. "It's okay," I say, even though it's not. "It was a long time ago."

"How long?"

"I was nine, so…fourteen years or so."

Avery says nothing for so long that I look up, wondering if I need to comfort him in some way. It's amazing how often discussions of my own grief have ended with me trying to make the other person feel okay. He just looks pensive, though. Calm and caring.

I look back down at the pile of crumbs in my lap. I laugh softly and shake my dress out. The tiny birds that have been hopping around the patio rush over in a little swarm.

"I'm glad you had Frederick, then. For those hard years."

I don't look up, but he sounds genuine.

"Seriously, Fran. I need you to know that I don't feel anything about the situation with my father anymore. You can talk about him, you can love him like a parent, it's okay. You aren't going to hurt my feelings. I'm happy to hear that he was able to be there for you as a support. I feel nothing but grateful that you had him when you needed him."

"You aren't angry that you didn't have him?"

Avery shrugs. "I used to be. But that was a long time ago. I had to let it go and move on."

"So you had no one growing up?"

"Not at all. I had a wonderful family. There was Stew, who probably would have been called the butler, but he was just Stew to me. He managed the house and drove me around, ran our errands. There was Miranda, she and her three kids lived in the house for my whole life, we grew up together. She was the housekeeper, but also my teacher and the person who tucked me in every night. And good ol' Phil, the groundskeeper. He was our gamemaster, always ready to play ball or set up the pool for us." Avery laughs to himself at the memory. "It was unconventional, I suppose, but I was a kid. I didn't know any different."

There's no way that's true, but I let it slide. "Where are they all now?"

"Phil passed a few years back. That was the last time I was there. We all got together for a service at the house. Miranda and Stew still live at the estate, Miranda's kids have families, two of them live in the area. Her youngest, Paul, moved to California. I stayed with him last year. We went surfing."

His tone is so nonchalant, like what he's saying is so normal. And I suppose it is. He's telling me about his aging family members, his siblings who he isn't particularly close to.

"So, you're an uncle?"

Avery smiles at me. "I suppose so."

I bite my lip and worry over my next statement, but it comes out anyway. "I'm an aunt. I have two nieces. My sister's kids. Suzie's three, and Freida's seven."

"Tell me more."

I can't help but smile as I pull out my phone and scroll to the last burst of pictures I took at my sister's house before I left to come to Faraday. The girls are showing off the new outfits we bought when I took them shopping with me for tropical weather clothes. Avery patiently lets me scroll through all the pictures, showing him who is who.

"Suzie's small for her age, just a little sprout. She still likes to be carried everywhere, which drives her mom crazy. She's going to be a tomboy, though, probably. She already likes black and blue best and chases her sister through the house throwing balls. Freida will always be my baby, my first." I go a bit teary-eyed as I think of my little bestie and how much I miss her. "She and I are one and the same. We've been going dress shopping together since she was in the Baby Björn."

"Sounds like you love those kids a lot."

I look up at his tone and find a question there. I look away, shutting down my phone and tucking it back into my bag. We can just skip right over wherever this is headed.

"I brought the list of measurements I need, and I wanted to run a few things by you about the buffet area and the welcome table."

"And…we're back to business."

I narrow my eyes at him. "We have a lot of work to do."

"Yes, indeed. Let's get to it."

I sigh. I knew it was going to be a challenge to balance the personal with work, but the only way to get used to it is to do it. "I thought we could start with measuring the patio, but there are so many people out here, it might be better to figure out the pacing between the patio and the place on the beach where we are going to set up the flower arch."

"Pacing?"

"Yeah, like how many steps it is. We don't want it to be too long, make the bride walk too far. It kind of takes away from the dramatic reveal of her dress if she has to walk half a mile to get to the aisle itself. So, we need to figure out how many chairs are going to be set up, which we can't know for sure until after the first of the year, but we can estimate it to be about a hundred." I stand and walk over to the edge of the pool patio to the top of the short steps leading down to the beach path.

"It's probably going to be five rows of ten on either side of the aisle. So, that would mean they start about here." I walk down to the place on the beach where I imagine the first row and draw a line in the sand with my foot. "And the last one..." I draw another line one chair's distance away and continue drawing lines until I have reached the last of the five rows. "Here. So that means the arch will be about here." I walk to the center of the aisle and stamp down a round area with both feet until I have a rough oblong shape marked in the sand.

I turn to find Avery standing back on the edge of the pool patio, arms crossed, grinning at me like I've lost my mind. "What?" I ask.

"Nothing, you're just adorable."

I scowl and cross my own arms.

"Adorably efficient that is." He hops down the steps and walks toward me. "So, what we need to figure out is how many paces it will take the bride to get from the door of Reef to the arch?"

I nod enthusiastically, happy that he's following my plan.

He nods back. "Okay, let's do it."

We walk back up to the door of the restaurant.

It's not totally ideal to have the bride enter from here, but it's the only doorway to the patio, so it will have to do. We can decorate the door frame so it looks less like a café entrance.

When we reach the wide-open door, standing aside to let people pass in and out between us, Avery puts his hands on his hips.

"I assume she isn't walking down the aisle to 'Here Comes the Bride?'"

I laugh and shake my head. "No way. She chose 'A Time for Us' from *Romeo and Juliet*."

Avery crosses to my side of the doorway and slides his arm through mine. "Do you want to sing it while we walk? So we can get the pacing right?"

I grin and stifle an eye roll at the thought of that. "I have it on my phone, hold on." I get the song started and slip my phone back in my pocket.

The old-fashioned, romantic orchestra piece plays from the tinny phone speaker, and I look up into Avery's face to see if he's ready.

He is giving me that look again, only this time it's got a charge to it that I can't quite place. I'm not sure how long I stand, locked in his gaze, but it must be a while because eventually he leans down and whispers, "Do you want to start it over?"

My gaze shoots down toward the phone in my pocket, and I realize that the song is almost half over.

"Oh. Yeah." I fumble to get it out and restart it.

New plan. Do not look at Avery.

I stare straight ahead. "Ready?"

"Ready."

We start to take slow, deliberate steps with the beat of the song.

I will freely admit that I had given exactly zero thought to what it was going to look like for Avery and me to walk down the imaginary aisle to this classic wedding song, but it becomes immediately apparent exactly what people think is going on.

"Congratulations!"

"Adorable couple!"

The calls from lounging vacationers makes heat rise to my cheeks. Avery must feel me stiffen because he pulls me closer. "It's okay. Just ignore them."

"Yeah," I say through gritted teeth.

"Ooh, aren't you two just the most adorable thing?"

Fuck. I have totally lost count of the steps. I start to panic, but Avery's right there, holding me steady.

"I'm keeping count, love."

I calm down and focus on putting one foot in front of the other. Slowly, the world fades away, and it's just us, walking down the freaking aisle to a classic wedding song.

No biggie.

Our feet move in perfect unison to the beat, and we sway slightly from one side to the other as we walk. When we finally reach the stamped down area representing the arch where the ceremony will happen, I feel like I haven't taken a breath in an hour.

I drop his arm and step to the side.

"Perfect. Great. That was…" I trail off, having no idea how many steps it was.

"Thirty-eight," Avery provides.

I look over at him gratefully. "Thirty-eight. Okay. That's pretty good, I think. What do you think?"

He shrugs.

I nod. "It's perfect. For now, anyway. Do you want to help me measure the buffet and welcome table areas? I would really like to get those tables secured." I'm jumping wildly from one project to another, but as long as I'm crossing things off the list, I decide it's okay.

Avery nods, and I practically run back up the aisle, up the stairs, and back to the bench where we left our discarded breakfast items and my portfolio.

I'm running from uncomfortable feelings, but he lets me. Maybe he's grateful. I still can't read his face, but if I'm being perfectly honest, I've avoided looking at it straight on.

That could be part of the problem.

As soon as I've packed up my stuff, and he's cleared away our garbage, I dare a look into those eyes.

Mistake! Retreat!

I look back down at my notebook. "Um, do you have a measuring thing? Tape. Measuring tape?"

Idiot.

Avery just smiles. "Not on me, but we can snag whatever you need from the maintenance room."

"Great," I say, following him out of the restaurant and through the lobby, down a long hallway that gets progressively less well-lit as we go.

Turns out, it's not great. The maintenance room is a vacant, almost completely dark, ten-by-ten closet at the end of a deserted hallway. He shuts the door behind us.

"Avery…"

"Oh, come on," he says, all of a sudden very close to me. "You had to see this one coming."

I shake my head honestly.

He laughs. "I'll let you measure anything you want."

It's my turn to laugh. "We're supposed to be professional when we're at work."

"I thought we were supposed to be professional when we were working around other people. Clearly, we need some further clarification of the rules." He isn't waiting for clarification, though, as his lips drop to my neck and graze upward toward my ear.

"Clearly," I whisper.

Who am I kidding? The tasks on my list for today are counting the paces in the aisle and measuring for two tables. We're already half done.

"I guess this could be considered a break?" I offer.

My shirt is off before I even close my mouth after speaking the words.

I laugh in surprise. "Avery!"

"Franny."

"You aren't supposed to call me that."

"You never told me what I should call you, so I thought I was off the hook."

The name battle is forgotten as my skirt hikes up around my waist, revealing the attached shorts.

"What kind of trickery is this?" he demands, scowling at the skintight Lycra.

"You have to pull them down, not up."

"You're the boss."

Down they go.

And just like that, I'm naked at work, getting my clit sucked in the maintenance closet.

It's a whole new cunnilingus experience, Avery crouched in front of where I stand, my hands gripping the shelves on either side of me, fingers digging into the metal, elbows knocking aside wrenches and tins of nails.

It never leaves my mind that we just walked through that door from a public hallway and left it unlocked, that anyone else could walk through it as well, but I can't worry about that right now. I just bear down on the shelving as Avery reaches up and inside me.

I should stop him, stop this. But, obviously, I don't.

He uses his free arm and one shoulder to push my legs farther to the sides and opens me up, sliding his tongue deeper into the folds of my flesh.

"Fuck, Avery, don't stop."

He murmurs something that I feel in my bones but can't hear.

I let my head hang back and just allow the feeling to overtake me. It does, very quickly. No sooner is he flicking my clit to the sides while curling his fingers deep in my pussy than I'm buckling at the core, biting my lip, and trying not to cry out.

I'm right in the depths of it, holding my breath and fighting back a scream, when the door opens.

Like a game of whack a mole, I drop instinctively to a crouch as Avery stands right up.

"Hey," he says, sounding casual enough that I know he knows whoever it is. Hell, he knows everyone.

"Hey..."

It's Sam. Shit!

Avery is standing about halfway into the room, behind a tall metal toolbox. I'm crouched behind his legs, and, luckily, behind the same toolbox. I can't see the door, so I know Sam can't see my naked ass.

"What's up?" Avery says when Sam doesn't go on.

"Just saw you head in here and close the door. Wanted to make sure everything was okay."

Does that mean he saw me come in, too?

And doesn't see me now…

"Oh, yeah. I was just grabbing a tape measure. It was hard to find in the dark, but I found it."

The men are silent for a long moment. I'm probably glad I can't see the look that passes between them.

"So, you can go," Avery finally says.

Sam knows. There is no way he couldn't. Avery just dismissed him in the most obvious way because Sam knows I'm hiding here naked.

"Okay," Sam says.

There is another long pause where the two men stand, facing off. Then the door closes.

Avery drops down beside me, laughing.

I smack him on the shoulder. "That wasn't funny! Get my shirt." I'm not actually mad, but I'm certainly feeling something.

"It was kinda funny, love."

"How was it funny? We are supposed to be professional, and then our first day on the job, we get caught doing it in a closet?" Okay, it is kind of funny. I let the laugh that bubbles up in me escape my lips.

"It's just Sam. It's not like we got caught by dad or anything." His face shoots to mine. "And by dad, I mean a general authority figure. I did not mean my actual father."

I shake my head. There is no way to make this not weird, so I just go with it. I slip my shirt back on and pull my skirt back in place.

"You don't think Sam's going to be mad?"

Avery shakes his head. "Not Sam. Now, if that was Ben catching us like this, that might be a different story."

I know of Ben, but I've never met the guy. "Why's that?"

"Eh, Ben is more like the dad of the group. Or he is to me, anyway."

There's something new in his tone, and I wait for whatever it is to come out.

"He went to Frederick's law school, works for the same firm now. He and my old man are kinda close actually."

It's bitterness, sadness, maybe even anger. Not things I've ever heard from Avery, even when he talked about being abandoned as a child by his own parents. I'm not sure what to do with this.

"Let's get out of here, okay?" he says before I can think of what to ask.

I want to know more, but we've already been hiding in the closet long enough, so I relent, making a note to ask about Ben later.

We tag team the measurements on the patio, dodging dripping wet children and women in giant hats.

I jot all of the numbers down in my notebook, doing some quick calculations as to how many tables will fit and where.

"What else?" Avery asks as I'm tucking the tape measure into my bag and wrapping up my portfolio.

"That's it, really. I'll use these measurements to draw up my table order and I'll figure out what linens we need to order as well. When I get a sketch of the configuration, we can look at it together and decide which tables should hold what—and what other decor we need." Avery is listening with rapt attention. "That'll all come after the menu meetings, though, probably. I'll need to know what kind of appetizer spreads the restaurant will set up and how much room they need, and we'll need to know where the bar is going to be and how large of a table they need. From there, it's just a matter of choosing a gift table and a welcome table and picking out the flowers and decorations for them."

"And the cameras?" he asks, referring back to our first meeting and causing a little skip in my heartbeat. How little I knew then about what was about to happen. I was still operating under the delusion that I'd be able to hide our masquerade party tryst forever, when the truth was, he already knew.

"Yeah. It'll probably work best to do a combo of Polaroids and disposable cameras, that way people can have fun with the instant prints, but we'll have a lot of shots to develop later on."

"Sounds like you've really got this all under control."

"Yeah, I mean, it's not my first time." My chest collapses into a full face-blush, and I shake my head. "Not my first wedding, I mean."

"I know what you mean, love. It is, however, my first one, so I'm lucky to have you here to show me the ropes."

I sigh, on the verge of telling him that I don't even really need him here, but the words just won't come. They may have been true in the beginning, but they aren't true now. I would rather die than spend the next few months planning this wedding alone—now that I know this option is available. What started as the opportunity of a lifetime to prove myself and establish my new business is turning into…something else.

And, while I probably should hate it, I don't. Not one bit.

Rule #14

LOOKS CAN BE MISLEADING. SOMETIMES

AVERY

Fran looks good enough to eat as we tuck into the golf cart, getting ready to head up the hill to the flower farm. Even though I did eat her—twice—before and after our afternoon nap, somehow, I'm still hungry.

"How do you know these people again?" she asks as I steer the little vehicle out of the paved drive and up the dirt road heading east.

"Ah, just spend enough time hanging around a tiny town like Saubry, and you get to know most of the locals." Sure, I may have schmoozed my way into a VIP floral arrangement for my own special guests at the resort a time or two, but there's no point in mentioning that.

Not when I have this special creature on the hook.

I don't know how exactly this happened, but the whole thing is definitely working out in my favor.

In my wildest dreams, I might have made friends with this woman, gotten to bask in the glow of her radiance for a bit while she tolerated my presence. Never, ever, did I see things going like this. What started with hostility, a "getting it out of our system" fuck, has morphed into something else entirely.

When I take her hand, she holds on.

When I catch her eye, she blushes.

When I slide my fingers inside her, she closes her eyes and opens for me.

Whatever this is, it's closer than I've been to anyone in a long, long time.

Possibly ever.

She's exactly the last person on the planet I should be involved with, but maybe that's part of the appeal. Forbidden fruit and whatnot.

Whatever it is, one thing is for sure. I am going down with this motherfucking ship. Consequences be damned. My body, heart, and soul are pinned to the sacrificial table with daggers through my limbs, preparing for the final blow—and not fighting for my own release.

We pull up in front of Marta's farm, and I park the cart next to a handful of others. I hop out and hurry to the other side of the cart to snatch Franny's hand as she emerges. She tucks into me and lets me lead her toward the opening in the vegetation that marks the entrance to the farm property.

"Wow," she breathes as we pass through the wild hedges, air ripe with flowers and fruit.

"Yeah, it's pretty incredible, huh?"

I catch her eyes, wide with amazement, and she nods.

My chest swells with pride for being the one to bring her here. I'm an undeserving explorer showing off someone else's riches and hoping some of the credit falls to me.

"Yoohoo," a voice calls out from the patio that wraps around the low, square house. I recognize Marta and wave, steering Fran toward her.

"You made it. I was wondering if you got stuck on the hill. I have got to do something about that road, but…" Marta trails off her apologies as she pulls me into a welcoming embrace.

Fran gets one next, so large and firm that I hear the breath whoosh from her lungs.

"It's about time, too. Pa is just getting the second round of drinks going—you almost missed the fresh pineapple," she chastises me, even though it's still early in the evening.

I smile. "Well, we wouldn't want to miss that, would we?" I claim Fran's arm with my own once more as we follow Marta into the house.

It appears to be a bit of a party, but I know from experience that this is just family and the group of seasonal workers who live on the property. Still, I'm sure it's more people than Fran was expecting. She moves closer to me as we enter the room.

"Everyone, this is Avery. You all know that, I know. But this," —she steps aside to motion to Fran—"is Franzeska. Isn't she something?"

The room certainly agrees and isn't quiet about it. I grin down at Franny's pink cheeks, watching her try to take the attention in stride.

"It's nice to meet you all," she says.

"It's nice to finally see a real woman on that handsome arm," one of the older ladies calls out from where she sits in a deep, padded chair with an oscillating fan blowing her wispy hair back. "If he stayed single much longer, I was going to snatch him up for myself."

The room breaks into laughter and chiding, all of the women offering themselves as my partner.

Fran is shaking her head, opening her mouth to protest, but she never gets the chance. Tall, iced drinks are placed in our hands, and we're led back out of the house into the gardens.

"Don't pay any mind to them, my dear. You've got no competition here." Marta eyes Fran sidelong. "Or anywhere, is my guess."

Fran doesn't respond. Just slips her arm out of mine under the ruse of walking over to admire some large, round, pink flowers. I let her go.

"These are beautiful," she says, tossing the words over her shoulder at Marta.

"Shampoo ginger."

"Shampoo?" Fran and I ask in unison, laughing at each other.

"Shampoo, yeah. You can use them in the bath. Or, just admiring them is more likely these days. But you want bougainvillea, right?"

Franny nods eagerly. "I was thinking it would be perfect for an arch. And you said there are lots of colors to choose from?"

Marta is nodding, leading us further into the gardens. "That's here. This red is lovely, but the fuchsia is the one everyone always wants. That and the cream. The two together are perfect. With the greens and blues of the hotel, this is what you should have."

Fran is nodding, clearly sold on the enchanting combo of soft, variegated purply pink, and the cream blossoms. "How many colors can we choose?"

Marta shrugs. "As many as you want, I suppose." She motions to the pots that the tall, vining flowers are growing out of, up the wooden trellis wall. "You choose the colors, and we will plant the vines, then grow them up the arches. When the big day comes, we'll bring the whole thing down in the truck and get it set up. It will always be alive."

I'll be damned if those aren't tears forming in Fran's lovely eyes. "They're so beautiful," she whispers.

"Nothing but the best for your big day." One of the farmers, an older woman in cut off shorts and a stained cream-colored tank, comes up behind Fran and me, clapping a hand on each of our shoulders and pulling us closer together.

"Oh, it's not—" Fran tries once again in vain to protest them calling this our wedding, but neither of the women is listening.

I briefly wonder if I should butt in, if I should be joining her in adamantly denying the idea that it's Fran and I getting married, but I don't. My jaw stays clamped shut so tightly that it's starting to get sore.

What the hell is that about?

I've never pictured my own wedding, never having imagined that there would be one. I've been to enough weddings to last me a lifetime, and the thought of having such a big deal made of my own life and love used to turn my stomach.

And yet here I am, allowing these women to talk about this wedding as if I'm going to be the one standing at the altar, watching Fran walk toward me in a white dress.

Okay, man. Time to reel this shit in.

"It's really perfect," I say suddenly, just to break the tension building in my chest. "Fran has some great sketches of how the whole thing will be laid out. I'm sure she can make you a copy so we can get the measurements correct."

We have the full crowd of farmers as our audience now, as they slowly trickled out of the house when our backs were turned. One of the younger women draws in close to Fran.

"You're so lucky he's taking an interest in the wedding planning," she says enviously.

"It's not—"

"Seriously. When I got married, I hardly even knew the date of the damn thing. My wife complains every time we see the pictures about how little help she had and on and on," one of the older farmers chimes in.

"It's not our wedding!" Fran finally gets her whole sentence out, and it rings through the golden dusk too loud, too forceful.

A hush falls over the gathered group, and Fran blushes, looking regretful. She looks to me to save the moment, and I happily jump in.

I'd save her from anything.

"It's Fran's brother's wedding we're planning. She's a professional wedding planner."

The silence stretches out for a long moment, and I notice Fran standing a little taller, tossing me a grateful look.

The quiet doesn't last, though.

"Will be yours soon enough," Marta's husband says.

"Who do you two think you're fooling?" one of the farmers adds with a laugh.

The good-natured muttering continues as the farmers trade knowing glances and laugh among themselves. I watch Fran's jaw tense up to the point where I'm concerned for the safety of her teeth.

I jump back in.

"Anyway, we'll get those measurements for you. And I'm assuming you will take the lead on building the arch frame for the flowers to grow up? Or is that something we will need to get our maintenance team to build?"

Fran looks to me gratefully as the whispers die down.

"We'll build the arch. Let's make sure we have the exact colors that you want, and then we can sit down on the patio and go over measurements," Marta says, starting to walk off deeper into what turns out to be a forest of potted bougainvillea vines.

Fran and I follow her—two feet apart—but the rest of the group wanders back to the house, excitement over for the evening.

Fran and Marta spend nearly an hour looking at particular plants and deciding which ones are the correct shades for the arch. When Marta has the desired plants tagged for cutting and planting, we head back to the patio and settle down at the big table.

My drink has been empty for a while, but Fran sets her glass down on the table almost entirely full. I pull the now lukewarm, melted, yellow liquid toward myself and start sucking it down as the women go over measurements and timeframes. Marta's husband swaps it for a fresh one when I have about an inch of warm, watered down booze left.

As we approach the golf cart half an hour later, Fran stops

short and holds out her hand. I place mine in her waiting palm and squeeze.

She tosses my hand off and holds hers back out. "The keys, Avery."

I twist my face questioningly, but I have a feeling I know exactly what's coming. "You want to drive?"

"Well, you're certainly not driving."

"Why—"

"You are not actually going to stand there and tell me that you think it's safe for you to drive a golf cart down a mountain in the dark after drinking three of those cocktails. I couldn't even take two sips of mine, it was so strong."

"Eh…" It's hard to argue with her there, but I'm still hesitant to hand over the keys.

Her palm persists.

I surrender.

It's one thing to follow along with the local "don't ask don't tell" drinking and driving policy, it's quite another to argue out loud for your right to do so.

We settle into our seats, and I watch for a long moment as she struggles to find the keyhole.

"Do you need any help?" I offer unhelpfully.

Fran sits back in her seat with a thud, arms falling resignedly to her sides. "Yeah, Avery. I am going to need a lot of help. I've never driven one of these things before, and it's dark, and the road isn't even a freaking road—"

She's freaking out, and I feel terrible. I slide over and pull her in close. She comes without a fight. "I'm sorry, love."

"You should be sorry," she says into my chest, her muffled words still filled with ire. "You drove us up here and then got drunk, so now I have to drive home. It's stupid."

The shame I feel at failing my role as protector is so great it nearly swallows me whole. "I didn't really think—"

"Yeah, that's clear."

"I mean, usually we just drive. It's just a golf cart—"

She's out of my arms and facing me in a flash, eyes blazing. "Just a golf cart? You're telling me you drive these things around drunk all the time?"

"No, I didn't say—"

"And that everyone else is doing it, too?"

"I was just saying that…" What the hell am I saying? She's got me there. "The laws are just a little looser down here—"

"Oh, that's real nice, Avery. Drunk driving is drunk driving. It doesn't matter where you are or what you're driving. Jesus, there are people walking everywhere on this island. Children, Avery! And you just drive around drunk?"

I have exactly zero recourse here. "Yeah, you're right. I just, I don't know. You're right. It's terrible. I'll never do it again."

"Good." She's exasperated, but on the way to letting it go—for now anyway. "Now put this fucking key in the ignition, please, so we can start this perilous journey."

"Oh, I'll put my key in your ignition—"

"Avery…"

"Okay, okay." I take the keys from her and slide it easily into the hole. "Now give it a turn, with your foot on the brake. There you go. The parking brake is just to your left. Yup, okay, now let off the brake and ease onto the gas." She follows my directions easily, and we set off down the steep road home. "There. You're a natural. Just take it slow."

Fran takes my words to heart, and we make our way down the gravel road at a pace I could easily beat on foot. I want to reach over and touch her, but she's concentrating so hard on driving, I doubt it would be appreciated.

"I don't know why they bother putting lights on the front of this thing. They aren't bright enough for driving at night."

"You're doing great."

She glances my way just long enough for a split second of eye contact before her gaze shoots back to the road in front of us. "You aren't even watching the road!"

"You're driving."

"Yeah, but I don't know. I would be watching the road if you were driving."

"You don't trust me?"

She shoots another split second look my way. "I don't know if that's it."

"So, you do trust me," I know she can hear the smile in my voice because her mouth tips up at the sides just a bit.

She shakes her head. "That was a lot back there."

"Yeah."

"And down at the pool this morning."

"Yeah." I know what she's getting at, but if the woman has something to say, she's going to have to come right out and say it. I find her thoughts too interesting to risk blurring them with my own.

"Did you always believe that you would just, like, not get married?"

I grin as she vocalizes a perfect Fran question. "My life isn't over, love." The answer is true enough, but not one I would have given even a week ago. I had, indeed, believed that I would never get married. But that was before.

"You know what I mean."

"It's not something I've given much thought to. I watched my parents get married a few times, I guess I just figured if it happens, it happens." Sounds much less pathetic than the truth, which is that I never imagined anyone would want to marry my irresponsible ass.

"You weren't at my mom and Frederick's wedding."

"I wasn't invited."

She turns to me, mouth wide open in shock.

I laugh. "The wedding before that, I may have gotten a bit carried away giving a speech."

"You did not." She sounds scandalized and definitely wants the whole story.

Too bad it's more sad than anything. "I was young."

She falls silent, deftly steering the cart around a curve. I notice that we've picked up speed—nearly to running pace—but I don't comment on it.

Finally, I can't stand the suspense. "Do you imagine getting married? I mean, with all of these weddings you've worked, and the ones you're going to plan. You must have thought about it."

She takes a while to answer, but I can see the thoughts churning in her mind, so I wait.

"I don't know. I guess everyone figures that they will probably get married, right? I definitely know what I would and wouldn't do at my own wedding after working so many of them. But I haven't dated anyone who I could imagine forever with."

"You've got plenty of time." I don't know what makes me say it, and I regret the words as soon as they leave my lips.

She sighs. I wait to be chastised for spewing another "you'll understand when you're older" type sentiment, but she surprises me. "My dad died when he was forty-six. When he was my age, he'd lived exactly half of his life."

Her comment from a few days back, about how she could be middle-aged, suddenly makes a lot of sense. "We never really know how long we have, huh?" I say.

"Yeah."

I can't tell from her tone if she's crying, but her words sounded stifled enough to make me lean over. She's dry-eyed but looking pensive. I sit back in my seat. "I guess I've always taken that to mean that I need to seize the day. Travel everywhere, go on every adventure. Life is short, so I keep myself busy."

Fran says nothing, steering us off the gravel road finally onto the paved road that will lead up to the hotel.

"Hey, pull over here."

Fran's head turns to me in surprise. "What? Why?"

"Because I said so, love."

With an exaggerated eye roll and a grin, Franny steers the

cart over to the side of the road, stopping next to a small forest of tall tropical plants.

"Turn in there," I say, pointing to a barely visible opening in the brush.

She tosses me an unsure glance, but follows my directions, inching the cart forward until we're moving at a snail's pace down the path through the trees. "Leading me off into the woods in the dark…" she mutters as she lifts up higher in her seat, trying to get a better look at the road ahead.

"It'll be worth it, I promise."

"…going to get eaten alive by mosquitoes," her muttering continues as the cart emerges from the foliage and stops in front of a large pond.

"Better than crocodiles, am I right?"

Her head whips to me, eyes as wide as her round little mouth. "Crocodiles?"

"Yeah. This isn't the place to go swimming."

She shakes her head. "Okay, what are we doing here, then?"

What are we doing here? I have enough tequila flowing through my veins that I can't keep my hands off of her, and the thought of going back to the hotel and going our separate ways is just too much.

So, yeah. We're totally going to get eaten alive by mosquitoes. I'll just have to make it worth her while.

"Just park here, and let's hop out."

Fran pushes in the parking brake and turns the key, pocketing the little palm tree keychain. I grab her hand and pull her out of the cart on my side, leading her right down to the water's edge.

"Whoa."

"I know, right?"

"How did you know this would be here?"

"I have an app on my phone that tells me the moon phases, so I knew it would be full tonight."

"But how did you know it would be right here, at the top of

the sky, reflecting down into this swamp and turning the whole thing into…I don't know. Something from a fantasy novel?"

I pull her close and watch over her head as a bird swoops close enough to the surface to cause a ripple. Franny gasps as the movement in the water turns the perfect reflection of the golden full moon into an otherworldly watercolor painting.

"It's incredible."

"The world is full of little things like this. Magic waiting around every corner."

"Is that why you travel?"

I pull her tighter and rest my chin on the top of her head. "It wasn't at first, but it is now. I'll hear about some ruin or natural wonder, or even a class or a unique, far-flung hotel. And off I go."

"Why did you go at first?"

I could've just left off that whole first bit and avoided this question. I mentally kick myself for saying it. But when the words start, I find I don't mind them all that much. Telling her doesn't feel like the gut-wrenching, tooth-pulling activity that offering personal information can sometimes be.

"I went on that first trip so I wouldn't have to go home for the long school holiday and be alone in that huge house."

I feel Franny tense in my arms, but she says nothing, apparently not wanting to get into the whole messy subject of my family drama again. That's more than okay with me.

When she does speak again, it's to change the subject, but not to one I was expecting. "Everyone thought we were a couple up there."

I smile, even though she can't see me. "And you sure told them."

She turns to look up at me then, catching my eye before turning her head quickly back to the fantasy scene playing out before us. I saw so many questions in that look. So much uncertainty.

There's no way I'm touching that with a ten-foot pole.

"It made me feel completely out of control," she says finally, stumping me even further.

"What do you mean?"

"I spend so much energy trying to control what people think about me. Back at the farm, it felt like they were just going to think whatever they wanted, no matter what I said."

I laugh softly, the sound surprising me. "You can't control what people think."

I get a little side glare for my laughter, and I eat it up.

She says nothing so I blunder on, determined to put my foot in my mouth.

"It's impossible to control what people think of you. Hell, the thoughts are in their head, so unless they say them out loud, you don't even really know what they're thinking."

"I'd love to know what you're thinking a lot of the time," she says softly.

"Well, you can ask."

"What are you thinking right now?"

"I'm thinking that it didn't feel as offensive as I would have imagined for all those people to think I was the one getting married." I shock myself with the truth of the statement, and the fact that I said it out loud. I quickly deflect. "And I'm thinking about an email I got this morning telling me that I'm only number 235 on the waitlist to purchase a ticket on the Darjeeling Himalayan Train Line."

"You're thinking about leaving."

It's not a question, but I feel the need to answer her anyway. I can't say what I'm really thinking again, so I offer up a worthless little quip. "I'm always thinking about something."

We stand in silence for a while longer while I wait for Franny to offer up her mysterious thoughts in exchange for the soul-baring I just did.

She does no such thing.

"I just got a mosquito bite."

I hold my ground, and my grip around her center, until she's wrenched herself out of my arms, laughing, and taken her seat in the golf cart.

"Come on, Ave. I need you to help me back out of here."

I take one last look at the magical moonlight and offer up a prayer to whatever god lives inside it.

Please, God, let this feeling in my chest be congestive heart failure.

Rule #15

SECRETS FESTER. LET IT OUT

FRAN

"I've been looking for you."

The voice comes up behind me as I sip coffee at the bar in Reef. I don't squeak in surprise—thank God—and turn to find Chef Dominic standing behind me, arms crossed like I'm about to get a scolding.

As if.

"Oh, hey, Dominic." I've only met the guy briefly when Avery and I dined at Raft, but I know I'll have to be working closely with him soon enough. He's a force to be reckoned with —the classic tall, dark, and handsome, but with an edge. Like you're always in trouble.

That feeling is driven at least partially by the fact that I've decided to use someone else for the main part of the catered dinner, and I'm not sure how he's going to react when I tell him.

"We need to get a meeting on the books."

I nod. "Yeah. We're free this afternoon if you are. Say two? Meet here at Reef?"

If he had any reaction to the word *we,* it doesn't show on his granite features.

"That's fine."

I let out a long, hopefully silent breath. "Okay, great. See you then."

He turns to walk back to the kitchen but gets held up halfway there by Reina, the breakfast server who brought me my coffee. The look and touch that passes between those two is not lost on me.

Holy fucking shit.

I may have an ally here at The White Sands.

"Hey, Reina," I call as she passes by the bar on her way to the dining room.

Her bright smile turns my direction, and she heads over. During our brief coffee exchange earlier, I hadn't given much thought to her, but with this new information, the question burns a hole in my tongue.

"How's the coffee?" she says brightly. She really is a doll, shoulder-length perky auburn waves and a splash of freckles across her nose.

"It's great. Listen, I couldn't help but notice you and Dominic over there." I glance toward the server station, unsure of how to proceed.

Reina's face takes on a rosy hue, and her smile intensifies. "Yeah, that's a thing, for sure." She holds up her left hand where a rock the size of the island we stand on glitters in the morning light.

"So, I hope you don't mind me asking, but why are you working as a waitress if you are engaged to the super rich owner of the resort?"

She laughs easily, not upset by my question one bit. "I don't usually wait tables. I'm filling in in a bit of an emergency. And I mostly do what I want, regardless of what anyone says." Her eyes flick back toward the kitchen, where I know I would find Dominic if I turned to look.

"Okay, but, you and he are, like…" I already know, but I just can't figure out the right way to form my question. I don't even know what my real question is here, other than the fact that I need this woman to be my friend.

Another of her soft, tinkling laughs. "We got together last season. You're Avery's new stepsister, right?"

"I'm Avery's father's wife's daughter," I say too quickly.

Reina stifles a smile. "Okay…"

"I…yeah. I'm sorry. Anyway, can we hang out?"

"Oh, sure. I guess we're both going to be part of this family soon enough, so we should get to know each other."

The blush her words inspire is not lost on this clever creature. She narrows her eyes and purses her lips. "We should get a drink in town later. I get off at about three. I'll be up at Raft."

"Sure, yeah. I have a meeting at two, I'll come find you after that."

"Bring Avery if you want," she tosses out casually.

"Oh, no. No. No." I'm shaking my head unnecessarily like a crazy person.

Reina nods once, eyebrows sky high. "Well, I'm looking forward to it." And then she's off.

That went pretty terrible, but I got what I wanted, so whatever.

I can't believe my luck. Another woman in her twenties who fell for one of the owners. She seems so nice and normal, too. I plan to squeeze her brain until the perfect advice for my strange situation comes out.

I finish the dregs of my coffee and scoop up my few items. I need to tell Avery about the meeting with Dominic, and the internet seems to be down resort wide. Since I have deemed this an appropriate visit, I take the elevator to the third floor.

Rule #16

THERE'S ALWAYS A BUT...

AVERY

"Holy shit, man. You scared the crap out of me," I say, laughing as I close the door behind me.

Ben is sitting at the bar in my hotel room, drinking coffee and reading a goddamn book. He wasn't here when I left an hour ago for my morning run and swim in the ocean, although, to be perfectly honest, I was so absorbed in my thoughts about a certain dark-haired beauty—and why she hadn't returned my text the night before—that there could have been a full-on surprise party in the kitchen as I strolled through, and I may not have noticed.

"Morning."

"I didn't realize you were coming to Faraday. Did you just get in?"

"I got here last night. I'm staying on Merit."

Of course he is.

All of us guys have a stake in the Merit Island house, but we know whose home it truly is. Ben took the lead in planning, decorating, and maintaining the property from day one.

He has an entire floor in the house all to himself and his... hobbies.

"And you decided to break in for an early morning visit to your best bud."

"It's eleven a.m., and the door was unlocked."

I pour myself a cup of coffee and settle on the sofa. Ben turns on his stool until he's facing me. There's something about his demeanor that I can't quite place, so I wait. Whatever it is he's here for, he can come out with it, or he can get out. I have a one o'clock meeting with my favorite person to shower and prepare for.

"I'm here because Sam called me." Unsurprisingly, Ben, the high-powered corporate defense lawyer, has no issue with getting right to the point.

"Oh, yeah?"

"He told me that you've given yourself a job working on your father's stepson's wedding?"

I sigh, knowing exactly where this is going. Considering my tenuous familial relations, there is only one person on the planet who would give me a lecture, and it's this man right here. "Yup. New job."

"And the girl?"

"Yup, there's a girl."

"Do you need me to tell you how fucked up this all is, or are you aware?"

A flare of white-hot anger shoots through me. I'm not usually one prone to having a temper, but something about that woman has all of my protective instincts online. "There's nothing fucked up about it at all. We're both adults. We are not related. We're just working together and having fun."

"Is she going to think it's fun when she finds out that you're just using her to get back at your father?"

The question seems so far out of left field that at first, it takes me off guard. The longer I think about my answer, though, the more I'm able to see his point. It would be very easy, considering the past thirty years of conflict between Frederick and me, to jump to this conclusion.

Here I was, worried people would think I was a pervert or a cradle robber, but what they really think is that I'm using her as a pawn in a decades-long family conflict.

Shit.

"It's really not like that," I say.

Ben says nothing, regarding me with a stern expression and folded arms.

"That's why you're here? To scold me for my bad behavior? Well, you can save it. I'm not on trial here, Ben. I've done nothing wrong. And, yes, I can see what you mean about how this could be construed, but it's not like that. She and I, I don't know, man. We just clicked. She's good for me. I've been here for weeks. I'm working on this project. I'm sleeping. I'm eating well. I'm talking about myself with someone. It's crazy, but it's like a relationship. Isn't that what you've always wanted for me?"

"What I wanted was for you to settle down in New York and have a relationship with my son. To find someone up there who you could be happy with and be a part of our lives. This? This is just you fucking off in a whole new way."

"How is Ainsley?"

"Don't try to change the subject. But he's okay. He's still not in college, but I think I might have made some headway with our last conversation." Ben sighs, adoration and concern warring on his stern, aristocratic features.

He's had a hard road of it, raising a son by himself while also climbing the ladder to partner at Frederick's firm. There have been too many long workdays, too many missed soccer games, too many nannies—and the indiscretions that seem to come with them—for those two to have made it to Ainsley's adulthood without a truckload of baggage.

"I heard he was going to be on Faraday soon for the wedding. Are you guys both staying on Merit?"

Ben nods then shakes his head and shrugs. "He has a room

there, but he's a nineteen-year-old kid. I'm sure he'll find himself a room here or an Airbnb somewhere close by." I can see the moment Ben snaps back into prosecutor mode. "But this conversation is about you. Are you really prepared for what's going to happen when the whole family arrives and finds you two shacked up here?"

"We aren't exactly planning to make an announcement at the rehearsal dinner or anything. We're just enjoying our time together. We both know this thing has an expiration date, and we are going to walk away when that time comes."

If looks could kill. Jesus fucking Christ.

"And you've talked about this with her? With actual, audible words?"

I laugh and shake my head. "Yeah, man. We've talked about it. She's an ambitious one. This wedding is the first of many for her. It's the launch of her new wedding planning business back in the States. She has no time to be shackled to a homeless old man like me." The words don't sting like they used to when they floated around in my mind.

Because I know damn well they aren't true.

Shit. When did that start?

"You know I want the best for you—"

"But?" There's always a but. We've been here before.

"But this just isn't it, Ave. This isn't the look for you."

"I think we look pretty damn hot together actually. Just wait till you see us in matching formalwear. You'll be singing a different tune."

"At the wedding. Where my son, your nephew, who idolizes you, is going to be."

"Ah. This is about Ainsley, then."

"Everything's about Ainsley."

I nod. I should have seen this coming.

Ainsley and I have always been close. To say that Ben harbors some disappointment that his only son grew up wanting to be just like me—and not him—would be a bit of an understatement.

"You're worried about him seeing me with a younger woman? Seems pretty par for the course around here. Yourself included."

"I'm worried that he's going to get the idea that it's okay to lead much, much younger women on when he has absolutely no intention of giving them the dream life they have definitely been planning in their heads. I don't want him to get the idea that women are just something to be used for his own amusement."

"Fuck, man. That is not what's going on here. I mean, it's not entirely what's going on here. I am amused, there's no doubt, but we have an agreement. One she came up with. Besides, at this point, if she pronounced her love for me, I would be on board so fast, I might capsize the damn ship. But it's not going to happen. She's using me, if anything." The words flow easily enough, but I have to wonder if they're entirely true. It's one thing to be harboring the crush of a lifetime on the sexy vixen in my bed. It would be quite another to commit to some kind of life with the woman. One that would certainly include my father.

Ben, having been my partner in crime since grade school, seems to read my train of thought as it crosses my face.

"Finally thinking things through, are you?"

I inhale deeply and sigh. "It's just going to have to play itself out, man. I'm taking it one step at a time, and I'll just see how it goes. The far-off future of what it could be like seems a little… out of character for me, but I'll cross that bridge when I get to it."

It's Ben's turn to sigh. "It's exactly that lack of plan making and goal setting that's gotten you to where you are. You never make decisions for the future. And look at your life."

"Um, I think my life is pretty damn perfect, thank you. Sorry if I haven't lived up to your expectations, but I'm doing exactly what I want with my life."

"You are setting a terrible example."

"Is that really true though? You keep saying it, but I see it another way. I'm offering Ainsley the idea that there's happiness places other than in brick mansions and eighty-hour work weeks. You'll stand there right now and tell me you think he'd be better off with *your* life? I'm not the only one who's alone, man. I'm just the one enjoying the benefits of freedom instead of trying to work myself to death as a distraction from my own loneliness and unprocessed grief."

Ben coughs out a laugh. "Shit, man." He shakes his head. "No, I don't want him to be alone like me, either. Can't there be some kind of happy medium? Like going to college, getting married, having kids, and living happily ever after?"

I shrug. "Maybe. Although I've never known anyone who's pulled it off."

"I know you're not the worst role model, Ave. I'm just pissed that he blew me off again. I don't know how to do this, and there isn't anyone offering advice."

"He's a great kid. My advice has always been to let him figure it out. He'll find his own way."

"I'm so scared of what that way will be. All I want to do is lock him up in a university dorm and do his homework for him."

I laugh, happy that my friend Ben seems to have replaced my father figure Ben. "Yeah? How's that going for you?"

"Bad."

"He's got this. He just needs to get something out of his system. We talked a lot when he was in high school about a gap year. You seemed okay with it then. What's changed?"

"The gap year turned into two, with no end in sight."

"Well, he can't actually follow in my footsteps because he doesn't have the bank account for it. Eventually, he'll get his act together. Probably when he realizes there are things in life he wants but can't afford. That's a big motivator. He's going to meet a girl and need the cash flow to keep her happy."

"He's so much like you. But, yeah, you're right. I'm not going to finance this fucking off forever. As much as he wants to be you, he'll have to get a job eventually. Right now, the only thing he wants to do is have fun. I mean, if he wants to be like Uncle

Ave so bad, why can't he be like you and go to fucking Harvard?"

"I'll talk to him."

"The time to talk to him would have been senior year of high school. When he was deciding that the Peace Corps was too much of a hassle because it requires a four-year degree and that he would just go off on his own with a backpack and a smile."

I smile at that, but it's the wrong move.

Ben is livid once more. "He isn't like you. He doesn't have the…I don't know, the street smarts that you have. When you head off on trips to far-flung corners of the continents, I don't worry about whether you're going to make it back alive. But Ains? He's so young and impulsive, and sure of himself."

"I didn't start my twenties as a safe, trustworthy traveler, man. I learned that stuff along the way." By not dying in any of the many, many sketchy situations I found myself in. But I choose to leave that part out. "He's young, but he'll learn."

"I don't want him to learn street smarts. I want him to go to fucking college."

I sigh. "He's lucky to have you, you know? You chasing him around the globe, holding his seat in class. It means he's going to come back eventually. And when he does, you two can sort things out."

Ben is quiet for a long moment, considering me with arms crossed. Then his whole body softens, arms falling to his sides. "It was shitty of Frederick to just let you go, Ave. I don't know what that was about, but he should have tried harder to keep you around. You're one of my, and Ainsley's, favorite people. We always want you around. You know that."

I just shake my head. I wanted to comfort Ben, not drag myself into family therapy.

A knock on the door draws both of our attention. I glance at the clock.

Eleven forty-five.

Either Fran's a bit early, or it's housekeeping. I pray for the latter as I cross the room to answer the door. I'm still sweaty and disheveled from my run and swim, and even though she's seen me like this plenty of times, I find myself wanting to look nice for her more and more as time goes on.

Besides, I have an angry lawyer taking up space in my kitchen. There's no way my gal has had enough coffee this morning to prepare herself for a meeting like this. I'll have to send her away, the last thing in the world I want, so that I can do a better job of facilitating their introduction later on, when everyone is ready.

Rule #17

YOU ARE A GROWN-ASS WOMAN

FRAN

He doesn't answer my first knock, so I give it one more go. Finally, after knock number five, the door opens—but only half-way. Avery's head pokes out. He's flustered. I can tell by the sheen of sweat on his brow and more color in his cheeks than normal. For whatever reason, my heart drops into my stomach.

"Hey." I don't know what else to say.

"Hey." He sounds rushed, and all of a sudden, I want to run. Avery has never made me feel unwanted before, like I'm interrupting something, and the feeling crashes over me like a sledgehammer.

"I can come back. If you're busy."

"Yeah, maybe that's a good idea."

My eyes go wide. I thought he would laugh off my suggestion and pull me inside, enveloping me in the carefree way he always does. Instead, he's sending me off.

He has a woman in there.

The realization is another hammer blow to my nervous system.

My mouth falls open and then snaps closed. I turn on my heel and try to make my escape, praying I can make it to safety before the tears welling in my eyes make their appearance.

What the actual hell?

I mean, yes, what the hell is he doing with a woman in his room after we decided…

But even more than that. What the hell am I doing crying about it?

I have to get it together. This was a casual arrangement. Either of us were welcome to end it whenever we wanted. So why do I feel like my heart is being torn from my body with an icepick?

"Fran," he calls after me, his voice much too close to be coming from the doorway. I glance back and find him close on my heels.

"It's fine. I'll just see you later."

His hand makes contact with my upper arm, and I try to shake him off, but he holds tight, pulling me to him. As my back hits his chest, his other arm snaking around my torso, I melt into him.

Why, body, why?

"What has gotten into you?" he whispers into the crook of my neck. I can feel the vibration of them in my bones. I want desperately to shake this off, to come back into the fold, but my anger has other ideas.

"Who do you have in there?"

Avery spins me to face him. I can only imagine what a mess I look, flustered, half crying, red from anger. He looks me long in the face, reading me like a book. Finally, after a pause that feels like it lasts a year but probably only lasts one second, he cocks his head to the side and smiles.

"Ben."

"Ben?" I say the word, but the meaning of the sounds doesn't register until a second later.

Oh, Ben.

"Yeah, he's on the island and got tipped off by Sam about our little closet adventure and came to read me the riot act. I thought it would be better for everyone, you especially, if you didn't show up in my room while we were figuring things out." He tosses a look over his shoulder, where the man in question is standing in his hotel room door, arms crossed. "But it's a little late for that. Come on, I'll introduce you."

I'm in no mood to meet a man who Avery thinks is going to disapprove of us, but what choice do I have? I follow Avery back up the hall to his room.

"Ben, the lovely Franzeska." Avery gestures to me where I hover beside him, still trying to get my act together.

"We've met," Ben's deep voice growls out.

My eyes shoot to his. "Excuse me?"

"I said we've met. At Frederick's house, a Memorial Day barbecue five years ago or so. You weren't looking so...adult then."

The anger I only recently tucked back down boils back up inside me. This fucking guy thinks he can cut me down to size? He's got another think coming. "Oh, right, sorry. All of Frederick's middle-aged work associates kinda blend together." I hear Avery snort softly beside me.

Before Mr. Perfect here has a chance to respond, I turn toward Avery. "We have a meeting with Dominic at two at Reef. We're going to go over the dinner menus."

Avery nods without speaking.

I turn back to Ben, giving the man one last tight-lipped smile. "Pleasure to meet you again, Ben. See you around?"

"Oh, you can be sure of that." His tone is slightly amused but still condescending enough that it requires me not to respond.

I do manage to hold in an eye roll as I turn and head back toward the elevator again, this time with my head held high. That motherfucker thinks he can intimidate me into behaving the way he sees fit? He's going to find out the hard way that isn't happening. I am a grown-ass woman.

I am a grown-ass woman.

I repeat the phrase in my head over and over as I bypass the awkward elevator wait and escape into the stairwell. I jog the full two flights down to my own floor holding my breath. It's only when I see the dusty rose of my own hallway carpeting that I let out a gasping breath.

That was a fucking roller coaster of emotions. I need to sit down for a bit. I pull out my phone and check the time. Hours before the meeting. Plenty of time for a nap.

The door hasn't been closed behind me for five minutes when it flies open.

I turn in surprise.

It's Avery, of course, looking handsome as ever with his tousled blond hair and big smile.

I stand, hands on my hips, while he stalks toward me. When he pulls my body to his, all of my fight melts away.

"Middle-aged man, huh?" Avery laughs into my neck. "You know we're about the same age, Ben and I."

"You're not the same age at all."

He pulls back and looks at me, head cocked.

"That guy's a stiff. You…well, you're something else."

"Is that right?" His face is back in my hair, nudging it to the side with his nose to make contact with the skin of my neck. I can barely breathe as his lips touch down. "What am I?"

You're mine.

But I can't say that, of course. For many reasons, but most importantly, that it's not true.

"You're Avery."

"Hmmm." The vibration of his hum makes my nipples stand at attention.

"And I'm Franzeska. We're just two people. Being alive. I hope you told him that."

"I told him something similar."

"And he told you that he was going straight to Frederick?"

Avery pulls back and takes my face in both hands. "He isn't

going to mention this to Frederick. Ben's not a bad guy, you know. He's my closest friend."

"I thought all of you guys were best friends?"

"We are, but it's always been Ben and me, Sam and Dom. We were closer as pairs, and then we came together as a group. Sam and Dom get to work together and that's perfect for them. Ben and I…worked together at one point, but that's ancient history. He went one way, and I went the other. Doesn't mean that we don't look out for each other, though."

"Does that mean you almost worked for your father?"

Avery laughs and shakes his head. "No, no, no. But I did get my undergrad in history and political science, planning to go on to get my law degree. Ben did the same degree at the same school. After graduation, he went on to Harvard Law, and I… well, I never showed up for class on that first day. We've been trying to figure things out ever since."

"You got into Harvard Law?"

"If by got in you mean there is a building with the Covington name on it on campus, then yes, I sure did." The humor in his tone only partially masks something underneath.

"But you didn't go."

"It wasn't for me."

"What did you do instead?"

Avery takes a step back. I'm cold with the loss of his touch, saddened by the idea that I erased the moment of closeness with my prying questions, but I want to know.

"I took my first solo trip. I rented a house in Bali, took up kite boarding, and never looked back. I've been more or less traveling ever since."

"And Ben went on to work with your father."

He sighs but shows no sign of being upset by having to share his past. "Ben suffered a pretty big loss his final year of law school. Lost his wife, Brianna, in an accident. She was an angel. Still is, I guess." Another sigh. "I came back for a while, but I couldn't really help. Not the way he needed. He had a six-year-old son at that point, Ainsley. I considered moving back, playing house with the two of them, but my father got there first. Brought Ben into the firm, moved him into his house, got him set up with a nanny. The two of them are a lot alike, and they get more alike all the time."

The sadness I heard before is back, and he's looking off in the distance behind me. I take a step closer, wanting nothing more than to ease this pain of the past. As my hand grazes down his chest, Avery's gaze comes back to me. It's another moment before I see his eyes return to the present, but when they do, the look there is nothing short of reverence.

My breath catches in my throat at the sight of him looking at me that way. I want to call it gratitude, but it could just be lust.

Let's go with that.

"We've got a couple of hours before our meeting," I start, using my fingers to undo one of the buttons on his short-sleeve shirt.

"Oh, really? And you don't want to go over the menus again? Make sure we're on the same page about what we're going to say?"

"I think there's time for both things," I say, placing my hand flat on his belly now that his shirt is wide open.

"Well, lucky me to have you keeping such good track of our schedule."

"It's easy," I say, keeping my hand on his stomach as I drop to my knees before him. "Twenty minutes for this, fifteen minutes for that." I graze my fingers down to the button on his shorts, popping it open. "Then twenty minutes for the other thing." I manage to get the zipper down over his growing bulge. I pull the shorts down around his ankles with his underwear, his freed cock bouncing. "And then an hour for a nap."

"I don't know what I'd do without your time management skills."

I land my tongue on his tip, swirling it around the sensitive skin. Avery sucks in a loud breath. I smile, the effect I have on him going straight to my head. This man is putty in my hands.

I bring those hands up and grip him at his base, sliding him into my mouth as I continue to work my tongue in soft circles.

"Fuck, Fran."

I can't even be mad about the name right now, not with the way he says it.

Like he's amazed by me.

Like I'm the sexiest woman on the planet.

I feel that way right now, kneeling before him, cock slipping in and out of my coral pink lips, a faint smear of the lipstick turning his skin a lighter shade of pink.

The sight of it, slightly trashy in a romantic, eighties movie kind of way, makes me moan in pleasure. I want to be that girl in the movie. I want to be so perfect that I get the guy.

I want the happy ending those stupid films always deliver.

Shit, I have got to get my mind back in the gutter.

It sure as hell can't stay wherever this is. Romantic movie land. What a ridiculous idea.

I take one of Avery's hands from where it rests at his side and bring it up to my head.

He gets the hint.

"Jesus, girl," he can barely speak, and it does things to me.

He starts working my head forward and back, gently at first, his cock filling my mouth so completely that it starts to butt the back of my throat, forcing my breathing to shift up to my nose. His fingers curl into my long, loose hair, getting a better grip. I'm craving the hard, punishing thrusts that should follow, praying that they erase these thoughts in my mind. Praying that they bring this back to surface level, where we're both safe.

But he doesn't do it.

Before I can even think about what's happening, his cock is gone, and I'm gasping in a long breath, watching him fall to his knees before me, using the grip he has on my hair to bring my mouth to his.

I come alive inside the kiss, the way he sinks into it like a drowning man.

I'm his only source of oxygen.

I press back, desperate to help him find whatever it is he lost.

Our hands are gripping each other's bodies, faces, hair, moving feverishly to match the pace of our tongues. Once again, I can't breathe, but this time, it's not because someone is trying to shove a cock down my throat, it's because I'm already shoving something down there.

Feelings.

So many goddamn feelings.

What am I supposed to do with this?

I break off, gasping for air, and pull his shirt the rest of the way off. "Get inside me," I order, dispensing with my own tiny dress and thong. When I look back up at Avery, he's smiling that sneaky, knowing, little Avery smile. The one I can never quite interpret so I make up meanings for.

This time, however, I don't want to guess what he's thinking. I want him fucking me so that I know what he's thinking.

I grab a little lube bottle from the coffee table and squirt a nice little pool into the palms of my hands. When I touch down on his erection in front of me, he gasps. It's my turn to smile now.

"Cold?" I ask, sliding my hands from root to tip with a featherlight touch, spreading the silicone gel over him.

"It's okay. It feels great."

"Are you okay on your knees like that?" I ask, worried as soon as the words leave my mouth that they'll be taken as an old man joke.

I should have worried for an entirely different reason.

"There's nowhere in the world I would rather be, love, than on my knees before you." His words suck all of the rational thought from my mind, if there was any left there in the first place.

He takes my stunned silence as an opportunity to turn me

around, his strong hands gripping my shoulders. When my back is facing him, he slides a hand down to grip my breast, fingers catching the nipple and causing me to gasp.

Then he's sliding his other hand around me, lower, just under my ribcage, lifting me just enough to nestle his slippery tip at my back hole. I tilt my pelvis toward him to spread my cheeks, pushing back and allowing the silicone lube to work its magic.

When he enters me, the thoughts do quiet a bit. I'm able to focus on the task at hand, which is to get this man further into my body.

My arms are pinned to my sides by his arms, but I manage to get both palms flat on my thighs, attempting to press myself back into him. To impale myself on his waiting cock. My palms are so slippery that I fail to gain purchase and let out a whimper of impatience.

"Girl, you are going to kill me with all this fucking," Avery growls into the back of my neck.

"You love it," I manage through gritted teeth.

"I do love…it. Yes," Avery stumbles over his words, sending my mind reeling once more.

There's only one thing I want to murder right now, and it's the thoughts in my stupid head. I engage my core and use those deep, strong muscles to do what my lubed-up hands failed to do. With one exhale, I press my hips down and back, crying out in pleasure as he finally slides inside of me.

My head dangles forward and I hold my breath, savoring every second of the blinding, mind-erasing pleasure of feeling him nestled in my body.

Avery leans forward and settles his teeth onto the meat of my shoulder in a soft bite, holding on as he pulls out and then slides back in.

I'm still pinned down by his arms, so I can't take charge of the situation any further. I can't lift up to my hands and knees, forcing him to rise up behind me and grip my hips.

All I can do is squeeze my eyes closed and hold my breath,

savoring the feeling of being fully restrained by this man, suspended in the cocoon of goddamn feelings I've been trying to escape since he entered my room.

He was going to say he loved me.

Don't be ridiculous. He's your stepbrother who you barely know. He doesn't love you. Not like that anyway.

But what was he going to say then?

"Avery, please," I beg, his slow, sensuous slide in and out of my tight ass threatening to send me over the edge.

And not in the good, orgasmic kind of way.

In the loony bin kind of way.

"I'm trying to last the full fifteen minutes allotted to this activity, love. If I move any faster, it's going to be all over, throwing our schedule off." He barely manages the words, speaking them right into my curled back, his forehead pressed to my spine.

I laugh. "When did you get so obedient?"

"When a beautiful girl started ordering me around."

"I'm ordering you to fuck me."

His arms withdraw suddenly, and my torso falls forward, my still slick hands not reaching out in time to catch me. Avery lifts up onto his knees, still inside me, forcing my hips up, so I'm on my knees as well, torso laying long on the floor in front of him.

I settle in for the mind-numbing pounding.

I press my forehead to the cool, hard floor and take him, reveling at the feeling of his fingers curled around my hip bones, the slap of his body against mine. The fullness of every strong slide.

When his hand curls under me to grip my pussy, I moan with pleasure.

I raise my head up just a bit, almost surprised to see that it's still daylight. I'm so lost in my own mind, time seems meaningless.

I press my knees to the sides as best I can, giving his hand an extra few inches to find the sweet spots. He finds my clit straight away, pinching the little bud at first, drawing all of my attention to that one tiny place as I gasp in pleasure and pain. Then his fingers are inside me, his thumb pressed flat on my clit, holding tightly as he continues to rock my body with his thrusts, my hips pressing up and down gently to add friction to his movements.

And I'll be damned if I'm not coming right alongside him, both of us trying to hold on to our motion long enough to get the other person all the way through their orgasm. The wave of pleasure passes through me to Avery and back again like the ocean tide.

When he finally stills, he slips out right away, collapsing onto his back on the floor. I rest where I am for a long moment, the floor tile no longer cool, but at least it's hard.

Steadying.

I breathe in and out and try to make myself move. Eventually, I do, pushing myself up to a kneeling position.

I can feel my own wetness on my thighs and feet where they are tucked under me. I can feel his wetness starting to drip from my body. I can feel every gust of ocean air as the breeze rustles the curtains, my skin a live wire of nerves.

"Nap," Avery growls out behind me, and I laugh, turning to where he lays.

He's absolutely gorgeous, lying flat, spread-eagle on the beige tile, naked and glistening with sweat. I can't take my eyes off him.

"Nap," I say, pressing myself up to my feet and standing slowly. I'm going to need a shower before anything else, so I start to make my way to the bathroom.

"Unscheduled activities?"

I laugh. "I'm going to take a quick shower. You're welcome to join me. And then let's take that nap somewhere more comfortable than the living room floor, okay?"

"You're the boss," he replies, eyes still closed, making no move to get up.

I turn the shower on to just the warm side of cold, letting the cool water wash over me as I stand, eyes closed, under the stream.

Some of the tension that had been building since I tried to run from Avery's apartment earlier has eased with my orgasm, but I feel it creeping back.

What was that about? I mean, it's been less than a week since we had the conversation in his room and decided that this was a thing—and that we would only be sleeping with each other.

Do I really think so badly of him that my mind immediately went to the worst-case scenario when I was presented with a confusing situation?

An even better question—why is that the absolute worst-case scenario?

I mean, this is just a casual thing, right? We're just having fun while we're both here. It's not serious. I'm purposely keeping it from getting serious because I know how that man works, and I don't want to be just another heartbreak on his world tour.

I'm going to be the strong one. The chick who can actually handle the no strings attached thing.

But try telling that to my stupid heart. The second I decided he had another woman in that room, I freaked out—and not in an angry, how could you be such an asshole way. In a broken-hearted, run for my life kind of way.

Shit.

My panic spiral is interrupted by the curtain sliding open, and the painfully beautiful, smiling man in question climbs into the shower.

He steps right up close to my back as if pulled there by an invisible force. I allow myself to relax into his warm, strong arms and let the manly scent of him envelop me.

"It's like a fancy little lingerie jungle in here."

His words are surprising and take me a second to process. When I do, I laugh. I've gotten so used to having my undergarments and clothing that I hand wash in the bathroom sink hanging around my bathroom that I almost don't notice them anymore.

"Yeah, I'm getting pretty good at handwashing. I just need to figure out how to dewrinkle." My current process of hanging items up to dry, beating them on the patio, and then ironing them is time consuming, but necessary to present a professional image—not the image of a person who lives in a van or something.

"You know, they'll wash that stuff for you."

I whip around in his arms so quickly that he takes a surprised step back.

"Really?"

It's impossible to hide my excitement at the possibility of having my laundry done for real.

Avery's smile twists to the side as he considers. "I mean, I think they will. They pick up my laundry from my room and wash it. I just assumed they did that for everyone."

Now I roll my eyes and groan. The promised land was so close to my fingertips, but now it's all slipping away.

"We'll ask at the front desk—I'll ask at the front desk, I mean. If not, you can just toss your dirty stuff on my floor, and they'll grab it when they come for mine."

Perfect. Now we're talking about doing our laundry together. Nothing but pure domestic bliss.

I nod, saying a silent prayer that the housekeeping staff will indeed pick up my stuff at my own room, but relenting to the fact that if they say no, I'm going to jump on the shared laundry offer full bore.

I've never appreciated my washer and dryer back home as much in my entire life as I have since moving here.

I guess that's how it goes, though. You can't miss something that you currently have. It's not until it goes away that you realize how good you had it.

Stop it, you freak!

"I'm done in here. I'm going to hop out and start beating myself a dress to wear to this meeting."

"Right behind you, love. Whatever the hell that means, I need to see it."

I choose a pale-green sundress and take it to task on my patio with a very amused Avery watching, then iron out the last of the wrinkles.

"What's the beating for?"

"If I just iron them straight off the drying rack, it's almost like I iron the wrinkles in. So, I started beating them against the railing out here to soften them up first."

"Very adaptable. You'd make a great world traveler."

I look up from the tiny countertop ironing board in surprise. Was that an invite?

Stop, Franzeska.

"Yeah, well…" I trail off, looking back down at my project.

"I'll meet you in bed, okay? I'm not going to make it through this meeting if I don't get a nap."

"Okay, yeah. I'll be there in a minute."

I watch through the glass door as he collapses on my mattress, pulling a pillow under his head and not moving again.

I finish ironing my dress and tuck in beside him, my phone timer set for forty minutes, even though I'm pretty sure I'm just going to lay here and worry the whole time.

When the timer goes off, however, it startles me awake.

Rule #18

YOU'RE NOT FOOLING ANYONE

FRAN

I pull on the green dress and tie my hair up, adding a bit of bronzer to my cheeks.

"You look great," Avery responds, coming up behind me and snaking his arms around my waist, undoing some of the tedious ironing I did before our nap.

But it's worth it.

"You always say that," I joke at his reflection.

"It's always true."

I give him a little smirk in the mirror, but the compliment sinks into my chest like sunshine. There really is nothing wrong with having a lover slash coworker who follows you around all the time giving you compliments. Every job should have one of these.

As I try to picture my next job, with a new lover, however, my brain protests. Straight up will not allow the fantasy to happen.

This has been happening more and more lately.

Whenever I try to look into the crystal ball of my future, something that's always been available to me, all I see is right now. This little bubble where I live in pretend domestic bliss with Avery. It's like time stopped when I got here and will never restart.

Would that be so bad?

"Let's head to Reef, love. Don't want to be late for our big meeting." He's teasing me now, but it's okay. It's the good kind, the kind I didn't even know existed before I met him.

Avery grabs my hand, and we take the elevator down to the lowest level, where Dominic is already waiting for us. The looks this man gives are seriously priceless. It's like he owns the entire world and has given us permission to use it—permission that can be revoked at any moment.

We slide into chairs, and Dominic regards Avery like a child he's sure has done something wrong. He's just waiting to find out what it is. "How's the job going?"

Avery smiles. "Best one I ever had."

Dominic grunts but says nothing.

"Thanks for meeting with us," I say, taking control of the table. All eyes are on me. "We still have about three months till the big event, but getting the menus finalized is a big step in the right direction, so I'm happy we're getting this settled."

Dominic seems to calm considerably when his attention is on me. Maybe it's just the lack of history between the two of us, but he is taking me far more seriously than he was taking Avery just a second ago.

"It's a big deal to do the first wedding here," he starts, hands folded on the table in front of him. "I was glad to hear that someone was taking charge of the project. This is the kind of thing that would just fall in my lap generally, but the timing on this one isn't super ideal. With Reef opening this season, though, and the new management staff, we should be able to handle it. And with you organizing, of course. That takes a lot off my plate." Dom gives his approval speech as if he's rehearsed it a hundred times.

It's not lost on me that he's talking to me as though I am completely in charge of the wedding. As if one of his lifelong besties isn't sitting next to me, legal pad at the ready. It only solidifies the fact that I'm going to be the one to tell Dominic the plan that we have come up with for the food.

I always planned on being the one to say it, but in the back of my mind, I know I have Avery here just in case I chicken out, or if Dominic reacts poorly. I'm no longer sure that's the case. If he doesn't take Avery seriously, would he take the plan seriously if Avery told him?

I take a deep breath and open my portfolio. "I—"

"Can I bring any drinks or snacks?"

I'm immediately interrupted by a well-meaning server arriving at our table. I bite my lip to hide my frustration. I just want to get this over with, and now I'm going to have to build the courage back up.

"Coffee," Dominic says to the server.

"Watermelon agua fresca," Avery says. I can feel him looking toward me to see if I want one, but I can't break my focus. He flashes two fingers to the server to let them know to bring me one as well.

I watch Dominic's sharp eye catch every second of it. He looks down at my portfolio and then back up to meet my gaze.

And just like that, I know he knows.

I try not to panic. This is absolutely not the time to panic.

The server walks away, and I take a deep breath. "I, I mean, we..." Dominic's eyes flick to Avery and then back to me. I keep it together but just barely. "Have decided that we're going to bring Chef Kuramo's pit barbecue out to grill on the beach for the main meal. They'll do the full spread with sides and sauces. We'll have the resort set up the bar, and Reef do the appetizers and the cake, probably." Shit, I'm rambling now, trying to soften the blow of my announcement that I am taking the biggest food order away from the hotel. I'm sweating, and my heart is racing, but I know I'm keeping it inside. I know I look great. I always look great. Avery tells me constantly.

Dominic's expression doesn't shift a single muscle, and he never takes his eyes from mine. I start to panic, just a bit, but then he speaks.

"Kuramo's going to pit barbecue on our beach?"

"Yeah," I say, firmly drawing down the word at the end so there's absolutely no way it could be perceived as a question.

Dominic sits back in his seat and folds his arms over his chest. After far too long of a pause, he nods.

"That's a fantastic idea," he says with the exact tone and expression you would use when telling someone that you wired their car with explosives.

My heart processes the words before my brain does, causing a bit of a disconnect in my emotions. It's like joyous terror.

"I'll talk to Kuramo when I'm in town tomorrow and find out what he needs to make that happen." Another couple of nods and I can almost see his brain working. "My guys can take that on. I'll let you know if we run into any problems, but I don't anticipate any."

I am silent for too long, my brain yammering on so loudly that I don't realize Dominic stopped and is waiting for me to respond. "Yeah, great. Perfect. That's perfect. Thank you. Okay."

I toss a look beside me to Avery, who's smiling. He nods, and I nod.

I turn back to Dominic. "For the appetizer spreads, we're thinking the majority of it will be passed because of the heat, but we still want to do a cold display of veggies, fruits, maybe some shellfish."

Dominic is nodding, making notes on his own legal pad.

"Passed apps can be hot or cold, probably a combination. I know we have a couple of vegans and at least ten gluten-free, but I'll have the exact numbers for that after the RSVP cut off after the first of the year." I glance up from my notes to see if he's going to say anything, but he doesn't, so I go on, my confidence building. "For the bar—"

"Reina's going to be your point person on the bar," Dominic interrupts smoothly, as if he does it to people all day long. "And Marcus is going to be the one who finalizes the appetizer menus. I'll give him what you gave me and have him come up with a couple of drafts. Reina you will need to meet with, the sooner the better."

He stands and tucks his pad under his arm, clearly finished with our meeting.

The server walks back up just then and places Dominic's coffee cup right in his hand as if they're used to him not staying put for long.

"Great. Okay. Yeah, I'll meet with Reina this week, and you can just let us know when Marcus is ready to meet up."

Another nod. He waits to see if I'm going to say anything else. When I don't, he turns to leave. A few steps away, he stops and turns back. "I almost forgot. You two are invited to dinner Saturday. Reina's throwing a party at our house."

The invite is strangely formal and not like an invite at all. More like a command.

I have to force myself not to look to Avery before I respond. "Okay, sure."

"Wouldn't miss it for the world," Avery chimes in beside me.

Dominic lets out another grunt and walks off.

I flop back in my seat and squeeze my eyes closed. "Holy shit."

"Yeah, that guy is quite the bore, huh?" Avery says.

"You mean like a nap or like a wild animal that is going to gore you?"

Avery laughs. "A bit of both maybe. Like the most boring goring you've ever gotten."

I let myself laugh in relief and shake it off. "I thought he was going to be so pissed about the barbecue thing."

"What? No way. That's totally right up Dom's alley. He loves that shit. And now he gets to dig a giant barbecue pit in the beach and someone else is gonna run it. The guy's in heaven."

Avery's sitting much closer to me now that Dominic's gone, and I sink into the warmth of his skin. "Besides, Raft is heading into yet another awards season, and that man now has a trophy to hold onto. I'm sure he came down to this meeting terrified that you were going to demand steak and lobster for a hundred people, and he was going to have to figure out how to make it happen while still running his tasting menu six nights a week."

I inhale deeply and let it all out in one big rush. "Is that why you suggested the chicken thing in the first place?"

He raises his eyebrows and smiles. "Also because it's delicious, but yeah. I figured it would give some much-needed stress relief to the kitchens here."

The relief I feel is like a living creature. It curls up in my lap and purrs.

I was so freaked about this meeting, but of course it went fine. "You could have said something. I've been freaking out about this."

"You should have told me you were freaking out. You hide it well."

Isn't that the truth.

It's a skill I learned over the years growing up in a family that loves to poke fun at every little weakness. You learn to show none.

All of a sudden, this whole thing is getting a little too heavy. I decide to change the subject, not realizing until the words leave my mouth that this might be even heavier. "He knows about us."

"Yeah."

My head whips to the side, and I gape at him. "You knew that he knows?"

"I mean, he and I know each other pretty well. I'm probably giving it away with my behavior."

I narrow my eyes at him. "What behavior?"

He laughs and pulls his tall, red, icy drink toward him. "Working, for one. Staying here so long also, I guess."

"You don't usually stay?"

"I mean, I stay for a bit. But I've been here since early September to help with the Reef opening, and they know I have every intention of at least staying through February for the wedding. It's not something I usually do. All you would have to do is look two inches to my left at the woman I follow around like a puppy dog, and you would be able to discern what's going on."

There is so much in that statement that I'm dying to unpack, I don't know where to start. I decide to go for the easiest bit—the one that isn't about him and me. "Do you stay in other places for long periods of time? Just not here?"

I hear him take a long breath and let it out. "Not really."

"Why not?"

He shrugs. "I just get restless, I guess. Being on the move makes me feel like I'm accomplishing something. And there's a big world out there. I'm never going to see the whole thing if I laze about in one place."

"Is that your goal in life? To see the whole world?" If that's true, it could explain a lot of things, but I have a feeling it's not.

"My goal right now is to get you into my hammock and wrap myself around you like a koala baby."

I feign a smile as he deflects the serious subject back to humor. As I turn back to my drink, though, I sip slow and long, trying to give myself a chance to think.

I should be used to this roller coaster by now, but it still gets me. Anytime I start to get worried about my growing feelings, I push the thoughts away. But as soon as I get the opportunity, I dig for any sign that he has the same feelings. That this thing between us might be growing. It's stupid, I know, especially when he goes and says things like he never stays in one place very long. It's as if he's trying to prevent me from forming any kind of connection to him. He's reminding me that he's going to leave.

That's the one thing I was supposed to remember in all of this —not to get attached because he leaves—but I find myself forgetting on a minute-by-minute basis. The closeness we've built in the last few weeks feels so…huge. It feels like it's real, even if I know damn well we're just playing house. I should be grateful for the reminder, but I just feel sick.

Avery reaches over and tucks my hair behind my ear. "You're having some big thoughts."

I smile down at my hands. "Yeah, I was just thinking about the wedding." It's a lie that I don't expect him to believe. But I know he'll let it go.

"How about that nap?"

"I'm heading up to meet Reina, actually. She gets off at three, and we're going to town to get drinks."

He says nothing, and I look over. His expression is as calm as the flat ocean, but I can see the depths sparkling in his blue eyes.

"I just…I want to make a friend, you know?"

"Yeah," he says finally, breaking eye contact to take a drink. "Maybe you can do some recon and find out what makes the mysterious billionaire tick."

My mouth drops open slightly, and I chomp it shut.

Avery's clever eyes miss none of it.

"Dominic, I mean," he says quickly. "Dom."

"Yeah, Dom," I breathe, locked in a gaze with Avery so intense that my chest feels like it's going to collapse.

I want to send him a message through my look that says, "what are we doing here?" but my eyes disobey, sending the words *don't leave me* instead. And I'll be damned if his eyes don't reflect the same SOS back to me.

But that doesn't make any sense. He's the one who does the leaving.

I need to leave. Like, now.

I stand so abruptly I have to steady my glass as it rocks a bit. "I'm going to be late."

Avery's on his feet as well. "Let me walk you up."

"No, that's okay." I need to breathe, and he's replacing all the oxygen in the room with his essence. I feel like I might die if I don't get a teeny bit of space from those eyes. From that look he's still giving me. "It's just upstairs."

Avery smiles. "Have fun, love. I'm sure you two are going to get along famously."

Rule #19

WHEN SOMEONE OFFERS A LIFELINE, TAKE IT

FRAN

I practically run to the restaurant upstairs.

Reina's in the dining room, going over something that looks menu-related with the Raft dining room manager.

"Hey," I call as I approach the two women. "I can hang out at the bar if you're not quite ready."

"I'm just wrapping up now." She's all smiles, mixed with a tinge of exhaustion. She jingles a set of keys at me. "Our chariot awaits."

As we climb into the shiny green golf cart, I spot Dominic out of the corner of my eye, standing at the back door of Raft, arms crossed over his chest. "What's up with him?"

Reina follows my gaze and laughs. "He is convinced that I'm going to roll the cart off the path and die of sand suffocation or something."

"I will one hundred percent save you from sand suffocation."

She looks over at me with that radiant smile. "I think you and I are going to be great friends."

I exhale deeply and relax into the seat. "I think so, too."

"Do you mind if we stop by my house so I can get out of my work clothes?"

"Not at all."

She drives us up the narrow path chattering about her workday and pointing out various things in the resort as we pass them. When she finally pulls into what is clearly the designated parking spot for her house, we climb out.

I shake my head in amazement at the steps in front of us.

I saw them before when Avery pointed out the house on one of our trips to town, but up close, they're even more mind boggling. "It's insane that you can't drive up to your house. You climb up and down these stairs every time?"

Reina's nodding. "Dom had this handrail installed when I moved in. Before that, you were really just taking your life into your hands each and every time."

She grips the sturdy rail and starts climbing. I follow close behind.

"Who buys a house like this?"

She laughs ahead of me, a little breathlessly. "He bought it after seeing pictures online. He bought a freaking dot on a map while in New York City. The realtors conveniently left out this little bit of information."

"Wow. That's crazy. Must be nice." As the words leave my lips, it occurs to me how often I have been saying them lately. Avery will tell me about something in his world, and I respond with "must be nice" as if I have been living my own life destitute and have zero future ahead of me. I really need to cut that shit out.

"These guys are definitely crazy. Each in their own way, of course. I chose mine, and it sounds like you've chosen yours." She turns to smile at me as she reaches the top and unlocks the door.

I blow out a huge breath. "Help me."

She laughs and leads me into the house.

The first thing that hits me is the cool air. I've gotten pretty used to being hot and sweaty all the time, so I almost didn't notice how hot I was until I walked into this perfectly chilled room. "Oh god. AC is a freaking miracle." I have it in my room, of course, but it's nothing compared to this ice box.

"It's on a timer to get the house down to this temp by the time I get home. After running in circles all day, I need it." She kicks off her shoes and strolls into the house. "I'm just going to change real quick. There's some iced tea in the fridge if you need a pick me up."

I make my way into the massive open kitchen. The cupboards are glass-fronted, so I find glasses right away. From there it's pretty easy to find the ice cubes and a large carafe of iced tea in the fridge. I pour myself half a glass and sit down at the kitchen bar.

Taking a massive sip of the lifesaving cold caffeine, I allow myself to check out the rest of the house, at least what's visible from my seat.

The place is wide open with dark wood floors, colorful rugs, panoramic windows, and recessed lighting. A comfortable looking brown sofa rests in front of one of the largest windows, aimed straight for the view in lieu of a television.

What a life this must be.

Living in this house, on this island, with a massively rich older man. Working in a management position at a five-star resort that's closed five months out of the year.

The endless travel destinations that come with a bottomless bank account—not just bumming it from hostel to hostel with your dirty clothes in a backpack. No way. The absolute best resorts, the most exclusive islands.

I shake my head to dispel the growing feelings in my chest. I can't decide if I would call it jealousy, but it feels enough like it that I'm uncomfortable sitting with it.

Am I jealous of her?

Is this what I want?

Three months ago, I would have laughed in your face if you

suggested settling down. Of course, I would have been picturing the type of guys I dated back home—standard, run of the mill recent college grads who were taking their first jobs as interns or law clerks or whatever. Would my opinion of the idea have changed if I knew that this was the kind of life that was waiting for me?

This life is so different from anything I would have imagined possible for myself, but even I can see the massive benefits. I could live and work in paradise and still be able to visit home—and the girls—anytime I wanted. Hell, I could live part-time here and part-time there.

I could take them on trips around the world.

I could buy them cars on their sixteenth birthdays.

When I swore off serious relationships, it was because I couldn't picture one coming with enough freedom for me to be able to show up for those girls the way I want to. This life, however—would make it easy.

But it's not that simple, love.

The words in Avery's easy drawl nearly bring tears to my eyes.

It's not that simple. Dom offered Reina this life. Avery isn't offering me anything of the sort. He isn't going to settle down in a huge house, work at a job, and build a life with me. That just isn't his style. He's on the move, traveling the world. He likes a new partner at every destination.

Okay, now the tears are getting harder to fight.

Shit! I have got to get it together before Reina comes back.

I hop off my stool and walk over to the window to give myself a second to calm down. I can see the whole resort from here, its two tall buildings, the beige stone path leading to the pool area. The massive pools with their little hangout nooks and water hammocks. The cabanas and chaise lounges.

I distract myself from thinking about Avery by trying to imagine the wedding laid out on the grounds before me. I can see the flower arch in my mind, placed on the sand past where the chairs will be set up. I imagine the aisle lined with driftwood, or maybe shells, or flowers of some kind. I make a mental note to ask Avery which he thinks we will be able to find in such quantity.

And now I'm thinking about Avery again. I let out a sigh.

"Big sighs over there," Reina says behind me.

I turn, grateful now that I took the time to walk over here and collect myself while she was still changing. "Just thinking about the wedding. You have the perfect view of the resort from up here. I can see how everything is going to be laid out."

"I can't wait to see it. I know the guys are pretty excited, too. This is going to be a big step for the property. I mean, we bring in high-end guests all the time, but to snag a high-end wedding or two every season? That'll be a massive boost to our sales."

She's not wrong there. I know as well as anyone the kind of money people are willing to spend on weddings. It's insane.

I have an enormous budget for Leon's wedding, and I'm not even having to pay for a lot of things, as the resort is taking care of some of it just for the pictures and the publicity. They went ahead and ordered the tables and chairs I wanted, clearing out a closet downstairs to keep them for the next wedding. It would have cost a fortune to rent those and have them shipped here, so that was really helpful.

"It's going to be beautiful," I say simply.

"Any chance you're considering sticking around and being the resident wedding coordinator?"

I let out a surprised laugh. "That is not a job I've been offered." While it's true that Sam and Avery have been talking about this wedding like it's the first of many I'll put on, there hasn't been any discussion of me coming on board full-time.

Would I even want that?

What a goddamn fool I would be to turn it down. I know my vision for Franzeska Events is to do weddings in the States, closer to my sister's house, and maybe some destination weddings. But an opportunity to be the resident wedding coordinator at The White Sands would be an incredible boost to my résumé.

I'm not allowing myself to get my hopes up about a continued contract with them, but now that I think about it, there is really only one way I'm turning down that job.

If I'm running from a broken heart after falling for the guy I am not supposed to be naïve enough to fall for.

And that whole fiasco is starting to look more and more likely.

"Well, you'd have my vote," Reina says with a wink. "And that counts for two, if you know what I mean."

I can't help but smile through my anxiety at her kindness and candor.

"Ready to go?" I need the drinks, truth telling, and advice giving from my new friend to start right now.

Reina and I pile back into the cart and bump our way to town down the long coral dust road.

I'm grateful for her cheerful chatter as we drive so I can watch the horizon and get my thoughts in order. There are so many things I want to ask her, and I don't want to come off as a crazy person.

"…right?"

Her question shakes me out of my own head. "Oh, sorry. What were you asking?"

She laughs kindly. "Head in the clouds?"

"Something like that."

"I was just asking if you'd been to town before."

"Oh, yeah. I came on my own the first day I was on the island, and Avery and I have come a few times."

"So, you've eaten at a few places, seen the beach and stuff?"

"We ate at Kuramo's and got coffee at the little window. He showed me some of the gardens and the beach."

"Perfect. I think we're going to hit up a place the locals just refer to as the sports bar. It doesn't sound like much, but it's actually really good. We can sit outside and have tacos."

"Sounds great."

We pull up to the same area where Avery parked and hop out. Reina treats her cart much in the same way Avery did, pocketing the keys but not bothering with any of the security features.

She grabs her bag and leads me down the sandy road toward a brown building with a large, open doorway halfway obscured with aged looking palapa palm leaves. There are brightly colored umbrellas, decorative nautical ropes and floats, and tables made of giant spools turned on end.

We settle into a table with high chairs and a view of the ocean, and it's only a moment before a tall, lanky man with a goatee and a huge smile comes over with a couple of menus.

"Reina," he greets her with a hand on her upper arm.

"Hey, Sal. This is Franzeska, she's working up at The Sands for a bit."

Sal's gleaming smile turns to me, and I can't help but smile back. "It's my pleasure, Franchesca."

He offers the French pronunciation, and I don't bother to correct him. It's a mistake I've gotten used to over the years.

"The pleasure's all mine. Is this your place?"

"Yes, ma'am." He sets the menus down in front of us with care. "How about a drink to start?"

Reina looks to me.

"I'm going to have a margarita."

"Blended or on the rocks?" Sal asks.

"Ooh, blended sounds great. And you can go ahead and make two while you're at it. I'm going to drink the first one before you even set it down."

Sal and Reina both laugh.

"Make it three, Sal. Thanks," Reina says, and he heads back inside.

"Okay, so it's a pounding margaritas kind of conversation, huh?"

I sigh and roll my face to the sparkling blue sky. "I'm so fucked."

Reina laughs. "Let's have it, girl."

"I'm sleeping with my stepbrother." The doom in my voice must be evident because she reaches out and takes my hand.

"I thought he was your mom's husband's son?"

"It's the same thing," I say sadly, giving up the semantics that have protected me so far.

"So…sleeping together as in, it's nothing serious? Or sleeping together as in getting together?"

"I don't know. No, I do. I mean it's nothing serious. Jesus, I can't believe I just said I don't know." I grit my teeth and let out a long sigh through them. "It's nothing. It's just sleeping together while we work on this wedding. Well, and pretty much living together and spending every waking moment together. So, you know. Fucked."

"He's not the guy you see on Instagram."

The statement surprises me enough to make me roll my head back in her direction. "What do you mean?"

"I mean that the internet makes him out to be someone I don't think is entirely accurate."

"A jet-setting billionaire heir playboy who doesn't have a home and parties all the time?"

"Yup. That's his image. Or how he's portrayed. But is that the man you know?"

I have to think about this for a second. "I mean…no. I guess not. Well, he definitely doesn't have a home, or that's what he says. He told me this morning that all the guys know something's up because he's been here on Faraday for so long. He talks a lot about traveling. He definitely has the money. He's always trying to spend it on me."

Reina laughs. "I know that one."

"And it's fine, I guess. I mean, he is Frederick's son, and Frederick has been a bit of a parental figure in my life since I was fourteen and he and my mom got together, so it almost feels natural to have Avery pay for everything. But at the same time that's not what I want. I graduated from college, moved out here to start my career, to launch my business with this wedding. I'm not supposed to have someone taking care of me like this."

"Oh, girl. I can understand the struggle. I moved here to take a job after crashing and burning hard in the city and racking up major debt. Of course, the first thing I did when I got here was hook up with Dom, who wanted to swipe his platinum card and make all my problems disappear."

My heart is practically glowing with excitement at Reina's story. It's certainly a different situation than mine, but I know there is something for me to learn here. I nod eagerly, and she goes on.

"We kept things super secret because he was my actual boss, and he had this idea that people would think he was a pervert and run him out of the industry if he was caught sleeping with a waitress. So, that did put a damper on what he could buy me, but oh, did he try. The staff got a lot of great perks that year because it was the only way he could give me certain things without raising suspicion. He had to give them to everyone."

"And you let him pay off your debt?" I don't mean any judgment by the statement, hell, I would let Dom pay off *my* debt if he offered, but I am curious how the whole thing ended up.

"Nope. I'm still working to pay it off. It's a whole thing, as I'm sure you can imagine. But in the end, it was super important to me to pay it off myself, and he is going to give me anything I want, so…" She shrugs.

"That's why you're not married yet?"

"Bingo."

"Well, the guy is head over heels about you. You can see it when he looks at you," I say with a smile.

Reina rolls her eyes. "Girl, look who's talking. Trust me. I've known Avery for a little over a year now, and while it's true that he isn't around a lot, when he is, he's never focused on one thing long. And I don't mean just women, although I'm sure there is plenty of that. He's always taking the helicopter to other islands for sailing classes or taking up windsurfing or something."

"Well, I guess my wedding is just his current project. He'll get tired of me and move on soon enough."

Reina shakes her head emphatically. "This is different. He's so…invested. I've never seen anything like it. Dom has been commenting on it as well. How strange he's acting. It's totally unlike him to go anywhere near a project that his father's involved in."

"Which is all fine. I mean, this could be a great way for him to grow as a person and possibly mend a few fences with his father, but I just worry it'll be at the expense of my own broken heart." Shit. Now that the truth is out of my mouth, the tears are out of my eyes.

Reina puts her elbow on the table and lays her head in her hand facing me, her face filled with kindness and understanding. "It's that bad, huh?"

I nod, full on blubbering now. "I am trying so hard to be the cool chick who can just have a fling with him and not get clingy, but I don't know if I'm that girl. I'm a mess, and it's hiding so close to the surface these days. I seriously almost tell him that I'm in love with him on a daily basis. It's making me sick."

Now that I've started with this whole truth nonsense, I can't stop. "But if I do that, it'll ruin everything, and he'll leave. Which would probably be for the best. Cut this off now before it goes any further, but we're doing this wedding together, and I know I could do it myself, but it's so great doing it with Avery. I want to stay in this little bubble we're in forever. If I tell him and he leaves and this wedding is ruined, then my career is ruined, and my family is going to be like 'oh, Franzeska screwed everything up again. There she goes following her silly dreams. What will she get up to next?' And I'll never be able to face them again. And Avery will be gone."

Reina takes my hand and uses it to drag me into a hug. I

close my eyes and allow myself to relax into her, my chest still heaving with sobs.

"Girl, those are some sad, sad stories you are telling yourself."

"They're all true," I manage through my tears.

"They are not one bit true. You can't predict the future. All you're doing is making up some ways that the future *could* go, and you've chosen the worst ones possible. Let's get you some new stories."

I pull back just enough to see her face. "What kind of stories?"

"Ones with happier endings."

I squeeze my eyes shut. "Those are impossible."

"Why? They are just as possible as the crazy stories you're telling yourself. Let's start with why you think the man who is currently putting his entire life on hold to live in a hotel room to be with you and plan a wedding for his estranged father's stepson-in-law couldn't possibly have a thing for you."

"I hear what you're doing there, but it's not that simple."

"Tell me."

"Well, first of all, he's never been in a relationship."

"Categorically false."

I sit up and look at her. "What do you mean?"

"I mean it's just not true. And why do you even think that? Did he tell you that? No. You just read a bunch of stuff about him on the internet and believed it. He's had lots of relationships. They have all been fairly short, it's true, but they still count. You're in a relationship with him right now, even if you want to deny it. Stepsiblings working on a wedding together with benefits is still a relationship, even if it's an unusual one."

"Fine," I huff, unable to find a defense against that. "He never stays in one place for very long. He is always leaving. He is going to leave me."

Reina folds her arms over her chest. "Do you see what I mean about how you take one little thing and make it mean that you can predict the future?"

This conversation is taking a frustrating turn, but she does seem to have a point, so I decide to throw myself at her mercy. "I can hear it, I guess. I don't know what else to do. If you know, tell me."

She shakes her head. "I don't know, same as you. We can't know the future. We can only know what we want and communicate those things clearly. Then we see what happens."

I shake my head. "I can't tell him."

"Tell him what? What is it that you want?"

"I don't know. To live in this little bubble forever. To plan weddings and have him with me always."

"What if he's out there agonizing over wanting to tell you the same thing and is too scared because you keep reiterating that it's only a sleeping together thing?"

"That's not what's going on."

It's Reina's turn to shrug. "You can't know that."

Tears prick the corners of my eyes again. This thing has baggage for me to unpack around every corner.

Reina's so sure that she's right, but she doesn't understand the situation. It could never go how she thinks it will go. Even if I got brave and told Avery how I feel, and he somehow decided that his twenty-three-year-old stepsister was the person he would break his lifelong habit of traipsing around the globe for —then we would have to face the family.

I am just about to lay out that layer of madness when Sal appears with a tray of margaritas. He's brought two for me, just the one for Reina, and a few small bowls of nuts and chips on the side.

"Be sure to have some of the snacks," he says casually, nudging the bowls closer to me. "The heat and the tequila can mix up real quick sometimes."

"Oh, we're going to do food, too," Reina jumps in, picking her menu back up. "Why don't you make us four birria and four carnitas tacos, and some chips and salsa and guac. We'll just share everything."

"Coming right up, my dear." With a small bow, Sal disappears back into the open restaurant.

"Tacos, huh? At a sports bar?"

"Sal's wife is from Mexico. She makes the absolute best tacos. And the sports bar thing, it's really more of a local nickname, although Sal does organize fishing tournaments and cornhole games and whatnot. Sometimes Dom will come down to watch soccer with the guys." She takes a long sip of her margarita, eyes narrowing at me. "Don't try to change the subject, though, we were just getting into the meat of this."

I'm halfway through my first tall, frosty glass, narrowly avoiding brain freeze with every giant sip. I already feel better, so I decide to let her keep me on track.

"I'm the youngest," I start, never setting my drink down. "And my siblings are pretty perfect. My brother, who's getting married, is an engineer, and my sister was a concert pianist before marrying her college sweetheart and becoming a stay-at-home mom. Her husband Richard actually works for the same firm as Frederick. They live in Hartford. Her two daughters are my favorite people in the whole world. When her oldest, Freida, was born, my whole life changed. I was sixteen, aimless, and probably on a path to no good, but then there was this amazing little baby, and it just changed everything. I moved to Connecticut from Colorado after high school, went to the University of Hartford, lived in my sister's house for the first couple of years, and then got an apartment a few blocks away." My heart aches with how much I miss those girls right now. This is one of the longest trips I've spent away from them, and it's not over yet. They will be coming down for the wedding, though, and I'll see them at Christmas. I'm counting the days.

"University of Hartford doesn't sound like anything to make fun of at Sunday dinner," Reina muses, taking a sip of her own margarita.

She could not be more wrong.

"All they ever do is make fun of me. Sure, U of H is a great school, but I chose hospitality management with a minor in interior design and worked for a caterer part-time all four years. I should have gone into business, they said. Or pre-law or pre-medicine. Whatever I do, it's not enough. And then, after I graduated, I went to work for the wedding caterer full-time as the assistant director, and they were appalled. How could I be working in the service industry? It was just so beneath them."

"Dang. Sounds like a bunch of jerks."

I shake my head and sigh. "It wouldn't have been that bad, honestly, but it's just that it didn't start there. It's always been this way. All throughout school, Leon and Anna had perfect grades, joined all the right clubs, had nice friends. Me, on the other hand, well, I was always in and out of detention for not paying attention or skipping class. I went through a goth phase, a jock phase, and a theater phase. I preferred to hang out at the park with my friends over joining French club or whatever. I was different from them, and they made fun of me. When my dad was around, he would always stick up for me." I break off and turn away. The thought of him shouldn't send me over the edge all these years later, but it does. He was my one ally in the family. Once he was gone, it was me against the world. And I guess it's felt like that ever since.

"You lost your dad?"

I nod, still looking over my shoulder, away from her. Finally, I take a deep breath and turn back. "Frederick came around when I was about fourteen. He was serious, but kind, and so different from the other guys my mom had dated. He was less needy, somehow. He was in charge. It was comforting, actually. After my dad died, we had a few years of really unsettled life. My mom would always talk about moving here or there for some job or some family member she wanted to be near. I can't imagine how hard all that was for her, becoming a single mother so suddenly. She had to go back to work, deal with all of the house stuff, and take care of us kids."

I take a moment to reflect on how strong of a woman my mother really is. Would I have been able to keep it together like she did?

"But then she met Frederick. He lived in Aspen. We were down in Boulder, but as soon as it got serious, my mom rented out our house, and we moved in with him. I loved Aspen. It was hard to leave my friends, but honestly, I was ready for a fresh start. I started sophomore year there, and I was a whole new person. That would have been fine but, of course, I'd already reinvented myself multiple times by then, so it was a long running family joke. What will Franzeska do next? Frederick never participated in that talk. He never criticized or made fun of me. Maybe that's just a male father figure thing, I don't know. Both of mine sure had it. I finally had an ally again. I remember this one time, I was in my room, throwing a fit because my mom had just dropped the bomb that she signed me up to go to an all-girl sleepaway camp that summer. Frederick knocked on my door like he always did, and when I answered, he came in and sat at my desk, asked me why I was so upset. I showed him the pamphlets from the sleepaway space camp in New Mexico that I'd found on the internet. He took the pamphlets from me, and the next morning, I was going to space camp. It was never even talked about. He treated me like a person. Still does. When Leon announced he and Cynthia were engaged, it was Frederick's idea for me to plan the wedding. He just believes in me. He believes me when I say I can do it."

"And your relationship with Frederick makes the Avery thing all that more complicated."

"It's not so much my relationship with Frederick, but Avery's."

Reina laughs. "No girl, you got that all wrong. If Avery and his dad were best buds, you would never have gotten yourself into this situation."

"Yeah, okay. You're right about that. I guess I would have grown up with Avery around. This would be extra weird then." We both laugh. "There's no way to make it not weird. Even if it's helpful that Avery mostly doesn't even consider his father a family member, I still have to face my family…our family."

"And that would be so bad? Sounds like you're pretty used to their judgment. And you don't even have to live with them now, so who cares?"

I inhale deeply and blow the breath out. How can I explain this to her? I can't even explain it to myself. "I don't know. I mean, I guess it doesn't really matter." I can tell by her face that my tone isn't convincing anyone. "Okay, fine, it matters. I just don't know why. I guess when you've spent your whole life trying to fit in with a group of people, it's a hard habit to break."

"What do you think you could tell them that would make them happy? What kind of life update would make them not make fun of you? This is just your mom and siblings that we're talking about, right? Not Frederick. So, what could you go to Sunday dinner and tell them that would make them proud?"

I pause to consider her question. Honestly, I've spent so much time worrying about how my decisions will impact my home life that I've never taken the time to think about what these people actually want from me. "I don't know. I'm not sure there's anything."

"Is it possible that they aren't actually making fun of you, per se, but it's just their way of communicating or relating to you?"

I roll my eyes. "If you're about to tell me I'm too sensitive, you can save it. I've heard that my whole life."

"I'm not saying that. I'm just saying, maybe you ended up with a different kind of communication style than the rest of your family. You got your father's style, and your siblings got your mother's. Do they talk to each other in the same way?"

I consider. "Yeah, I guess they do. But when someone questions their life choices, they don't even bat an eyelash. They are so sure of themselves."

"Okay, okay. I think we might be getting somewhere. What I hear you saying is that your family members are all very confident in their life choices, but you aren't feeling that way. So, when people question you about what you're doing, you feel attacked and don't know how to defend yourself."

"Are you sure you're not actually a therapist?"

Reina laughs. "I just read a lot of books." She finishes off her margarita and sits back in her chair. "What will it take for you to be sure that what you are doing is what you really, truly want to be doing?"

"I guess I need to be good at it. I mean, I've wanted to have my own wedding planning company since before I even started working for the caterer. I remember the wedding planner at my mom and Frederick's wedding just being so…badass, so cool. She was in charge and totally chic. Everyone listened to her. I followed her around like a shadow. I'm sure she thought I was totally annoying." I take a pause to reminisce and laugh. "But this is the first wedding I'm doing on my own. I won't know if I'm any good at this until it goes well. Or goes terribly, I suppose. If I pull it off, though, then I'll have proven to the world that I can do this. So, what do I do? I immediately start up a relationship with Frederick's son, distracting me from my project and further jeopardizing my chances of becoming an adult in the eyes of my family." I let out a sad sigh. "I'm hopeless."

"Girl, you're crazy, that's what you are."

I laugh. "Is that your professional therapist opinion?"

"No, it's my human woman opinion. I don't know where along the way you picked up the idea that your job in life is to prove your worthiness to your family, but that ain't it. Your job is to find happiness and cling to it like a life raft. Your job is to be exactly who you are. If those people don't like it, they can shove it."

"It's so easy to say that."

"No, it's easy to live it, too." Reina holds her hand up to

silence my interruption. "It's easy to live it if you're confidently going after what you actually want. If you're sure of yourself, you won't have any problem defending your choices."

I'm saved from answering by Sal appearing with our feast. We dig in and both have a few minutes to think. Once I have devoured my first taco, I pull my second margarita close and take a deep breath. "So, how do you know when you're sure?"

"I was sure about Dom when I realized that the thought of spending a day apart from him would literally break my heart. I was sure about Reef the very first time he brought me down there, back when it was a storage floor, filled with broken kitchen equipment and junk. I just knew. Have you ever had that feeling?"

I nod. "Yeah. That's how I felt when I met the wedding planner at my mom's wedding."

"How old were you then, seventeen?"

I nod again.

"So, you've been chasing the same dream now for six years? I'd say that sounds pretty sure. And look how far you've gotten. You've got years of experience working for that company under your belt, and now you're launching your own business with this wedding. Girl, you've got it made."

I nod again. She's so right. But since meeting Avery, my dreams of having my own company just don't seem like enough. "I'm just not sure…"

"About Avery?"

"No, I'm sure about Avery." The words leave my mouth before I can think about what they mean. I bite my lip and look up at Reina, who's grinning at me.

"Okay, then. Just stop worrying about it."

"What? How am I supposed to stop worrying about it?"

She shrugs. "If it's meant to be, it will be."

"Oh my god, are those lyrics to a country song?"

She laughs. "Probably. But it's true. Just keep on doing what you're doing, plan the most epic wedding ever, and don't freak out. And when the dust settles and the families all go home, you and Avery can decide what happens next."

"It's the not knowing that kills me."

"Yup, I can see that. This will be an excellent growth opportunity for you."

I groan.

"Or you could just break it off now and concentrate on the wedding."

Shaking my head and laughing, I don't even need to answer.

"So, there you go. Just chill. It'll work out. I'm telling you, the guy is having the same feelings and worries as you are."

My laughter quiets but my head continues to shake. "This is going to kill me."

She shrugs. "Maybe. But if not, you'll come out on the other side better off."

"You mean, what doesn't kill you makes you stronger?" I tease.

"I wasn't going to say it, but yeah. That's the idea."

I let my mind drift the whole drive back and as I climb into the elevator to head back to my room. All I really want to do is climb my three-margarita ass up to the third floor and let Avery take care of me, but I know taking tonight to myself will be good for me.

I can't get a lot of thinking done with this much alcohol in my system, but I can think clearly enough to make one decision.

I'm going to take Reina's advice.

I'm going to chill.

Enjoy the hell out of this time I get with Avery and work out the rest as we go.

It nearly kills me to think that I'll have to wait months to find out what happens, but maybe that's just how life goes. All we do the entire time is find out new things—live each day as it comes.

I laugh to myself at my deep, existential thoughts as I drift off to sleep, fully clothed on my sofa.

I might just be growing up.

Rule #20

PEOPLE CHANGE... DON'T THEY?

AVERY

"Are you sure you're ready for this?"

Franny looks down the stairs at me like I'm crazy. "Ready for a dinner party with your lifelong friends? Yeah. I think I'll be able to handle it."

I sigh, resisting the urge to pull her closer to me. We agreed to avoid any PDA or any mention of what's going on. Not because we're ashamed or trying to hide, but because Fran doesn't want our pseudo relationship to be the focus of the evening.

"It's Reina's party. We're not going to steal her thunder with a scandal," she told me as I watched her get ready in her room. "Besides, I think getting a chance to talk about the wedding in a more casual setting like this will benefit us. Get a few drinks in them, find out what they really think. Then we can talk about it later."

I like the part where we're back in one of our rooms after the party, sharing our recon conspiratorially. I want to skip right to that, but I suppose there's no way to get there without actually doing the social part first.

Usually I'm all for a party, and it feels strange to be approaching this one with such dread. It's just that I've taken quite a liking to having this woman all to myself, and I know this evening is going to require a lot of sharing.

"Welcome to the party!" Reina squeals as we pass through the heavy wood door of her and Dom's hilltop mansion. "Come in, come in. Can I get you a drink?"

Fran and I share a grin as we follow Reina into the house. When we emerge from the hallway into the open concept kitchen dining room area, however, my smile falters.

It's just the three guys waiting in there, all watching us enter with their arms crossed.

Is this a dinner party or some kind of intervention?

Luckily, Fran doesn't seem perturbed. She follows Reina into the kitchen while I head over to stand with the guys.

"Hey."

"Hey."

"Hey."

"Hey."

Okay, now that we have those riveting greetings out of the way.

"Smells great in here." It's the dinner party equivalent of commenting on the weather, but I'm struggling to find anything appropriate to say to these guys right now. I've spent the last few weeks so absorbed in my life with Fran—the wedding, our bodies, the sun, and the ocean. I feel like I just poked my head out of the sand for the first time in a while and left my formerly grand conversational skills buried.

"Reina's reheating food I cooked earlier," Dom growls.

I turn to him with an incredulous look. "What the fuck, man. Why would you say that?"

He huffs. "It's true."

"Who cares if it's true? Would it kill you to let her have some of the credit?"

"Mr. Sensitive over here," he says without taking his eyes off his lovely fiancée, who's pouring Fran and I tall glasses of pink wine.

I accept mine with a gracious smile. "Everything looks lovely, Reina. Thanks for inviting us."

I hear Dom huff again beside me but ignore him.

The girls are whispering and giggling together in that girly way that they do, and all four of us guys shift uncomfortably on our feet. I marvel at the power the women hold over the room—over us. How have I never noticed that before? I've been in plenty of rooms with giggling groups of girls, and never once have I even considered demanding that they tell me what's so funny.

This is the first time you've had one you cared about enough to want to know.

The truth of that thought is a cold splash to the face. I want this girl to like me, and I'm terrified she's somehow going to get talked out of it.

Before I can interrupt, they clasp hands and disappear back down the hallway into the house.

"'Bout goddamn time." Dom crosses into the kitchen and starts adjusting all of the things Reina was doing in there, muttering to himself.

I laugh softly at the way my control freak friend waited until his woman wasn't watching before he did things his own way. I guess even the most alpha of us guys doesn't want to cross the females.

I turn to Sam and Ben, who are both cradling large glasses of the same wine. "Are we waiting on more people?"

Sam shakes his head, tight lips holding back a smile. "Nope, this is it."

I join him in stifling a smile. So much for a dinner party. This is just the same ol' crew. Plus the ladies, of course. "We got the flower thing sorted," I start, offering up the only conversation I am capable of these days—wedding talk.

Sam and Ben both turn to me with curious eyes.

"It's going okay, then? You two working together?" Sam dares.

"Yeah. It's going great."

Ben doesn't react a single bit, but Sam lets out a sigh.

"Ave, this is concerning."

"What? What do you mean?"

"I mean, having this wedding go well will be great for the resort. I just wish you weren't...you know..."

"Enlighten me." I do know what he's trying to say, but I'm not going to concede the point.

"Doing the Avery thing where you swing in and fuck things up and then leave us to pick up the pieces," Dom joins the conversation.

My mouth drops open and then snaps closed. "That's not what I do. When have I ever done that?"

"Christmas 2017."

"Well, that was different. I mean, the fire wasn't my fault, first of all. And second, I wasn't running off on you guys, I had a six-week watercolor class in Milan to get to."

Ben is just shaking his head, but Sam's face softens. "We weren't blaming you for the fire, Ave. Or anything. It's just...this is kind of a pattern of yours. You find something you like, get really invested in it for a bit, and then bail. But this time the project you've chosen is one that could turn out to make millions for the resort or cost us millions. And the girl—"

"The girl whose heart you're going to break is your father's stepdaughter," Ben cuts in.

"I'm not breaking anyone's heart. If anything, it's my own heart that's going to get annihilated here."

I'm convincing no one.

"People change," I say, trying for a different angle.

"They don't change," Dom says from his side of the kitchen island.

"Oh, really, Dom? You didn't change for your new love? Come on. I distinctly remember ninth grade when you lost your virginity to Misty Robinson—what did you do? You stopped by Ben's house on the way home, where we were all hanging out, and told us all about it. And now here you are, engaged to a woman who you *secretly* dated for almost a year."

"You guys knew the whole time."

"That's beside the point. And on top of that, she's still working to pay off her own debt before you get married? That's the least Dom arrangement I've ever heard. Honestly, I wouldn't be surprised to learn you're actually an alien body double and the real Dom is being held hostage on some planet."

Dom rolls his eyes but doesn't comment. There's nothing he can say. I'm fucking right.

I turn on the other guys, flames shooting out of my ears as I prepare to continue the epic takedown of all of my closest friends. "And you two—"

"Okay, Ave. We get it." Sam, ever the peacekeeper, holds up his hands in surrender. "People do change. But you have to understand where we're coming from here. We've all seen how that girl looks at you. And you two certainly have some kind of relationship going on. It's just...we're concerned about the fall out."

"How she looks at me?" I'm baffled now. "How about the way I look at her? You guys got this all wrong. I'm just a rest stop on her journey to stardom. It's me you should be worried about."

"Yeah, Ave, it's you we're worried about," Dom chimes in from behind the stove, where he's hurriedly seasoning things in pots before replacing the lids.

"You know what I mean, dick. I'm going to fall for her, and she's going to leave me. I'm going to be a crying mess when this whole thing is over, just you guys wait."

"If we didn't have twenty years of evidence for the opposite happening, we may just believe you."

I don't get a chance to defend myself because the ladies reappear.

"What are you doing?" Reina chases Dom out of the kitchen with a swat on his ass.

"Nothing, nothing," Dom mutters as he joins us on the living room side of the island.

Fran stays in the kitchen with Reina, but her eyes catch mine. She sparkles with some kind of mischief, but I'm not brave enough to get excited about it. Not when I've got these three watching my every move.

"Will you all go sit, please? You're making me nervous," Reina says as she re-checks the pots Dom was just checking. Seemingly satisfied, she takes her own wineglass in hand and comes around to tuck into Dom's side.

My own empty side burns with jealousy, but I don't reach for Fran.

"How about the deck?"

Reina nods at Dom's suggestion and allows him to lead us out there.

Sam catches my arm just as I try to make my escape into the warm evening air.

"Hey, man. Sorry if that seemed like an ambush."

"It didn't just seem like one, it was one," I reply, trying not to sound like the gaping emotional wound I am after learning just how highly my closest friends think of me.

"We just want you to be happy. We want you to find whatever it is you're looking for, it's just…" He trails off and gives me a pained smile. "This is concerning."

"Well, I guess I should be grateful to have so many father figures looking out for me." The thought of them all talking about me before this dinner and deciding how to handle the situation is annoying. But also, kinda nice. Reassuring. "No, seriously. I…always feel on my own, but I do have you guys, and I should remember that. I appreciate you looking out for me."

"And Franzeska."

I huff out a laugh. "Sammy, you don't need to worry a lick

about that girl. She's on course to take over the world. I'm just a foundation stone in that castle."

"I want to believe you, we all do. Just…keep in mind that this is all going to change drastically when the family arrives for the wedding. No matter what either of you think right now, that's going to be the end. You might consider ending it on a good note before the big day."

Over my dead, rotting, bird-picked corpse am I ending anything, but I smile and nod. "I'll talk to Fran about it."

The sky is just turning pink and gold with the setting sun as we rejoin the group relaxing on the deck. Dom kicks on the gas firepit and we all sit down in soft chairs surrounding the dancing flames.

"So, what's the latest on the big wedding?" Reina takes the lead on starting some conversation she thinks will be safe.

The silence after her question extends so long that finally Fran pipes up. "Well," she starts, tossing a confused look at me. "We got the flowers squared away. We went up to Marta's farm, and I got to choose the colors. It's going to be incredible. And we decided on Kuramo's pit barbecue for the main meal, which I'm sure you heard about, so it's nice to have that settled."

"I got a call from Mackenzie that the tables and chairs will be coming over next week," Sam adds.

Fran and I both turn to him in surprise.

"What? You didn't tell me that," I say.

Sam nods. "I just heard from him before I headed over. The barge gets in next Thursday."

I turn back to Fran, and we share excited eyes.

"So, all in all, things are going pretty well?" Ben asks, the first thing out of his mouth in a long time.

"It's going really great. We're on schedule, things seem to be arriving in a timely fashion, which was one of my main concerns, and the RSVPs have been flowing in back at my brother's house in the States. He's been sending me updates on that. We'll have a final number soon."

"Is it still under a hundred?" Sam asks.

"So far, yeah, but I imagine we'll end up right at a hundred."

"Are you going home for Christmas?" Reina asks Fran, who nods.

"Yeah, I leave in less than a week. It's crazy how quickly time has gone by!"

I hold my smile fixed but say nothing. I'm not excited about her leaving and am absolutely terrified that things will be different when she gets back. Luckily, she's going to her sister's in Connecticut, not back to Aspen, but still. Her mom and Frederick will be there.

I could go.

I smile wider thinking of what a mess that would be—if I just randomly showed up for Christmas for the first time in my whole life and tried to share a bed with Franny.

No, better sit this one out.

Not to mention the fact that she didn't ask me.

I'm going to have a typical Avery Christmas—sleep late, swim, drink, eat. All the guys will be on the island, even Ben's son Ainsley, so I'll be in good company.

"When you get back it's gonna be game on," Sam says good-naturedly.

"I know." Fran tosses me an excited look, and I smile back at her. "This whole thing has been kind of a whirlwind. I mean, I had an idea of what I wanted to do before coming, but being here has changed a lot of that. The actual location, measurements, as well as the availability of stuff—" She turns to me suddenly. "Speaking of which, I still need to order the cameras to be delivered to my sister's house so I can fly them back with me." She grimaces at no one in particular. "I can't believe I forgot about that. I hope they arrive in time, with it being the holidays and whatnot."

I lay a hand reassuringly on her thigh. "If they don't, I can fly back in a few weeks and grab them. Or we can fly to Texas or something. It'll work out."

She calms and nods, glancing down at my hand and smiling. I don't pull it away.

Fuck the guys.

"I met with Kuramo about the barbecue," Dom starts, clearing his throat. "We're going to get Mackenzie's excavator out the week before the party, so we're going to need some fencing for that."

"Okay," Sam says. "We have enough downstairs, I think, from when we did the pool renovation."

Dom nods.

I could not be enjoying myself more. Fran really was right about getting to talk wedding in this casual environment. With everyone so relaxed, information is flowing.

I'm beside myself with excitement at being included.

I generally stay on the sidelines of things like this. Even as one of the owners of the resort, as much a partner as any of these guys, I never feel like anyone is particularly interested in my opinion. They are often just working things out among themselves. I can't remember the last time I was asked for my input about something that didn't involve an international trip one of them was planning, or a guest who was coming in from some far-flung location and needed assistance with logistics.

I feel useful. I feel smart and capable.

It's a good feeling. My chest swells with pride as I listen to the conversation. Each time someone mentions my name in conjunction with some project or idea, I feel myself glow a bit more.

And I know exactly who's responsible for this—the woman to my right.

She swept in and changed me. For the better. I never even knew what I was missing, but I know I have it now. I wonder if I'll be able to keep this up after she's gone.

And…there it is.

Couldn't just let a good feeling go on too long, now could you, buddy?

Because the hard truth of this work situation is that it's just as temporary as my relationship. And everything in my life, really. I'm usually so good at just enjoying things while they last, not taking it too seriously when it's time to move on. This time, I not only see the epic heartbreak coming a mile away, I'm doing exactly nothing to prevent it. I'm running headlong into the breaker.

"...Ave?"

I snap myself out of it and find Franny looking at me expectantly. "Oh, yeah." I nod in agreement, having zero idea what I just agreed to.

She narrows her eyes suspiciously but goes on. "It's a reddish shade, so it will look really nice next to the whitewashed walls, and it's thick enough that it should cover the molding that's already on the doorway."

Oh, the mango-wood planks we found in town the other day to use to camouflage the café exit for the bride's entrance down the aisle. I nod and smile. "Honestly, we might even consider keeping it up after the wedding. The wood is gorgeous. Much nicer than the plywood molding we put up."

I'm probably overstepping by commenting on the fate of the café entrance, but hell, I do own the damn place. Luckily, none of the guys call me out.

"What are you going to wear? Did you bring an outfit with you from the States?" Reina askes Fran.

She shakes her head. "No, I kinda thought I would get something here, but there aren't a lot of shops with formalwear." The group lets out a polite laugh. "I might look when I'm home for Christmas."

"How about you, Ave?" Sam tosses my way.

I shrug. "I'm sure Franny will pick something out for me." I realize too late that I called her the name I usually only say in my head. I glance over at her to see if she's going to be mad, but she's giving me a look I can't quite read. Narrowed eyes and pursed lips, but not pursed in the mad way, more like the "inside joke" way. I shift closer to her.

"Well, it seems like it's probably dinnertime. What do you think, baby girl?"

Our attention shifts to Dom as he tosses out the adorable endearment to his fiancée. A look passes between them, incredibly similar to the look Fran and I just shared.

I take a deep breath and try to keep it together.

"Yup. Let's eat," Reina agrees, climbing to her feet and leading us back inside.

They have the dining table set up in the sunroom, a half floor down from the kitchen and dining room. We all carry a dish to the already laid table.

The wine flows throughout the lovely meal, starting with sparkling and transitioning through white to red. By the time Dom carries down a tray of coconut ice cream with mangoes, I'm feeling a little tipsy.

"Limoncello?" he offers, already pouring into the tiny glass in front of me.

"Oh, sure."

Fran smiles as he fills hers but doesn't lift it to her lips.

We say our goodbyes soon after dessert and escape into the dark.

I walk down the steep staircase in front of her, walking slowly and keeping her close to my back so I can break her fall if needed.

I try not to glance back up at the figures watching us go from the top of the stairs, but snippets of their over-served voices carry in the night air.

"Collision course…"

"Trouble…"

"Let them be…"

There's no way Franny hasn't heard as well. I try to catch a glimpse of her face as we head hand in hand down the sandy path, but it's too dark.

Finally, she speaks. "Do you think they like me?"

It's the first time I've heard anything but confidence from those lips. Anger at my nosy friends reignites. "Of course they like you, love. They just…sometimes don't like me all that much, I guess."

She stops short, and I have to follow suit to avoid letting go of her hand.

"Avery, those guys love the shit out of you."

I let out a surprised laugh and shake my head, then nod. "Yeah, I know they're just showing their love in their own way, but sometimes it feels pretty judgmental."

"Love is kinda judgmental, I guess."

Her eyes are downcast, so I lift her chin with my hand until she's eye to eye with me. "It doesn't have to be."

The look we share is so loaded that I can't breathe until it's over.

"Yeah, maybe," she mumbles as she finally looks back at her feet.

Tell her you love her, jackass.

But that is the exact opposite of what we're doing here.

"Come on," I say, leading her down the path behind me. "I've got somewhere I want to show you."

Rule #21

THE CURE FOR ANYTHING IS SALT WATER—SWEAT, TEARS, OR THE SEA

AVERY

The absolute last thing we should be doing in this state is giggling our way up to the rooftop deck to look at the stars, but alas. The girl just inspires something wild in me.

"Can I ask you a question?" I ask, once we are settled on a blanket I found tossed over a chair, taking in the night sky.

"Anything." She's quite drunk and apparently feeling very open.

"What's with the pregnancy thing? I mean," I say quickly when I feel her start to tense up, "don't get me wrong, I have no interest in getting you pregnant. It's just that, between your IUD and condoms, it's pretty darn safe. I've been using condoms for my whole adult life, and it's never failed me." I consider this for a moment. "At least I don't think it has. No, I would know." I let out a dark laugh. "I would definitely know."

She's lying on her side on the roof, facing me, her lovely eyes looking far too sad for such a perfect evening.

"I'm sorry to bring it up. It's just that you love your nieces so much, it doesn't seem like you hate kids. I just wonder why it would be the worst thing in the world."

I watch as she rolls to her back, facing the brilliant spray of stars. I do the same.

"I love those girls so much." Her voice fills with emotion, and I glance over. "I'm a little drunk, so I'm probably going to cry this whole time, but I'm fine, okay?"

"Okay," I say softly.

"And I love my sister. I have spent every second with them that I could since the girls were born. I moved there after high school, went to college nearby. I'm always there. It's very important to me to be a part of their lives."

She pauses, and I wait. When she goes on, I can hear the tears in her voice. I want to grab her and pull her to me, but she said that she's okay, and I have to believe her.

"But my sister is so busy, with her house and her volunteer work and her husband and her kids. They have two dogs and a cat. It's a busy life."

Silence falls again. I think I know where she's going with this, but I wait for her to break my heart anyway. "I don't know if they would visit me."

There it is.

"If I had a baby, and I got busy with my own family, and I lived somewhere else, would I ever see them again? There's no way they would visit me like I visit them. It would be the end of my relationship with the girls. And my own babies wouldn't know them. Not like I know the girls. They would be strangers. It would be so obvious that I'm not as important to them as they are to me." She finally cracks, a sob escaping and her words coming to an end.

I do reach for her now, and she lets me pull her close. We lay like that for a few long moments, just two warm bodies, wrapped together in silence.

I don't want to tell this story, but it feels necessary. "I'm not sure what age I was when my parents' sporadic work trips turned into something more permanent, but I have memories of these phone calls, starting when I was really young. Miranda, my housekeeper, my pseudo-mother, would dial the phone for me every night. I would talk to one or both of them every day. As I got older, it slowly slipped into every few days or once a week. But Miranda would always dial the phone. It wasn't until I was an adult that I realized they never called me. But as long as she dialed, they would answer, and we would talk. I wouldn't know that they didn't call."

Fran is quiet and still in my arms now, and she turns her tear-stained face up to mine. "But that's such a sad story."

I laugh softly. "Yeah, I guess it is."

"It's the same sad story as mine." She's crying again, and I hold her tighter. "Your story is supposed to have an ending that helps me know what to do. But your ending is just that you grew up and now you see how sad it was. That's not helpful."

I can't squeeze her any tighter, so I press my lips to the closest spot on her body, a place on her head, right above her ear. "Sorry, love. I don't have all the answers. I responded to my family problems by avoiding them for my entire life. It's not the worst solution. If you need some advice on how to do that, I'm an open book."

"I don't want that, Avery. My family is important to me. I'll just, I don't know. Move next door to them. Never have a family of my own."

"Those aren't solutions, though."

She pushes away and rolls onto her back once more. "There's no solution. If I want to have them in my life, I have to be the one to do the work. They aren't going to."

"You can't just live your entire life for other people, though."

"But how do I do it then?"

"If I knew, I'd tell you, love."

After a long silence, she makes her way back to my side, curling her body around and over me. I pull her in and hold her there so tightly my muscles ache. It's not long before she's asleep.

I'm so filled with feelings and booze that I'm incapable of processing everything. Between the joy of finally feeling like a useful part of the resort team and the sadness of not being able to clear away my girl's problems with a wave of my magic wand, I'm caught in some kind of emotional limbo.

It's completely exhausting.

How do people do this on a daily basis?

Moving so often that I never get attached just scored a point, I think.

But even as the feelings try to eat me alive from the inside, I can't help but notice how full I feel. I'm full of sadness and nervous anticipation, sure. But I'm also full of gratitude, excitement, and curiosity.

How could this go?

What other kinds of things are possible for me?

It's like by moving here and dragging me into this bizarre arrangement, this woman has opened me up to a world I never even knew existed.

It makes me feel like doing a lot of things.

But for the first time ever, running isn't one of them.

Rule #22

YES, PEOPLE CHANGE

AVERY

After a few glorious weeks of sun, swimming, cake tasting, and orgasms, it's time for the dreaded Christmas break.

I take Fran all the way to the airport in the city, rather than just putting her on the boat at Faraday like I've done with every other person.

I sweet talk the customs agents into letting me walk her to the gate.

"Avery, I'm fine. You don't have to stay with me for the next two hours. I can read my book."

She's been trying to get me to let her go since we stepped onto the water taxi.

"It's fine. What else do I have to do?"

Truer words have never been spoken. The two-week trip home she scheduled might actually kill me.

What am I going to do without her?

Possibly the same things you were doing for the last thirty-some years? You know, all the ones that came before you met her?

But it's like those years are a gray blur in my mind, unretrievable no matter how hard I squint my eyes off into space searching for them. When she gets on the plane…it's time to man up. I leave the airport with a new resolve to be fine. Totally fine.

Maybe…

Christmas is lovely, as expected. We take the long weekend to head over to Merit Island and shack up in the house there. Ainsley, Ben's son, has flown in from Cambodia, where he's currently driving his father crazy volunteering to build a school. He and I spend long hours laying out by the pool, swapping travel stories.

Franny and I message nonstop. I catch nearly as much shit as nineteen-year-old Ainsley for always being on my phone. And I care exactly as much as he does about the flack.

He met a girl while in Southeast Asia and thinks he convinced her to move to Faraday next to teach yoga or whatever it is she does. The prospect of having him on the island lifts my spirits, but only until his father catches wind of it. I guess taking one more year off college wasn't the Christmas surprise Ben was hoping for.

When it's finally time to scoop Franny up at the airport, I arrive two hours early and then try to play it cool when she finally strolls out of customs.

"Franny," I breathe out as I finally lay eyes on her.

She walks straight into my arms. It's all I can do not to cry as I pull her warm body into mine. Her dress is crumpled, and she smells like she just spent ten hours traveling, but she's perfect… and she's home.

"How was your trip?"

She laughs, and it's music to my ears. "We texted the whole time, Ave. I don't think there's anything that happened that you don't know about."

On the boat ride home, she shows me all the pictures that she already messaged me, telling me who's who and laughing over how many gifts her little nieces got. She seems happy to be back. I can't ignore the closeness of her—the way she sits with her legs crossed in my direction, how she leans into my side as she holds her phone out.

It's a homecoming.

And I waited here for her to come back.

I waited here for her. I didn't leave.

We didn't go our separate ways. I didn't move on to the next thing. She went on a trip, and I waited for her to get home.

Avery, you're crossing some dangerous lines here.

But it's too late to go back.

And weirdly…I don't want to.

Rule #23

AVOIDANCE IS AN ART FORM

FRAN

Just the sight of The Sands peeking over the horizon as we make our way down the sandy street brings tears to my eyes. I wasn't expecting this to feel so much like a homecoming, but there's no denying it. The feeling of running into Avery's arms when he picked me up at the airport was…everything.

I let myself into my room for the first time in two weeks, and a few tears do actually fall. The smell of it, the feel of the cool tile beneath my bare feet. The bag of freshly folded laundry waiting just inside the door.

Avery is watching me like I might disappear again at any moment, but I manage to shake him off long enough to shower and take a nap. When I wake, I find flowers in my kitchen and a bag of takeout from Chef Kuramo's place on the counter.

Sneaky little elf.

This is certainly enough food for two…

Avery
I'll be right down.

He knocks on my front door five minutes later, something he never lets me do at his room anymore, but somehow, he still feels the need to do at mine. I open the door wearing a big smile —and nothing else.

"Franny," Avery coos in surprise, putting his arms out to block my body and backing me into the room, kicking the door closed behind him. "Everyone's going to see you."

"So what if they do? They can have a little show," I tease, knowing damn well that there's no way anyone could have seen me.

"That's my little show you're talking about. I have the only ticket."

His hands are everywhere all at once, and I close my eyes and lose myself in the feeling. The warmth of him, the salty, musky smell of his beach life. It fills my senses and makes me hesitant to let my breath go. I want to hold this feeling inside me forever.

Those were two long, long weeks of being alone again. A harsh reminder of what's waiting on the other side of this whole wedding extravaganza. As much as I've been looking forward to the big day, to showing off all the work we've done, I also wish it would never come.

The tears swell in my eyes before I can shut down my feelings and stop them. Avery, of course, notices right away, halting his full body fondle and pulling me into a tight embrace. "What's going on, love?"

Love. That's what the fuck is going on. And it's going to kill me.

"God, nothing, ignore me. I'm just happy to be back."

"Your trip wasn't all you were hoping it would be? Sounds like your family was happy to have you."

I search his voice for traces of the kinds of things I'm feeling

—the heart-breaking, soul-splitting fear of the loss that's now visible on the horizon. But I find none. He's happy to see me. He's concerned that I'm upset. That's it.

"It was great. I did love getting to see everyone. And the girls grew so much." And now I'm crying for an entirely different reason. Because the absolute truth of the matter is—it was nice to be back and know that I was visiting. It was really special. Everyone paid me a lot of attention, the little girls especially. I spent the days doing fun activities and decorating for the holidays and baking. It was nothing like the day-to-day regular life I was participating in when I lived in their house, driving them to and from lessons, rationing out ice cream and screen time.

Needing to go home to those girls is my lifeline in this whole Avery mess. Sure, being here with him is great, but there's a life that I have to get back to. People who need me.

But what if that's not true? What if everyone is fine without me, and I can just visit and have an even better time than I did when I lived down the hall from all of them?

If I have nowhere I have to be when the wedding is over, then I am in a lot deeper shit than I ever expected. It's going to hurt all that much more when he leaves—and I have nowhere to go.

I must be breaking down on the outside as well as the inside because Avery is leading me slowly to the sofa and sitting me down.

"What's this all about? You seemed so happy to be back a few hours ago."

His concern makes me feel guilty. I shouldn't be putting this on him—especially since he's more or less the cause of it all, and I'm not going to tell him that.

"I am happy to be back, it's just..." I flop back against the cushion, wishing I'd just kept it together. We would probably be getting it on right now if I had. "It was nice to visit. It was so fun. Like I was special for being there because I'm not around all the time. Before I left, I kind of started to feel like the babysitter, which was fine. I was happy to help, but this time I was the most exciting guest. Even my sister, who can be really critical of what I'm doing, just chatted with me about her own life and the wedding. I had something to talk about. It kind of felt like I had a purpose, a direction finally. Like I wasn't just her burden. I didn't realize how much better that would feel until I experienced it."

"Absence makes the heart grow fonder?"

I laugh and wipe the last of my tears away. I'm calming down just being in this man's presence, just having him listen to me. "Yeah, I suppose so." There's so much more I could say here about the complete existential crisis I'm having, but I decide not to. What's the point in laying all of my early-twenties craziness out for him when it's probably just going to scare him away sooner?

No. We have an arrangement. Fun while we plan the wedding. I plan to get my full allotment of fun—all the way until the wedding is over. I'm not going to cut it short now by going all girly on him.

"What about this guy?" I slide my hand up his bare thigh and over the sleek material of his shorts until I'm cupping his half-hard cock.

Okay, make that fully hard.

"Did my absence make this guy grow any fonder?"

Avery doesn't respond right away, and I glance up, expecting to find him smoldering with desire, and find questions in his eyes instead. He doesn't want to let it go, but I'm already too far gone to go back to that sob story.

I land my lips on his as I pull myself up and over his legs, straddling him and grinding my naked pussy into the bulge in his shorts.

Just try to have a serious conversation now, buddy. I dare you.

His hands on my ass let me know that I talked him into moving on.

He pulls my hips down tightly so my body grinds against his as I slowly slide my hips up and down his length.

Now, don't get me wrong. I brought my vibrator home to Connecticut with me and had more than my fair share of sessions—most of them picturing this man right here—but nothing compares to this.

With my eyes closed and his strong hands gripping my body as I stimulate every aching nerve between my legs on his massive erection, I feel like I come back to life in a way the little silicone buzzer just can't simulate.

Maybe it's the smell of him.

I inhale and moan out my pleasure. Yeah, that's probably it.

I wonder if I could mix myself a bottle of this fragrance to spray before solo sessions, so I can better pretend that he's with me.

Pathetic, Franzeska.

"What are you thinking?"

My mind is spinning so quickly he must be able to hear the gears working.

"I love how you smell," I manage as he grips my hips impossibly harder.

Avery laughs softly into my hair, tilting his hips just enough that I get more of his length to grind on. "I was just thinking the same thing."

"About how great you smell? Cocky bastard," I try for humor, but my voice betrays me. Every word sounds like a moan. I'm so close, and the man hasn't even taken his shorts off. I allow his strong arms to support me as I lean my head back, hands finally living out their dream of running down his firm chest.

My body is so turned on and open, I nearly melt into his lap with every stroke of my hips. I allow myself to imagine him pulling off those shorts, freeing the erection trapped inside as I've watched him do so many times. In my mind, I slide back into his lap and the tip of him disappears right into my wet, waiting pussy.

Wait, what? Hold up.

It's one thing to have this fantasy solo, but here, only a millimeter of fabric separating his tip from…

That's just straight up dangerous.

I would never actually do something like that.

Would I?

I've spent a lot of years of saying no—sometimes over and over and over—to getting fucked there. It's just not my thing. I tell myself I'm not ready. I tell the guys I'm not ready. We do other stuff.

So far, the same thing has played out with Avery. I told him to stick his dick elsewhere, and he did—happily.

I'm happy too. I love when he fucks my back door. He always gets me off. It feels so good I find myself craving it right now.

It's just…

Maybe I've stopped being not ready.

I mean, all the reasons for not doing it are still there. They just seem less…reasonable now.

Maybe it's time.

I try to calm myself down. The adrenaline shot I got from imagining him fucking my virgin pussy is nearly too much to handle. I'm very close to coming just from the thought of it.

Avery senses the shift in me and starts to grind me against him more quickly.

I lose the battle against my approaching orgasm, curling into his chest and dragging my fingernails up the sides of his ribs as I come.

He's still holding me tightly, working my body against his to keep me in the state of pleasure, so all I have to do is ride it. I clench my teeth and float there, suspended in the ocean of his scent, my nerves firing, the image of him slipping into my pussy still playing out in my mind's eye.

When I can finally breathe again, I release my claws from his sides and bring my lips up to meet his, feverish with desire now. That orgasm should have sated me, but it did no such thing.

"Let me get these shorts off, love." His low, growly, desire laced whisper brings my mind back to the present moment. I rise off him and watch as he lifts his hips, making quick work of the shorts.

And there he is, sitting on my sofa, in my room, in the resort I now call home, if only to myself. His cock is free, and so hard, waiting for me against his stomach. Oh, that tight, flat, tanned stomach that I know he works so hard for.

I'm salivating just looking down at him.

This is the exact image that I just orgasmed to, except for one important thing.

He was in my pussy.

How easy it would be for me to put him there now.

I would place one knee on either side of his thighs.

I would place my lips on his to distract him, maybe bring his hands up to cup my breasts as my hip hovered over his.

As he was busy with two of his favorite things, I would slowly lower myself straight down, until his tip caressed over my clit and slid through the wetness he already created there. Down until it nestled right at my waiting entrance—

Nope.

No, just no.

Jesus. What am I even thinking?

I take a step back, trying not to let the crazy in my head show. I look wildly around me until my eyes fall on a discarded bikini bottom draped over a chair just to my right. I snatch it up and pull it on. It's still damp and the material sticks to every part of me as I drag it onto my body, the cold, clammy nylon a sufficient wet blanket for the fire between my legs.

"Everything all right?" Avery asks, having just watched my little display of madness with curious concern.

"Yup. Everything's fine."

And it is. I have a plan.

I take the few steps back to the sofa and crouch down between his lazily spread knees, tucking the entrance in question safely away from any threat of penetration.

I take his cock in both hands and land my tongue down on his tip, giving him my sexiest eyes as I peek up at him from behind his cock, from underneath my wild hair.

"Love," he starts, his hands sliding down his thighs toward me as if he's going to stop me.

As freaking if.

I suck his tip into my mouth, and his hands curl into fists instead. A little smile perks the corners of my mouth as I revel in the power I have over him.

If men ever actually thought they were in charge, I have news for them.

I slide his tip further into my mouth, twirling my tongue over the hard shaft as I grip his base tightly with my hands. He tastes just exactly like Avery, salty and sweet. The scent of his skin still invades my senses, causing my brain to short circuit. I dive into my task like I'm on a scuba mission.

"Fuck, Franny, that feels so good."

I don't even flinch at the little nickname that's been escaping his lips more and more over the last few weeks. I kinda don't mind it so much anymore. The idea that he calls me that name in his mind—a name that only he is allowed to even think—well, it's kinda special. Hot, even.

Romantic?

Stop, girl.

I tip my head forward and tap the back of my mouth with his tip to chase that thought out of my mind.

Nothing romantic going on here.

"You're perfect. You're doing so great, love."

I ram his tip at the entrance to my throat harder at his words, trying desperately to distract myself.

"You keep going just how you like," he says in his tortured voice.

I can feel the *but* coming, and I wait for it.

"But if you want me to be a little rough, just let me know."

The words send a shiver down my spine.

I mean, I love getting it rough—during other kinds of sex. But with him in my mouth? I'm nervous and excited at the thought. No one has ever taken charge of me like that before.

How rough would he be?

How far would he go?

The devil on my shoulder is telling me to go for it. I mean, I was two seconds away from offering my virgin pussy to this guy, why not compromise and give him my virgin throat?

I nod up at him before I can talk myself out of it, his dick still as far inside my mouth as I've dared to take it so far. Our eyes meet, and his flash with desire. I hope mine do, too.

He makes no move to start ramming his cock down my throat, so I look back down to the task at hand, literally, and keep up my action of pulling him in and out of my mouth, up and down my tongue. I have a firm grip on his base, and I pump him in the slickness of my own spit as he slides between my lips.

When I start to feel the creep of his hand on the back of my head, I try not to stiffen with excitement and anticipation. I keep myself soft and flexible under his strong palm.

His fingers curl into my loose hair, and the pull is a shot of delicious pain.

"Keep breathing, love."

I suck a long, slow breath in through my nose.

"Yeah, there you go." He presses my head just enough to tap the same place at the back of my mouth that I'd been tapping a moment ago to keep from thinking romantic thoughts.

Perfect.

This is going to be just the distraction I need.

"You ever done this before?" he asks in his gentle, caring voice.

Damn it, why can't he stop being so sweet and fuck my throat already!

I shake my head as best I can with his cock lodged in my mouth.

His grip on my hair lifts me right off said cock, forcing me to face him.

His eyes hold such a dangerous blend of desire and caring that I can hardly stand it. I try to look away, but he holds my head steady.

"I'll go slow, and you can stop me anytime by tapping your fist on my thigh. Got it?"

I nod, the action sending the same sharp pain from my scalp straight to my no doubt dripping pussy.

"Do it," he says, his voice lowering into a rough whisper I hardly recognize.

I clench my clammy palm into a fist and tap it on his thigh just above the knee.

"Good girl."

Oh god.

"Now open up."

I obey, obviously, and my head travels back down to his lap, mouth first, faster than I was expecting. He fills me quickly and then pulls me back off of him.

"Fuck, you're so damn sexy. How am I going to last a single second of this?"

I can tell he's just talking to himself, so I don't bother trying to respond. Not that I could anyway.

Down I go onto his cock again, this time slightly better prepared. I suck at him as he slides through my mouth, inhaling right at the moment his tip touches the top of my throat.

"Good girl," Avery murmurs again.

I squeeze my eyes closed, insane with the pleasure of pleasing him.

The next time his cock touches my throat, it breaches just a bit.

It takes a bit more concentration to keep from gagging, but I pull it off.

The next thrust goes even farther. My naïve plan of staying calm goes out the window as my body's reflexes take over and try to dislodge the invader from my throat. I flush with embarrassment at the gagging sounds coming from my own mouth, but Avery practically growls with pleasure above me, so I try to let it go.

My eyes are brimming with tears I can't control. They spill down my cheeks and hit the corners of my mouth in salty rivers, mixing with the taste of him and blurring my vision.

My swallow reflex is on high alert, closing fruitlessly around his tip over and over, eliciting noises from the man's mouth that don't even sound human.

It's me causing those sounds. Fuck, it's so hot. He's using my body for pleasure in the dirtiest possible way, and I love it. I am completely out of control here, and I'll be damned if I'm not about to come again, just from the idea of being his fuck toy.

I let out a small moan as he slides past the clenching top of my throat, the feeling so foreign it's all I can focus on for a second. The moment passes, and I'm still alive, so I take another slow breath through my nose.

Instead of pulling out to thrust again, Avery slides himself farther into me.

His grip on my hair is as tight as ever, leaving me no way to lift my own head, but my eyes flutter up toward his lap, dislodging a whole new river of tears.

He's so deep.

"Fucking hell, girl," Avery growls as he presses himself a bit deeper, then slides out an inch, only to press back in.

The feeling of him filling my throat is the most visceral experience of my life.

All of my senses are on high alert, every instinct in my being screaming out warnings about imminent death. There's so much adrenaline in my bloodstream right now, I could probably lift a car.

I keep breathing, keep crying, my throat spasming uncontrollably as it tries desperately to keep me alive. Avery pumps his tip in and out of me a few inches at a time, growling and moaning like a goddamn maniac.

All I can do is hold on. At one point, when he's been in there for what feels like forever without giving me a break, my brain tells me to tap out. I give him a warning sound, the low, strangled moan the only one I can manage. I am a millisecond from bringing my fist to his thigh when he contracts.

I know he would still pull out, even in the middle of his orgasm, if I was to give him the fist signal, but I don't.

I know somewhere deep in my rational brain that I'm not actually going to die. I can hold on.

And boy, is it worth my effort.

Avery is gripping my hair so hard I wonder if some of the liquid I feel running down my temples is blood.

The fiery feeling of him owning me like this keeps me so focused on his body—I get to experience his pleasure through him.

He's deep in my throat, so deep that I can't taste a drop of what I know must be shooting straight into my stomach. As he spasms, his tip slides in further than it has before, further than he dared to press on his own volition, his thrusts overtaken by the throes of ecstasy.

I am fully suspended in time and space, the life preservation chemicals flooding my system. But with nowhere for them to go, nothing to actually fight off, they simply pool between my legs.

Just when I think I can't take another second, as the excitement and interest of getting to feel Avery's orgasm inside my skull wears off, he pulls out.

He releases my hair as he collapses back onto the sofa.

I lose sight of him as my eyes flood anew with gallons of salty tears. I swallow over and over and over, so many times that it starts to sting, and I place a hand on my chest to try to help myself regulate my own breathing. To calm myself down enough to actually take a full breath.

When my throat finally accepts the fact that the invader is gone and it can stop trying to save me, I get the breath I've been waiting for. It's long and slow, deliciously cool against my raging hot skin. I wipe my arm over my face, clearing away some of the tears and sweat, hoping that the eye makeup I foolishly put on before boarding the plane in the States isn't too much of a mess.

After what feels like an eternity, I look up at him.

And have to look away almost immediately.

The man is worshiping me with his eyes like I'm the savior come to earth. His expression glows with what cannot be called anything but freaking love. His mouth ticks up at the sides in that adorable Avery half smile that I find myself searching for all the time.

He's perfect. He's everything.

And he's mine.

Nope. Not mine.

Let's just stick with the perfect thing, okay?

The man is perfect. I already knew that. He's perfect, and he's going to continue to be perfect forever, and I'm just going to have to deal with that fact once he's moved on to whatever comes next for him.

"Fucking hell, girl."

I can't help but smile as his words draw my mind out of its doom spiral.

"Yeah?" I say this because I can't think of anything else right now.

"Um, yeah."

"That was…a lot." I finally find a few words and offer them up with a timid smile.

"Too much?" he asks, his lovely face falling with concern.

"No, no," I say quickly. "Not too much. Well, maybe a bit too much, but not in a bad way."

His eyes narrow as he decides whether to believe me or not.

"I am so turned on right now. I'm sitting in a puddle."

All thoughts of my wellbeing fly out the window with that statement. Before I know it, he has me under the armpits and is tossing me on the couch next to him stripping my wet bikini bottoms off.

I let out a surprised laugh as he licks my slit from asshole to clit. But I don't know why I'm surprised. He moans in pleasure, and I laugh again.

"What can I do for you right now?" he asks, peeking up at me from between my legs.

"Fill me," I say, the words flying out of my mouth before I can consider them.

Avery's hand slips back to my tight hole, where he's accustomed to fucking me and starts to work me there.

"No," I say, taking his hand with my own and dragging it back up to the ragingly wet entrance to my pussy. "Here."

He cocks his head and narrows his eyes at me.

"With your hands or…whatever."

Avery bites his lip and considers me for a long moment. I know I just gave him an impossible decision, but I wanted it off my own shoulders. I can't decide what I should do, so I'll let him.

I'm not sure what I'm hoping to get out of that move, but he definitely decides on hands.

I'm not disappointed. Well, maybe a little, but it's for the best.

But those hands…it's impossible to be disappointed for long.

I get the first two fingers along with his lips sucking my clit into his mouth, a signature Avery move that always makes me scream.

I can feel him smile when I do without even having to look down.

A third finger enters me, stretching my body open, as his thumb lands on my clit, roughening up the play a little. I suck in my breath and arch my back as he presses into me with all parts of his hand, his mouth hovering just over the action, blowing softly on my exposed nerves.

"More," I say, although the voice definitely doesn't belong to me.

He takes that to mean more fucking, and I don't complain. However many fingers are now pumping in and out of me are the perfect number, filling me and satisfying my every fantasy… until they're not.

"More," I moan again at him.

Avery doesn't let up on his penetration of me, but I can feel his attention become divided. When I hear the telltale rip of a condom wrapper, I almost look up to see what he's doing.

Instead, I squeeze my eyes closed.

I let him decide.

Whatever he decides is fine. It's perfect.

No, it's not.

Just as I feel the larger object touch down next to his fingers at my entrance, I tense up. "Avery, I—"

"It's not me, love. It's okay."

I catch his eyes, and he's calm. He's telling the truth. I hold his gaze as whatever he just wrapped in a condom slides deliciously into my body. I bite my lip at the feeling of fullness, and he mimics my expression, sucking his beautiful lip into his mouth and biting down as he pulls whatever it is out and presses it back inside me.

I glance down, but all I can see is a flash of green pumping in and out of my spread pussy. I should have known he wouldn't let me down. He found a way to fill me, and right now, that's enough. I'm sure I'll learn what the object is soon enough. Right now, I'm squeezing my eyes closed and pretending it's that gorgeous cock pushing in and out of me.

"Harder," I manage.

He obliges me, fucking my body with his hand and whatever helper he's employed. I can feel his face grow closer to my clit as his breath lands down first, and I brace myself, knowing damn well that I'm not going to last ten seconds once his tongue starts.

Not with the fantastic fullness of his motion.

Not with the forbidden fantasy playing out behind my clenched eyelids.

Just a little tickle of his tongue, and I'm coming so hard I can't even cry out.

My core clenches, and I nearly sit up with the contraction, but I don't open my eyes. I come long and hard with his hardness inside my pussy, the friction of that stiff length giving my body all the action it needs to wring itself out completely.

When I collapse back onto the couch, I feel him slide out of me.

Still, I don't look.

I just pretend.

Avery tucks himself beside me, shoving me over until we are side by side on the much too narrow sofa, over and under each other in a tangle of sweaty limbs.

When I can't stand it anymore, I break the silence. "What was that?"

Avery huffs into my chest, where he pressed his face. "I could ask you the same thing."

I lift just a bit so I can catch a glimpse of his face. "What do you mean?"

He looks up at me for a moment and then shakes his head and tucks back into the side of my breast. "You know what I mean."

I do know exactly what he means, and the shame being called out is nearly too much. "I'm sorry."

He props himself on an elbow and really looks me in the eye. "You don't need to be sorry, love. That was all amazing. But you can't possibly expect me to sheath up and fuck you without even talking about it first. Not after all you've told me."

I nod, words escaping me.

"I mean, if that's what you're ready for, we can certainly talk—"

"I'm not," I say quickly before I convince myself to say the opposite.

Avery just nods. "Okay. I didn't think so."

He tucks back in, and it's not long before he's asleep.

Perfect. Now I can lay here, stuck beneath him, and ruminate over how stupidly I just acted. Well, almost acted.

I can't believe how close I was to giving it up just then. If he hadn't been the level-headed one, we would have had real, actual sex.

Would that have been so bad? Really?

Yes. Yes, it would have.

I mean, I do understand that it's a bit crazy to be holding onto this one thing for so long. To be waiting for some undetermined date or criteria before I go all the way there. But the fact that it's been so many years, and I have waited, just makes it seem all the more important.

It started as fear. Back in middle school, before I was ever in a position to be worrying about such things myself, one of my sister's friends got pregnant. It really scared me. Listening to what she went through, how her life changed. I just knew that wasn't for me. I couldn't live with the kind of shame she was having put on her. I couldn't have my own family members have to "deal" with me the way hers did.

Not a year later, another of my sister's school friends got pregnant, and it was the same situation.

When I was in high school, three of my own friends had big scares. One of them ended up going secretly to the big city with her mom to get an abortion. She came back a different person.

My own sister got pregnant when she was twenty and gave up her lifelong dream of being a concert pianist to marry her boyfriend and settle down.

So, while I understand that logically, the condoms and IUDs

are pretty safe, it's never been enough for me. I have too much on the line. I'm not giving up my life.

But I almost just did.

The gravity of this moment rests heavily on my chest, and I let out a long sigh.

Avery, the far too observant man who always has me in his sights, pops one eye open. "Big sighs coming out of you, twinkle toes."

I smile at the funny nickname and snuggle in deeper. "Yeah. I'm just happy to be home."

"Franny, you don't fool me for a second. I let you slide by on all of the excuses not to talk you throw around because I can totally understand not wanting to talk about things, but I know there's more going on."

I wait for him to ask a more specific question so I can answer it, but he doesn't.

I write the whole thing off in my mind as some kind of homecoming craziness. Maybe jetlag.

Yeah, jetlag. That's probably it.

I shift toward Avery to tell him, but he's already drifted off to sleep. It's for the best. He has this uncanny ability to see right through my bullshit—and call me on it. That's the last thing I need right now. We are in the home stretch of wedding planning, and I need to keep my focus there.

My hopeless love story might be a lost cause, but the wedding needs to be epic.

Rule #24

POWER LOOKS GOOD ON YOU

FRAN

Three weeks later, I wake to the golden dawn, groggy and stiff from spending the whole night tucked over, under, and around Avery on my sofa after yet another wild, passionate night. There's no way to not wake him as I rhinoceros myself off the couch.

He smiles up at me. "It's game time."

He could not be more correct.

The last few months have been spent planning, measuring, casually talking with people about plans, sketching out ideas, choosing cocktails. Now, with only a week left until the big day, it's literally game time.

The energy of the resort is different as we make our way out of the sex cocoon that is my hotel room and down to the lobby.

Sam and Ben are both waiting there, making me extra happy that I took the time to properly shower and gather all of my official-looking wedding planning items before being chased out of the room by the golden god himself.

Who, by the way, looks and smells amazing because I

happened to have a full outfit of his in my laundry. I even fixed his hair after the shower. He has a bit of a faux hawk, and it's all I can do to keep from grinning every time I look at him.

Professional, Franny.

"Morning," we exchange all around.

Avery and I snag paper cups of coffee from the cart next to the front desk, and then we're all walking. We pass a doorway, and Dom steps out, joining our group as we head toward the pool patio for a full run through meeting.

Questions are coming my way, and I'm fielding them like a pro.

I'm in charge. I am so freaking in charge, and it feels incredible. The five of us empty out next to the pool, stopping to admire the mango-wood trim Avery and I added around the roll-up door where Cynthia will be making her first appearance.

"We have a final count?"

"A hundred and six. It ended up being more gluten-free than expected, but I already sent those final numbers to Dom." I nod at the man, and he nods back. A thrill shoots through me at the power exchange. "But that's not a huge concern, considering that the meal is almost entirely gluten-free anyway. The vegans are another story."

"We have a plan for them. Did you decide about gluten-free cake?" Dom asks.

I nod. "Yeah, we're going to have a selection of the corn flour cookies from Ava's Bakery, along with the option of the ice cream that we planned for kids, so if they want dessert, they'll have those to choose from. Honestly, though, they're all adults, so I'm not expecting anyone to be expressly put out by not having a special allergy-friendly cake made for them."

Nods all around.

"I think the biggest thing we need to go over right now is table set up so we can get a plan in writing that can be distributed to the team who's going to be setting things up the day before."

"You don't want to wait for your brother and the bride to get here before we finalize all that?"

It feels totally surreal to think that Avery and I will be picking them up at the ferry dock in less than a day.

I shake my head. "I've been keeping Cynthia and my mother in the loop about some of the plans, but she still insists on being surprised by most of it. As for the structure of the party itself, we've made the best decisions for how that's going to flow, so we're going with it."

The meeting continues to go well, with the four resort owners following me around, nodding at everything I say.

I thought that party back in October when I got fucked by a masked stranger in a mysterious mansion on a tiny island was the hottest thing that ever happened to me, but honestly, this is giving that memory a run for its money.

I'm alive and firing on all cylinders. I know everything. I have a plan and an answer for every question. I'm the boss. I'm the queen.

This wedding is going to go great.

Now I just have the family to deal with.

Rule #25

PARTY'S OVER

AVERY

When we wake up the next morning, Franny is a whole new creature.

I lay, still naked, on the bed and watch her try to curl the ends of her hair for the millionth time, the humidity foiling her plans and drawing her ire.

"What the fuck..." she mutters under her breath as the latest strands fall flat against her back, not a curl in sight.

"Come back to bed, love."

She whirls to face me, a Tasmanian devil of nerves, now all directed toward me. "I can't go back to bed. I have to get ready."

I hold up my hands in surrender, holding my smile in, luckily.

She's been like this all morning, freaking out about her brother and his fiancée's arrival. Her mother, Frederick, and the rest of the family and guests won't be here till next week, but the love birds booked their room a bit early to relax before the big day.

My little bird is freaking out about their arrival in a way I hadn't expected.

"You look amazing," I say, coming up behind her in the bathroom, catching her eyes in the mirror.

"I can't believe you're not even dressed."

With a sigh, I retreat and start following the trail of discarded clothing until I have all my clothes from the night before. "You know, if you really want to be ready for their visit, you could pick up some of this stuff."

The trail of complicated, hyper-specific girl mess that covers most surfaces of this room is comical and mysterious. I often find myself reading the backs of bottles when Fran is otherwise occupied, just to find out what all this shit is for.

She flies around the corner, eyes wild. "What do you mean?"

I open my mouth to answer, but I don't need to. Her panicked gaze is no longer shooting daggers into me, it's floating around the room, taking in all of her stuff. She figures out exactly what I mean. "Oh my god! I have to clean this place up!"

Great job, Ave.

As if she wasn't freaked out enough.

"I got it, okay? You just keep…curling. Or primping…" I trail off as she disappears back into the bedroom.

There's a good reason for her tiny items to be piled all over the various counters and tables—there really isn't much storage in the room.

I decide to put it all in one of the kitchen cupboards. Relocating the only thing inside—a blender—to another cupboard, I start carrying the bottles and tubes and sunglasses and purses and snacks and trinkets into the kitchen and lining them up on the shelves.

Once the whole living room is clear, I look around in satisfaction. Then I pick up the shiny white room phone.

"Good morning, front desk, this is Julia, how can I help you?" the cheerful voice chirps out on the other end of the line.

"Morning, Jules. It's Avery."

"Oh, good morning, sir. How can I help you?"

"I'm in a friend's room, two seventeen, and she's got some important guests coming. Could you send the housekeepers up now? We are just about to head down to Reef. If they could be in and out in thirty, that would be ideal."

"No problem at all, sir. I'll send them up now."

"You're a jewel."

She laughs on the other end, and I hang up smiling.

Fran appears and looks around the now clear living space in surprise. "Where is everything?"

"I put it away."

She opens her mouth and closes it, narrowing her eyes at the now empty coffee table as if it somehow stole her stuff.

"And the housekeepers are on the way up to clean and do the bedding and stuff. So, grab your phone and let's go get breakfast."

She nods. "I'm ready."

This girl is always a stunner, but right now? She could murder me, and I wouldn't complain.

She's traded in what I've come to know as her signature beach babe look of tousled long hair, short dresses, and flip-flops, golden skin free of makeup, for a more urban look—tight, high waisted dark denim shorts and black tank tucked in, hair half up, face painted to magazine worthy perfection.

This must be what she looks like in her real life.

I have a sudden twinge of pain at the thought that I don't really know this girl at all. That we're just a vacation from her actual life.

I push through the hurt and rise to my feet. I have not dressed up. My signature beach bum attire is not a vacation look, and I have zero intention of changing it for these people.

Slipping my hand into hers, I pull her to me. She holds herself stiffly, no doubt protecting the hair and makeup that just took her over an hour to complete, and I give in, letting our clasped hands drop between us.

She holds tightly to my hand all the way to the elevator and for the whole glorious ride. As the doors open, however, she drops it.

Rule #26

YOU CAN'T RUN FROM YOUR PROBLEMS (BUT YOU CAN TRY)

AVERY

They're already here, of course.

I don't know why I expected anything different with how this morning has gone so far. Fran spots them as we walk into Reef and freezes. Then, as I've seen her do before, she transforms into a big smile and carefree attitude.

I follow her over to their table, dread growing with each step.

"You're here!" She's bright and chirpy but doesn't sound like herself at all.

"Yeah, of course we're here. We flew in last night."

"I thought you were coming on Thursday. Today. We were going to go down to the dock and meet your boat."

"Wednesday the fourteenth, Jellybean. It's always been Wednesday. You need to get a planner or something. I can show you how to work the calendar on your phone if you want."

This fucking guy.

"I know how to work my phone calendar," Fran mutters, face turned toward the ground.

I've had just about enough, and they've only been here for two fucking minutes.

I step forward, blocking Fran slightly with my body. "Avery," I say, putting out my hand.

The man takes it with eye contact so direct that I'm transported back to Harvard. It's been a while since I met someone with so much to prove.

"Of course you are. Jeez, it's like someone did an AI mashup of Frederick and one of those surfer guys from *Endless Summer*."

I stumble for a moment, trying to decide if he meant that as a compliment or a dig. Before I can speak, he goes on.

"Leonard. You can call me Leon. It's nice to finally meet you. You know, when your father showed up and married Mom, I thought I was getting a brother out of the deal."

Dig, then. Definitely a dig. "Oh, yeah. Sorry if he gave you the wrong idea."

Leon narrows his eyes slightly, probably trying to decide if I'm sneaking in a dig of my own. He recovers nicely. "This is Cynthia, my lovely bride-to-be." He steps back, and the woman still seated at the table comes into view, with her short, curly blonde hair and pale, freckled skin. I make a mental note to remind Fran to keep this woman covered in SPF 100 until the big day.

Wow, Avery, since when do you worry about women's skincare?

Since Franny here needs a perfect wedding, that's when. And a perfect wedding requires a non-lobster bride.

She rises and smiles the polite, closed-lipped smile of society. I take her offered hand and bring perfectly painted pink nails to my lips.

"It's a pleasure to meet you."

Her smile softens a bit. "Will you two join us?"

I look to Fran, who's still wearing her Bloomingdale's mannequin smile, before accepting. "Sure."

Everyone shuffles so that Leon and Cynthia sit side by side at the rectangular table, leaving Fran and I to sit across from them. I make a point to take the seat opposite Leon, instinctively feeling the need to block Fran from whatever energy this guy is putting off that's making her shut down like this.

The server shows up when we're settled, and we order coffee and eggs.

"I can't wait to walk the grounds with you and hear what you've been up to," Cynthia has perked up a bit since being sequestered to the girl's side of the table. I let the two of them sink into wedding talk and focus my attention on the man in front of me.

"I've heard a lot about you," I say, a bit awkwardly, but I can't think of anything else.

"You're joking, right?"

Er…

"You literally just learned that we existed, what, three months ago? I, on the other hand, have been hearing about you for almost ten years."

"Oh. Yeah, I guess—"

"You're like a legend."

"Well, I don't know—"

"Seriously, man. This is so cool. When Franzeska told us you were here helping with the wedding, I didn't believe her. I figured she was full of shit. But here you are."

"You figured what?"

"That she was just making it up."

"Why would you—"

"She does that sometimes. Makes shit up."

"I do not, Leon," Fran cuts in from beside me.

"The men are having a conversation over here, Franny. Stick to your girl talk. It doesn't concern you."

"You're talking about me and saying things that aren't true. I would say that concerns me."

"Whatever," the man replies, looking down at his coffee.

"No, not whatever. You can't just say something like that

without any evidence. Name one time that I have just made something up. One time!"

"Jeez, Jellybean, don't freak out. It's not a big deal. You're making a scene."

Franny is simmering with rage beside me, and yet…she's going to let it go.

I want to punch the guy right in his fucking mouth.

I'm rising out of my seat, a few carefully chosen words on the tip of my tongue, but Fran pulls me back down with a firm hand on my shoulder. When my butt hits the seat, I look over at her.

No, her eyes say.

Goddamn it.

Biting my lip, I turn back to Leon. "You look pretty fit, Leon. You like to run?"

Get the man alone and stage an accidental death falling off of a cliff onto the ocean rocks.

Unfortunately, Fran sees right through me and cuts in again. "Cynthia and I were just talking about the menu, and I thought it would be fun to take them into town so we can eat at Kuramo's and meet the grill masters who'll be cooking at the wedding." She's back to her bright cheerful self, and for some reason, that makes me even angrier.

I'm angry that she's not angry.

"Not tonight, we have plans," I hear myself saying.

Fran's head turns sharply, and her eyes bore into the side of my face. "We do?"

"Yeah," I reply, not elaborating since I have no idea yet what those plans are. All I know is that we are not spending the evening with these two. "Besides, I'm sure Leon and Cynthia want to rest and recover from their flight."

"We got in yesterday," Leon says.

"Jetlag," I reply, looking him right in the eyes, daring him to argue with me.

"Yeah," he says. "I am still pretty tired, and I know Cynthia is, too." He doesn't glance over at his bride-to-be as he speaks.

Which is just as well, she doesn't seem inclined to argue with him. "And I'm dying to get into that pool."

Breakfast is a pretty quiet affair.

We escape soon after, Fran following me out the doors and up the outside stairs, not catching up or saying a word until we reach the elevator in the lobby. I feel her warm presence next to mine as we wait. Close but not touching.

When the doors finally swing open, I stalk in and lean against the back wall, arms crossed across my chest, feeling like a toddler throwing a tantrum compared to her cool, calm demeanor.

And she was the one getting gaslighted down there for fuck's sake.

"That guy's a dick."

Fran laughs and curls into me, resting her cheek on my shoulder. I relax my arms down and swing one around her back.

"Yeah."

"You just take that from him?"

She shrugs. "What am I supposed to do? Getting more hysterical when someone accuses you of being hysterical only proves them right. I learned long ago that arguing is futile."

"When you told me that they all make fun of you, I had this picture in my mind of you fighting back."

"Yeah, well. You got that wrong."

Goddamn motherfucking—

"What are we doing tonight?" she asks.

"Escaping," I say, a plan already forming.

When I glance down at Fran, she raises her eyebrows.

"Go get an overnight bag packed. Meet me in the lobby in twenty. We need to go pick something up for the wedding on another island."

The elevator door dings open on her floor, and I push her out. She turns in the hallway, her face filled with questions, but I just give a little wave as the door closes between us.

Rule #27

CAREFUL. YOU'RE STARTING TO BELIEVE IT

FRAN

"Where are we going?"

I'd like to say that I speak the words while refusing to get into the waiting helicopter, but that's not how it goes. I let Avery lead me down to the launch pad and settle me into the seat farthest from the door. All the while having no idea where this whirlybird is taking me.

"San Pedro."

"Belize?" I exclaim, the answer more surprising than I expected—even from Avery.

"Yup."

"You're taking me to another country? Just like that? I didn't bring my passport."

"It'll be fine."

Of course it will. Why would I even question him? Have I ever seen a closed door when walking hand in hand with this man?

The pilot greets Avery like an old friend and gives me enough direction to make me feel comfortable, and then we're off. I watch the island get smaller and smaller, and then it's ocean in all directions.

"Why are we going to Belize so suddenly?" I have a feeling I already know, but I'll be damned if this man is getting off the hook without saying the words aloud.

"I just had to get away from that guy."

"That guy is my brother."

"Yeah, and he's a bit of a tool."

"That doesn't mean we run."

"What would you have done? Given them a tour of the resort while he criticized everything you said?"

"I mean, yeah. Probably."

"Vetoed."

"I'm still going to have to do that when we get back. We can't hide in Belize forever."

"Oh, love, that's where you're wrong."

"The wedding, Avery."

"Well, I guess we'll go back for that."

I shake my head and turn toward the window, not feeling like continuing to battle this out. The pilot told me that we'd be in the air for just under two hours, so I settle in for the ride. Avery snuggles in beside me, and when I glance over, I see him starting to doze off.

"Avery!" I exclaim, tapping his chest.

He jumps to attention, grinning at me. "What?"

"How can you sleep right now?"

A casual shrug. "Seems like a pretty good time to sleep, actually."

I shake my head and turn back to the window. The horizon is hard to follow with no land mass in sight, so I focus on the water below.

I can see when we fly over sections of reef, the water tuning a pale aqua and the bottom nearly visible. We then cross over deeper ocean, and the water sinks into a dark, nearly blackish, blue.

The surface wind creates little white caps that stand out in contrast to the dark ocean, and at one point I think I spot a group of whales. When I turn to point them out to Avery, I find him fast asleep. Rolling my eyes, I continue my task of single-handedly keeping the helicopter in the sky with my own attention and anxiety.

By the time we land, I'm feeling a lot calmer, and if I'm being completely honest, a little excited. No one has ever whisked me off to another country on a whim before, and I plan to make the most of it.

There's plenty of time for hotel tours and playing nice tomorrow.

We're taken by golf cart to a tiny little high rise a few blocks south of the bustling downtown. I get to see enough of the town to know that there are too many golf carts and a lot of things I'm dying to go back and see. One shop in particular caught my eye.

The condo is incredible, of course, fully stocked and ready for our arrival, even though the owner couldn't have had more than a few hours' notice. I stretch out on the bright yellow bedspread and take in the view. The ocean is different here than on Faraday. The waves don't break on the beach, and the tides bring in a lot of plant matter. It's still lovely, but I don't find myself dying to go for a swim.

"Swim?" Avery asks, reading my mind.

I shrug. "I don't know. The beach doesn't look quite as swimmable as home." I bite my lip as I realize the word I used to describe Faraday, hoping Avery won't catch it and give me too much shit.

If he notices, he lets it slide. "Pool?"

"Oh, yeah. Definitely pool."

We swap sweaty clothes for swimsuits and parade up the winding staircase to the rooftop pool. The view up here is even more epic and combined with the ocean air and brilliant blue sky, it has all the makings of paradise.

"Tell me you own this place," I say, closing my eyes and letting the sun hit me with its full power.

"It's here for us anytime," Avery replies, which is not an answer, but I decide to follow his lead and let things slide for the time being.

I slip into the water and let myself go straight under, all concern for my hair and makeup gone. As the stiff curls and gold eyeshadow wash away, leaving only the waterproof mascara behind, I slide back into myself.

When I surface, Avery is inches away, reaching for me. I allow myself to be pulled into his arms.

"Isn't this better than all that?"

"It's certainly different."

"Bah," he scoffs. "You don't mean that. It's better."

"It's better. But it didn't solve anything. Those people aren't going anywhere. The conflicts I have waiting for me are always going to be waiting for me."

"I think you're starting to get an idea of why I never went home again."

My ability to let things slide drifts away on the soft wake we create with the movement of our bodies. "I've always understood why you never went home again, Ave. I just...feel differently about family, I guess."

"You like the conflict? Those people terrorize you."

"They're my family. Things are hard sometimes, but they're good sometimes, too. We have history. That's how you build community for yourself. How you plant roots. By participating in the good and sticking around for the not so good. Everyone has their ups and downs."

He's not going to argue with me on this, I can tell.

I can also tell that I have in no way convinced him.

"We'll go back tomorrow," he finally says into my neck, his hands sliding lower as he drifts us closer to the edge of the pool.

"I know."

"And I'll try to be nice."

My feet find the tile bottom, and I push myself off his body, turning to face him with my hands on my hips. "You're damn right you'll be nice. That man is our client. Family relationships aside, it's our job to make him happy. Besides, I've never seen you be anything but kind to everyone we've ever encountered. You would seriously start your mean streak with my own brother?"

"No, no. I said I'll be nice. He's our client."

"And my family."

Avery says nothing to that. He reaches for my body again, and I let him pull me back without a fight.

"This isn't just about escaping our needy clients, anyway," Avery says into my wet hair, his chin resting on my shoulder as I float with my back in his arms.

"Hmm?" I ask. I know I'm about to be fed some line, but you know what? I'm hungry.

"No. I've been thinking about how many damn people are in the pool at The White Sands."

"Oh, really?"

"And how I never get to do this." His words accompany his hands as they slide my bikini bottoms down. I curl my legs, allowing him to pull them free with ease. He sets them on the side of the pool and reaches back between my legs with a soft caress.

I sigh with my entire body when he touches me, his warm hands contrasting with the cool water and kindling my fire.

"Yeah, we definitely need our own pool," I manage to get out as Avery presses deeper, deftly slipping inside me.

He's supporting my upper body, so I relax and let my legs drift apart. His fingers press even deeper as his other hand slips into one of the triangles of my bikini top.

I had a feeling that thing wouldn't last long. As soon as his hand is fully inside the wet fabric, he pulls up and slides it over my head.

"There we are. Just as nature intended."

I can't help but laugh at how ridiculously casual he is about all of this. Here I am, naked in a rooftop pool where anyone could walk out and see us, and Avery's making corny jokes.

I'm still distracted by his words when he surprises me by rotating us so that my chest is against the wall, his strong body pressing me into the blue tile. His fingers hold tightly to the walls of my pussy as he brings his hips forward and drags his erection the full length of my ass.

"Feels like that thing wants out," I say, folding my arms in front of me on the pool deck and resting my cheek against them.

"Nah," he replies, not letting up the motion of his fingers in and out of me, paired with his grind against my backside. "He's not in charge here."

"Oh?" I ask, a bit surprised by his words. "And who is?"

"Yeah, love. That's something we're going to have to figure out one of these days, isn't it?"

I raise my head and open my mouth to retort, but I'm already being lifted high on my thighs by two strong arms. My legs bend, and I use my arms to help me twist and come to a seat on the tile beside the pool.

"Lay back," he commands, giving a tug behind my knees to drag my bare butt to the very edge of the pool.

I obey, obviously, crossing one arm over my eyes to shield them from the afternoon sun. Avery presses my knees to the side and dives in headfirst. The touch of his tongue to my clit brings me upright with a gasp and a laugh.

"Avery, are you sure no one can see us?"

"I'm sure," he says, reaching up to press my body back down on the tile.

He does sound awfully sure, and I'm dying to ask how he knows, but his tongue and his fingers…I let it go.

With his free hand, he brings my heels up one at a time to rest on the interior ledge of the pool, taking the bend out of my lower back. I instantly relax into him even further, the leverage of my heels helping to tilt my pelvis forward.

"Mmm," he growls, tongue buried inside me.

I agree.

With his tongue traveling back up and around my bare clit, he finally gives me the full combination I've been aching for since this all started. He works my clit softly and quickly, while using his fingers to drag up and down my G-spot.

Sounds escape my mouth and float up into the open air, mixing with birdsong and sounds from the street below. This feels so decadently naughty, like we could be caught at any moment, even though Avery has assured me we won't be.

Somehow, just the thought of someone coming up here and catching us has me ramping up quickly.

The thought of someone seeing us—together.

I'm very close now, holding my breath as he pumps me faster.

The thought that he's mine.

And…that does it.

My hips buck forward as I tip over the edge. I don't need to announce myself. Avery always knows just when to pick up the pace and lay on the clit pressure. He works me deep and fast through my spasms of pleasure, growling at every cry that escapes my lips.

When I finally still him with a squeeze of my thighs around his head, he slips his fingers out so slowly, pressing one last kiss to my achingly sensitive skin.

I stretch my arms out beside me, lost in the aftermath of hormones and chemicals pumping through my bloodstream.

This might be it. I might have actually found paradise on earth.

The one place where I am really and truly happy and carefree.

The one place I can live peacefully forever.

Except that it's not mine.

And it can't last.

Jeez, Franzeska. Way to kill the vibe.

I roll halfway to one side and prop myself up on an elbow, looking for Avery.

He's just surfacing from the crystal-clear pool, tossing his head back to clear the water from his face like someone in an underwear commercial or something.

"Come back," I say, and he obeys, swimming back over to the edge of the pool and hooking his hands on the ledge beside me.

I curl forward until his face is close enough to kiss and do just that, my eyes closed tightly, pretending this is something that it's not.

With that fun thought fresh in my mind, I pull back from his lips and panic just a bit. "Your turn," I say, trying to sound cool and seductive.

Avery just smiles and swims off backward, never taking his eyes off me. "Nah," he says when he's a few feet away.

"I'm sorry, did you just say nah? As in you're turning down a poolside BJ?"

His feet find the bottom, and he stands, shoulders coming out of the water just enough for me to see him shrug.

I'm surprised and a teeny bit rejected, so I should say nothing, but obviously, I do. "I don't know how I feel about that. Should I be offended?"

Avery swims back over and brings his face close once more. "It doesn't hurt to get all riled up and have to wait sometimes. I kinda like it."

I open my mouth and close it, considering my next words. I don't want to sound like a complete dork, but I also want to know. "I thought, you know, that it could hurt." *Welp, dork.* "If you guys get hard, and then no one takes care of it. I thought that could cause problems."

Avery's face turns stern. "No. It does not need to be taken care of. And I swear to God, Franny, if you tell me who told you that it does, I am going to find that guy and punch him in the dick."

I laugh in surprise, my cheeks flushed with poorly concealed embarrassment at being called out on something I probably should have known was just a line. "Man, being a dick to my brother and now threatening bodily harm to someone? This is a whole new side of Avery."

He laughs and shakes his head, pushing off the side and drifting halfway across the pool. "You just bring something out in me."

"Something good?" I ask.

"You tell me. Do you like it?"

I nod.

Another shrug from Avery. "Me too."

Fuck! Fuck, fuck, fuck.

There are so many follow-up questions I want to ask, but I just can't bring myself to be that girl. Instead, I stand as sexily as I can on my unsteady legs, gather my wet heaps of swimsuit, and walk over to one of the gorgeous, cushioned chaise lounges.

There's no way to pull this wetsuit over my damp body without looking like a total fool, so I stretch out completely naked, trying to make it seem like I intended to do that all along.

As I expected, it doesn't take long for Avery to appear beside me. I sneak a glance at his wet, clingy shorts and find that the erection that was rubbing against my ass earlier is indeed starting to take care of itself.

"This town has some incredible restaurants," Avery says, seemingly unaffected by the emotional bombs dropped just moments before.

I try to follow suit. "I can't wait to try one. Also, I saw a shop I want to go in on the drive here." I've been dealing pretty well with shopping withdrawals but having cute new tropical weather clothes just a few blocks away is too tempting to pass up.

"Perfect. Head out in an hour or so?"

I nod and close my eyes.

When I open them with a start, I'm not sure how much time has passed. I glance over at Avery, who is solidly in a nap, and take a moment to watch him. His golden skin has dried in the sun, leaving him with just a glisten of sweat to make him sparkle slightly. I trace the lines of his tattoos like I always do, the shapes becoming as familiar as if they were my own.

After a full moment of ogling, I realize that he's asleep in the full sun and rise to angle the blue striped umbrella so that it shades him. Then I grab my suit and head for the stairs.

Rule #28

YOU KNOW HOW THIS ENDS

AVERY

I pat barefoot down the tile steps to the condo, still shaking off an epic nap. Coming in through the glass doors, I find Fran's suit draped over a chair in the dining room and hear the shower shut off.

Just as it's been every second since the first time I met her, I walk to where she is, the magnetic pull of her presence too strong to fight.

"Hey," she says, looking over at me with a smile as I come up behind her in the bathroom mirror. "I was just going to come wake you up."

I walk until I press against her, wrapping my arms around to pin hers to her chest and nuzzling my face into her clean, wet hair.

"Avery, you're getting me all sweaty!"

And…there's the erection.

She feels it and laughs, pulling away. "I thought you liked to wait," she teases, leaning over farther than she needs to lift her hairbrush from the counter.

"I do. Doesn't mean this guy gets the memo."

"Is that what you're wearing to dinner?"

I look down at my faded blue swim trunks and frown.

"Get dressed, okay? I'm hungry."

Well, we can't have that, can we?

I strip and shower, pulling on the only other clothes I brought with me—black shorts and a pale-green tee. Franny is already wearing a dress that I could slide my hands up in one motion, and so I do, making her squeal and run into the other room.

I chase but surrender when I find her braced against the door, hands holding the short skirt down.

"Dinner. Then whatever you have in mind, okay? I'm going to get mean if I don't eat."

I have a feeling she isn't referring to the good kind of mean, so I lead her out of the condo and down to the dirt street.

We're on the top floor of a yellow building just on the south side of town. It's only a block and a half before we're sharing the small space between the buildings and golf cart traffic with groups of other people, bikes, and dogs.

Fran never lets go of my hand, even when we have to go single file.

The red and white sign for El Fogon comes into view around a corner, and I pull her inside the open gate behind me.

"Good evening," greets a host I don't recognize.

"Hello. Two for dinner," I say with a smile.

"You're lucky you came early. We're full tonight, but I can sneak you in if you promise to be finished in an hour."

"No problem at all," I respond.

We follow the young man to a lovely table away from the dusty street with a great view of the open pits they use to cook the food.

As we settle into wooden chairs, Fran eyes the fire. "I am seeing a bit of a pattern forming here, Ave. You have a thing for fire?"

"I have a thing for barbecue, yeah. Every culture has their

own form of cooking meat outdoors over a fire, and I always find the best one everywhere I go."

"This is the best one here?"

"Best I've found."

When the server, an older man, arrives at our table, I order us shrimp, chicken, and steak to share. Fran jumps in to ask for a vegetable dish and a pina colada.

As it seems to happen with everything we do, everywhere we eat, every moment of my days now, we fall into a comfortable chatter, talking about the wedding and the town we're in and trading stories about past travels.

I am excited to hear that Fran has gotten to do some traveling with her family and with friend groups. She's been to Bali and Turkey. She took a school trip to Ireland and once took the Pacific Northwest Alaska ferry from Washington to Juneau by herself.

I tell her about swimming with sharks in Polynesia and freezing my balls off in Poland. The food arrives, and I get to watch her eyes dance over the glorious dishes, eating them up long before the food enters her mouth. We share the meats and veggies, serving each other and moaning with pleasure at the freshly cooked barbecue.

I stuff myself, and Fran doesn't, a common occurrence for us at meals. She has just one drink while I nervously sip down three old-fashioneds. I don't even know what I'm feeling so apprehensive about. All I know is that I got a taste of what it's going to be like to share this woman with people she knows, and I didn't like it. I want to go back to having her all to myself, all the time.

But that's not possible, is it?

She's on a stop-over from her life, doing this project with me tagging along. The expiration date on our relationship is stamped into my skin with invisible ink. The only problem is—I can see it. I can feel it. I want to scrub it from myself, but I don't know how.

"…ready?"

I snap back to attention and try to catch up. The waiter has returned the small rectangular bill tray with my change and Fran is sliding her chair back expectantly. I nod and sift through the bills, leaving a solid tip before standing and walking to her side of the table.

She doesn't need any help getting up, of course, but I take her hand anyway, guiding her to her feet and into my arms. "Where to now, love?"

"Shopping." The word rings out in a singsong tone, and her face lights up.

Suddenly, I'm inhaling to find my chest swelling with gallant determination. I will buy this woman each and every thing that she desires. I will provide for her and take care of her…

Ay yi yi, Ave. Getting a little carried away there, huh?

I can't help it. Some kind of instinct has kicked in that I'm powerless to fight.

"Lead the way."

It takes wandering around in circles for nearly half an hour before we finally decide to retrace the route the golf cart took from the dock to locate the shop Fran saw on the way to the condo earlier this afternoon.

I can see why she singled this one out. In a street lined with brightly lit storefronts filled with mostly the same touristy junk, this shop has a bit of an edge to it. The artfully crafted window display screams taste. And money.

We're greeted by a young woman and given the usual direction—take our time and let her know when we're ready to try things on. Fran is in heaven, and I follow close behind, absorbing the energy trailing behind her as she runs her fingers through racks of flowy pants and brightly colored dresses.

"What do you think of this?" She turns to me holding a black two-piece outfit—loose pants with a matching black crop top.

"Let's add it to the pile," I say with a smile.

When she's chosen her size in nearly half of the styles in the store, we follow the salesgirl down a short, dimly lit hallway to a circular bank of dressing rooms. Mirrors surround us, as well as hanging pendant lights that give the room a bright white glow.

Fran's dressing room is large and has a long bench, so she drags me inside as soon as the woman leaves us alone. I settle on the seat, leaning against the wall and watch her. The walls of the changing room are made entirely of mirrors, so from my seat I can see every angle.

I could get used to this.

Her long dark hair swings side to side as she pulls the dress over her head and hangs it on a hook, leaving only a black thong, so now I get to admire her shapely ass, breasts, and every other curve of her in the 360-degree mirrors.

"Did you bring me in here to torture me?" I ask with a soft laugh as she starts covering her lovely parts with the first of the fancy outfits.

A look tossed over her shoulder shows me smiling eyes. "Yeah," she responds simply.

I have to smile at that. The girl certainly knows how beautiful she is—and what an effect she has on me.

I'm once again struck by the contrast between this confident, wild creature and the one I got to meet at breakfast with her brother. I never in my wildest dreams would have expected Franny to just shut up and take it when faced with that kind of asshole behavior.

I guess that's what family does to you. It brings out the worst.

All the more reason to avoid those people like the plague.

But what she said about putting down roots, about sticking around for the good and the bad, really stuck with me. That's never been my MO. I am a short visit kind of guy—that way I never have to get into these complicated dynamics. When good will starts to wane, I'm out and onto the next place, where feelings are fresh and new.

After twenty years of this, I would have told you that I think it's a pretty good system. I never have to deal with people's hard feelings or navigate cohabitation conflicts. Three months ago, I would have told you that. But now? All I want is the cohabitation conflicts with this woman. I crave learning each and every thing about her, the good and the bad.

But I wonder if that's even true. If I've never been around someone long enough to get through the bad, do I even know what I'm signing up for?

I've had relationships in the past, short ones, but I consider them very successful.

I think it's a societal flaw to only give gold stars to the people who have stuck through relationships for decades. Short relationships can offer value to the people in them as well. You never have to fight, for one thing. You never have to deal with the grossness of people's messy lives. You just enjoy the honeymoon phase and then move on.

I've always appreciated the time I get with women.

I just head out when shit gets real.

I can't help but wonder now if the women I left behind would consider our relationships as successful as I always have.

I can't even imagine saying all of this out loud to this particular woman. I've been pinned under her sad, almost pitying gaze one too many times already. She thinks there's value in sticking around, even when things get tough or messy or not fun.

And, for the first time in my life, I am starting to see why she thinks that.

I want to stick with her forever.

It will be Fran and me, alone, no one else ever speaking to us or bothering us. For the rest of our lives.

"What do you think?"

Fran's voice pulls me out of my impossible fantasy.

She's standing with her hands on her hips, posing in a white two-piece—short flowy skirt with a wrap and tie crop top.

And fuck if that white dress isn't sending me into wedding fantasies.

What is wrong with me?

"I think you're going to have to take those undies off."

She glances behind her in the mirror, where the line of her black thong is clearly visible under the see-through fabric of her skirt.

I could bottle and mainline the look she gives me as she lifts the skirt and slips the thong down, tossing into my lap.

"Better?"

"Turn."

She does a slow spin, wiggling her hips as she goes to make the skirt sway side to side. I am able to keep eye contact with her the whole time in the mirrors. There's something there, something so poignant, but I just can't quite place it. She's back around and facing me before I fully grasp it.

"Looks amazing." I like them all. I have no idea why she's still asking for my opinion when it never changes.

"I got something for you, too."

I raise my eyebrows as she starts sifting through the hangers, looking for whatever she hid on the way in here. When she turns, she's holding two hangers. One contains a pair of cream linen shorts, the other a white short-sleeve button-down that I can see from here has white embroidery on the front. How the fuck she managed to pick these out and add them to the pile with my eyes never leaving her is beyond me. I don't argue as she holds them out, I just hang the garments beside me and start stripping down.

The clothes fit perfectly. I turn to face Fran where she has paused her own trying on clothing and stands watching me in the white dress. I button up the front of my own white shirt and hold her gaze. The look I saw before reflected in the walls of mirrors is now staring me straight on, but I still can't quite put a name to it.

Or maybe I'm just too chickenshit to try.

I finish with my shirt and step beside her, turning us so we stand side by side in the large mirror. I watch in our reflections as her hand snakes down and takes mine.

"Probably best not to choose these get-ups to wear to the wedding, huh?" I try to lighten the moment with a joke, but it falls flat.

I don't try again.

Fuck it. I won't dispel whatever this is. It can kill me if it must. I'll take it.

"You know what the saleslady would say?"

I glance down at Fran as she makes her own little joke. I wonder if she's feeling the weight of this moment as much as I am.

I nod. "That we're a beautiful couple." I want to smile, but I see my own reflection, and it looks more like my dog just died, but I'm trying to be a good sport about it.

It's what everyone says. They've been saying it since day one with us.

It just can't be true.

That's the hard fact of life.

Fran nods, holding my gaze in the mirror as she holds my hand.

"Do you want to try on the next one?"

She shakes her head, still not looking away.

"What do you want?" I don't think before I say the words, but I hear the desperation in my own voice. This is the real question. The one I want answered more than anything but have never been brave enough to ask.

Because I'm not ready for this to be over.

And I can't give this woman what it is she's going to ask for.

Or maybe she would reject me. Maybe I've gotten this all wrong after all. Honestly, that seems like the better option right about now. She can walk away, back to her real life, and I can send myself out to sea on a burning ship like a dead Viking.

Damn, Ave. Get it together.

Franny turns to me, her gaze falling to my chest. I feel her fingers on the button of the shorts, but I don't look away from her face as I feel them fall to the carpet beneath us. I step out and kick them to the side.

It seems she's decided to skip answering the question altogether.

I can't decide if it's mercy or not.

"Sit," she directs, pushing me back slightly until my bare ass is on the cool bench, back against the mirrored wall. She kneels before me, unbuttoning the white shirt slowly, still not catching my eye.

I watch her below me, I watch her in the mirror behind her, beside her. She's kneeling, bowed, intent on her task. The silence is deafening.

After finishing the buttons, she slides her hands into the shirt but doesn't remove it. Her warm palms caress over my chest and torso. I want to close my eyes and bask in the feeling of her touch, but I can't look away.

She reaches up to trail her fingers along both sides of my neck, her arms coming closer together and squeezing her breasts into a perfect crack of cleavage in the low-cut neckline of the white top. My fully bare cock starts to respond to all of this touch, all of this closeness.

Fran glances down at it and finally meets my eye. "This guy still waiting?"

I nod my head, feeling fairly sure that it'll grow an extra three feet just to strangle me in my sleep if I deny it any longer.

Her fingers find the sensitive skin on the underside, and I nearly choke on the breath I'm taking.

"So good to wait," she coos.

I smile to myself at her boldness, at whatever kind of character she's chosen to roleplay in this moment. She's so free and open when we're alone. It's not something I'm going to forget soon.

Her fingers drag up and down, alternating between soft

touches, soft nails, and firm little grasps at my tip when they reach it.

I breathe deeply and steadily. The last thing I want to do is come all over the carpet in the fancy room. The clothes are one thing—we can take those with us—but I don't want to explain any puddles to the shop owner.

Turns out, I don't need to worry.

I watch her in all of the mirrors as she lowers her soft lips to my tip, tongue darting out to lick the notch on the underside before it disappears between them into her mouth. She's leaning forward enough to nearly give me a peek under her skirt in the mirror across from us, and I focus my attention there.

"I can see up your skirt, love." The words come out strangled, and I laugh softly at my own unbridled desire.

She pauses her exploration of my tip and sits up a little, glancing over her shoulder at her own ass. She wiggles it and watches the white fabric expose her in flashes as it swings side to side. Then she reaches back and flips the whole thing up around her waist, baring herself completely.

I groan as the full view of her, head in my lap with my cock sliding into her mouth, mixes with her spread legs, bent over from behind. I can see the glisten of her arousal. I can see the tight hole where she always wants me to fuck harder. I can see her clit between the pink folds as she moves her knees to the side, settling her upper body further down in my lap, sliding my cock just a bit deeper into her mouth.

My eyes shoot back and forth between that mouth and the ass show, pleasure and amazement swirling inside me as this woman once again shows me that I know nothing.

I lose myself in the depths of her pussy once more when all of a sudden something starts to sneak in from between her legs. I watch, breath caught in my chest, as a red fingernail slides over her engorged clit and down her wet slit. She adds another finger, pressing them both inside her own body with a few slow pumps, dragging the wetness she finds there out and back up to her waiting nub.

As if her sucking my cock down like a starving person wasn't enough, she's now moaning on it, finger banging herself while I have a front-row view of the whole thing.

I watch her fingers deftly work her clit. I can feel her pulse rising in the arm braced against my knee, the hand gripping the base of my cock and feeding it in and out of her wet, hot mouth.

I can't even bring myself to care if she gets off first. I know I can always trade places and suck her into oblivion. Besides, I'm in no way controlling the speed of this situation. I'm strapped in and along for the ride.

Franny's driving the bus.

It's not the first time I've felt us heading straight over a cliff and done nothing to stop our free fall.

Her fingers perform perfectly for me and for herself, I can see her ramping up as she starts to swirl her own clit faster, harder.

My cock is grazing the back of her throat, the urge to take her hair in my fist and hold her head in place is nearly overwhelming. My hands rest at my sides in tight fists. She drives her mouth down as much as she can, gripping my base and digging into my rock-hard cock with the tip of her tongue as she makes each thrust.

This is how I might have imagined my own wedding day ending. The white dress, the blow job, the fierce, wild woman owning me like I'm her goddam pet.

If I had ever actually imagined my wedding day. Which I have not.

Until now.

Jesus fucking Christ.

In a desperate attempt to get out of my own mind, I bring a hand up and cup the back of her head. Fran responds by loosening her grip on my base and pressing her head into my hand.

Fuck.

I take the direction and slip my fingers into her wild locks, getting a full grip as I tilt my pelvis forward, driving into her now stationary mouth. I feel like an absolute madman, with dueling voices in my head shouting at me to look at my cock fucking her mouth and also to look at her own hands fucking that sweet, sweet pussy.

It's nearly too much to handle, and I catch myself trying to close my eyes several times, both voices in my mind agreeing that would be the worst move ever, and dragging my eyelids open.

"Franny, I gotta come, or I'm going to die. I'll finish you off after, okay?"

She makes some kind of noise. I don't know what I was expecting her to say with the tip of my cock lodged in her throat, but I have to take whatever she tried to communicate as a sign of agreement.

I focus on that pussy, spread and juicy before me, filled with her fingers, and start to careen into my home stretch.

"I'm coming down your throat, baby, just hold on." The words grunt out of me in a voice I don't recognize.

I let my gaze shift to her stretched mouth and up her gorgeous face. Her eyes spill with tears but hold my gaze with the same determination and love I saw there before this whole thing started.

I didn't mean love. I meant lust. Lust.

Fuck.

I love you.

The words sit on my lips as I tip over the edge, holding her beautiful head steady as I empty into her, my tip just far enough passed her gag reflex and into her throat to feel my seed going down and not pooling in her mouth. Her throat spasms through swallows as the liquid invades, and the pulsing squeeze of the muscle unlocks a whole new level of my orgasm, sending me into darkness as I cry out and hold her tighter.

I'm gasping for air and concerned about my sudden loss of

vision when the wave finally passes, and I am able to think clearly, realizing that I had just closed my eyes.

I rip them open as the final throes of ecstasy rise from my shaft to my groin to my aching, sweaty body, and focus back on Franny's pussy. Her hand is gone now, I can feel both sets of nails digging into my thighs where she braced herself for my orgasm.

That pussy is wide open and waiting for me.

I lift her head off of my cock in one smooth motion. The cold air rushes over my drenched lap and sends goose bumps skittering over my body.

I don't give her a second to recover, simply pressing her down on the floor and crawling over her body. I find her mouth and invade, searching for my own taste. I find it and lick the salty remnants from her tongue.

My hand finds her wetness and slips inside, following the path laid for me by her own fingers. A few more long, desperate kisses, and I'm dragging myself away, slipping down her body and burying my face between her legs.

She's gotten herself pretty worked up already, so when my tongue touches down, I can feel her core buck up to meet me.

No need to start slow this time.

I press her favorite three fingers into her soft, waiting body, and curl them inward. The flat of my tongue introduces itself to her clit, and I follow the moans of pleasure around each side, swirling and flicking until she stops making any noise and braces.

I hold my position, moving consistently in the same back and forth, in and out pattern, until her breath finally comes rushing out, and she curls inward as she comes.

I keep it up, holding her on her back as spasms overtake her, licking the sweet nectar of her orgasm as it's offered to me.

She holds on to the orgasm so long that I'm impressed, as always, finally stilling me with her thighs and collapsing against the floor of the dressing room. I take one last lick, smiling at the jolt it sends through her body, before slipping my fingers out and sitting back on my heels.

Before either of us have caught our breath enough to speak, there's a soft knock on the door.

I grin down at Fran's shocked face.

"How're you doing in there?"

I raise my eyebrows at her, waiting to see if she's going to speak. When a full beat passes, I take the lead. "We're doing great. She found many things she's going to get."

"Oh, that's wonderful," the voice behind the door rings out. "Do you need any different sizes? I would be happy to grab something for you."

"I think we're okay for now," I answer, never taking my eyes off of Fran's.

"I'll be right out here if you need me."

"Thank you," I answer, grinning down at the puddle of a woman in front of me.

I reach down and grab both of her hands, standing her up as I rise to my own feet. She's still dressed, and now that her skirt is flipped back down, looks surprisingly well put together, considering all that we just went through.

I hold her around the middle as she stands unsteadily in front of me, wiping her eyes and running her fingers through her hair.

"You could never get away with this with your big girl makeup on," I say.

She lets out a breathy laugh. "Yeah. That's for sure."

She stops fixing herself, but I don't let go, making for an awkward moment. Finally, I let my arm slide back to my side, releasing her.

"You better put some shorts on, or that sales lady's going to be so embarrassed."

Her sass is so perfectly Franny that I can't help but shake my head in amazement. "You know, this is the kind of confident, boss bitch I was expecting to see at breakfast with your brother. You took me by surprise by turning into that timid little girl."

"I know you didn't just tell me that you wanted me to drop to my knees and suck your cock in front of my brother."

"Jesus, Fran, of course not. It's just..." What is it? "I've come to know you as one person, and then your family arrived, and you turned into someone else. It just surprised me, that's all. I was scared I lost you. That all of that time we spent together was a figment of my imagination."

"Different people and different relationships require different things from you. It's like your three besties. Wouldn't you say you have a different relationship with Sam than you do with Ben? And with Dom? All of those guys have their own personality, and you all have history together that created the relationships you have today. You interact with them all differently based on that shared history and each of your different personalities."

I consider this for a moment. It's not something I've ever gone looking for, but I suppose it's true. There are things Ben knows about me that the other guys will never know. I would invite Sam to go out for drinks alone, but I probably wouldn't do the same with Dom.

I concede with a sideways head nod.

"So, there you go."

Her words suddenly make me feel like I've given that douche of a brother a free pass. "But my friends aren't purposely trying to be assholes. Okay, maybe Dom is sometimes, but not like that breakfast. That guy was trying to get you to react."

"Yeah, that's just the way he is. Even difficult people deserve love, Ave."

Straight to the goddamn heart, this one.

What about scared people? What about people who always run when it gets hard?

Do those people deserve love, too?

"You were right about this outfit. There's no way I can wear this to the wedding," she casually moves back to talking about the task at hand.

Fran is stripping off the white two-piece, hanging the garments up and looking around at the rest of the clothes as if a chasm of emotional wreckage hasn't just opened up in the dressing room floor.

Women are too good at this. They don't understand what this kind of thing does to us.

"Yeah," I say, knowing I need to say something.

She catches my tone and shoots me a sidelong glance. Questioning.

I give a nod and look away, catching sight of my own ridiculous reflection for the first time since standing up. I grab for my shorts and slip them on.

"What about this one?" She's holding up a calf length dress in soft turquoise, with cream-colored beading along the bodice. She's going to look spectacular in it, of course.

"Better try it on," I respond, just wanting to prolong this little bubble we're in.

She arrives at the checkout with a mountain of clothes. We add both of our sex outfits to the pile, even though we agreed that we will probably never have an occasion to wear them. It just feels wrong to put them back on the rack.

I have to physically remove her hand from the credit card machine to get my own in before she does, and she puts up more of a fight than I expected.

The walk back to the condo doesn't allow for much talking, with the narrow, overly crowded streets blaring too loudly for even the shortest shouted exchange. I'm grateful for the space, even if it comes with a load of shopping bags and the bustle of people and golf carts all around me. Fran holds tightly to my hand, and I let my mind drift.

The woman in that dressing room—the badass, confident, sex vixen who showed this old dog a few new tricks—that's the girl I know. The girl I want to be showing herself to the world.

Well, not the sex part. I could live with knowing that she never showed that part to another human as long as she lives.

But wait, could I really? I know that the thought of her being with someone else is trying to hack its way out of my skull with a machete, but that girl is not mine. I'll have to get used to the idea eventually. Don't I want her to go on and spend her life being pleasured and having fun?

Fuck no, I absolutely do not…unless that pleasure is coming from me.

With the arrival of the first of her family, I feel more and more like the timer is ticking down. The sand through the hourglass or some dramatic shit like that. It's no wonder I went and threw a fit when faced with them. The guy was a total douche, sure, but he's also the one who gets to spend the rest of his life knowing Fran.

And I don't.

Talk about jealousy.

But it's too late. We have an agreement, and I have to stand by it. If she can't stomach the idea of telling her family she's sleeping with me, how on earth is she going to admit to them that it's more?

And there I went, my first ever meal with them, and I showed my cards. Proved right off the bat that I'm not someone you bring around your family. Not part of the family at all. I'll likely never score another invitation to share a meal with them, clients or not.

This is when she starts to pull away.

I can't feel it yet, but I know it's coming.

The past few months, she's had no one but me. Now her whole world is going to arrive. The need for my temporary company is going to be screeching to a halt.

Rule #29

YOU DEFINITELY NEED A SAFE WORD

AVERY

The morning sun brings me back to life with my arms wrapped around Fran's naked body in the gloriously large bed of the condo. I don't move a muscle, even though my bladder is aching, knowing the second I move, she'll wake up, and it'll be time to go.

Alas.

I slip my arm out from under her slowly, hoping she'll stay asleep as I pad across the tile floor to the bathroom. When I come back, her green eyes are on me.

"Morning," I say, slipping back in beside her and pulling her close.

"Morning," she replies, head tucked into the crook of my arm. "We'll probably have to head back soon, yeah?"

"Yeah."

"I love it here, though. I wish we had longer."

Keep it together, Ave.

"Yeah, me too. We can come back whenever, though."

"Is this where you're going to come? I mean, after the wedding?"

I haven't actually given a second's thought as to what I'll do after the wedding is over and Fran goes back to the States. I'm more or less pretending that day will never come, even as the wedding planning gets more and more specific as we home in on the big day. "I'm not sure."

She doesn't respond, and we lie silently for a long moment before she finally sits up and looks back at me. "I'm going to hop in the shower."

Without waiting for me to answer, she slips out of bed and disappears into the small, tiled bathroom. I wait until I hear the water running before following her inside.

It takes a full minute for her to notice that I've cracked the curtain and am watching her enjoy the hot stream coming out of the waterfall shower head. When she does, a little squeak of surprise escapes those pink lips, followed by a laugh.

I smile as her posture changes now that she knows she's being watched. Her spine straightens, her arms squeeze in a bit to cup her breasts from underneath. Her face goes full-on sass as she reaches for the soap.

"Here for the show?" she asks, lathering the bar between her hands and holding eye contact.

I slip in behind her and take over the task of soaping her from head to toe. When I finish with each of those toes, she kneels and takes the bar from my hand. The moment is intense, both of us crouched together in the steamy spray, eyes locked in a knowing stare.

But what does she know? Does she know what this is doing to me? What I'd like to do to her? How many years I'd like to do it?

The heated moment ends before I can ask.

I stand and lean back against the wall, allowing her to wash me, savoring every second of her attention.

We decide to leave a bit early to grab smoothies on the way back to the helicopter pad, rather than call a golf cart taxi ride.

Settling onto the wooden bench at the airport, waiting for our helicopter, I finally get the nerve to broach the subject that's been weighing on my mind. "I want a promise from you that you aren't going to forget what a total badass you are when we get back to the resort."

Franny narrows her eyes at me. "Well, I want a promise from you that you aren't going to be a total asshole to our clients when they are difficult or needy."

I fold my arms over my chest and smirk at her. "Promise."

She looks down at her smoothie, fussing with the straw and avoiding my gaze.

"And you…" I prompt, refusing to let this go.

Her eyes finally meet mine. "I promise to do my best to stand up for myself and remember that I'm in charge of this wedding. I did a great job. I'm an adult, and no one can call me Jellybean or tell me that I'm being too sensitive."

Eh…what am I supposed to do with that?

"Franny, you're killing me."

She lets out a stiff laugh. "Yeah, well. This is hard. It's hard to just change the dynamics of lifelong relationships. You must know something about that." Her eyes flash to mine, and I give a little nod. "I took on this wedding knowing that I was going to have to deal with all of this—with these people, who see me as one thing. I knew I was going to have to be a different person in front of them. And I knew it was going to be hard. Now that it's here, it's just…harder than I expected. But I've gotta do it. I have to show them that I can do this wedding because I'm already doing it. There's no backing out now."

The idea that she had even considered backing out takes me by surprise. "It's that bad with them? You thought about backing out of it?"

"No. No, of course not. It's just…when you do things for or

with strangers, you can act differently than you do with your family, you know?"

I nod. I definitely know about that.

"So, when I'm doing weddings in the future, for my business, I'll just be Franzeska, the boss wedding planner. And that's who I've been all these months planning here with you, and with the guys. You all see me as an equal. My family just sees me as a little girl. I'm so scared they're all going to show up here and start questioning everything, and I won't be able to convince them that I've got it under control."

"They wouldn't have put you in charge of the wedding if they didn't think you could do it."

She just shrugs, convinced of nothing.

"I'll be there."

That draws not a look of confidence from her dazzling eyes, but one of ire. "Yeah, you'll be there and so will your father, the man you've avoided for how many years?"

"Frederick and I are both adults, Fran. We aren't going to cause problems."

She looks at me long and hard. I try to read whatever those eyes are trying to tell me, but I fail.

"I'm an adult, too," she says softly.

"I know you are. I never said you weren't. That's not what I meant at all."

"I know. I know you know that. I'm just not sure if my family is going to fully agree with you."

"You just have to show them. You did an amazing job on this wedding. It's going to be the party of the century. They're going to be blown away."

"Promise?"

I tilt my head back and suck in a long breath, trying to keep my frustration with her self-doubt at bay. She's sharing important feelings, and I shouldn't be so annoyed with them, but I can't help it. Is this really how families are around each other?

What's the freaking point of being in one if all they do is make you feel shitty about yourself?

"Franny, I promise that I'll be beside you for this whole event, reminding you of who you really are. If you ever forget, or feel insecure, just look at me. Do we need some kind of signal or safe word or something?"

She nods, tears starting to brim at the edges of her eyes.

"Okay, what should it be?"

She considers her smoothie straw again for a moment. "Iced tea," she says finally.

"Iced tea?"

"Yeah. If I ask you for some, you'll know I need a boost. And you can ask me if I need some, and if I say yes, rescue me."

I nod, satisfied with the plan.

Hell, a plan that involves me never leaving her side and us having a secret code between us—it's no surprise I'm on board.

Rule #30

TOO BAD YOU'RE NOT A MIND READER

AVERY

"Where the hell did you go? We looked for you for dinner, knocked on your door, but you weren't there."

"Oh, yeah. We took the helicopter to San Pedro to pick up some table linens I commissioned to have hand embroidered by a local artist and ended up staying."

I smirk behind my coffee cup. While it's not entirely true, I'm happy to hear the confidence in her voice as she tosses some sass at her big brother.

"Oh," is all the poor guy can manage in the face of my boss beauty.

"We walked the whole grounds yesterday," Cynthia chimes in, looking far more awake and perky than she had at breakfast the day before. "And ended up having dinner with Sam at Raft. It was incredible."

Good ol' Sam.

"I'm so glad you had a good time. That restaurant won the Pendleton last year. Did they tell you that?" Fran asks, her attention focused on the lovely bride now.

The girls fall into excited chatter and lead us down the path toward the pool area, where we were headed to look at table layout diagrams over coffee.

I fall into step beside Leon. "You two settling in?"

"Yeah. We have a really nice room." He pauses and then looks over at me. "This resort is top-notch. You've done a great job getting it turned around. Frederick showed us the before and after pictures. All the ones from when it was open in the nineties and how it looked when you bought it, and then the slideshow on the website from opening day. It's pretty incredible what you were able to do with it."

There is so much to unpack there, I don't even know where to start.

I decide to grab the lowest hanging fruit—and save the interrogation about how and why my father knows so much about my life for another time. One when I have at least three drinks in this guy.

"Thanks, man. We followed our vision, and it all manifested. The locals were on our side, which was really helpful. Everyone wanted to see the place reopen, and they helped us pull off some projects we might not have had the know-how to do without them."

I smile, thinking back to our flummoxed contractor from the States, and how much the local builders had to assist in basic construction projects. Things are just different down here. We would've been lost without them.

"Cynthia's so excited about the wedding."

I glance over at him. "You're not excited?"

"Oh, yeah. I am. But it's her day, you know? I would have been happy with anything. Or nothing. But she wants this whole thing. All the pictures with family, and the beach, and the party. She's really getting the wedding of her dreams, and I know she was much happier not having to make all of the day-to-day decisions. And I have you to thank for it."

"No, you have Fran to thank. She planned the wedding. I'm just here to look good."

"Yeah, she planned it. At your resort. With your dad's money, for the most part. I mean, I know she did a lot of the decorating, but without this spectacular place to decorate, it would be just another wedding."

I am beyond irked to hear him refer to what Fran has been doing these last few months as "decorating," but I made a promise to be nice to this dickbag,, and I plan to keep it. "You're going to be blown away by what she has in store for you."

We turn the corner, and the beach comes into view. I spot the guys out there helping the small backhoe down the beach. "Want to go watch them dig the hole for your authentic Caribbean pit barbie?"

"What? Really? That's so cool. Wow. Cynthia's going to be stoked."

He rushes forward to grab his bride's hand and points down the beach to where the commotion is starting. I can hear him explain what's going on and why, and the two share an excited moment before clasping hands and heading down toward the action.

Franny walks beside me as we follow them.

"Everything good?" I ask, just to have something to say.

"Yeah. They settled in nicely. The rest of the family's going to start arriving tomorrow and keep arriving all the way up to the wedding."

This is the part I'm looking forward to least, so I keep quiet.

"I need to go to the front desk to check on some of the room availability times with checkouts to make sure we don't need to set up a welcome area for people who come in on water taxis earlier than their rooms are ready. You know what, I should just set that up anyway."

"I can do that. I'll go get that taken care of while you and Cynthia are going over table decor. We can set it up in the meeting room off the lobby. That place isn't really used for anything anyway. People can put their luggage in there, and then we'll have the deck opened up for them to have drinks."

"Perfect. Thanks, Ave."

There's a long pause where I realized that I just volunteered to leave her side but don't want to. "You going to be okay?"

She smiles and nods. "I'll text you if I need any iced tea."

I pull out my phone and make a big show of checking to make sure the ringer is on. Then I give her shoulder a little squeeze and turn to head back up the steps to the lobby.

As soon as I hit the first hallway, however, I detour to Sam's office. The door is open, as usual, and I find him behind his desk. Thankfully, he's alone.

"Hey Ave. How's it going?"

"Eh. You know."

He smiles broadly, telling me he was waiting for a little meeting like this. "Enlighten me."

"Leon just told me that Frederick showed him pictures of the resort from the nineties when it was still the old White Sands, and pictures of the abandoned resort when we bought it. He showed them all the slideshows from the website when we first opened. Are those even still on there?" I consider, shaking my head. "They aren't. He must have saved them. Oh, holy shit," I have to pause, my mouth gaping, as the truth dawns on me. "He must have been showing them that stuff as it was happening."

My confusion turns sharp as I try to picture Frederick caring what I was up to. I mean, sure, I had just transferred more money out of our family holdings than ever before—possibly more than anyone else had ever taken—but had the man even called me about it?

I flop back in the chair and try to think back to that time. What had been going on in his life? Franny has given me a bit more context for his timeline, so I think I can place the purchase of the resort and the subsequent construction project right about the time he and Mimi were getting married.

I imagine him hanging out with her and her teenage kids,

showing them all the pictures of my project, and it nearly breaks my brain.

Sam, the fucking saint, is just sitting there quietly, allowing me to go through this.

I finally find a few words. "Did you know about this?"

He shrugs.

"I need to talk to Ben. Is he still here?"

"He's on Merit."

I let out a sigh. Of course he is.

"Okay, so what was going on during that time? My mom flew in for the opening day party, I remember that. She stayed in the room next to mine. Frederick definitely didn't come, but did he call?" I absolutely cannot remember.

Sam shakes his head. "I don't remember, Ave. Sorry. There was a lot going on."

I nod. "Yeah. There really was."

That period of time, less than two years, is one of the most memorable times of my life. I was so into the project. It consumed me night and day. I would have called it the most alive I'd ever felt. Until Franny, of course.

Thinking back to those years, when four city boys took a huge leap of faith and purchased a ghost resort on a tiny island in the middle of damn nowhere, thinking all it would take was a boatload of money to get the place ready to open. We had the money. We thought we had it under control. I have to smile to myself at the naïveté, hell, the stupidity, of those four guys. Taking the tropics by storm with absolutely none of the necessary skills or experience to actually get the job done.

But somehow, we pulled it off.

We had epic amounts of help. Without the local builders, all of whom are still on the payroll, we would have been shit out of luck. Those teams stepped in and guided us through the process, the messy regulations and red tape. Mackenzie, the local import guru became our best friend. We single handedly paid for the guy's kids to go to college. Probably bought him a second home.

God, I haven't thought about that time in so long.

I thought this resort was it for me. I thought I was going to stick around and be part of the operation forever.

How long did that last? A year? Less?

I let out a sigh and look up to find Sam watching me go through the process. "That was so fun." A ridiculous way to sum up the most transformative period in my life, but I can tell that Sam gets it.

"Yeah. It was quite the ride, wasn't it?"

"I should have stayed."

"Let's focus on today, huh? You're here, and there's going to be a huge wedding. Now is all we've got."

I nod, trying to shake off the nostalgia and get on board. "I actually need to get the meeting room off the lobby cleared out so I can set up a welcome area for guests who arrive too soon to check into their rooms. I'm going to get the deck setup, too, and I need someone to work out there, getting drinks for people and answering questions."

"That's a great idea, Ave. I can help."

"I can't take the credit. It was my boss's brilliant plan."

Sam smiles knowingly. "How's that all going?"

"Terrible."

He raises his eyebrows.

"I mean, the wedding is great. The working together is fine. But, hell, this is all going to end, and I'm not ready for it."

"Why does it have to end?"

I shrug, thinking the answer to that is pretty obvious. "She's just here for the wedding. When the wedding ends, she leaves. And that's that."

Sam just waits for me to go on.

I don't want to, but after a long enough pause, I can't help it. "I wish I could keep her here forever."

"If she was here forever, would you stay?"

"Of course. I mean, I think I would. Yes. I definitely would. As long as she would have me."

"It's getting pretty serious then?"

I consider this. How to put into words what's been happening between us? "Yes and no. Everything that happens when we are together is so serious. Like, we are *together* together. But we both still treat it like it's going to end. So, I guess it has to. I mean, she can't imagine telling her family that we're a thing. We have to hide it when they are all here. And if she can't tell them, then it can't be real. Right?"

Sam shrugs unhelpfully.

I sigh and continue digging my hole. "I am so deep in this thing. All I do is imagine whisking her away with me and being alone with her forever. But that's not what she wants. She's really invested in being close to her family, although God only knows why. They sound like really difficult people. She's launching her wedding planning business, so she's going to need to live somewhere permanent to build that. And I have not exactly been invited to come with her. I don't know how to do this. All I can do is plan another trip. I don't know how to stop moving. To settle down. Not that anyone's asking me to. But still." I run out of words and flop back in the chair.

"Sounds like you need to get through this wedding without any drama, and then you will have to have a conversation about what comes next."

"When have I ever caused any drama?"

Another raised eyebrow look from Sam.

"Okay, you're right. And that's my plan. I'm keeping it together really well. I know it's going to get a little hairy when Frederick and his new family arrive, but I've spent enough years getting used to the idea that he's just some guy that I think I'll be able to get through it."

"Franzeska knows all of this? The part about your family history and what you are going to be dealing with when the guests arrive?"

I nod. "She knows everything." Now there's a statement I've never been able to make before.

Sam nods and rises from his seat. "Okay. I think that's all you can really do for now. Let's just get through this weekend, show these people one hell of a good time, and then you'll have some space to sort out what happens next with your lady."

I nod, rising much more slowly. I'm feeling safe in the office and not quite ready to face the outside world.

Sam comes around and puts his arm around my shoulders. "I'm here for you. We all are. If you need anything, you can ask me or Ben or Dom. Really. We've got you, Ave. We're going to stand by you no matter what."

Well hell.

Now I'm going to have to get back to work fighting back tears. I blow out a breath, letting the emotions go with it. "Thanks. Okay. I'm ready."

And I almost believe it's true.

Rule #31

EVEN THE BEST-LAID PLANS GO TO HELL

FRAN

The quiet sanctuary that the resort has been for the last few months is officially gone. In its place is a mass of guests, employees, and family members, all asking me questions.

It's incredible.

I'm not sure I've ever been so happy in my life.

Everyone wants to know things, and they all have questions and concerns, and I am the one with all the answers. I walk around the resort with my clipboard, fielding question after question, the answers flowing out of me like I was born for this.

I'm starting to think I was.

Avery is still my rock. He's at my side anytime I look over. He's always ready to help me with a project or a guest or an orgasm. Whatever the situation requires.

Although, there've been a lot fewer orgasms in the last few days.

We're mostly sleeping in our own rooms, which I can tell is torture for Ave, but there's not a lot that can be done about that.

Between my mom, my sister, the girls, and all of the female cousins, there are a lot of girl eyes on me at all times.

I know damn well what kind of vibes Ave and I give off—we've had to convince people that it's not our wedding we're planning so many times.

And I can't have these people picking up on that.

The last thing I need right now is for this perfectly planned launch of my company—I mean, my brother's beautiful wedding—to go down in flames because of my own personal scandal.

Avery is cool as a damn cucumber all the time, greeting guests like the gracious host that he is, showing people around the resort, picking special guests up at the water taxi.

Frederick got held up at work and won't be arriving until later today, so Avery's attitude might change a bit then, but who knows. The man is such a good actor, I honestly don't think anything could shake him.

I'm just dropping the little girls off at their mom's room after our sleepover in my suite when I spot Frederick following a hotel employee carrying his bags up to his and my mom's room.

"Frederick," I call and make my way over to him.

He embraces me, and I can feel the tension of travel in his body. "Hey there, Franzeska. Glad to finally be here." He pulls away and looks me right in the eye, as he always does.

And…I just about shit myself.

If I thought there was a passing resemblance in the right light when I was conjuring up this man from memory, the real, live man standing two inches from me is the spitting image of Avery.

I suck in a breath and try to maintain my calm smile. "I'm so glad you're here. The trip was okay?"

"Long, but yes. It was fine. This place is gorgeous. The pictures don't do it justice."

I flash back to when I was sixteen, sitting on the couch while my mom's new husband showed off pictures of his son's Caribbean resort.

That was before we understood that we'd never meet the guy, of course.

Frederick was so excited. Now that I think about it, he seemed proud as hell.

How could I have forgotten that?

I wonder if that's the kind of thing I should tell Avery, but then I stop myself. I need to keep Frederick and Avery in different parts of my mind—for my own sanity.

"I'll let you get settled in. You heard about the dinner plan?"

"Mimi's in charge of plans, but I'm sure she'll let me know when and where."

He disappears into his room, and I can finally breathe again.

Must get to room. Must be alone to freak the fuck out.

But that's not how it goes.

"Hey, I've been looking for you."

Avery is waiting for me when I get to my own door.

"What's up?"

"Marta just texted me that they're leaving the farm now. We should be able to meet them downstairs in twenty or so."

I nod, remembering that I penciled the flower delivery into this afternoon's schedule. We'll store the arch and all the bouquets in the cool room next to Reef until it's time to set them up in the morning.

Tomorrow…holy shit…the freaking wedding is tomorrow!

I take a deep breath to calm myself. "Great, okay. I just need a minute."

He follows me inside and closes the door behind us. "You good?"

"Yeah, yeah. I just…" Should I tell him about Frederick being here? I mean, he's going to find out soon enough. And should I invite him to dinner with us? Oh god, I hadn't even thought about that. Will I have to lie to him about my plans, so he doesn't feel left out? Or maybe he should come to dinner. He is part of the family, after all.

I am officially freaking out.

"Franny, whatever's going on, it's okay." Avery tries to calm me like he's done so many times before.

Only this time, I'm not sure he's right.

Up until this very moment, I was still holding on to the fantasy that I could make this work. I mean, I know he and I haven't exactly talked about making this thing between us more permanent, but obviously that's always been my secret plan.

Until now.

Now that I'm actually faced with having him here—in my room—and my whole family, his father included, right outside, I don't know how I would actually make it work. I can't be the perfect daughter that they want me to be, the perfect sister and auntie, the perfect stepdaughter, and also be the perfect, badass, world-traveling, wedding planning partner for this gorgeous, kind man.

I would have to be two people. And lie to both parties about the other for the rest of my life.

The thought nearly sends me to my knees.

Avery is half carrying me to the sofa and sitting me down.

"Whatever this is, love, we can get through it."

"Your dad's here."

"I figured."

"I said hi to him."

"That's good."

"I'm having dinner with them."

"That seems appropriate."

He is so unflustered by this whole thing that it does actually start to calm me down a bit. "Do you want to come to dinner? It'll be the whole family."

"Do you want me to come?"

"Avery! That's not an answer."

"Sure, I'll come."

"I haven't told them you're coming."

"Franny, this doesn't have to be weird, okay? We're all adults, and we all know the history here. We're going to be polite, and it's going to be fine. I'm excited to meet everyone. It's been so hectic around here that I haven't felt like I had a moment to stop and really meet your family as they arrived."

"The girls are excited to meet you." It's true. Everyone is. This man is a legend.

"I'm excited to meet them."

I sink into him and let him hold me for a long moment. I stay as still as I can, trying to make it last. I know once we head down to receive the flowers, it will be hours before we have another chance to sneak away. "Will you stay here with me tonight?"

Avery pauses and I look up into his kind but concerned expression. "Not tonight, love. We have the wedding tomorrow to get through, but once it's over, everyone will leave, and we can enjoy the quiet again. Better not risk it before then."

It shouldn't feel like rejection. It is, after all, just plain common sense, but it does. In my current state, I'm not processing things well.

"Okay," I manage.

"Franny, you know there is nowhere on earth I would rather be—"

"I know. It's okay. It'll all be over soon." I'm already disentangling myself and climbing to my feet. "And you're right. There are too many people who could pop by unexpectedly. Wouldn't want to have to hide you in the closet."

I watch my joke land and the crater it causes in his steel resolve.

He nods and follows me to the door.

Right before I open it, he places his palm flat on the wood, pinning it closed. Then he's on me, his lips on mine, his hands holding my waist firmly in his grasp.

I melt into him.

I had no idea how badly I was craving his touch, but now that I have it…

The flowers might just have to receive themselves.

I let him touch me for as long as he wants, frantically feeling over his clothes for as much contact with the man as I can get. There's something so final about this moment, it takes my breath away.

When he releases me and reaches for the door handle. I straighten my dress and try to keep myself upright.

"Iced tea?"

I shake my head. "I think I'm good."

Avery nods. "I'll meet Marta with you, but then I need to run back to town to pick up some fruit that was forgotten, and there are a couple of guests coming in that I'll bring back as well."

"Okay. So, I'll just see you at dinner then?"

Why does it feel like a chasm has opened between us? I am speaking to him over a river of questions so wide, I almost feel the need to shout.

"Yup," he answers simply.

The family has a big table waiting in the Raft dining room, consisting of all the small tables pulled together and draped with tablecloths. The staff really made it beautiful with flowers and small candles in crystal cups. I'm so happy and grateful that they thought ahead and treated this dinner as what it is—a rehearsal of sorts.

We hadn't planned any events other than the wedding at the request of the couple, who wanted things to be more free flowing. But this dinner, with the core family together, the night before the big day, is something so special that I'm grateful we're getting to experience it.

I immediately count chairs and do a mental headcount. We need at least one more. "Avery's going to join us," I say to my mom, who's helping the little girls into their chairs.

"Oh, lovely. I look forward to getting to talk with him. Everything was so busy when we checked in and met him, I didn't get the chance."

I nod and smile before hurrying away to let the server know to add another chair.

Everyone is happily talking and laughing, finding seats, getting drinks, and humoring the two little girls who are now performing a song while standing on their seats.

I greet my sister and her husband with hugs, share an excited little dance with Cynthia, who looks like she's on the verge of overwhelm, and high-five my brother. I see my aunt Linda and one of her daughters, a cousin I was close to growing up but have mostly lost contact with in the last few years. I seat myself close to her so we can catch up.

The energy of the group is a living thing, pulsing around me.

I'm happily taking it all in when a hush falls over the table. I look up from helping Frieda squeeze a lemon in her drink to find Avery standing at the foot of the table, his hand on the back of my aunt Linda's chair.

I meet his eye and then my gaze shoots around the table, searching for the empty seat that should be waiting for him.

It's not there.

His smile is unfaltering as he greets familiar faces and accepts introductions to new ones. There's no denying the fact that he looks like an outsider, however. A man who wandered up to a table filled with family.

A family that he isn't a part of.

I'm halfway out of my chair, trying to push it back and escape to find the chair that should have already been here, when he speaks.

"I just wanted to pop in and say enjoy your meal. The chef here is famous. The food will be incredible." His kind, gracious voice shows not a hint of sadness at his own exclusion. He's just one of the owners, come to pay his respects to high paying guests.

But that's not right. He's part of this family.

"Avery, I'll get a chair—" I'm still struggling to get out of my own with the two beside me so close, but he stops me with a look.

"That's okay, I actually have to take care of a few things that came up. You enjoy your meal, and I look forward to seeing all of you in your tropical best tomorrow for Leon and Cynthia's big day."

His proclamation causes the group to start talking excitedly among themselves about the wedding, people calling out congratulations to the couple from opposite ends of the table.

I think I might be the only one who notices Avery sneak out, but when I glance toward the head of the table, I catch Frederick's eye for just a moment before he turns his attention back to his drink.

The look on his face is uncannily like the one on Avery's that just broke my heart. Stoic. Unruffled.

I see it for the lie that it is.

Rule #32

LETTING GO SOUNDS SIMPLE. IT ISN'T

AVERY

I head straight for my golf cart, having exactly zero interest in explaining why my face looks like this or trying to make words come out around the boulder-sized snowball lodged in the center of my chest.

I know every goddamn person in this resort and one of them is going to want to talk to me. I have nothing to say right now. I don't want to talk about this. I want to shove it deep, deep down in the depths of my mind where it can go back to sleep and never bother me again.

I swing the cart out onto the sandy road like a madman.

The long, dark, bumpy drive does little to soothe me.

I don't need soothing.

I'm fine.

Nothing happened.

Everything's fine.

I pull up in front of Mackenzie's and hop out.

"Hey, Ave," Sal greets me with a smile as I pass through the sports bar's open doors.

I should have picked one of the tourist bars. What was I thinking?

"Hey," I call back, plastering on a smile.

It's never felt more like a mask.

"I'm just gonna grab a table. Will you bring me a beer?"

"Sure thing."

I'm one sip in when I feel someone sit down across from me. I don't even need to look up from where I'm peeling the label off my bottle to know that it's Max.

Max is the caretaker of our Merit Island property and a wise old sage. I've spent the last near decade showing up on his doorstep with every problem or heartache—and he always talks me through it.

I thought about heading over there to get his take on this whole Franny thing early on, but once it became clear how tenuous it was—and how high the stakes were—I didn't want to share the truth with anyone, not even Max.

I just want to blink and have the whole waiting, wondering part over.

Talking isn't going to do any good.

"Hello, Ave. Fancy meeting you here."

But I guess I'm going to be talking.

"Hey."

"I had the most interesting conversation with Ben this evening."

I let out a sigh, trying not to get angry. I know the guys want the best for me, and I know for damn sure Max only wants the best for everyone on the planet, so I don't want to let my temper take over and say things I'll regret.

"Yeah?" I manage.

"Tell me about it."

I grind my teeth and focus on the label once more. I may as well get this over with. "Well, I met a girl—"

"No. Skip to the part where you got in your cart and drove here."

I look up at him in surprise. I figured he'd want the whole sordid love affair.

"Okay, it was the rehearsal dinner…"

Oh. I get it now.

How did I not see this before? These last few months I've been able to keep it together, even when I wanted to proclaim my love for Fran and lock her in my hotel room. I worked through it. I practiced patience and restraint. I grew as a fucking person.

I thought it was all fine.

I thought my escape and journey to town tonight was just a tiny mental break from the stress of the wedding or something.

Leave it to Max to get to the root of my distress with one fucking sentence.

"There was a family dinner. Fran invited me, and I decided to go, against my better judgment. When I got there, the table was full."

I close my eyes as I remember the feeling of walking up to that table and realizing the situation. I told myself in the moment that I needed to get out of there to make the whole thing easier on Fran, but that might not have been the entire truth.

"I said hello, and Fran was freaking about the missing chair, but all I saw was Frederick. He had his wife on one side, his grandchildren or step-grandchildren or whatever to his other side. And he just sat there, watching me look around for my chair. The one that wasn't there. He could have gotten up and helped. He could have said hi. He could have pretended it wasn't happening. Even pretending would have been better. But he just looked at me like this is my family, and you don't belong here."

I break off and take a drink, shaking my head. I can't believe I'm saying these things. I can't believe I'm allowing a door like this to open, especially right now with such an important day tomorrow. I hope I can force it back closed in time.

"He was right, too. I don't know those people. I would have

been a complete outsider seated at that table. I only went to the dinner because Franny seemed to want me there, and I've got the world's biggest blind spot when it comes to that girl. It was stupid to go at all. I've already learned that lesson. Do you remember that Christmas when his second wife insisted that he have me over for Christmas morning, but then there were presents for everyone but me?" My voice finally cracks, and I break off, shaking my head at my own weakness and stupidity. "I don't even care about presents. I buy myself everything I want. I don't need a pair of slipper socks or whatever junk you buy someone who you don't know at all. But it's like—why invite me, then? Why not just leave me alone? I was fine. I'm fine now. I'm fine."

Silence drops between us, heavy in the humid air.

"You've been avoiding facing one heartbreak, and you've found yourself another," Max says, more than a hint of kindness in his voice.

"Which is which?" I offer with a small, huffed laugh.

"What is it that you want, Ave?"

I take another drink and avoid the man's eyes. If I knew the answer to that—

"It's okay to say you don't know, Ave. But if you did know, what do you think it would be?"

I sigh, clearly not going to get away with avoiding the question. "Okay. I want Franny's first wedding to be spectacular."

Max nods.

"I want her to get investors and be able to have a huge launch. I want Ainsley to head back to New York and talk to his dad. I want Ben to ease up and let the kid be himself. I want Dom and Reina to live happily ever after. I want the perfect wife for Sam. I want world fucking peace."

Max doesn't laugh at my joke. "Do you want anything for yourself?"

I shake my head. "If everyone else is happy, I'm happy."

"And the girl? You want her to head home and have a nice, happy life?"

"No. I mean, if that's what she wants I can't stop her. But..."

"But you want that relationship to continue."

"I just don't know if I get to decide that. It seems like people decide for themselves whether to stay or go."

"So, this is about your father."

"I didn't say that."

"You did."

I sigh again. This is exactly the shit I don't want to talk about. "It's fine. He had...other things going on that were more important, so he took off. I survived."

"And you get to go through life wondering when everyone is going to leave you?"

"I've never really cared all that much."

"Until now."

I nod. "Until now."

"What's your plan? I know you have one."

"Wait until after the wedding and then talk to her about how I feel."

"That's actually not a bad plan."

"Thank you. I am capable of rational thought sometimes."

"And if she still leaves?"

"Then I'll go wherever she goes."

Max raises his eyebrows in surprise. "Oh, really?"

I shrug. "I'm very mobile. It's one of my most defining personality traits."

"You feel that if you were capable of following your father when he left, then things would have been different. But you were just a kid, so you couldn't," Max offers.

"It was better to imagine that he just couldn't stay at the estate for work reasons or whatever. Sure, I always dreamed that if they would just let me get on a plane, I could go to wherever he needed to live for work and things would be different."

"But you understand that if that was the case, he would have taken you with him."

"Yeah, Max. I understand that."

"So, no amount of you chasing him around the globe would have changed the nature of your relationship."

"He didn't want me. If I showed up on his doorstep, he would have probably slammed the door in my face."

"And if Fran leaves, and you chase her to wherever it is she goes..."

"It's different."

"Tell me."

I'm angry now...and sad. I don't want to be speaking these words into existence. "It's different because I'm going to make it different. I'm going to tell her how I feel. That's not something I ever did with my dad."

"You never told your father that you missed him or wanted him to come home?"

"No. No, I tried to always be happy. I thought that if he thought I was happy, that the house was a happy, fun place, that he would be more likely to visit. Who wants to visit a sad, clingy kid? No. I never told him anything. I just pretended to be so happy all the time. Like things were great and I had the best life. I thought it would make him love me more and come home. God, this is so fucked up. I hope I never have children."

"Taking up with a twenty-three-year-old woman tells a different story."

"Max, you're killing me here. Can we just let this go?"

"I don't know, Ave. Can you let it go? Can you let go of the resentment you carry toward your father and be in a relationship with someone who is going to require you to interact with him on a regular basis? Can you let go of the idea that everyone who loves you is going to leave?"

"Jesus, man. I thought you were here to help me."

It's Max's turn to shake his head. "I just came to have a nice

Diet Coke." He holds up his mostly untouched bottle, the condensation dripping into a ring on the wood table.

"So you're not going to help me."

"How should I help you?"

I gape at him in frustration. "Tell me what to do, man."

"Let it all go."

I scoff and shake my head. "Easier said than done."

"Yes."

"Yes what?"

The man smiles. Actually freaking smiles at me. "Just yes. It's very hard to let go of the wounds from our past, especially ones that run as deep as yours. But if you don't want these things to keep controlling your life, it's your only option. If you want to be free of it all, just let go. Forgive and move on with your life."

"Forgive Frederick for abandoning me." I shake my head. "He doesn't deserve my forgiveness."

Max nods. "Maybe not. But forgiveness isn't for the other person. Forgiveness is for you. You alone carry this pain, and you alone can release yourself by deciding to forgive."

"Fine. I forgive him." I huff.

Max laughs loud and long, drawing amused looks from neighboring tables. "That's a good start, Ave."

"But it's not enough?"

He shakes his head and smiles. "You decide now to forgive, and you will keep deciding to forgive each and every day. Some days it will be easier than others."

"And I just do this, what, forever?"

He shrugs, still smiling at me. "You do it until you're free."

"Tomorrow's going to be a hard day to practice forgiveness. He's going to be there with his perfect new family."

"You are choosing this pain, Avery. The adults at tomorrow's event are not your father's children. Your father did not leave you to go off and have new babies that he loves more than you. He married this woman when she already had mostly grown children. Choosing to tell yourself any other story is only adding to the stress of tomorrow. I encourage you to also let that go."

"It's a lot to let go of at once. I usually just avoid thinking about it, now you want me to forgive and tell myself the truth all of a sudden."

"All of a sudden, you have a reason to tell the truth about the past and offer forgiveness. If you want this badly enough, it will be a small price to pay."

"I like when the price is money."

Max laughs again, so loudly that people around us laugh along with him. "You silly men and your money. You make everything so hard on yourselves."

"Okay, let's just stop at truth telling and forgiveness. We can save giving away my fortune to become a monk for another day."

His eyes grow serious as he leans forward and pins me in his gaze. "I believe you have finally found something worth giving it all away for. Tell me the truth now—am I wrong about that?"

I shake my head. "No, you're not wrong. I'd give everything away. Every cent. If that's what it took."

He sits back in his chair and shrugs. "Well, if that's the case, you have nothing to lose."

Spoken by an old man who views pain and struggle as learning experiences.

"I could get my heart smashed, and you're telling me to just go for it."

"You're here on this planet for a limited time only. I'm telling you to go for it all."

Rule #33

ONLY LOVE COULD HURT LIKE THIS

FRAN

As soon as I can get away without looking too suspicious, I escape to the bathroom to text Avery.

Sitting there on the toilet, waiting for his little text bubble to pop up, I nearly lose my mind.

This is the last thing I needed tonight. I was feeling so confident in my party-planning abilities. Everything seemed to be going so great. And then my emotions—and the emotions of that man—stomped that flame right out.

I can't be worrying about this right now. I have an entire wedding to worry about. Over a hundred people. All of the resort employees. The launch of my business. The rest of my career.

This is exactly why getting involved with him was a bad idea in the first place. I knew it, and I did it anyway.

With a sigh, I tuck my silent phone back into my purse.

He's not going to respond.

And that's just going to have to be okay. I can't hold the

space for him emotionally right now. Why was it ever my responsibility to do that in the first place?

Uh, maybe because you're in love with the guy?

Yup. That's a problem.

One I have to slide to the back burner.

Avery may have just gotten his feelings hurt, but he's going to have to just deal with it for the next forty-eight hours.

Rising to my feet and putting myself in a power pose, I repeat the words inside my head, trying to suck the confidence out of them.

He's going to have to just deal with it.

I can't be responsible for him right now.

I make my way back out to the table and try to let it go.

It gets easier when the food starts to arrive. God, the food is just glorious. The best I've ever had. I could definitely get used to this lifestyle.

I'm just finishing off my passion fruit mousse when I feel my phone buzz with the telltale WhatsApp three pulses.

Avery
Hey, sorry I missed your message. Just got back from town, met a friend for a drink. I'll bring coffee up at 6.

Okay. Sleep well, see you in the morning.

And I'll be goddamned if all is not right again in the world.

Fucking love.

Rule #34

IT'S FUTILE TO FIGHT AGAINST GIRL CODE

AVERY

I juggle the cups and muffins in my grip like a pro as I tap on Fran's door with my foot. I'm not expecting her to still be in bed, so it's no surprise when the door flies open two seconds later.

She's dressed in the turquoise shift with cream-colored beading that we picked out in San Pedro. I sing my dick a little "don't get hard" jingle in my mind as I say good morning.

"Everything's perfect so far," she says, leaving me at the doorstep to hurry back to her room.

I grin and follow her in, setting breakfast down on the kitchen bar. "Great. Anything I can do right away?"

She pops her head out, flat iron in hand. "We're meeting with the setup crew down on the patio at seven. Kuramo and his people will be arriving a little bit after that. We need to make sure there's room in the Reef kitchen for them to start prepping."

We've gone over this schedule so many times that I have the thing memorized. I sip my coffee and listen patiently while she goes over the entire day again.

I was a bit worried that we'd have to have a conversation

about the failed family dinner party, but it seems like she's going to save that for after the wedding.

That's a relief.

The processing I did last night during, and after, my heart-to-heart with Max left me in a good place. The last thing I want to do is get into anything heavy with her right now.

Not this morning. We have enough on our plates.

She struts out again a few moments later, shoes on, clipboard in hand.

God, she's so perfect.

"Is that coffee I smell?"

"And muffins."

She falls on the food like a starving person. "What is it about fancy restaurant food that makes you so hungry the next day?" she muses into her muffin before catching herself and looking up at me with wide, apologetic eyes. "Ave—"

"Nope." I nip that in the bud. "We're not doing this right now, love."

Franny nods like she gets it.

She does get it. She gets me.

Fucking hell.

A knock at the door interrupts our intense eye contact. It flies open without waiting to be answered.

"Good morning!" Mimi sings as she strolls into the room. "Oh, Avery, I'm so glad you're here. I missed getting to talk to you at dinner last night."

"No rest for the working man," I joke, and then wish I hadn't as Frederick enters the room on her heels.

"Morning," he says, not looking at me, but not not looking at me. He casually scans the room and the people in it as if he's on a stage.

"Morning," I reply.

My voice causes him to turn to me, and our gazes meet.

For a long moment, I'm not sure what's going to happen, but then he puts out his hand and takes a half step forward.

I barely glance at it before extending my own and giving him a good ol' professional shake.

Three pumps and we release our grip, both slipping our hands into our shorts' pockets, practically in unison.

He turns to Mimi as if awaiting her direction.

I turn to Fran.

She has paused her coffee drinking with the paper cup halfway to her lips, a look of mild shock and amusement on her lovely features. Our eyes meet, and she smiles, raising her eyebrows as if to ask, "Are you good?"

I nod, and she nods back.

It all happens in the span of a second, but it's everything to me.

How did I make it through this life without her for so long?

"I just stopped by your sister's room, and the girls are up. They're going to head down for breakfast in about a half hour and then take the girls swimming to get some of their energy out."

"Sounds great, Mom. You should join them. Avery and I have a full morning of meeting with people and getting set up. We may not see you again until it's time to gather everyone on the beach for the ceremony."

"Anything I can do to help?" Mimi asks, and it sounds like she means it.

"We can definitely use your help with setting up the welcome table at around ten. But mostly I need you to be in charge of keeping Cynthia calm and making sure she's ready when the time comes. I'll be up there before the ceremony, but I'm not going to have time to really take care of her. Do you think you can do that?"

"I won't let you down," Mimi responds, so filled with pride at her special position that you would think she'd been asked to take a bullet for the queen. "I'm so happy to be welcoming a new child into the family. I always wanted four, you know."

As she finishes speaking, I watch her face transform into a

look of pure horror. She tries in vain to scoop the words up and put them back in her mouth.

"I mean, I didn't mean..." She turns to me, an apologetic smile on her tightly pressed lips. "There were always four. I always knew that. I just meant another daughter. I always wanted another daughter."

I feel for the lady. She's going to be rehashing this slip of the tongue at three a.m. for the rest of her days. "I know what you meant, Mimi. And now you're getting that daughter."

She takes both of my hands and gives me that old lady thank you look. "It's so nice to finally get to meet you, Avery. You should really come visit us in Aspen sometime. We would love to have you."

I should say that I will. It would be the polite thing to do. I'll never do it, but that doesn't really matter in a moment like this. We would both be saying things that aren't true.

But I say nothing.

The moment drags on. Finally, she drops my hands with a sad little nod and steps back to her husband's side.

I take a step toward Franny and then remember myself and take a step away.

"Okay, well," Fran decides to take charge of the situation, and I'm grateful to her. I'm not sure how long we all would have just stood there awkwardly. "We'll definitely see you down at Reef. We'll be in and out all morning."

"Come say hi to the girls," Mimi responds, looking between us with her kind smile back in place.

"We will."

Once they're gone, Fran busies herself with her coffee and muffin, not meeting my eyes. It's the most concerning thing that's happened all morning.

"If it would be better for me to just take off, let me know, okay? It won't hurt my feelings. I want what's best for the wedding and Franzeska Events."

Her face shoots to mine, a look of pure horror written across it. "Don't be ridiculous."

I shrug, hands held up in surrender. "I'm just saying, we're two for two in awkward family meetings."

She's shaking her head and rolling her eyes while shoving blueberry muffin into her mouth as quickly as she can. "I don't have time for this, Avery," she manages around bites. "We're here to do a job, and I can't do it without you."

I'm speechless.

For one thing, of course she can. Her entire plan in life is to plan weddings—without me. She would be fine. Another thing…I think that may be the closest she's ever come to telling me she wants more from this relationship.

Even if that more is just keeping me as her working stepbrother with benefits forever, I'd take it.

I should argue. Tell her she's being ridiculous now. That she doesn't need anyone.

But, of course, I don't.

"Let's get going then. I want to swing by the kitchen to make sure Marcus is ready for Kuramo's team before we need to be out front to meet Marta."

The kitchen looks spotless and ready.

The flowers arrive and are beautiful.

The team sets up the party tables, buffet, and bar without issue.

Fran has just rushed off to double check on the outfits for the wedding party, and I make my way down to the pit dug in the beach, where Dom is hanging out in shorts and a tank top, looking like the cat who caught the canary.

"Looking good, man," I say, glancing down at his flip-flops.

"This is the fucking life, Ave. I may close Raft and just open a pit barbecue joint out here."

I breath out a small laugh at the sheer absurdity of that statement. Us co-owners had been trying to get Dom to offer a more casual fare menu for years before we finally got Reef opened. To think all we needed to sway him was a big hole in the beach.

"I'm glad you're enjoying yourself."

He huffs but says nothing.

We watch the team work to get the fire built up enough to create the coals they're going to need for dinner for a few minutes before a familiar laugh draws both of our attention.

Reina runs to Dom first, but she's at my side pretty quickly after that.

"Everything looks amazing, Ave."

I nod, a big smile on my face. "Yeah. It's all going great."

"It's only a matter of time before you and Franzeska start planning our wedding." She tosses a look over her shoulder at Dom who's pretending not to be listening. "And then you guys will be planning your own!"

I have to laugh in surprise at the bold statement, coming seemingly out of nowhere. "What? We aren't getting married, Rein. We're just working friends. Of a sort."

Reina huffs and rolls her eyes in annoyance. "Are we seriously still doing this whole pretend you two aren't perfect for each other thing?"

My heart soars as my mind sinks.

This is not the time for this.

I shake my head, but don't have a chance to argue before she's going on.

"You know you're in love with her. We all know it. Don't we, Dom?" Another glance over her shoulder at the stoic man gets her a grunt but nothing else. "That was a yes. And I know for a fact she feels the same way—"

"Hold up. Hold up." I just need her to stop talking for a second so I can process. "What do you mean you know that for a fact?"

Why I'm asking this right now, I don't know. But there's no way in hell I'm letting this opportunity slip by.

"Because she told me. And if you just told her how you felt, she would tell you, too. I'm sure of it."

"When did she tell you this?"

"When we went out for drinks back in November."

"In November? You've known about this the whole time, and you never told me?"

Reina scoffs. "Girl code."

Girl fucking code.

"So how come you can break the code now?"

"Because it's the wedding. We decided that it would be best to wait until after the wedding to have any kind of big discussion, especially since she wasn't one bit convinced that you were going to tell her you felt the same way. So, anyway, the big day is today."

The warring emotions in my body shoot at each other with automatic weapons and lasers. And crossbows.

This is the end for me. I'm just going to fall over dead right here.

Killed by his own feelings.

It'll make one hell of a tombstone.

"She didn't think I was going to tell her I felt the same way, meaning…"

"Oh my god! You men are so freaking dense."

"Please, Reina, for the love of god—"

"You're going to have to talk to her."

This morning went from even-keeled to spiraling out of control real quick.

I'm going to have to get it together.

But trying to convince my mind to think about anything other than the fact that Franny might be in love with me and planning to ask me if we can stay together after the wedding? Fat chance of that.

"Anyhoo, I've got to get back to the bar set up. We're going to be good to go in just a few minutes if you need a drink or something."

And then she heads off down the beach, smiling and waving at people as if she hadn't just atom-bombed my entire psyche.

"Girls always have some fucking thing going on."

My head shoots to Dom as he speaks. "You knew about this?"

He shrugs and huffs. "You two are never not touching each other. Connected at the damn hip. I know you don't like to talk about your personal stuff much, so we've mostly left you two alone, but it does seem like there's something going on there. Even if you chose the most complicated fucking person on the planet to fall for."

I head off down the beach toward the resort, not bothering to respond to that particularly unhelpful comment.

Franny loves me.

It's a song I could listen to on repeat for the rest of my life.

I'm terrified but also elated. This is everything I'd ever hoped for but never let myself imagine was actually possible.

The wedding is going to come and go, and we're going to stay.

Here, there, wherever.

We get to be together.

Franny comes up beside me so quickly, I jump. "It's a go upstairs. My aunt Linda is taking on the task of making sure it runs smoothly. I know my mom said she'd help, but her mind is all over the place. Linda will be…what?"

She trails off, narrowing her eyes at me.

I want to grab her and pull her into my arms. Drop to one knee and shout my love for her to the world.

But I can't do that. Not here, with all of her family and friends around us.

Hmm. In my euphoria, I managed to skim over the actual reason why we may not have had this conversation already.

Fucking Frederick.

Her family.

Her age—oh god, how easy it's been to forget that she's only twenty-three when we're isolated out here.

Her bright and shiny future.

Fuck. Way to rain on my own parade.

It's fine. We'll get through all of this. There's a solution to every problem. That's my life motto. Why can't it work for this situation?

"Are you having a stroke or something?"

My eyes finally focus on her, standing in front of me, a look of complete bafflement clouding her beautiful face. "No, sorry, I was just thinking—"

"Okay, perfect. Well, we need to get back up to the patio to supervise the table set up. I have no idea if my mom is actually going to come…"

She's three feet away before I realize she's walking, and I have to jog to keep up.

The little jolt of exercise snaps my brain back online.

Focus on the wedding, Ave. You can deal with all of this later.

Nothing has changed.

Except…everything has changed.

Rule #35

BETTER WORK ON YOUR POKER FACE

FRAN

Not a dry eye in the whole freaking crowd.

Job well done, Franzeska.

Not that I had any hand in writing those super sweet vows—although to be honest, it seems like Cynthia might have written both sets, but who am I to judge?

The guests are getting up and starting to follow the lovely new Mr. and Mrs. back down the aisle and onto the patio.

I watch from the sidelines, the satisfaction of a smooth flowing procession almost turning me on. I don't need to direct people at all. The party is so well laid out that they just corral themselves. Like perfect little sheep.

God, this party is so epic.

I am doing the best freaking job.

I mentally pat myself on the back.

And then, through the crowd, I spot something that isn't part of my perfectly laid plans.

Skirting the edge of the crowd, I make my way up to the patio to have a little chat with the offender.

"Excuse me, hi."

She turns as I lay my hand on her arm.

"Hey. You must be Franny."

Okay…at least we know whose guest she is.

"Yeah, I am. I was just wondering about the camera. We have a professional photographer—"

"Franny," Avery says behind me. Close enough for my body to want to dive into his arms, but not so close that it actually does so without my permission. "This is Kendra. She's a professional branding designer and photographer. I hired her to shoot the wedding for your website and new brand."

I turn back to the woman, feeling a bit sheepish for how close I just came to throwing her out. "Sorry, Kendra. Someone,"—I toss a look over my shoulder at the man in question—"didn't tell me you were coming. Thank you. I'm so excited to see what you come up with. Let me know if you need anything, okay?"

"The wedding looks great, Franny. Your website is going to be epic. I'm just trying to get the angles right so it looks like at least a dozen different weddings, that way we can sell this whole package,"—she gestures around herself at the party—"as your brand."

Excitement threatens to overwhelm me, but Avery seems to sense that. "We'll let you get back to it, Kendra. We've got some catering things to attend to."

The woman heads off with a smile, and I turn on him.

"You hired a branding designer and didn't tell me?"

He shrugs, not looking one bit apologetic. "She's a friend from way back. She has some seriously big-name clients. This is going to be great for you."

All of a sudden, his behavior this morning starts to make more sense. "This is why you've been acting so weird all morning? Because you had a surprise?"

He doesn't confirm or deny, but a shadow crosses his face that I can't quite read. It's replaced with his sly grin so quickly that I decide to let it go.

"You're going to have to work on your poker face, mister."

"Yeah, I guess so."

His tone is too serious for what we're talking about, and I'm about to grill him further, but we are interrupted by literally my entire family.

"Such a beautiful ceremony, Franzeska. The flowers were incredible." My sister is pulling me into a hug, and I go a bit teary, forgetting all about the look on Avery's face. "I wish you'd done my wedding." She tosses a look at her husband, who grins and nods in agreement.

"Yeah, we had regular old lilies." He makes a ridiculous gesture miming gagging himself with his finger in his mouth.

"Daddy! You can't do that! Mommy said I wasn't allowed to do that, so you aren't allowed to either."

Good ol' Freida, not letting anyone get away with anything.

"Well, what do we have here?"

We all turn to Avery as he kneels down to address my nieces. "Two fairy princesses?"

It's an easy mistake to make. They are, after all, dressed in pastel tulle that glitters in the sun.

Freida's hands drag slowly up to her hips as she regards him. "We aren't princesses. We're astronauts." Her matter-of-fact tone and dagger glare makes me stifle a grin.

"I'm a werewolf!" pipes up little Suzie.

"My mistake. Sorry, ladies. I didn't recognize astronaut werewolves because of the glare. The sun is shining in my eyes." He holds a hand up to prove his point. I can see the hidden smile just under his serious expression.

"She's a werewolf astronaut. I'm a witch astronaut," Freida corrects him.

"Do witches and werewolves like watermelon juice?" Avery takes the easy way out.

The girls turn to each other and confer silently with their eyes.

Finally, they face him once more and nod in unison.

The whole group of us barely contain our laughter now. Luckily, Avery takes one little girl by each hand and leads them toward the refreshments.

They don't make it two feet before we're all busting up so hard that we're in tears again.

"That man is a gem," my mother says, still wiping at her eyes.

"Yeah, it's a shame we're only just meeting him," my sister says, turning her gaze to Frederick who, I notice now, isn't cracking up with the rest of us. "Why hasn't he come around? He wasn't at your wedding, was he?"

She looks to me to make sure her memory isn't just failing her, but I shake my head.

"We don't really get along," Frederick offers, as if that answers everything.

"Seems odd not to invite your own son to your wedding. Or Christmas." My sister isn't just going to let it go, and I'm grateful. I have a load of similar questions I'm not sure I'd be brave enough to ask right now.

"We have *this* lovely wedding to focus on right now, don't we, my loves?" Mother dear, ever the peacekeeper, steps in between my sister and Frederick, effectively ending the interrogation. "And what a great job Franzeska has done." She looks around the party with a broad smile on her face. "This wedding could not be more perfect."

"Just wait till dinner," my sister's husband pipes up. "I've been watching the crew set up that barbecue all day. I can't wait to eat whatever they're cooking."

I allow myself to be distracted, if only because we're now discussing my favorite topic. The wedding.

"It's going to be incredible. But right now, you should all get drinks." I glance over toward the bar, where Avery is kneeling next to the girls again, being shown a better way to fix his hair. My entire being burns with the desire to walk over to him. To be part of whatever he's doing.

"We were going to wait until after pictures to start drinking," my sister says, and my mom nods in agreement.

"But surely one little drink won't hurt?" her husband asks gently.

"Go on, then," my sister says with a laugh. "But get something we can share."

Pictures. Of course. I glance down at the clipboard I'm holding and spot the place on the schedule where we're going to head off to the beach with the whole wedding party and close family to have the professional portraits done.

Oh, the best laid plans.

I thought I had this all figured out. How could I have overlooked something so critical?

"Okay," I start, just to draw the attention back to me. "Let's all take a few minutes to cool off and get a drink, then we'll meet down by the flower arch in ten. We need to get the pictures out of the way before everyone starts melting."

"Or covering their werewolf astronaut dresses in barbecue sauce." My sister laughs and follows her husband toward the bar to wrangle her kids.

Frederick goes with her.

I snag my mom's arm before she can follow.

"Mom, what about Avery?"

Her look tells me this is something she's considered. "I'm not sure, sweetie. I thought we might all get on the same page at dinner last night, but when he didn't stay…I'm not sure where the whole thing stands."

"Shit." The word escapes my lips before I can stop it. "Sorry, I just…"

"I understand. This is not an easy situation. It's terrible to think of him being left out of the family pictures, but it's just as concerning to imagine hanging those pictures up at the house with him in them. I mean, the men aren't exactly working toward a solution to their problems. I would hate for Frederick to have to live with a reminder of their strained relationship on the wall every day."

It's an impossible problem.

One I should have seen coming a mile away.

I was just too blinded by my own feelings. Too wrapped up in that man's arms. I allowed this nuclear situation to fall through the cracks.

"Well, he'll just have to be in some and not others." With a huge sigh, I settle on the only possible solution. "I need to go talk to the photographer."

My mom gives my hand a loving squeeze, and I run off.

It's not as painful as I was imagining, but it's a little awkward.

If Avery wasn't a complete saint, it would be a total shit-show.

He stands in photos when directed and graciously stands aside when asked. There's no missing what's going on when he's left out of a photo with all the rest of us, but I can't see a smidge of feeling about it on his face.

Maybe he has perfected the freaking poker face after all.

When we walk back up to the party to make sure the restaurant staff is getting the hors d'oeuvres out and is ready for the feast to begin soon, he finally lets me off the hook.

"That was awkward."

I laugh in surprise and relief. "Yeah, a bit."

"I wonder which family portrait your mom is going to choose to hang over the fireplace."

I glance over at him, but he's looking straight ahead. "Ave, I know this is strange and hard. We knew it was going to be."

"Yup."

"Are you doing okay?"

He looks at me then. "Of course. Are you not doing okay?" The concern in his voice is loud and clear.

"I'm okay."

"No iced tea?"

I exhale with a huge sigh. To be perfectly honest, there's nothing I want more in the world right now than iced tea, but it no longer looks like the perfect solution we planned. Back before this all became real, I imagined him whisking me away to somewhere quiet when I got overwhelmed and helping me calm down.

How had I not understood that the overwhelming part would be him?

"No, I think I'm good on tea. I could definitely use a cocktail, though."

"I'll grab you one and meet you by the Reef kitchen. I just saw Kuramo's crew head up there, so they are probably getting ready to throw the meat on the grill."

I nod, and he's off.

Well, hell.

I guess that's that.

Here I was, stupid, naive little twenty-three-year-old Franzeska, thinking that she could somehow heal a thirty-year-old rift between these two men and manage to keep them both.

It somehow never occurred to me that I would have to choose.

I want to choose Avery.

But what if choosing him means losing the connection with my mom?

Losing the family home where I go for holidays?

Losing the dream I've always had of taking my own family home for Christmas? Sleeping in my childhood bedroom with my own kids. Showing them all of the pictures and trinkets my mom has held onto all these years.

Is that something I'm willing to give up?

I actually thought I wouldn't have to. I never thought it would come to this.

But if there's one thing I've learned over the last three days, it's this. I am definitely going to have to choose.

I can't live in this awkward, peacekeeping mode for the rest of my life. Hell, I can barely stand the idea of doing it until the end of the weekend. I need everyone to get along because when they don't, I have to fix it. And it's exhausting.

I can't live like that forever.

And I can't live two lives, leaving Avery at home—wherever that is—to fly home for visits on my own. It's too much.

I knew this relationship was impossible. I told myself—promised myself—that I wouldn't get attached.

For this exact freaking reason.

And yet here I am. At the epic wedding that I threw to launch my new company, lost in my own morose thoughts about how something I knew better than to get involved with is going to break my heart.

Screw that.

I am going to boss bitch my way through this wedding.

There will be plenty of time for my broken heart tomorrow.

Rule #36

THE DEEP END ISN'T A METAPHOR

AVERY

Well, that went well.

No, seriously.

I wasn't expecting to be called down to the family portrait session at all—never even crossed my mind, as a matter of fact—but when Franny and her mom looked at me with those eyes…I knew I was going to be in some shots.

There was one particularly good one of Fran and I—the wedding planners—where she's holding up her clipboard and grinning. Hopefully I can email the photographer later and get a copy for myself.

But maybe Fran will just give it to me herself. After all, it's officially possible that there's going to be a Fran and Avery after this whole thing is over. I try not to get distracted again thinking about it.

Just gotta keep this epic wedding flowing through the midnight hour, keep the people happy, keep the drinks pouring. Keep the pictures coming, too. I smile at a group of guests enjoying themselves with the Polaroids, adding their candid shots to the book laid out for that purpose on the welcome table. It was such a brilliant idea. I can't believe I thought it was stupid at first.

I have a lot to learn.

"Avery, thanks again for the invite. This wedding is absolutely gorgeous. I don't usually have so much to work with, but I think your girl really has something going here."

I smile over at Kendra, who just finished shooting the same Polaroid moment I was watching. "Yeah, it turned out great. Just wait until the meat hits the grill. Those guys usually sing reggae while they cook."

She gives me another grin and a shoulder pat, and she's off, chasing down the supernatural astronauts to try to get a pose out of them.

Hiring Kendra was a last-minute burst of inspiration, but one I'm pretty proud of. It's not an expense that Franny would have thought to splurge on before her company even begins, but having the dedicated brand photographer here, rather than just relying on the regular wedding photographer photos, is going to set her apart from day one.

My mind is reeling with ideas for how we can work with Kendra in the future to create logos and brochures. It's not every brand-new business owner who gets to have consultations with the absolute best branding consultant in the business, but mine does. After this party, Franny's going to have investors throwing themselves at her feet.

One in particular.

And I could not be more excited. She and I worked so well together, I can only imagine what we'll be able to pull off once we have a few more under our belts.

Sure, it's a little presumptuous to assume that I'm just going to be included, but I'm okay with that. I'm done being a silent investor like I more or less have become at The White Sands. I'm ready for a more hands-on life. At The Sands, at Franzeska Events, and in my relationship with Franny.

This is a turning point for me.

It's funny, I always wondered if I would ever settle down. Even while telling people it would never happen, I wondered. It's not something people like me plan for—at least not out loud—but I've watched it happen to enough lifelong travelers to know that you don't have to plan.

It can take you completely by storm, steamrolling you into submission.

I've been to the weddings. I've heard the stories. Men and women just like me, independently wealthy playboys and digital nomads who expected to keep on adventuring for the rest of their days—sidelined by love.

I always knew it could happen.

And then it did.

It's hard not to consider myself one of the lucky ones. For so many reasons, but mostly because the one I found is so special, so freaking perfect, the decision to settle down wherever she decides and work with her isn't even a decision. It's just another step down the path. One I'm happy to take.

Growing up, ol' boy.

I'm grinning as I swing into the kitchen.

"I want to smack that grin off your face so bad..." Dom grumbles as he hauls a heavy hotel pan of raw chicken onto the cart they'll use to pull it all down to the beach.

It only makes me smile harder. "What? You do not. You're happy for me."

Another grunt. "Are you here to help or just watch?"

"Do you need help?"

"No."

"Okay, perfect. Then I'm not here to help. I just want to check to make sure everything's on track for dinner, then I'm going to go deliver a cocktail to a very deserving wedding planner."

"You are coming in here to make sure I'm doing my work right." Dom's shaking his head. "Never thought I'd see the day."

I clap him on the back. "You're going to be seeing a lot more of me, buddy. It's just a matter of time before The White Sands brings me and my love on as the resident wedding planners, and we'll be all up in your business on the daily."

He pauses then, looking at me with raised eyebrows. "Yeah?"

I shrug. "Yeah. I mean, why not? I've got an in with the owners. I have a feeling they'll give her the job if I ask real nice."

"Well, I can't say I'd vote against having her on staff. She did an excellent job with this wedding. But that'd be a big step for you."

"A huge step, but I've already taken it, mate. I'm completely off the deep end."

"That much is clear," Dom mutters as he turns to get back to work.

Deciding that my job of checking in on them is complete, I head back toward the bar to snag an elderflower margarita for the woman of the hour.

I find her helping a young server spread ice over the base of what will soon be the seafood display.

"Your drink, milady." I pass over the cocktail with a bow.

She takes it gratefully. "Not too strong?"

I shake my head. "I told the bartender just a splash."

"Everything's going so great. Dinner's doing okay?"

"Yup. Dom was actually a little offended that I was checking up on him. Can you believe that?"

She laughs a bit, the sound feeding my soul. "Yeah, I guess I can see that."

We stand side by side and watch the party for a minute.

"You know, this whole thing is pretty much running itself. And you have such a capable assistant. You could probably go enjoy your brother's wedding for a bit. I'm sure there are a lot of people who would love to talk to you."

She smiles over at me. "I might do that for a bit. Do you want to come? It's not exactly your family—I mean, because it's mostly my side. I mean, shit. You know what I mean."

She's so perfect, even putting her foot straight into her mouth is adorable. "I know what you mean. I think I'm going to go make sure the guys don't need help with the barbecue."

"Okay, well. I'll see you at dinner probably."

"You're going to sit and eat?"

"Yeah. I'm going to sit with my family."

"I'm probably going to sit off to the side with Sam somewhere."

She looks over at me, forehead creased. "You sure?"

Sure that I don't want to struggle through another awkward meal with the fam? Definitely. "Yeah, I want to check in with him anyway."

She nods, probably as relieved as I am that she's off the hook for this one. The family is something we're going to have to deal with eventually, but there's been enough of that already this weekend.

Baby steps.

"I'll see you on the dance floor later. If you need anything, just text me. I have my phone on."

She nods but says nothing.

The dance floor is absolutely rocking. I'm helping Sam get the last of the white string-lights plugged in, fielding compliment after compliment about how excellent the meal was.

They're not wrong.

Kuramo's crew pulled out all the stops and came with a meal fit for royalty. People are going to be talking about it for years.

I didn't make my way over to the head table during the meal, although I kept Franny in my sights. Sam didn't even complain when I spent the whole time I talked to him watching her.

She laughed and ate and drank. Got so many hugs. Cried three times.

And now she's dancing with her nieces to some ridiculous eighties song.

When the DJ throws on a slow jam, I make my move.

"Mind if I cut in?" I ask Freida, the older of the two astronauts.

The little spitfire turns her glare on me, hands balled into fists on her hips. "What does that mean?" she demands.

"I'd like to dance with your auntie here."

The girl softens a bit and glances up at Fran, who nods.

"Okay. But we're still going to be right here so don't step on us with your giant feet."

I stifle a laugh. "I wouldn't dream of it."

Fran steps into my arms, and we fall into a soft sway together.

"Are you happy it's almost over?" I ask and feel her whole body tighten.

I spin her and pull her back, not too close, but close enough. She still says nothing. Her face is downcast, unreadable.

"There's going to be another wedding soon, love. Once you get that website up and running. Once these pictures hit Instagram, you'll be booked solid."

"Yeah," she says finally. The sadness in her voice takes me by surprise. I mean, sure, I'm sad this chapter is coming to an end, but the next one looks just as bright.

I'm just about to say so when I feel a firm hand on my shoulder.

Fucking Frederick.

"May I cut in?"

I'm about to tell the guy to back off, or he's going to get something else cut, but Fran drops my hands and steps back. "Sure," she says, and walks over to take his hands.

Not a lot I can do but step aside.

"Meet you at Reef in twenty?" Fran says to me. "We can make sure the cleanup crew is all here and knows what to do?"

I nod and watch as the crowd swallows them up.

Rule #37

GET A LITTLE PERSPECTIVE

FRAN

The irony is not lost on me as I let go of one Covington man to take the hand of the other.

"This has been a lovely party, Franzeska."

I smile up at him. "Thanks. And thanks again for this opportunity. I know it wouldn't have happened without you."

He shrugs, but I can tell he's pleased. "I do what I can to help." He twirls me exactly like his son did, pulling me back to the same appropriate distance. "Speaking of which, I know we're going to need to talk about a possible investment in your company when we get back to the States. I'd say you sure earned yourself that meeting with this event. I'm very impressed."

It's unexpected, but welcome. "That would be great, Frederick."

I should be ecstatic that he is all but offering to fund my startup. Just a few months ago, I would have been.

Right now, though, all I feel is exhaustion.

It's probably just the events of the day. This has been a bit of a doozy.

As soon as the song is over, Frederick pats my shoulder kindly and returns to my mother's side.

I should go find Avery and start planning for the party cleanup, but I'm not ready. I told him twenty minutes, and I need all of that time to get my shit back in order.

I'm feeling all kinds of discombobulated right now.

Swiping my champagne glass from the table, I sneak down to the beach and find a quiet, dark spot far enough away from the commotion at the fire pit where I can be alone for a few minutes.

I flop into the sand, worry about keeping my dress pristine long gone. The weight of my decision is sitting heavy on my shoulders.

Because I have made a decision.

The hardest one I'm ever going to have to make.

I briefly consider just running. Sneaking up to my room and gathering some essentials, paying someone at the boat dock to take me over to the mainland where I can wait for the airport to open.

I laugh sadly to myself at the idea.

It's a fun fantasy, but only just that. There's no easy way out of this one.

I comfort myself with the knowledge that I'm not going to be altering his life plans in any way with my pronouncement. Hell, he could already be planning his next escapade across the globe as we speak. He hasn't mentioned it, but that doesn't mean anything.

Or it could mean everything.

If he doesn't want to tell me what his plans are, chances are they don't include me.

It's for the best.

For the goddamn best.

It's no use. I can't make myself feel better about this.

I flop back in the sand, letting my now empty glass fall to the beach beside me. The stars twinkle away above me, completely undeterred by my minuscule personal drama.

And maybe that's the answer.

I'm feeling like this is the biggest thing in the universe, but it's so not. Not even close.

My silly little feelings mean nothing in the grand scheme of things.

Maybe I can somehow adopt that attitude for the next few days. Calm, kind detachment. I mean, it was always going to end, right? The only thing that's changed about Avery and my initial agreement is my feelings.

I can woman up. I can adult my way through this.

Yeah. I can do it.

As a matter of fact, when I look at the situation objectively, I have kind of a great opportunity here.

I am in a benefits-only relationship with someone I trust with my life.

This could actually work in my favor.

I mean, I never really thought that I would be launching my stratospheric wedding planning career debut as a freaking virgin. Those old fears just kinda got out of hand. Once I spent enough years telling myself I was only safe as long as no guy went there, I convinced myself that it was true.

When will I ever find a guy I trust this much again?

Not soon enough.

What a brilliant idea. This will be such a fun sendoff, he and I getting to share something special after working together on this project. And he's no doubt going to be a friend for life, after some of these feelings have a chance to dissipate. It can be a cute story I someday tell my adult daughters.

You are never going to believe what I'm about to tell you about Uncle Avery!

I laugh to myself again, but this time it's less melancholy.

This could actually be fun.

I think he's going to agree.

Rule #38

THERE'S A FIRST TIME FOR EVERYTHING

AVERY

"You ready to head up?"

The last of the cleanup crew cart away the remaining tables, making way for the overnight cleaners to work their magic.

It's wild standing here on the patio, in the sparkling moonlight, looking around at the empty space. It's almost like it never happened.

"I'm ready when you are." As if I was going to leave her down here.

"You go ahead, 'kay? Leave your door unlocked, though. I'm going to sneak in after dropping my stuff in my room."

I turn to her then, eyes wide with surprise and pleasure. "You sure about that?"

She shrugs, tired and happy. "No one's gonna come looking for me tonight."

Well, I'm certainly not going to turn her down. "My door's always open."

"See you in a few."

And so I do leave her standing there.

My room is an oasis of familiar smells, of calm, still, quiet. I hadn't realized what a rambunctious day it really was until opening that door and being so grateful to close it behind myself.

I'm sitting on the couch, thinking with my eyes closed, when the sound of her coming in snaps me back to life.

"Falling asleep over there, old man?"

"Never."

I open and accept her entire body at once as it slides over mine. She's warm and soft and wearing entirely too many clothes. I slip my hands up the backs of her legs and right up her dress, pushing the material up as I go until her fancy dress bunches around her waist.

The way she just settles into me. The ease with which she sits up just a little to allow me to slip the garment over her head and then falls back onto me, lips finding mine.

It's like we've been doing this for a million years.

People like to say that talking is the best way to get on the same page, but clearly Franny and I have eclipsed the need for that.

We exist on the same page, on the same beat, on the same breath so naturally.

Her fingers are in their favorite home, tangled in my hair, as my tongue presses deep into her mouth. My grip on her ass tightens as my need to take this further grows.

"I think I'm going to lock the door," I murmur, face still buried in her neck.

"I thought your door was always open."

"Tonight may have to be an exception."

I stand, bringing her with me and cross the few paces to the front door. Pressing her back into the solid wood, I grind into her center, and she moans.

I slide the lock into place and slip the same hand between us, cupping her soft, wet heat. "Damn, girl. How long has it been?"

She laughs lightly, arms pressing into my shoulders as she lifts my face back to hers. "A day?"

"At least two."

"Well, I'm ready."

"I think I could give you your first one right here against the door." I move against her slow and hard, just to prove my point.

"No. Bed," she manages with her breath held.

She's not wrong there. I am freaking exhausted after the longest day of work in my life, and I'm sure I would be regretting any kind of acrobatics in the morning.

I throw her down on my bed and watch her body bounce. Watch her hair leap up to cover her face before she brushes it to the sides and pins me with those eyes.

She's got me.

I've let go of any ideas I had about my life, how it was going to go, what I wanted.

All I want now is to see where Fran will take me.

She's splayed out before me, her hot, exhausted body writhing on the bed, begging for my touch. I don't make her wait.

Her little undies come off, and I press her legs open further, the scent of her nearly sending my eyes rolling back in my head.

Mine.

I lick her, rosebud to clit, sliding my tongue gently around the soft folds of her body. She moans and relaxes even more, her legs falling further open and giving me full access to her body. I accept the privilege and add my hands to the mix, using two fingers to hold her little nub in place while I flick the tip with my tongue.

When she cries out, I bring the other hand to her opening and slip two fingers inside. "God, you're so wet, love."

She answers by arching her back off the bed and pressing her body harder into my face.

I obey her command with more force, flicking and sucking, pressing and curling inside her. She comes apart in my grasp after only a few short minutes, expelling the tension of the day into me. I accept it and push her on and on, waiting for the telltale tightening and laughter before I let up.

I can't say that I'm not excited for my turn on that ride. This whole event has been nothing if not a bit tense, and I'm craving the relief I now see on her face.

I start to get up. To begin the usual process of finding the lube bottle, flipping her over, but she stops me.

Places me flat on my back and climbs me like a tree.

Whatever this is, I'll take it.

Her lips land on mine as her naked body hovers over me, and I offer her a taste of herself. One she devours as her tongue slides against mine.

My shirt comes off easily with a pull from Franny and one enormous core contraction from yours truly. She's on the button of my shorts now, fingers working feverishly toward their prize.

My raging hard-on smacks against my stomach as she pulls the shorts off and tosses them to the side. I watch her face as she grips my cock, eyes focused, lip clasped between teeth.

I'm content to just lay back and let whatever she has in mind unfold. There's no way I could be disappointed with this little vixen taking charge.

"Condom?"

Um…

My mouth opens and then closes. Opens again and closes again. She's still watching me with those impatient sex eyes.

"Um, yeah. Bedside table."

I watch as she crawls over there. I listen to the crinkle of the familiar wrapper in her hand. But I still don't quite get there.

She rips the package open and fumbles to get the thing turned the right way. I should help but…help with what?

"Franny—"

"I got it, just give me a second…"

She does indeed got it.

The latex slides over my still hard cock right to the base. She looks up at me triumphantly.

"What—"

I don't get to ask my question, not that I know exactly what I was going to say anyway, because her lips stop me with another passionate, all-consuming kiss.

Damn, this woman is great at distracting me. My hands slide up her naked body, and my eyes slip closed as I lose myself in the feel of her.

Wait. Hold up.

I grip her shoulders and pull her lips away from mine far enough that I can look her in the eyes. "Franny, why am I wearing a condom right now?"

She bites that lip again and raises her eyebrows. "I want to do it."

"Do…it?"

"Yeah. I'm ready. I want to do it. And I want to do it with you."

My mind is reeling. Half of it is screaming at me to just go for it, the other half jumping up and down, waving red flags.

"I thought we were going to talk about this." I'm just stalling, and I know it. Whatever she wants, she's going to get.

"Ave, it's not that big of a deal."

"It's a big deal for you."

"Everyone does it."

"You don't."

She sits back on my stomach, arms crossed over her chest. My poor cock is alone down there, sheathed and confused, bumping up against her ass where it rests just out of reach.

"I'm ready. I trust you. I want to do this."

I am at a total loss for words. Obviously, I want to do this as well, but I'm terrified at the same time. This is a huge step for her. For us.

Well, I have been taking a lot of big steps lately, I guess this is just one more.

"Don't make this weird." She's on the edge of being annoyed with my stalling, and I can't have that.

I bend to her will as easily as grass to the wind.

"You...you gonna be on top?"

She nods.

"Okay."

Her lips meet mine once more, and I press into her mouth, gripping her ass with both hands, trying to let the awkwardness of the last few minutes slip away.

Franny seems to be over it. She seems as excited as ever. I decide to join her there.

One hand slips between her legs and dips into her wetness. "My wet girl."

"Do you think I'm wet enough for you?"

Fucking hell, we're going to play this game, huh?

Now I wish I was the one on top, slipping my tip inside her virgin pussy. But I have to let her do this her way.

"You feel so ready. You wanna take my cock, love?"

Her eyes flash as she gives a little nod.

"Well, slide on down there."

Her wide eyes hold mine for another hot second before she glances down at where our bodies meet. I watch with rapt attention as she shuffles down until she's on my thighs, my cock now between her legs. She takes it in both hands, and I nearly come just from the force of the contact after so much anticipation.

"There you go. Now lift up a bit on your knees."

She obeys, eyes darting back and forth between my face and where her fists have a death grip on my shaft.

It seems she's happy to take my instruction, so I continue.

"When you're ready, you can slide forward a bit, yeah, like that." My voice cracks as she lands my tip down on her clit and slides it back through her wetness. "You know where it goes."

She presses her hips forward a few inches until my cock lines right up.

"Is that the spot?" I ask, barely able to breathe through the intensity of the moment.

She nods, not looking up.

"Okay, then. When you're ready."

Her head lifts, and our eyes lock. I can feel my mouth hanging open, feel my lungs screaming at me to breathe, but all I can do is watch.

She never looks away as she slowly lowers her body onto mine.

The sound that escapes my lips as my tip slides into her an inch or so does not sound human.

Franny makes a similar noise and presses down just a bit more.

I risk a second of looking away from her eyes to take in the sight of my cock penetrating her body as she slowly, so slowly, settles her weight down on me.

When I'm fully inside her, I meet her eyes once more. We just stare for a moment, neither of us daring to move.

"Feel okay?" I ask.

She nods.

I reach back and take her ass in my hands, the movement of my body shifting the angle of my cock just a bit, and she gasps.

"Still okay?"

Another nod.

"Say something, Franny."

"Fuck me."

Fucking hell.

"You…you fuck yourself for a few minutes, and then I'll take over, okay?"

She nods and begins to rock her hips with a movement as smooth as a boat on the ocean. She's got her clit rubbing right on my pelvic bone, and I know she can feel it.

I would give anything in the world to know what that feels like. To know how my cock compares to my fingers, or my tongue. To understand what it is to be breached like this for the first time.

She leans forward and places one hand on either side of my shoulders. I have to bite back a moan as she pulls me out almost all the way, and then slides me back in. She does it again and again, playing with me, playing with the way our bodies work together.

"You feel incredible," I say, never taking my eyes from hers.

She sits straight up, and I can tell by the surprised look on her face that she wasn't expecting the way my cock shot deeper inside her when she changed angles so suddenly. With another of those orgasm-inducing lip bites, she swirls her hips around a bit, exploring how my tip moves deep inside her body.

"I'm going to get on top, okay?"

She nods, and I roll us with one heave.

Franny laughs as she lands on her back with her legs splayed. I slipped out when we rolled and I'm now kneeling before her, marveling in the perfection that is her body.

There's no need to check to see if she's still wet and ready, I can see her entrance glistening for me.

I dive right in.

With my hips in charge, I'm driving into her with a force that she hadn't managed to find on her own, although I know she'll get there.

Her tits bounce, and her mouth freezes in a wide O as I grip her hips and work her.

"Fuck, Ave, that feels…insane."

I take that as a compliment, one that I could easily offer to her in return. Her tight, wet body wrapped around my cock is easily the greatest feeling of my life. Her muscles churn and massage me as I pump in and out.

It's all too much, and I pull out suddenly, trying to edge myself just a bit. There's no way I'm coming before she does.

Franny looks down as I slide my tip back inside her, working the shallow area of her body where she always likes my fingers.

"What do you need, love?"

"I need you closer. All the way inside me, holding me close."

I pull out again and crawl over to sit with my back to the headboard, knees bent. Grasping Franny's hand, I pull her up and guide her into my lap. She seats herself on my cock like a goddamn queen, and I wrap my arms around her.

I let her get the motion started and then add my hips, moving counter to her movement and adding to the friction. With her legs splayed against me like this and her body leaning forward against my chest, I know she's feeling it. The breathy little moans that won't stop escaping her lips are music to my ears.

Reaching up, I slide the fingers of one hand into her hair. Not to grip and pull, but to cradle her head and keep her looking at me. Her eyes open, and we stay locked in the intense stare as we both continue to move.

"Do you want me to come?" Franny asks breathlessly.

"Yes, love. That's just about all I've ever wanted in life."

She smiles. "I'm sure that's not true."

I shake my head, holding her gaze. "It's the truest thing I've ever said. Come for me, love."

She bites her lip and sucks in a breath, pressing herself against me as she moves slowly.

The moment her orgasm begins, I feel her body tighten. Her face transforms with an expression of sublime pleasure.

I hold her head gently in my hand, keeping up the steady rock of my hips as her core clenches, and she tries to drop her head back. I don't let her, keeping her face straight to mine, our noses nearly touching as the breath finally whooshes out of her. Her eyes go wide as the sensation grows, and she presses her cheek to mine.

The movement feels like completing a circuit. I feel completed. Complete.

Franny slowly drags her face across mine until our lips meet. I sink into the kiss, my hands still holding her hips steady as she comes. My tongue slips out to taste her, and it's so sweet, so salty, so Franny. I could die in this moment as a happy man.

Her body stills and releases its stranglehold on my cock, allowing us both to take a breath. It feels like the first one I've taken in an hour. I feel as breathless as Franny looks—and I haven't even come yet.

"It feels so different like this. It's like…I don't know how to describe it. It's like I melt into you. I don't even have to try. My body knows just what to do."

"You ready for more?" I ask and she nods immediately, eyes bright and happy.

"Give me all the crazy positions. I'm ready for it."

I laugh at her unabashed eagerness. Flipping her over onto her belly, I land a hard slap on her ass, smiling as it jiggles for me. Then I haul her up on her knees and place her hands on the headboard.

Behind her on one knee, one foot on the bed for leverage, I hitch myself inside her once more. She knows the program from behind and tilts her hips forward to allow me to sink deeper. I'm not sure what she was expecting to happen, but I know for damn sure it feels different than when I'm fucking her ass because her voice takes on a note of surprise and excitement that nearly does me in.

"Oh my god, Avery, yes!"

I grasp her body like a lifeline, sliding in and out, praying that I can hold on long enough to get her off again. I slip a hand between her legs, pressing one finger to the side of her clit and holding tightly as I fuck her. That seems to be the right move because her cries build with every thrust.

We're both surprised by the sudden banging on the wall behind the headboard, but I don't know why. We're loud as hell. We've probably woken the whole floor.

I pull her away from the wall, and we collapse on the bed in a fit of giggles.

"Who's your neighbor?" she asks breathlessly when she gets ahold of her laughter.

I shake my head and shrug. "Doesn't matter."

"I feel bad that we woke them."

"They're just jealous."

Her bashful smile turns sly as she rolls herself fully over to face me. "What's next?"

"You were liking it quite a bit from behind."

"I did like that. But let's do it face-to-face again. I love looking at you."

Lord, take me now.

The fervor of the last position seems to have dissipated a bit. I keep my eyes locked on hers as I slip slowly back into her body. She accepts me like it's always been this way. The feel of her muscles gripping at my tip as it enters her is like something I remember from a past life.

I don't pick up my pace this time but keep gently massaging the inside of her as my mouth finds her perfect nipples. As my tongue traces every inch of her that I can reach, she clings to me and rocks her hips with my motion.

When she comes again, it's intense and passionate, her body curled around my body. I hold her close as she grinds herself into me, stealing every bit of pleasure from our coupling.

When she finally stills below me, I brush her hair to the side and take in her happy, relaxed face.

"That was...wild," she breathes, her eyes still dark with desire. "Oh, you are going to come now, right? Do it, Avery. Fuck me until you come."

I pull right out and sit back on my heels. "I can come a different way. That's a lot for your first time." It's the coming inside her that was the basis for all the years of fear. I'll never forget that.

"No, no. I want it all. I want the full deflowering experience. You promised."

I don't recall promising anything, but hell if I'm going to say no to her.

"You got my orgasms, Avery. I want yours."

My cock slips itself back inside her before I can fully think this through.

"What do you like best?" she asks, her voice still heavy with pleasure.

"I like when you're so wet," I start, slipping myself out just to the tip. "Like you are now."

"Oh, yeah? What else?"

I start a steady pump, leaning over her body, pressing my forehead to hers. "I like when you murder me with those fingernails."

The request lands quickly, and it's not even a full second before the delicious pain of her grip shoots through my shoulders and back.

"What else?"

"I like to look down and see how much you like it when I fuck you."

"Like this?" she answers, rolling her eyes back as she presses her head into the mattress, her mouth in a round O.

I don't even need to answer. One look at her adorable porn star expression has me contracting with a moan of pleasure. I know the condom is good to go—I triple checked after she came, and I pulled out—but there's still a lingering concern in the back of my mind as I spill into her. I fight through it and let her absorb all of the energy radiating out of me as I come.

She does absorb it. Grips me tightly and holds my body so close. Her strong inner muscles milk the last spasm out of me until I'm completely spent.

I collapse on the bed beside her, unsure if I can even manage to deal with the condom before sleep attacks me with its steel club.

Franny sits right up, though. "Wow."

I roll to one side and peek up at her through half dead eyes.

The same activity that has completely wiped me seems to have only energized her. I watch with amazement as she crawls off the bed. "I'm going to grab some water. Do you need anything?"

"Yeah, a towel."

I catch the hand towel from the bathroom as it flies in my direction.

She wakes me up sometime later when she crawls back into bed and takes the used towel from me. "You okay?"

I curl my body around her where she sits beside me. "I'm more than okay, love. I'm the best I've ever been. More importantly, are you okay? Franny—"

"I'm the best, Avery. Better than I ever could have imagined."

The next time I wake, the world is still and dark, signaling the deepest part of the night. I'm still curled around Franny's body, half covered by the white sheet. I take a moment to trace my eyes over her tan lines, the curve of her lips, and the outline of her loose hair on the bed.

I memorize every inch of her in the moonlight.

When I realize that's what I'm doing, I smile to myself. It's become a habit, but not a habit I need anymore. I'll get to have and hold the real thing every day. No need for committing her to memory.

I drift back off to sleep with her taste on my lips.

Rule #39

THIS IS GONNA HURT

FRAN

I lie still for as long as I can but waking him is inevitable.

"Hey."

"Morning," Avery replies, yawning and rolling to his back to stretch.

I watch him greet the day like a wild cat, yawning and huffing and rolling this way and that like sleep has been torn from him.

I'm going to miss waking up beside this man. But all good things must end. Right?

After I use the bathroom and freshen up, I put on coffee in his tiny kitchen and then make my way back to the bed. Avery's sitting up now, smiling at me.

"We did it."

I laugh. That could mean so many things. "We sure did."

"I meant the wedding."

Shaking my head, I laugh again. "I'm sure you did."

"But the other stuff, too."

I just shake my head once more. There's a lot I could say, but

I'm worried I won't be able to hold back my emotions if I do. "You about ready to face this day?"

"You mean to get rid of all these pesky guests so the world can go back to just me and you? Hell yes, I am."

I put my hands on my hips and narrow my eyes into a glare. "That's my family you're talking about."

"I know it is. And I've been so nice to them." He walks to the edge of the bed on his knees and tries to capture my waist.

I take a step back, knowing exactly what will happen if he succeeds.

Plans foiled, Avery sits back on his heels and grins up at me. "But now it's time for them to go."

"And then what?"

When they go, I go.

He goes somewhere else.

Right? Isn't this the end?

"And then you and I can live forever in my hotel room."

"That's not what we agreed on, Ave."

My statement hits him square in the jaw, and I watch the shockwave ripple through his features. "What do you mean?"

"Kind of but not really stepsiblings with benefits while we worked the wedding. That was the arrangement." I'm amazed by how level my voice sounds. It doesn't match the tsunami going on inside.

He's on his feet, rushing toward me. I back into the kitchen.

"That was a long time ago, love. I thought things were different now."

"What made you think that?" I thought it too, and I had a feeling he was starting to change his mind, but it's too late for that now. I learned how things have to be over the last few days of the wedding, so I stand my ground.

"Because we…I…" He's at a loss for words, and I can't blame him. If he'd blindsided me with this, I would feel the same.

I might not have shown it, but I would be devastated.

Hell, I'm devastated now, and I've had a full twelve hours to get used to the idea.

"You just gave me your virginity." His voice is soft and hard all at once.

"I mean, only technically."

"Well, yeah, but technically…"

I shake my head, unable to meet his eye.

"Ave…"

"No. This can't be real. You can't be serious."

"I'm serious."

"You're just going to leave? And then what? Never see me again?"

"I don't know yet. All I know is that I have to go back to my life. And I think we both know my life is not what you want."

"I want what you want."

Anger flares inside me. Why is he making this so difficult? Sure, he may have thought we had a few more months of fucking ahead of us, but surely, he has his next adventure in mind.

"No, Ave. You don't. You don't have a home. You don't speak to your family. You won't speak to my family. You can't commit to anything or stay in one place long enough to build trust with people. I can't live like that. I'm not like you."

"I'm not like me, either. I mean, not like that. I'm not like that. I've been torturing myself my whole life waiting for someone. Waiting for you to come and save me from myself."

I shake my head, sadness settling over me like a mist. "I can't save you, Avery."

"I'll be different. I'll change."

"You had a chance to change last night at the fucking wedding, and you didn't. You politely ignored all of the important people in my life when you could have used that party as an opportunity to get to know them. And now, all you want is for them to go away so you never have to see them again. That isn't you being different. That's you being exactly the same."

I may have killed him. If he wasn't still standing, I would walk over and check his pulse. All signs of life wash out of his features.

"I'm going to go," I say.

He shakes his head but says nothing.

"Let's talk in a few hours, okay?"

My hand is on the doorknob before he speaks.

"I was in the pictures."

I turn to look at him, still standing where I left him, not facing me as I prepare to walk out.

"What?"

"The family portraits. I was in them."

I almost run back to him and curl him in my arms. I almost decide right then and there that maybe I *can* save him. Maybe it would be worth it to sacrifice myself for him. To make him happy. But I can't.

"You were in half of the family portraits, Ave. Not the half they're going to use."

He doesn't turn around as I slip out the door and close it gently behind me.

Rule #40

IT AIN'T OVER TIL IT'S OVER

AVERY

I'm not sure how long I stand there. Time has lost all meaning. All I know is at some point, I can't feel my legs anymore, and I collapse on the sofa.

I'm utterly wrecked.

If I'd seen this coming, it would have been one thing. But nothing in the world could have blindsided me more.

Blind.

That's exactly what I was. This whole time, I was catching feelings for someone who I had no business catching feelings for. Telling myself it was going to be fine. That I was going to walk away and get over it.

Until things changed last night.

The wedding, my conversation with Reina, Fran and my special night together. I added it all up and interpreted it exactly the way I wanted.

The way that worked out in my favor.

I failed to add in the parts about Franny and what she wants. My lifestyle of avoiding family in order to avoid family problems has worked fine for me, but I knew from the get-go that it wasn't what she wanted. I just chose to skim over that fact when I decided I wanted a long-term thing between us.

Homeless, family-less, jobless. Aimless. Goal-less.

Pointless.

What have I been doing with my life?

I'm on my feet in an instant. This is exactly the point in a problem when I would usually bail and lose myself in another adventure. Another distraction.

Not this time.

This time, I'm going to do what it takes to make it right. To prove to her that I'm not all of those things. Or, at the very least, that I'm not going to be them anymore.

I make a mental list of the things I need to do to make this right and decide to tackle the easiest of the bunch first.

The one that involves spending money.

I'm out the door before I can talk myself out of it.

I should stop by the lobby to share my heartbreak—and current plans—with someone. Anyone. But I don't. I'm out the front door and into my golf cart before anyone can stop me.

"Avery! What a surprise. What can I do for you this morning?"

"I need a house. A really good one. And fast."

"Okay…" Karen, the real estate agent who helped us through the years acquiring staff housing and who helped Dom buy his house, eyes me suspiciously.

But she won't turn me away.

"I have a couple of choice properties across the island. Do you want to set up a time—"

"Nope, you just choose the best one and get it for me, okay? Choose the one that you would want. And make sure it's full of furniture and homey stuff. Just leave the key under the mat. Text me when it's ready, yeah?"

No, actually, is the answer to that.

You can't buy a house by dropping your black card on the

desk of a real estate agent and asking her to fill the fridge with groceries on her way out.

By the time I'm leaving her office, having chosen what she tells me is the best of the properties and signed off on an offer for her to submit—one she assures me will secure me the property—it's been hours.

I drive back to The Sands like a madman with a grainy computer printout of my new home—our new home—as the only proof I have that I'm now officially a responsible adult.

It's not much, but it's going to have to be enough.

After nearly having an aneurysm waiting for the elevator during the busy checkout hour, I take the stairs two at a time and arrive at her door a sweaty, grinning, mess.

She always told me I didn't need to knock anymore, but I feel like things are different now. I give the door a rhythmic knock, rehearsing my speech in my head.

It swings open just moments later.

"Yes? Can I help you?"

The young housekeeper doesn't recognize me, but that's probably for the best. "The woman who was staying here? Is she in there?"

"No, sir. She checked out."

What. The. Fuck.

It takes half the time to get back down to the lobby as it took for me to get up, as my feet slide dangerously down the carpeted stairs. I scan the busy lobby but don't spot Fran or her family.

Slipping past the line and behind the counter, I have the agent bring up her information. She's been gone for almost an hour.

The chances that she's still at the water taxi dock are slim, considering the boats run every half hour this time of day, but certainly not zero.

Unfortunately, Ben's in my golf cart when I jog back to it.

"Slide over, man. I gotta drive to town."

"No."

"What the fuck do you mean no? You look like you've got something to say, so you can say it while I drive."

His arms cross over his chest, and he doesn't budge. "Karen called me."

"So the fuck what. You aren't my parent. I can buy whatever I want."

"Sure. But running in off the street and demanding that she pick you out a house and just buy it for you raised some suspicions. What's going on?"

"Fran left me. She went home with her mom and family. She doesn't want me because I'm a homeless waste of space who's never committed to anything in his life. She doesn't think I can be the kind of person who will show up and be part of her family. So, I bought a house. A really good one." I hold up the picture, which is terminally crumpled from being grasped in my fist for so many stair runs. "And I just need to show her."

Ben watches me for a long moment, the look in his eyes so sad that I have to look away.

"I don't need your pity, man."

"Get in, Ave."

I do, but only because it's what I wanted to do in the first place.

At the end of the drive, he turns left, however, rather than right to head to town.

"Where are we going? The water taxi is the other way."

"I know where the water taxi is, Avery."

I flop back in my seat, resigned to whatever fresh hell this guy has in store for me. I would argue more, but I know she's not still at the dock. I knew it before I even left the hotel. I just couldn't not chase after her.

Now that I'm stuck in the cart with Ben, my mind has a chance to settle down and think a bit.

She left.

I went to the real estate agent's office, and while I was there, she packed her bags and got on a plane.

The last thing she said to me was that we'd talk in a few hours. I took that to mean she was sticking around.

Okay, well, the actual last thing she said was that bomb about how they just took a bunch of fake pictures with me in them to make me feel included, a little piece of information I haven't even begun to process.

But before that, she said she would talk to me.

And now she's gone.

I'm jolted out of my own head by Ben turning the cart to head down a long, paved driveway into the jungle. We pass through an open gate and continue on.

"Where are we?" But as I ask, I spot Karen standing in front of a large white brick house.

The place looks even better than the pictures, with a garden of native plants circling the large, covered porch and big windows along the whole front draped with cream-colored curtains. I spot a tree heavy with lemons and another thick with pink blossoms.

Home.

"Fat lot of good it's going to do you to show up with your girl to a house you've never even been to."

I climb out of the cart instead of answering. Karen holds the front door open for me as I walk inside.

The heat from the day seems to dissipate as I cross into the dim room. It's wide open, with tile floors and arched doorways that open into hallways and other rooms. I can see through the windows at the far end that there's a big backyard with a swimming pool. A curved white staircase leads to the upper floor just to my left, the banister made of white stone and topped every few feet with a painted stone seashell.

Home.

I had a home back in New York, one where all of my childhood memories took place. But it didn't feel like this. This place is more like the quiet end of a day, when I'm tired and hot. The smell of meat cooking on a grill. The sound of laughter and bare feet on tile.

This is where I can build a life for myself.

I've never felt this way about anywhere before.

"Nice choice, man." Ben comes up behind me and puts his arm around my shoulder, pulling me in.

"Do you think she'll like it?"

"Do you like it?"

"I love it."

"Well, that's really all that matters."

He's wrong, but I don't have the energy to argue.

"Are there beds and stuff upstairs?"

Karen's voice pipes up from behind us. "The house is fully furnished, but the furnishings are, of course, as-is. You'll have to check on the quality of them and make sure they're up to your standards. This has been a vacation home for a number of years. It was a private residence before that."

I walk up the stairs, not caring if anyone follows me, poking my head into each and every room.

Home.

I choose our bedroom. I choose an office for Franny to run her business from.

When I come back to the top of the stairs, Ben's waiting at the bottom, looking up at me.

"I think I'm ready."

"Oh yeah?"

I nod, walking slowly down the steps until I'm standing beside him in the foyer. "Yeah. This feels like home, man. Can you feel it?"

He nods.

"I guess I'm going to hang out with my dad. Oh, I should take some pictures to show them." I pull out my phone and see the notification. It's from fifteen minutes earlier.

Fran: Sorry I just left. I went to your room, but you weren't there. It's probably for the best. I'm going to go back to Aspen and get settled for a bit. I can't tell you how much I appreciate having your help over the last few months. I've enjoyed our time together more than I could ever say. Maybe in another life it would have worked out between us. I just don't know how to make it real.

"Damn. With a text? That's cold," Ben says, reading over my shoulder.

I shove the phone back in my pocket and scowl at him. "Changes nothing."

"Give her time."

"No. Nope. Not happening. She doesn't get to leave. This is not how it ends."

"Ave, you've got to give her time."

"I don't have to do shit. You can't tell me what to do. You're not my father." It sounds childish, but it's a long running joke between the two of us. I actually say it to try to lighten the mood.

Ben fails to take my joke as a hint to back off. "No, Ave, I'm not your father. But sometimes I wish I was. I wouldn't have left you like that. I have a son of my own, and I can't imagine leaving him. I don't know how the man did that to you. But you have to know that was his own shit. It wasn't about you."

I turn to face him, even though I'd rather run. He holds my wavering gaze with his steady one.

"You are a worthwhile man. You are strong and loyal and loving. You take care of people and look out for those who can't look out for themselves. You are the best friend a guy could ever ask for. You will make an incredible partner. An even better parent. I would trust you with my life and my son's life."

"Shit, man," I say, eyes falling to my feet as they start to mist over. I rub them with the crook of my arm. "You're just saying that."

But I don't mean it.

Ben doesn't bother to defend his words. He gets it.

"Whether it works out with this girl or not, you have got to stop looking at yourself like a man without a family. Without a home. You've got this home now," he gestures around us at the grand, vaulted ceilings of my new house. "But you always had a home. You have it on Merit, and at The Sands. You have a home in New York. And you have homes all over the globe. The homes of people whose lives you've made better by just showing up and being the glorious human being who is Avery Covington."

I'm crying now, even with Ben's dry, stern face pinning me to the spot. Nothing new there. I shake my head and look up at the ceiling.

"Fine. So, you think I should give her some time?"

"No, man. I misspoke. I think you should do the most Avery thing you can possibly do in this situation. That's the only thing you should ever do."

"So, the helicopter then."

Ben just shakes his head and laughs.

When we get back out to the driveway, another golf cart is pulling up. I smile as Dom and Sam climb out and head toward us. I should have known these guys wouldn't be far behind.

We always were a pack.

"Sweet digs, man," Dom whistles, shading his eyes to look up at the house.

"It's bigger than yours," I respond with a grin, earning me a rare one from Dom in return.

"I brought you a housewarming gift," Sam says, looking down at the small potted plant in his hands. "The Sands donated it, I didn't have time to, you know…"

"Thanks, man. Do you want to put it inside? I've got to go rally the helicopter pilot."

"I already called him," Sam responds. "He'll meet you there in half an hour."

My mouth drops open in surprise. "How'd you know?"

Dom laughs. "This ain't our first Avery rodeo. Besides, we like the girl. She's good for you. Whatever it takes to make it work, you can count on us."

I shake my head, eyes misting up once more. "Thanks. That means a lot."

"You'd do the same for us," Sam chimes in. "As a matter of fact, you have. Remember when my college girlfriend Samantha wanted to go to that show, and it was impossible to get tickets? You just happened to know some guy who could get us in."

"And last spring when Reina's bag was lost by that Indian airline—accidentally put on a plane to Thailand—and no one we could get a hold of knew what to tell us? You just flew over there and found it. She was so happy when you showed up at our house with that damn bag."

"And every time Ains needed someone to be home with him when I had to go away for work, you were there. No matter where in the world you were, you flew back to New York to stay with him. Up until the day he graduated high school, that kid never needed an overnight babysitter."

"Bet you wish I was babysitting him now, huh?" I do the obvious thing and try to deflect the heavy emotions with a joke.

The guys just shake their heads, almost in unison.

"We're serious, man. You may not have taken the same path as us, or as anyone else, but you are the glue that holds all our lives together. Each and every good memory I have is in some way connected to you. I know these guys feel the same," Sam says.

"Why didn't..." I trail off and look up at the trees, trying to get my emotions in check.

It's a lost cause.

I look back down at my three best friends and have to wipe away a tear as it rolls down my cheek.

"Why didn't you ever say any of this stuff? I've always thought you guys just kinda tolerated me."

Sam's crying too, and the other guys are about as close as I've ever seen them.

"I'm sorry for that, Ave. It just...I don't know. Life goes by, and you don't say the important stuff. You just think everyone knows." Sam's voice is rough as he gets the words out. "I should say these things more. We all should." He looks around at the other guys, and they nod. "Life's too short not to tell the people you love how important they are to you. It's a mistake I won't be making again."

"Same." Dom's voice is strong and steady. "But this isn't the time for a full-on brotherly love fest. Ave's got a helicopter to catch."

I smile and nod, giving my eyes one last wipe.

There's time to pause for a tight hug with each of the guys as I make my way back to the golf cart.

As I head back down the driveway, I can hear Dom calling after me. "Go get your girl."

Rule #41

NO ONE LIKES A MAD WOMAN

FRAN

What seemed like such a sound, logical decision on Faraday now feels like absolute madness at thirty thousand feet. What was I thinking leaving him there without saying goodbye?

My mom found me in tears in my hotel room after I stormed out of Avery's and dragged the whole sordid tale from me, bit by bit. Her advice? Head on home with them that afternoon and take some time to think.

It sounded perfectly reasonable. I mean, what doesn't sound reasonable when spoken by your mother while she rubs your back and dries your tears?

But now that I'm locked into this seat, I want to demand they turn the plane around.

I stare at my phone nonstop until the very second the stewardess politely tells me I have to turn it to Airplane Mode—for at least the tenth time. Avery never responds to my message.

When we land in LAX to catch our connecting flight, there's still no reply.

On the plane, I sleep fitfully and dream that he texted me

back, demanding to know where I'd gone. Telling me that we'd make it work.

When the plane touches down in the winterscape that is Colorado, however, there's still no message.

I start to feel stupid. After all, I checked in with Sam before I left. Avery could have easily learned where I went. Hell, I told him where I was going in the damn text.

And then I told him that maybe we could be together in another life.

What a stupid ass thing to say.

It was all but admitting defeat.

And it appears he accepted my resignation.

He probably read that text and laughed about it. Laughed at my melodramatic, twenty-three-year-old feelings. I mean, sure, he was confused and a little bit pissed when I bailed, but he probably just wanted us to hang out and fuck for a while longer, right? I pulled the plug on his good time too early.

Those are just some of the many lies I keep feeding myself to keep the truth from settling over me.

The truth that I had something there.

And I left.

Waking up the next morning to a winter wonderland outside my window is a bit of a shock. I stand, holding the curtain back for a long time, thinking morose thoughts about my future.

I mean, my future is still hella bright. Like the damn sun bright. But I can already tell it's going to take me a few weeks to feel that way about it again. My little White Sands Avery bubble was filled with nonstop confidence building and power moves—by yours truly.

All he did was build me up. All I did was show the world what I was capable of. It was supportive and solution-focused and happy and fun and fucking goddamn it.

I just left.

For the millionth time since getting on that plane, I remind myself of why it just couldn't work out.

He refuses to hang out with my family.

Not entirely true, after all, he did hang out with them at the wedding, and a few times in the days leading up to the wedding.

But it's the best defense I have, so I keep repeating it. He wouldn't fit in with my family.

They all loved him.

Stop.

Okay, next reason.

He can't settle down.

This one holds more weight. Again and again people reiterated to me that Avery was doing something pretty out of character by sticking around The Sands long enough to make me fall in love with him. His normal life includes a flight every few weeks—and a lot of little flings.

And goodness knows, I could never be the kind of person who travels the world all the time. Not sensible, responsible Franzeska. No. She's gotta get started on building her business.

Her business that will involve flying all over the world to throw epic destination weddings for the rich and famous.

And who better to have by your side for that than a man who has spent his life traveling?

If you're just going to shoot holes in all of your reasons, maybe you should quit.

With a sigh, I throw myself back on the bed.

It's a really nice bed.

Okay, now there's one I can get behind.

Hotel rooms and Airbnbs are super fun to visit, but there's no denying the comforts of home. Like, for instance, your own bed. Oh, and the shower.

The shower in my en suite here at the Aspen house is to die for. I spent a half hour in it last night, and I'm gearing up for another round now. That's not something you would ever pull in the tropics. Not with their water conservation rules and terrible, terrible water pressure.

Sorry, Ave. We could have lived happily ever after, but my parents' house has this shower…

Not that the guy has returned my message. And I only check my phone constantly all day every day.

With a huff, I drag myself off the bed and pull on some sweats. Feeling sorry for yourself in bed is great, but downstairs, there's an espresso machine and oat milk. Now there's something to walk away from a perfectly good relationship for.

I can hear my mom fussing about somewhere in the house, but I manage to avoid her as I make my way into the kitchen. We haven't talked again since getting back, and I'm not ready for another heart-to-heart. She promised not to tell Frederick about the situation—for now—so at least I don't have that awkward conversation waiting for me.

It's nearly noon, but I have jet lag and exhaustion to blame it on, so I don't try to keep it down while making coffee. Not that these two would come right out and judge me, but I can always see it in their eyes.

I'll always be the lazy, sleep all day teenager. No matter what a boss bitch I am in other situations.

That was something I could have gotten used to with Avery. He may have had more than a decade on me, but he never made me feel like I was less than for being so young. It was like he understood that we knew different things because of our ages, and the things I knew were strengths, not weaknesses. He definitely didn't think there was an age a person would grow to when they would suddenly understand all the mysteries of life.

Coffee in hand, I pause in the dining room and perch on a chair. From here I can see into the sunroom at the back of the house where Frederick is reading the paper. He took the day off to get settled back in from the trip. Seeing him home in the middle of the day is not a common occurrence. The man lives at his office.

Another point for Avery.

Somehow, I had just resigned myself to the fact that I would find and marry a man who worked at a job like Frederick's. Someone who made a lot of money and worked hard for it. It's what my sister did, and she seems happy enough. I mean, she is raising two kids with a nanny as her partner, but still. That's what people do, right?

Not Avery. He was always around. Always willing to go for a swim or sleep the afternoon away. He's a man who's enjoying the entirety of his life—the complete opposite of all the men I've ever known. No wonder I didn't even realize it was an option.

Frederick turns then and catches my gaze through the window. He waves. I wave back.

Now I'm just sitting awkwardly behind him, creeping from the window, so I get up and walk into the sunroom. Setting down my coffee, I curl up like a cat on the couch near his chair.

"How're you settling back in?" he asks, setting his paper aside.

"Good. My shower is so amazing."

He smiles. "Yes. There's a reason people vacation in the tropics but don't move there."

"Because of the showers?"

His eyebrows go up. "That and the Wi-Fi signal. I wasn't able to take a single meeting on that island. The internet was never strong enough."

The man has his priorities, I'll give him that.

And those priorities have built a great life for me. My life went from living with a struggling single mom to this massive estate, where none of us ever have to worry about a thing. This man put us all through college without even a discussion about it. He introduced my sister to her husband. He funded a destination wedding for my brother.

He's fully prepared to write the check that launches my wedding planning business.

I want so badly for him to be the villain here.

How good would it feel to lash out at him for being who he is —the very thing standing in the way of my happiness with Avery?

Because, even with all of my silly excuses, that's the real reason, isn't it?

If I didn't have to tell this man that I was sleeping with his son, would this all be so monumentally difficult?

I doubt it.

I just can't face the judgment.

My mind flashes back to things Avery said over the last few months about family.

He chose to deal with the complications of his familial relations by just avoiding them. I judged him so hard for that. My mom raised me with values that told me family is the most important thing. Fitting in with your family is your goal in life. When you grow up, you create a family of your own and then merge with the larger family. Extended family holidays and events. Christmas presents and thank-you cards. Generations of smiling, well-off people all politely avoiding talking about real issues.

Families are hard, but they also teach us about life and support us when we need it. Every person has their good side and bad side, and sticking around for both teaches you to communicate and compromise.

I just don't know if I can actually imagine a life with a man who isn't willing to pay that cost of admission.

Because if he's so quick to blow off relationships when they get hard, what would that mean for ours? How long before my emotions or my needs became too much, and he runs?

Frederick isn't the bad guy here, but I'm still pissed at him.

I know families are complicated, but this guy straight up abandoned his. Avery's father leaving when he was so young was the defining moment of his life. It set him on the path he's on now, for better or worse. How can you possibly claim to stand for strong family values when you walked out on your first family?

I shouldn't say anything, but I have to. I need to know why.

"Can I ask you a question?"

Frederick looks up from his phone and tilts his head. "Of course, Franzeska."

"Why did you leave Avery when he was a kid?" It's a crummy place to start, but I want to get right to the meat of this.

"Franzeska!" My mom, who came up behind me in the doorway too quietly for me to notice, is outraged that I would question him like this. She certainly never would.

"No, no, Mimi. It's okay. We're all adults here. That's a fair question." My confidence rises a bit and then sinks back down as he turns to face me. "You got to know my son pretty well over the last couple of months?"

Just the mention of Avery has my emotions rising high in my chest. I have to be able to keep it together to have this conversation, for Frederick to take me seriously, so I fight them back down. "I did."

"How's he doing?"

The question surprises me. After the way the two men treated each other at the wedding, I would not have guessed this was something on Frederick's mind. I take a deep breath and decide to answer as honestly as I can. "He's lonely."

Frederick is unmoved. "There are a lot worse problems to have."

"He knows that. That's why he never complains about anything. He just goes through life with a smile on his face hiding everything inside."

"Again, not the worst life to inherit."

"You didn't answer my question."

Frederick takes a sip of his coffee and sets the mug down. "It's a complicated issue, Franzeska."

"Seems pretty simple to me."

"There is nothing simple about the relationship between parents and children. When you have some of your own—"

"Don't do that. I may not have children, but I have parents. I know that relationships are hard."

"Avery and I never really saw eye to eye."

"You don't have to see eye to eye with a child. As the parent, you take care of your child. That's how it works."

It dawns on me then that I'm describing unconditional love. The love I used to feel when I was younger, and my dad was still alive. Before things got so...complicated. Before my siblings grew up and started offering me their not-so-subtle opinions on my life choices.

I guess I've been trying to prove my worthiness to them—and to everyone—ever since.

I have to hold back the emotions that start to rise when the thought smacks me right in the forehead—I never once had to prove myself to Avery.

He believed in me from the very first second. He didn't even know me, and he knew I could pull that wedding off. He did nothing but believe in me from the get-go.

And what did I do? I abandoned him and ran right back to the people who have been making me feel like shit and jump through hoops for their love.

After a lifetime of that style of relationship, I guess I didn't recognize unconditional love for what it was.

Until it was too late.

"Avery was perfectly safe. I traveled a lot for business, and he had people to care for him," Frederick is more interested in his drink than this conversation.

"He needed you."

"I think I know a little bit better than you what my son needed."

"Unbelievable. You aren't even going to try to defend yourself? You don't have a single reason for abandoning your child for his whole life?"

"Franzeska, that's enough." My mother is more insistent now, coming into the room and standing beside the arm of the sofa.

I stand up too. "I really thought you were going to have such a great reason. I thought I was going to come home and ask you about this, and you would just explain it to me, like you've always done with everything."

Frederick is staring straight ahead, as if admiring the scenery. No time at all for a hysterical woman.

"He was right about you." My words land like shots fired.

Frederick's head turns slowly to me, his eyes blazing. "*I* was right. I made difficult choices, but they were the right ones."

I shake my head, but I have nothing else to say.

Back up in my bedroom, I sink into a chair as the realization of what I've really done threatens to kill me.

I'm so upset with Frederick for not being there for his son, but it hurts me so deeply because I feel like an abandoned child myself.

I've always been the odd one out. The one who wasn't quite good enough to win awards at school or be the center of attention at holiday dinners for my achievements. I just wanted everyone to see me and love me for who I was. When that didn't seem to work, I set out on a path to prove to the world just how good I was.

What I see now is that it was never going to work.

Everyone did love me, in their own way, but I was the one who had to learn to love myself.

And for a minute there, I did.

I loved the me I could see reflected in Avery's eyes. For the first time in my life, I could really and truly be myself. I didn't worry about saying or doing the wrong thing. I didn't worry about how my actions would reflect on my image, or whether my outfit was on trend enough. I just existed as a human in my own skin.

It was gloriously freeing.

But also terrifying.

Because if I don't have these people's expectations to live up to—how will I know if I've made it?

You've already made it, love. You made it the second you were born.

Avery's sly voice sneaks into my thoughts, but it doesn't do a lot to comfort me.

I had what I always wanted. What I desperately needed.

And I left.

I fall asleep with my phone in my hand, waiting for the familiar beep of a WhatsApp message I know isn't coming.

Rule #42

I'LL ALWAYS COME TO WHERE YOU ARE

FRAN

I sleep fitfully and wake from a dream to raised voices downstairs.

I crack my eyes open and check my phone. Just after seven a.m. I drag myself out of bed, still fully clothed from the night before, and head toward the stairs. I'm about three steps down when I see him.

Avery is standing in the entryway being fussed over by my mom and the housekeeper. Frederick stands to one side of the foyer, arms folded.

My brain doesn't think fast enough to stop my body from running to him. He sees me coming and scoops me into his arms. I wrap my arms and legs around him and hold on for dear life. I don't know if him coming here means that everything is going to work out, but for this moment, having him back in my arms is enough.

"Thank God, Franny. I didn't think they'd let me in. I thought I would have to scale the back wall of the house and break you out," he says into my neck.

I just laugh and squeeze harder.

"Avery, put Mimi's daughter down."

I feel Avery laugh, but other than that, he has zero reaction to his father's command.

"I flew all night. Connected through Seattle. There's so much snow here. I'm freezing."

I finally let my legs slide down until my feet touch the floor but relinquish none of the hug. "You're in shorts," I say into the fabric of his jacket.

"Yeah, that's all I had. I didn't have time to stop and get something. I needed to get here…to you."

I can hear voices around us, my mother, Frederick, but it's like Avery and I exist in a world all our own. They can't reach us here.

"Why did you come?"

"What do you mean? You're here. I'll always come to where you are."

"But I left you." I'm crying now. My words sound ridiculous considering the fact that I'm holding him so tightly that he must be struggling to breathe.

"Yeah, well," he says noncommittally.

I laugh out my breath and breathe him in. It feels so right, so perfect to be in this man's arms, all of my well thought out reasons for leaving fly out the window.

And then come slamming back.

Sure, it was easy to think about running off with the man who offered me unconditional love when I was alone in my room, but now? With the watchful eyes of my family on me?

It's all I can do not to look to my mom for guidance. But I know in order for this to work, I'm going to have to start making decisions for myself. Start standing up for what I really want in life, not just what I claim to want so they will accept me.

As I pull away enough to look up at him, the bubble cracks, and voices start to leak in.

"…think for a while about what to do here."

"Completely inappropriate."

I take a step back, but he won't release my hand, so we stay connected. "This scares the hell out of me," I say just to him, trying my hardest to ignore the outside world.

Avery nods. "Tell me what you need."

I decide to start with the easy things. The request I know I can make with judgmental ears listening. "I need…I need a home, Avery. I can't live out of a suitcase."

"Fine, great. I bought a house on Faraday. Let's go live there."

This is interesting news, and my eyebrows shoot up while I process his words. I beg my chattering mind to let that be enough. To let this kind, generous man's obvious feelings for me be enough. But it won't. "Okay. That's…a good step."

"Tell me."

I don't want to do this here, surrounded by all of the tension and questions, but I'm afraid if I don't say it now, I never will. "I've spent so long trying to be the person I thought my family wanted me to be." I motion around myself, to the house, the people standing around us. "So, it's going to take some time for me to figure out how to do this for myself." Tears are forming now, and I can feel Avery's need to pull me back in, to comfort me, but he lets me speak. "Are you sure you want to wait for me?"

That's the real question burning its way out of my mind. Will this confident, self-assured man really have the patience to stand by while I try out being an independent adult for the first time?

"Oh, Franny. You've got nothing to worry about there."

"What do you mean?"

"You have this idea that you have to become perfect before you can be loved. I don't know where you got that. I mean, I have a guess, but that's a convo for another time. For now, all you need to know is that we're both coming to this relationship as we are—and that's enough. We both have plenty of room to learn and grow, but that's what we get to do together."

"But my growth…has to start here." My eyes flick up and catch Frederick's glare. I look quickly away, back to the gentle understanding in the eyes of the man I love. "It's important to me not to run from the challenging relationships in my family. I know I need to find my own life, my independence, and I want that with you. We'll make our own home. But I'm not going to be able to live a life where we have to avoid my family."

"Fine."

"Fine, you'll come live here with me, in this house?"

It's Avery's turn to catch Frederick's eye and drop his gaze. "Sure. When's breakfast?"

I laugh and shake my head. "Thank you, but I don't actually want to live here. I do need at least a week to get stuff settled here, though, and then I need to head to Connecticut."

"To see the girls."

I nod, tears pricking again just thinking about them.

"Great. Let's go get a house there. Preferably one with nice thick walls to keep out this frozen hellscape."

"I thought you just bought a house."

He shrugs. "Doesn't matter."

I shake my head. "I don't know how you got a house on Faraday so quickly, but let's take some more time to think about future houses. Although, I do like the idea of living in Faraday for the winter weddings and living in Hartford for the summer."

"Whoa, is this Franzeska's first ever compromise?"

I smile. "I guess so. Lucky you."

"Lucky me."

"Okay, okay, now that you two have your entire lives figured out, would someone mind explaining to me exactly what's going on here?" Frederick asks, his voice not amused.

"We're in love," I say at the same time Avery says, "Nope."

Avery's face shoots to mine, and then back to his father. "What she said. The love thing."

Frederick rolls his eyes—actually rolls his eyes. He must have learned that move from me. "Avery, Franzeska is almost twenty years younger than you."

"You're, what, seventy? And how old is your new wife? The stunning lady doesn't look a day over forty."

"It's different."

"How is it diff—"

"That's enough." I finally find my voice. Both men look at me. "Avery, go upstairs and put your stuff in my room. Get ready, and we'll go shopping. Get you some pants." I smile down at his shorts before turning to Frederick. "I'll be happy to answer any questions you have."

Avery gives my hand a squeeze and disappears up the stairs with his duffel.

"Franzeska," my mom starts, her voice filled with hesitation. "Are you sure about this?" She's the only one who knows how hard it was for me to leave. I can imagine she's concerned about seeing me like that again.

"I'm sure, Mom. It's crazy, but it's crazy right. I'm going to find my own life, and I'm going to find it with Avery. We'll still visit, I promise."

She has tears in her eyes, but I can tell by how she looks at me that she understands. Her concern is a show she's putting on for her bull of a husband, who is practically blowing steam out his nose.

"He never thinks things through," Frederick proclaims.

"You wouldn't know," I say defiantly.

The man gives me what could only be described as a pitying look and disappears up the stairs after his son. I try to follow, but my mom grabs my hand and pulls me close to her.

"Let them work it out, okay? You and I have our own things to talk about." Gone is the skeptical tone, replaced with the conspiratorial voice of my lifelong friend, who wants nothing more than to hear all the exciting details.

I feel a momentary pang of regret that I allowed myself to interpret looks just like that as judgmental for so many years.

That I hid from her curious questions and brushed off any interest in my personal life. How hard would it just have been to open up, to let her know me?

I guess it's time to start finding out.

I grin and let her pull me into the kitchen.

Rule #43

IT MAY BE CRAZY, BUT IT'S RIGHT

AVERY

I've only just located what must be Fran's room and tossed my duffel on the bed next to what could be everything she owns when I hear Frederick clear his throat behind me.

I turn, and he's leaning on the doorframe, arms crossed. The look on his face is not friendly, but it's far less domineering than when he was looking at Franny downstairs. Anger rises in me at the thought of him thinking he can make decisions for her. He would never consider pointing that kind of control at me.

"You're really gonna do this to me, huh?" Are the first words out of his mouth.

His statement does nothing to dispel my irritation.

"I'm so sorry all of my love and happiness inconveniences you."

"That's not—" He breaks off, not even managing to convince himself that's not what he meant. "There are millions of girls in the world. Why do you have to pick that one?"

"I've met all of those women, Dad. None of them were the one."

He laughs darkly. "I guess you have met them all, haven't you?"

"I've met a lot of them. And now I never have to meet another one. I guess I have you to thank for that."

"Wow, was that a thank you? That's not something I ever expected to hear from you."

"Why is that?"

"You hate me."

I don't..." My first instinct, of course, is to argue with him, but I freeze with the words on my lips. It's true that I no longer scream those words into the phone or at family pictures. The sharp feel of the hate has settled over the years into something I would call resentment. Or confusion. But there's no denying the truth. "You left me."

My father scoffs. "Are you still rehashing all this old stuff?"

I shake my head in disbelief. "Never mind."

"No, wait. I didn't mean that. Shit. I never thought I would be having this conversation, but after Franzeska took me to task about it yesterday, I guess I should've been prepared."

I raise my eyebrows but say nothing. I love the idea of Fran standing up to this guy, but I hate that it was to protect me.

"Listen," he starts, sounding like he would rather be stoned to death than speak the next words. "My father, your grandfather, was a real piece of work." He holds up his hand, stopping me as I start to argue. "Not to you, I know. He was the perfect doting grandfather to you. But as my father, it was different. He was mean and controlling. You think it was bad to have me gone all the time? My father was around for every second of my life. He wanted me to turn out exactly like him. He got his wish. I turned out the same as him when it comes to business. I followed him into the family firm, bought the houses and the cars. Married the woman he picked out for me."

I watch him struggle with emotions from the past and do nothing to help. I have my own versions of these old stories. My first memories are of dressing up in one of his suits and pretending to go to work with him. I looked up to him that much. He yelled at me so harshly, I hid for hours while the staff searched the house for me.

That was the exact time he stopped being around, if I remember correctly.

"When your mother got pregnant, I was so excited. Things were going to be different. I had plans. Wasn't until you were born that the fear set in. I was so scared I would do to you exactly what he did to me. So, I did the cowardly thing. I left. I removed myself from the situation."

I'm shaking my head, but I can't find any words. This from him, after all of these years of silence? I don't know how to process it. Finally, I conquer the feelings with my old friend sarcasm. "Bet you wish you would have stayed, huh? I know how you feel about how I turned out."

"Are you kidding me, Avery? You turned out perfect. You're everything I always wanted to be in life. I never could because I have this sense of responsibility. The whole world rests on my shoulders. But you? You're a free bird. I'd be lying if I said I wasn't a little jealous. Everyone hates me, but no one hates you. You're friends with everyone you meet. You have this easy way with people that I find baffling and exasperating because I could never be that way."

"You don't really know anything about me."

"It may seem that way, but it's not the truth. I pay very close attention. I follow all your social media accounts. I watch you, even though we never talk. Your life is so fun, so free. I know that it's hard for you to accept, but the best thing I ever did for you was leave."

"That's sweet but also really fucked up."

He laughs. "I know. You should hear what my therapist says about it."

"You have a therapist?"

"Not anymore. She fired me when I refused to even try loving myself as a solution to all my problems."

"Is that why you're always trying to find someone new to love?"

He shakes his head and sniffs out another dark laugh. "When you work as much as I do, there has to be someone waiting for you at home."

"I wonder what she would think of your glowing description of marital life."

"It may sound bad, but I promise she's getting what she wants out of the deal. That's how it is for me, even in love. My life is just one long business transaction."

I can't fall into the pit of pity he's trying to open up for himself. We're too far gone for that. My anger, however, is far from dissipated.

"The house staff raised me while you hid somewhere, and you expect me to believe you did it for my own good? You know who I played ball with as a kid? The gardener. You know who taught me to read? The housekeeper. She and her kids were my family. The butler gave me the talk about the birds and the bees. I don't know what would have happened to me without those people."

"Do you think it was just a coincidence that our gardener was a retired minor league baseball player? Or that our housekeeper had an education degree and three well-adjusted children your age? I scoured the world and found the most qualified people I could and offered them exorbitant salaries to come live in our house and raise you. And look at the kind, generous person you've become. I know that sounds insane. Hell, I knew it was insane back then when I was doing it. But you know what? I'd do it again. The life I live, the one where everything I have was earned the hard way and every single person on the planet is always trying to take it away from me, I wouldn't wish on anyone. Least of all my son. You can go ahead and hate me. I'll take it. If that's the cost of your freedom, I'm happy to pay."

"Jesus, Frederick. What do you expect me to do with that?"

He just shakes his head.

I take a deep breath, holding the bridge of my nose and trying to shove down the rising emotions. I don't want to ask, but I may never get another chance. "If I had told you, back then, that I missed you. That I wanted you to come home. Would it have made any difference?"

"No. I left for your own good. Telling me that you wanted me to come home wouldn't have made any difference." He finally looks back at me and the eye contact physically hurts. "I knew, son. I knew you wanted me to come back." He looks older now than I've ever seen him look before. Frail. Tired. "Just…just come for Christmas next year, okay? Bring Franzeska."

After a pause, I nod. The calm feeling blooming in my chest might not be forgiveness yet, but it's something like it.

The man holds out his hand.

I stare at it for a few long moments before taking it in my own. I use our grasp to pull him in for what starts as a very awkward embrace but settles into a casual hug.

It's a start.

"Oh my goodness! Do not move. I need to grab my camera," Mimi's voice rings out behind us, and we jump apart, smoothing our clothes out in the exact same gesture. He catches me doing it at the same time I catch him, and we share the tiniest smile.

"Well, I'll leave you to it, then," Frederick says, no longer meeting my eye. On his way out the door, he takes Mimi by the hand and pulls her along with him. I catch Fran's eye from the doorway, and the tears I've been fighting off start to rise once more. Hers are filled to the brim with emotion—happiness and sadness. Understanding.

She comes in and closes the door, leaving my father, the conversation, the whole world, outside.

"You get a few answers?" she asks finally when I fail to find any words.

I nod. "And a ton more questions."

"Well, maybe you can ask some more next time."

I offer a tight-lipped smile and another nod. I don't want to think about having another conversation like that as long as I live, but I do like the words next time on this woman's lips.

"And look at you. Didn't burst into flames when your dirty little secret got out to the fam. You okay?"

Her sheepish smile is hiding a much larger one as she shakes her head. "I don't know why I thought they were going to be so mad at me."

"Well, live and learn, I guess."

She walks over and stands directly against me, cheek to my chest. I wrap her in my arms. "What's next?" I don't want to ask, but it seems like the right move. There's no way she doesn't want to talk about this, not now that we've come this far.

I wait while she inhales deeply and exhales before she speaks. "Well, first thing is probably the mall to get you some clothes."

I wait, unconcerned with my outfit.

"And then, I guess we just see how it goes. I mean, I'm still processing the wedding and everything that happened. I have a call with Sam scheduled for later this week, and I know he's going to want to talk about doing more events at The Sands. I still have the material from Kendra to sort through. A website designer to hire."

I continue to wait silently, holding her close to me.

"I'm excited to head to Hartford to see the girls."

She peeks up and looks at me from where her chin rests on my chest. "What about you?"

This is where I would generally tell her that I'm game for all of that. Whatever she wants or needs to do, I'll just join along.

But I see now how wrong of an answer that has always been.

This woman doesn't need me to follow her around aimlessly. She needs me to be my own person so that she can be hers.

That's a real partnership. Two people with their own lives coming together to share in the good times and bad.

"Well," I start, planning my words carefully. "I bought a house, and I'm pretty excited about that."

She smiles up at me, waiting for me to go on.

"I'd like to do some shopping for furniture and other house things while we're in the States. I can do that here and in Connecticut and have it all shipped to Houston. I'd love to have your help."

"I can't wait to see it."

"Want to see the pictures?"

I'm grateful now for the dozens of shots I took before I left the house. Franny oohs and aahs over them as she holds my phone, scrolling. She asks questions and points out things I hadn't even noticed.

When she reaches the end, she looks at me, eyes narrowed. "How'd you get a house so fast?"

I shrug, sly grin starting to spread across my face. "When you want something bad enough, you can make it happen, I guess."

"Well, I approve. And it's super close to the resort, which will be handy for work. We'll probably need to get two golf carts, though, so you don't always have to drive me around."

I nod. This world she's describing is officially my favorite thing ever. It includes her and I, building a life together.

I can't think of a better future.

Rule #44

LIVE AND LEARN

AVERY

Lami Bay, Fiji
Three months later

"Do you have time to drive Richard's grandma into town?"

I glance up from my bowl of chicken chop suey and smile. "Of course. Is she ready to go now?"

Franny nods. "He's bringing her down the stairs, which is a long process, so you have a few minutes. She wants to change some money, so she has Fijian cash to spend at the shops and tip people."

"He told her the resort is all-inclusive?"

Franny shrugs. "She can't be deterred."

"It's no problem at all. I can pick up the tablecloths when I'm in town. I was going to drive in later for them anyway."

Her face lights up. "That's perfect. Just make sure they brought that one out to fifty-six inches, okay? And make sure the two blue ones match?"

I abandon my lunch and rise to pull her into my arms. Touching this woman is sustenance for my soul. "Yes, dear."

We've taken up temporary residence at the Novotel Suva Hotel on Lami Bay in Fiji, where a couple of investment bankers from Iowa decided to have their wedding. The family is lovely, even if they're a bit overwhelmed by the change of scenery. I've chatted with more than one person who told me they applied for their very first passport to come on the trip.

In the months since purchasing the house on Faraday, it feels like the world shifted into warp speed. We've visited Aspen twice since the day I came to rescue her, and more or less made our peace there. Frederick came around to the reality of the situation quicker than either of us expected. Kendra and her team finished the website and social media for the wedding planning company, and we've been booked solid with requests for meetings with prospective clients.

Fran's sister is on the lookout for the perfect property for us in Hartford, something she's taking as seriously as a full-time job, and we're happy to wait. Between The White Sands, where we're booking a wedding a month for next season, and the small, exclusive destination weddings around the world that we're being hired to organize, we don't have a lot of down time anyway.

Franny is the confident, glowing face of the company, walking around with a clipboard and pulling fantastic ideas for decor and ceremony styles seemingly out of thin air for each new couple we meet.

I'm more of the support system, and I couldn't be happier with my position. Turns out a lifetime of international travel perfectly qualifies me to help pull off weddings around the world. I deal with logistics, angry locals, and grandmas who want a handful of local currency to spend on daiquiris at the poolside bar.

It's so nice to be needed in this way—to have a job. I guess I finally understand why they're so popular. I wake up each day with a purpose—and a beautiful woman next to me. There's no need to plan elaborate trips or seek out adrenaline shots. Our life is one long adventure together, making sure all of the pieces fall into place to create absolutely spectacular weddings in places where most people would be flummoxed by red tape.

When Franny first got the draft website back from the designer, and we sat down to look over photos and click links together, I got my first glimpse of the name she settled on for the company. Paradise Events.

I teased her about pigeonholing us into only ever working on far-flung islands, but she assured me that the name covered anywhere anyone could ever want to celebrate their love surrounded by family and friends.

"Paradise is where you make it, Ave," she said.

And I couldn't agree more.

"...just don't understand why you had to get married somewhere so hot."

I swing into action, sliding my arm around the old lady and pulling her toward the waiting truck—and away from her exhausted looking grandson. "There's no better AC on this island than in this truck, little lady."

She softens immediately at my display of charm, offering up the first genuine-looking smile I've seen from her all week.

"I didn't know *you* would be taking me," she says as she allows me to help her into the seat.

"Only the best for the family matriarch."

I can tell I hit the right note with that one because tears of love and pride begin to swell in those big brown eyes. I close the door behind her with a smile and walk to the driver's side.

"You two have fun now." Franny grins at me from beside the groom on the sidewalk in front of the hotel.

I tip my hat and drive off, waving toward her reflection in the rearview mirror.

I've learned a lot of things this year, but the most important one is probably this—home is where you make it.

After a childhood spent waiting for my life to look like the lives of my friends, I guess I got the idea that I wasn't meant for family life. I tried so hard during those years to make everyone think I was okay with the patchwork family I had, instead of the normal, nuclear one everyone else seemed to have, that I just got used to the emotional barricade.

What followed was decades of acting like I loved not having a home or anyone waiting excitedly to meet me at the airport.

Well, I don't pretend anymore.

I've thrown myself so headlong into nesting that I know I even drive Franny nuts sometimes. I chose plates and silverware. I ordered sheets from France. I had a custom standing desk built for Franny by a local craftsman.

Any spare moment that isn't taken up by wedding stuff is spent thinking about ways that I can make our home better. I've really sunk my teeth into this whole home thing, and I'm not letting go.

I really couldn't have chosen a better partner. Fran grew up in nearly the exact opposite kind of family as mine, so she's equal parts excited to have a home base and happy to let me make a lot of the choices about paint color and chaise lounge cushions.

I'm a shopaholic. Who would've guessed it?

"Your wife is quite a special lady," Richard's grandma pipes up from the passenger seat.

I smile over at her. "We're not married, but you're right about that. She's the most special lady on earth."

"So why haven't you married her?" The woman sounds incredulous.

I shrug. "We haven't known each other very long."

She shakes her head and rolls her eyes. "You know, in my day, you didn't need ten years of cohabitation to be sure about someone. You just knew."

I smile at the road, thinking about how much simpler life must have been back then.

But then it hits me—isn't love still just as simple?

"I know she's the one. I knew it from the first time I met her. We just...don't need rings right away to prove it. We both kinda like not having anything to prove to the world right now." I've never thought about it before, but as the words come out, I know they're true.

"Ridiculous kids and your newfangled ideas. Always have to be unique." She's shaking her head, looking out the passenger window, apparently no longer interested in this conversation.

It's just as well. I have no interest in defending what we have. Fran and I are solid—rock solid. We're creating a world of our own choosing one day at a time. I wouldn't trade our crazy life for anything.

Rule #45

THIS MOMENT IS EVERYTHING

FRAN

Faraday Island

As always, the post-wedding exhaustion is a surreal state of limbo.

After months of planning, texts, lists, frantic phone calls, bribes, and heavy lifting, all we have to do is pull our suitcases up the bumpy driveway and into our house.

I could not be happier to call this my home. I know that Avery bought it on a crazy whim, but it really couldn't be more perfect.

Sam came over and opened the house up earlier this afternoon in preparation for our arrival, so the place is filled with a sweet-scented breeze from the fruit trees in our backyard.

But the house, the unpacking, the dinner plans—everything—are going to have to wait.

I roll my suitcase against the wall in the front foyer and head straight for the patio doors.

I need to get in my pool naked, and I need to do it right now.

My crumpled green traveling dress and underthings fall onto a chaise, alongside the leaves that have fallen since the pool cleaner got the place ready for us the day before.

The cool, clear water washes away the grime of airports and golf cart rides, the stress of being portable, until I'm just me again.

"Damn, girl. Didn't waste a second, huh?"

I swim over to the edge of the pool where Avery is kneeling.

"Get in."

"Don't have to ask me twice."

His wicked grin and flashing eyes disappear briefly under his shirt as he pulls it over his head.

There's no sleek, quiet pool entrance for Avery. He takes a running leap off the edge and hits the surface of the water with a cannonball.

I laugh as the wave crashes over me. By the time I can open my eyes again, he's inches away, pulling my naked body around his.

"Do you remember that pool in San Pedro?" he asks, moving my wet hair off my shoulder so he can access the skin of my neck —his favorite place to bury his face.

I nod. "That was our first private pool."

"And all I wanted in the whole world was to be alone with you at that pool forever."

I laugh. "That's not all you wanted. I seem to remember you wanting to take over the top floor of The Sands, so we'd have the rooftop pool there all to ourselves."

"Okay, I wanted to be alone with you in *any* private pool."

"Well, you manifested it."

"I guess I did."

Avery and I have had several big talks about us and what we're doing. Having frank discussions about the reality of our future together was something he had to warm up to at first, but once he got going, he talked for hours. It seems that he had the perfect partner version of himself hidden deep down all along, too scared to stick around long enough to let it be known to anyone.

Honestly, I'm still getting used to the transition myself. It was a huge step for me to admit to everyone, myself included, that I was going to be with Frederick's much older son. After a few phone calls and conversations with family, it got easier to talk about, but I still have to breathe deeply sometimes to help dispel the growing feelings of fear and shame that try to pop up when I talk about my choices in life.

It's scary, but necessary. And very freeing. I no longer get paralyzed with indecision when it comes to making choices for myself—turns out all of that fear just stemmed from worrying about what people would think of me. Now that I'm living my life for me, I know just what I want, and I ask for it.

Avery has been more than helpful in that department. I still stare at him wide eyed sometimes when one of the family members asks him how he's doing, and he just tells them the truth, the whole truth, but it really does inspire me to do the same when I see them nod and smile—and like him anyway.

Turns out you don't have to be perfect to be loved…or even liked.

Why don't they teach stuff like that in school?

"How long do we get to stay here before the next thing?" he asks, one hand on either side of my shoulders where I hold onto the edge of the pool in the deep end.

"Excited for the next thing, or excited to have some time to stay put?" I tease.

Avery flashes that sideways grin. "Both, I guess. As long as I'm with you." His eyes move behind me to the house, though, and I can see something like longing there.

"We're here for almost two weeks."

He nods and disappears back into the crook of my neck.

"But come October, we're staying put for the full season. Over seven months."

"Wow," he murmurs into my skin.

"Is that scary? It's not like you to stay put for so long."

"I'll stay wherever you are."

"Is that all you've been doing this whole time? Searching for love?"

"No, love. I was searching for you."

I smile and pull him closer. His stiff erection against my stomach is no surprise, and I reach for it, quickening his breath as I stroke him under the cool water.

"You sure you have the energy to be starting this?" he teases, moving his hips playfully into my hand as I grip him.

"It's you who needs energy. I plan to just lie there," I tease back.

He answers me with his hand sliding between my legs, and suddenly, there's no need for any more talking. I keep hold of his cock as he slips his fingers through my folds and into my body.

I arch my back against the rough side of the pool, barely able to hold on with my one free hand as his movement in and out of my pussy intensifies.

"I'm going to drown," I whisper.

Avery lets out a soft laugh. "Well, we can't have that, can we?"

And then he removes his hand and swims off.

"Hey!" I call, watching him get further and further away as my now abandoned core aches for his touch. "Bring those things back."

"They're right over here," he calls back, standing up in the waist deep shallow end of the pale-blue pool and wiggling his fingers toward me.

I grin and push off the side, swimming toward him.

I grasp his wrist as soon as I can reach it and pull it back between my legs.

"Needy, huh?"

"Very."

"Well, what are we going to do about that?"

"You know what to do."

"Oh, really?" he asks, pressing me back against the wall in the shallow water, lowering to his knees to get on my level as I curl to keep my shoulders under. "Should I do this?"

He presses right back inside me, my body warm and open to him, reaching out for his touch. I lift my hips to allow him better access as he penetrates me, his thumb grazing over my clit.

"Yeah, that's a good start."

"A good start, she says…" he murmurs, his face tucked back into its favorite spot.

He works me until I'm in a frenzy, struggling to control my breathing as my orgasm builds.

"Yes, Ave. Faster. Yes."

I tip my head back with my eyes squeezed closed, breath held tightly as I bite down on my lip. As the bright, electric energy of my orgasm begins to erupt through my body, however, I open my eyes and look up at the deep blue sky, the canopy of palmetto trees. I spot an oriole, its golden body stark against the dark foliage.

There's only one word on my lips as the pleasure overtakes me.

"Home."

Avery fucks me with his fingers at a steady pace until I'm laughing and pulling away, the overwhelming sensation of having just come making my nerves ultra-sensitive.

"God, I love it when you say that," he murmurs, chasing me down where I slipped away and pulling me back into his arms.

I don't need to open my eyes to find his hard shaft, and I take it in my firm grasp.

Only to lose my grip as he lifts himself out of the pool.

The loss of his body, and with it the promise of even more pleasure, leaves me with my mouth hanging open in surprise.

"Are you going to make yourself wait again?" I ask, only

slightly teasing, remembering the pool in San Pedro where he withheld his own orgasm.

I get a cocky grin in return as he flops, wet and naked, into one of the padded lounge chairs, his gorgeous, tanned body gleaming in the sun. "Not this time, love. This time, I'm just going to make you chase it."

He wiggles his hips to make his cock flop back and forth, and I laugh.

Well, I'm not too proud to chase down what I want.

I lift myself out of the water and flip my hair like a bikini model. Then I stalk toward him, wiggling my hips side to side in an exaggerated strut.

"Hmm," Avery coos, shielding his eyes from the midday sun to get a better look at me. "That's exactly what I had in mind."

"Oh, really?" I offer, hand on my hips. "This was your plan all along?"

The mixture of desire and love in his eyes is something I'm slowly getting used to. It's one thing to imagine having a man like this—handsome and charming and rich and accommodating—completely gaga over you. It's quite another to get accustomed to it on an actual day-to-day basis.

I had to shed so many insecurities to get to where we are right now. I had to quiet down the voice in my head that would tell me he was just going to leave. I had to work up to the trust I needed to accept this life with him.

Avery, amazingly, didn't seem to need to work up to trusting me at all. You'd think a guy with that kind of past, that history of being left behind by those he should have been able to count on, would have been more hesitant to offer up his soul on a platter. But not my guy. Avery loves full throttle. Boundlessly. Shamelessly.

And I aspire to do the same. I know it will take time, but I trust now that I'll have all the time I need.

I place one knee on either side of his hips and lower myself until I'm sitting with his stiff cock jutting up between my legs.

"Did you plan for me to climb up here and ride you, too?" I ask, taking his cock in both hands and sliding them up and down, the water from the pool allowing my skin to glide over his.

He nods, and I laugh out loud.

"Well. I approve."

I lift just enough to touch his tip down on my still sensitive clit, sliding it back and forth in the combined wetness from the pool and my orgasm.

"Shit, girl. You are the hottest thing alive."

"Oh, really? Just alive, huh? There have been hotter thi—"

"Hottest thing that has ever lived," Avery corrects himself quickly as I find my entrance with his tip. "You put me in there, love, I can't be responsible for what happens."

I laugh again and slide him in another inch, my grip still firm on his base. "That's okay. I approved the plan. I'll take responsibility."

He just smiles and shakes his head, surrendering to me as I wiggle my hips and seat myself down on his cock.

We both let out audible breaths as he slides deep inside me, Avery's eyes falling closed. I keep mine open, though, watching the absolute perfection that is him as he holds my hips, waiting for me to take the lead.

We still enjoy our fair share of backdoor sex—it will always be a favorite of mine—but we've been exploring pussy sex more and more. And more and more. I've decided it's possible to have two favorites. Maybe even three or four.

With Avery, it seems every touch is my favorite. And I know he feels the same.

Feeling him inside me like this still gives me a thrill. It's a forbidden fruit. The pleasure I denied myself for so long that I still crave like a drug. I wake in the night sometimes and need to pull him inside me.

The first time he went bare I couldn't let him fill me with his orgasm, but over time I started to crave that as well. With the growing trust that he wasn't going to leave me came a trust in him when he said we would be safe.

And a brand-new kind of trust developed from the joining of those two—the trust that we would figure things out, no matter what happened.

With Avery's cock filling me, my legs spread wide to open my clit up to his pelvic bone, I know I'm not going to last long. I hold onto the back of the chaise and grind myself up and down, back and forth. Avery matches my pace and motion, providing the perfect counterpart to my thrusts. The perfect base for me to press myself against.

I lean my forehead down to press against his as I tip over the edge, keeping my pace just how I like it and coming for so much longer than I expect. When I finally still, I open my eyes and find him watching me in amazement.

"What are you looking at?" I tease.

"That was so fucking hot. I'm going to come in two seconds."

I smile and shake my head, my wet hair sending a shower of water over his still glistening skin. "Go ahead."

His grip tightens immediately, and I feel his legs slide up behind me until his feet are flat on the chair. His powerful thrusts fill and lift me until I have to hold on as he turns our sensual lovemaking into a wild ride.

He wasn't kidding about being on the edge. I've only just relaxed into his pounding pace when he's holding me close and gasping, emptying himself deep inside my body.

I don't know if it's the long denial of this, or some kind of primal instinct—maybe a combination of both—but being filled with Avery's seed is becoming a bit of a fetish of mine. It's an act so natural and yet so raw. It's a powerful bond, a merging of our two selves much deeper than we could ever accomplish buying furniture for our new house or running a company together. It's a connection on an ancient, animalistic level, and there's no denying what it does to me.

I grip his hand as soon as he stills and press it onto my clit, rocking my hips slowly, deeply, grinding our bodies together until I'm coming once more. I close my eyes and release his hand, trusting him to keep me here, and he does.

I lean back and take him deeper as he rubs my clit and waves of shuddering pleasure crash over me.

I become sensitive quickly as soon as my third orgasm passes, and I bat his hand away and catch my breath. When I look down, I find him smiling, completely content to be underneath me, naked in the afternoon sun, used for my pleasure over and over. He doesn't clamor to get up or get onto the next thing. I know from experience that he'll just rest there forever, cock still inside me, until he goes soft and slides out. Until he drifts off into a nap still covered in the evidence of our sex.

And maybe that's been the biggest surprise—and lesson—I've gotten from Avery. All the time we worked on my brother's wedding, I thought he was just waiting to head off to his next adventure, but in reality, he was right there beside me.

It was always me preparing for what came next—my mind already planning for some future upset or holiday or errand. It's necessary to think two steps ahead in my business, where there really is always something looming in the near future that could derail everything, but I'd never noticed how much I spent every waking moment thinking about the future.

Avery may have spent his life traveling, but when he's somewhere, he's there. One hundred percent in the moment.

For all my big talk about family and putting down roots, I've always lived with one foot out the door. Part of me already living in some imagined future. My mind drifting off to what could happen next, at the expense of the present moment.

With Avery, there almost isn't a future. There is only now. It's a far extreme from how I've always lived my life, but I know his point of view will be good for me. And mine will be good for him. We ground each other, balance each other out.

I smile as I let go of the dinner plans in my mind and slide my body down beside Avery's on the chaise. The oriole is back, and we watch it hop from branch to branch around the yard, collecting grass and other plant matter to take back up to build its nest.

After a while, my eyelids grow heavy, and I don't fight them, drifting off into a calm afternoon nap with Avery's favorite word still echoing in my mind.

Home.

Epilogue
PLAYING PIRATES

FRAN

"All aboard!"

I grin up at Avery, who's ringing the yacht's deck bell in his Bermuda shorts, tan chest bare and sandy-blonde hair wild in the wind.

Reina shoves her duffel into my arms and hoists herself onto the boat, grumbling good-naturedly. "I still can't believe you're making me play extra in your little photo shoot. I haven't even been home from Japan two days."

"We need all the beautiful people we can get, Rein. The pictures just wouldn't be the same without you."

I toss the bag up to Avery, who's stowing cargo under the deck. It's only an overnight trip, but everyone brought plenty of stuff.

My mom and Frederick just happened to be on the island with my sister and nieces, so we invited them to join. The little girls look adorable—and murderous—in their matching pink life jackets, completely appalled to be the only ones wearing them.

Victoria comes aboard next, lifted from the dock by Ben, who never takes his hands off her as he guides her to the wide, comfy seating area, like she's the most precious piece of cargo.

"Thanks for flying over for this," I tell Ben again.

"I was told it was mandatory," he replies with a sly, slightly suspicious smile.

Not that we've given anyone anything to be suspicious about.

We're adding intimate, high-end yacht weddings to our event portfolio, and we need a photo shoot for the website and socials. Reina—still glowing with actual marital bliss from her own dream wedding just a month ago—graciously agreed to play the bride. We planned to hire a model for the groom, but you can imagine how well that went over. I just pray not too many people recognize Dominic, the celebrity chef and co-owner of the resort, in the photos.

Kendra and her best photographer, Wren, have been prepping the boat all afternoon. The plan is to sail out about three miles, to the buoy we had installed, and stage a magical mock wedding—complete with flowers, cake, and champagne. We'll then spend the night out there, capturing the utter perfection of the tropical night sky with The White Sands lit up onshore in the background.

Sam is last to board. He fought harder than anyone to stay behind, but Avery won him over in the end. I watch with a smile as he settles on deck and accepts a beverage from the one server we brought for the shoot—who is doubling as our mock officiant.

The mood aboard relaxes as everyone enjoys the ocean breeze on the way out to the buoy. Drinks are flowing, our best friends are all together, and everyone's dressed in perfect resort casual. The pictures are going to be epic. Who wouldn't want this magical experience for their special day?

Kendra and Wren attach a wide mesh panel sewn with tropical flowers between the mast lines. It blows gently in the wind, our floral ceremony backdrop.

Avery slides in beside me as we watch Reina and Dom prepare to exchange pretend vows. It's not going to be hard—they're still looking at each other like there's no one else in the world.

"They look so happy," Avery murmurs in my ear.

I nod. "Yeah. I'm happy for them. They deserve it."

He pulls me closer on the padded bench. "Are you happy?"

I turn to face him, trying to keep my expression neutral in case our photo gets taken. "Avery, we've been over this again and again."

"I know," he says quickly, kissing my forehead. "I'm just… making sure, you know?"

"I'm sure," I reply confidently. "Are you sure?"

Avery's easy smile melts any remaining doubt I could have had.

"Never been so sure about anything in my whole life, love."

Dom actually gets a bit misty-eyed as Reina bawls her way through the fake ceremony, and the two kiss and accept our congratulations in shot after shot of hugs, smiles, and laughter.

When they finally flop down next to the rest of the guests on the green benches, spent from an hour of re-living their own emotional vows, Wren hops up to stand in front of the flower veil.

"Sam, could I get a shot of you up here?"

Sam agrees, of course, leaving the comfort of his seat to be a good sport and help us get all the photos we need.

Wren places him centered on the top deck.

Avery hops up to stand beside him. I see the two men exchange a whisper, and a happy, slightly disbelieving grin spreads over Sam's face.

It's time.

"If I could have your attention, please," Avery calls out.

The quiet chatter on deck fades as everyone turns to face him.

"I just wanted to thank you all for coming to our photoshoot. You lot are some of the most important people in the world to us." His gaze finds mine, and I'm not surprised to see him already getting emotional.

Avery holds out his hand, and I climb up top to take it.

A round of hushed whispers spreads through the small group of guests as they all take in the sight.

"I want you all to know," Sam starts, quieting the crowd once more as he takes the lead. "I'm just as surprised as you are."

The whispers become murmurs, but Avery has both of my hands in his now, and he's the only person in the world I can see.

It's funny—after watching countless couples stand in this very spot, preparing to do this very thing—it never occurred to me how it would actually feel. I always imagined it would be sort of a blur. Going through the well-planned motions. Like the mock ceremony we just held.

But it doesn't feel like a blur at all.

In fact, I'm not sure any moment in my life has ever felt as crystal clear as this one.

Avery's hair blowing in the wind. The smell of the ocean. The warmth of the afternoon sun.

The feeling of standing on the precipice of the rest of my life.

The knowledge that I'll never have to be alone again. That I have someone who will walk beside me through every high and low. Someone I can trust with the truth.

And there are the tears.

Avery grins and wipes under my eyes with both thumbs, fixing my makeup perfectly, as he's learned to do in the last year of being my emotional support everything.

"Without further ado."

Sam's voice cuts through the moment, and I'm back on the boat, surrounded by the people I love most.

"I don't have anything prepared, so we're going to have to wing it."

Avery and I laugh along with the crowd, never breaking eye contact.

"Since I first stumbled upon these two…hiding in the maintenance closet," he pauses for laughter, "I knew there was something special going on. Along the way, there were obstacles that would've been too much for most people. Any sane person probably would've bailed." More laughter. "But these two never even considered taking the sane, normal route. I've known Avery since he was skinning his knees climbing trees to build forts so high, none of the other boys were brave enough to go up. And let me tell you—he's always been this way. I just met Franzeska last year, but it's easy to see she's just as disinterested in taking the easy road. Which is how I now find myself in the middle of the ocean, officiating a wedding that was a surprise even to me."

Sam turns back to us. "The joy you two have brought back to this resort, to this family, cannot be overstated. It's only been a year. A year of having one of my best friends living here full-time. A year of watching him finally get the love and care he's always deserved. One short year—and already I can't imagine life without you two at The White Sands."

"I suppose there are rings?" he asks, glancing side to side like a wedding planner might appear.

Kendra hops up and hands him the tiny red envelope we slipped her before launch.

Sam dumps the rings out into his hand and nods. "There's probably a million dollars' worth of gold and jewels here, dumped out of a paper envelope that someone's just been carrying around in their pocket all day." He grins at the crowd. "And that is the Fran and Avery magic."

He holds out a ring to each of us, and we accept them, preparing to deliver the short vows we wrote last night.

But we get interrupted.

"Excuse me!" a voice rings out from the crowd. "Are you forgetting something important here?"

All eyes go to Freida, standing on her seat, hands on hips, life jacket riding so high she has to stretch her neck to keep her face from disappearing inside it.

"Yeah!" her baby sister calls, scrambling to stand on her own seat. "You forgot the flower girls!"

Freida prowls over to Reina and snatches the bouquet from her hands, her fierce glare daring the adult to challenge her. Reina does nothing of the sort, trying to keep a straight face.

The girls climb up to the top deck and proceed to pull the bouquet to pieces, grabbing it back from each other as they go, littering the ground around our feet with petals, stems, leaves, and, finally, ribbons.

When Freida holds nothing but a handful of bare stems, she tosses them carelessly behind her. "Okay. Now you can do the wedding."

Victoria catches the bundle before it lands on her head, laughs, and quickly hands it back to Reina. But no one misses the look that passes between her and Ben as they cozy closer on the bench.

Freida and Suzie make their way back to their seats, clearly very satisfied with their contribution.

"Well," Sam says, fighting a smile, "now that we are properly flowered…I assume you two have prepared some vows?"

I nod, a laugh-sob escaping as I open my mouth.

Avery takes my hand and slips the delicate, handmade, diamond and opal ring onto my finger. "We did it, love," he whispers. "We're doing it," he continues, finding his voice. "We made it here." He shakes his head, like he still can't believe it. "I've been everywhere on this whole planet. Searching for something. So, I can say, without a doubt, the only place I ever want to be is where you are. I don't need to make plans. I just want to bask in your glorious light and let the rest fall into place. You're the only choice I ever needed to make. And the simplest choice, love. Because the world is messy and strange—but in our home, things are clear. You allow me to be safe standing still. You see me, and I don't need to hide." He lifts my hand and kisses the back, so gently. "Here's to forever."

Tears are streaming down my face, but somehow, I have to

build the courage to follow that. "You promised if I let you go first, you wouldn't make me cry," I choke out. The crowd laughs gently, giving me the moment I need to collect myself.

"It's funny—you talked so much about a wedding. Asking me what kind we'd have, where it would be, all of it. And I always said no wedding. I didn't want to share you. I still don't. I'm still happiest when it's just you and me, like it was at first. Alone in our quiet bubble. But then I realized...when I said no wedding, you thought I meant I didn't want to marry you. And that couldn't be further from the truth. Because this is it, babe. Just like you said all along. We get to do it our way. Life doesn't have to be a long series of things we don't want to do while we wait to go home and curl up on the couch. Life *is* the couch. I didn't know that until you showed me. I didn't understand I could just *choose* my life. Love what I love. Be who I am. You gave me that freedom. And that's exactly what our marriage and our life can be. Freedom and peace. Together."

I slip the simple gold band on his hand and hold it tightly.

I can't let go. It's still sinking in that I never, ever have to.

"Forever, babe."

The (almost) end

I just had to know what Avery was thinking when he first saw Franny at that Masquerade party…so I wrote it.
head to **www.loretownsend.com/bonus** to download the first chapter from Avery's point of view.

If you loved *Shameless* as much as I do, please consider leaving me a review! Nothing helps small, indie authors more than your kind reviews.

A Look At Book Three:

LYING FOR KEEPS

I confronted my billionaire boss to expose his cheating son. I didn't expect to end up in his bed.

I only wanted to settle the score—to tell Ben Adams exactly what kind of man his son turned out to be. But the powerful resort owner and sharp-tongued attorney misread my boldness as flirtation… and to my surprise, it worked.

What should have been one impulsive night turns into something far more dangerous. Ben is nothing like I expected—dominant, relentless, and devastatingly charming. He makes me feel seen, desired, powerful. Every time I try to run, he follows. Every game I start, he plays to win—turning my defenses into ash with nothing more than a look.

But I'm hiding more than just my heart. The truth about who I am—and why I really sought Ben out—is a secret that could destroy everything: my job, my home, and the only man who's ever made me feel alive.

I should walk away.

But walking away was never my style—*and neither is surrender.*

AVAILABLE FEBRUARY 2026

Acknowledgments

I honestly still can't believe this book exists.

Now, don't get me wrong, I love all my books…but this one is special. Maybe you felt it, too.

As an author, every book I write, every character, every drama and trauma, every emotional "arc" is in one way or another my own. I'm working out my own questions about life on the page and never has it been so profound as in Shameless.

Family stuff is deep and old and hard to work through. For me, it's always been about proving myself worthy. Where I got the idea that I needed to become worthy of love is up for debate, but regardless, it took me to the age of 39, standing here at my desk in the dark at 5 a.m., putting these characters through the wringer for me to finally get it.

One of the comments I got a lot from early readers of this book was that Fran's family seemed perfectly nice (with the possible exception of her brother), so why did she think they were so critical of her? But that's really it, isn't it? It's not how people actually are that we're reacting to, it's how we perceive them. Franny was unsure if she was good enough, so when someone asked a question, even a soft, kind, well-meaning question, she perceived it as an attack. It's a feeling I know well.

When I started writing this book, it was going to be about escaping your teasing, critical family and living a life of freedom. Only, when it came down to it, it couldn't be about that at all. It had to be about unconditional love—that we have for each other and that we have for ourselves. Without that, it doesn't matter who we're around, we'll always feel like not enough. Every word will always be criticism.

Here's a little story for you. It was the summer of 2023, and I was just starting to play around with these characters in my mind. I already had most of the action and conflict between the lovers worked out, but I was still wrestling with the family drama. That summer I really got into the ten-minute version of "All Too Well," and sometimes when I needed just the right feels, I'd put it on repeat in my headphones.

So, there I was, paddling around the middle of the lake in my inflatable kayak with "All Too Well" on repeat, and the scene at the end with Ave and his dad starts coming to me. I hurried back to shore and dragged my boat up onto the grass, already crying behind my mirrored sunglasses.

For the next twenty minutes, I sat in my beach chair and dictated that scene in bits and parts into my phone, bawling my eyes out, while bathing suit-clad families milled around me. It would be fun to say they all looked at me like I was insane, but I'm sure no one noticed me at all.

And isn't that how it is.

All this to say that, if you cried at all while reading this book, I did that on purpose.

Shameless would not be what it is today without the loving care of Karen Washo. She worked with me over several months to get the story just right. At least one of your favorite scenes is one she suggested I add (promise).

My gratitude also goes out to the courageous, inspiring team here at LT: Morgan my lionhearted PA, Cathryn—eagle-eyed proofreader, my whole beta team, and Melanie for being the first to bring the unconditional love thing to my attention. Mylee my friend and first real-life reader. Chipp, my patient, understanding partner in life, who puts up with my endless hours of typing and helps me put my phone down at the end of the day.

It takes the time and perspectives of others to get to the deep emotional places in ourselves we have to go to do the real work. Thanks to everyone who helped me. And thanks to you for reading. It means the world to me.

Lore

You can learn plenty of normal things about me in my various platform bios, so here's some things you can only learn in the back of this book:

Q: Where did the idea for this book come from?
A: I knew I wanted to do Avery next after Secret, and I wanted that scene at the beginning where she meets him in the crowd at the mask party. I also knew it was important to her to not get pregnant so she wouldn't learn that no one would visit her and her baby. This is a sad bundle of real feelings I've had in my life. This book was taking shape during a time when a brand-new baby had just been announced in our family (not mine), and I was having a meltdown about not being able to love it as much as I had the other babies because of how far it was away from me. Being an auntie is hard.
Q: Which character surprised you the most while writing?
A: I'm obsessed with Avery calling Fran's underwear undies. Like, I can't even.
Q: Do you base your characters on real people?
A: Only myself lol.

Q: What's a detail in this book only *you* would notice?

A: There are a couple of really deep, sad things Avery thinks in his head that I wasn't sure people would get. Like the scene where he's sorting his feelings into piles…I cried when that came out of me because it is so, so true. A couple of my ARC readers highlighted it, though, which made me really happy.

Q: How do you write your steamy scenes—music, candles, locked door?

A: Same as any other scene. I stand here at my desk and type what I see happening in my head. I write my books in order, from start to finish, so there are times when I have to hit pause… and come back to a spicy scene later if there are people around or I can't get through to the end without being interrupted.

The best place to find the most current info about my books and events is here:

linktr.ee/authorloretownsend

www.loretownsend.com

Join Lore Townsend's Romance Club

www.ingramcontent.com/pod-product-compliance
Lightning Source LLC
LaVergne TN
LVHW040214110826
845146LV00005B/1279

* 9 7 9 8 8 9 5 6 7 6 3 3 2 *